Stuff the Turkey

by

Tara Ford

When Christmas isn't all it's cracked up to be...

© Tara Ford 2016
All rights reserved

ISBN-13: 978-1540559975

ISBN-10: 1540559971

No part of this publication may be reproduced, stored in a retrieval system, or transmitted in any form or by any means, without the prior permission in writing of the author, nor be otherwise circulated in any form of binding or cover other than that in which it is published and without a similar condition including this condition being imposed on the subsequent purchaser.

Cover design by Jacqueline Arbromeit
http://www.goodcoverdesign.co.uk/

Other titles by Tara Ford

Calling All Neighbours

Calling All Customers

Calling All Dentists

Calling All Services

Acknowledgements

Thank you to all of you who continue to support me in my work. I want to particularly send my heartfelt thanks to those of you who have kindly left a review on Amazon. They are hugely appreciated and a vital tool to learn from, whether the reviews are good or not so good.

Thank you to my wonderful family for putting up with me and my mumblings (at those crucial moments), I couldn't have done any of this without the strength I gain from you.

Thanks to those of you who give me inspiration to write what I do (I think you probably know who you all are).

Thank you to three special ladies (CF SC & JH) who have helped my writing come alive this Christmas.

Last, but not least, thank you to everyone who likes and shares my posts and/or likes and retweets my twitterings.

Tara Ford

http://taraford.weebly.com/

Twitter: @rata2e

Facebook: Tara Ford - Author

For my wonderful Woking family

*** 1 ***

Oh, great. How could I have been so stupid?

I stare down at my crinkly orange legs and cringe. Orange is really not my colour, yet my legs are covered in a bright – no – practically fluorescent orange, ruched fleece which is a little itchy and highly unpleasant to look at. Highly unpleasant for me anyway. Highly amusing for others. At least the plastic shoes are comfortable, almost as much as slippers, but that's not the point – I look ridiculous.

I peer up at the gilt framed, ornate mirror, in front of me and muster up a half-smile. Maybe I'll look better if I grin my way through the rest of the evening. I force a cheesy grin and peer at my reflection.

No, it doesn't work – I still look pathetic.

Peeling the red crested hood from my head, I run my fingers through my flattened hair. To think that I paid £40 last night to have my long blonde hair cut into a stylish, shoulder-length bob. It was supposed to be my new look for Christmas. New hair – new me, that kind of thing. Now it's stuck to my head and rather greasy looking. Whoever was the last person to wear this stupid outfit had obviously not cleaned it very well, as my hair has gone from neat to nasty in less than 60 minutes.

OK, I *can* and I *will* keep calm about this. I *can* laugh this off. I *will* keep smiling. I'll keep laughing about how stupid I look, and everyone else will admire me for being so brave and self-effacing. Yes, that's exactly what I'll do.

Although, the fact that there are still those at work who laugh their heads off every time my name is mentioned, it's probably making matters much worse that I fell into this evil trap tonight.

My name is Susie Satchel, which, on its own strength, is not a bad name I suppose. I should be proud to have come from a long line of Satchels who date back to pre-Victorian times and who excelled in the business of making straps, belts and all sorts of other leather accessories. I suppose I am proud, a little, but it's not something I ever mention to anyone.

There is a problem with my name though... and I didn't give it a second thought when I applied for the job... and it wasn't until my interview day, when I saw the smirk on several people's faces in the staffroom...

Anyway, the problem is, I work at a school, and not just any school, I should add. The real problem is that I work at Baghurst Primary School. I'm a teaching assistant and known as Miss Satchel – obviously. So, there you have it – Miss Satchel works at *Bag*hurst school. Ha ha, very funny.

Not.

And to make it even worse, guess what the latest craze is for school kids these days? Yes, trendy satchels. In fact, it isn't just the kids who *must have* these highly desirable, trend-setting satchels. There are men-satchels too and *Disney* satchels, women's Italian leather satchels, leopard-print and retro satchels, *Game of Thrones* and *Marvel* satchels, soft leather and designer denim satchels. Satchels, satchels everywhere. Hence, I can categorically say that I do not have a satchel. How could I own one? I would then be Miss Satchel, who has a satchel and works at Baghurst school. There would be far too much baggage going on there – can you see?

I've only been at the school for six weeks but I've had at least ten of the older children ask me where my satchel is. 'Miss Satchel, have you got a satchel?' 'Where's your satchel, Miss Satchel?' 'What kind of satchel do you have, Miss Satchel?' *Snigger, snigger, snigger.*

My replies have been as simple and sweet as, 'I don't have a satchel.' 'I don't like satchels.' 'I don't want a satchel.' While all the time, I give a sickly-sweet false smile which helps to hide my peeved irritability.

Hmm, peeved irritability, that's exactly how I feel right now as I stand here, in this posh ladies' room, staring into a large rectangular mirror, which some of my fastidious colleagues might describe as being a quadrilateral. Maths – huh. They all seem to eat, sleep, live and breathe mathematical supremacy and literature mastery. As for me, I'm going with the flow as I get my head around their way of doing things in schools these days, compared to when I was at school, some 12 years ago. I mean, I've barely learnt every child's name in the class (there are 30 of them for goodness sake), let alone mastered anything. Things have changed a lot in education and I have got a lot to learn – and that's without all the names. There are children's names, teacher's name (I need to know them by their first name and by their last name) and everyone else's name – God help me.

It's a big school consisting of over 700 pupils and more than 70 staff. That's an awful lot of names, but I guess I don't have to know all the children's names, just my class would be a start. I had worked in a pre-school for eight years previously (far fewer names) but felt the time had come to move on to my preferred profession as a teaching assistant.

So, that's where I am now – the new TA, Miss Satchel, at Baghurst Primary. To be honest, I wish I'd picked a different school that didn't have any possible resemblance to 'a container in which to carry things in' but I guess it's too late now.

"Susie, I wondered where you'd disappeared to..."

Jade Smith has just walked into the ladies' room. She's quite nice. In fact, she was the first person to say hello to me when I started at the school and the only one who didn't smirk at my name. Although, she does have a very cool, turquoise, turtle-shell satchel which I quite like and if I were to ever own one myself, it would be one like hers. But that's not going to happen as I don't want a satchel – ever.

"I was hardly going to stay out there when everyone was laughing at my expense," I say, bitterly.

"Ignore them hun. They'll soon find something else to amuse themselves. Give them another hour and they'll all be drunk. Then you can laugh at them when they're falling over themselves."

I smile at Jade. She's a kind and caring girl. I haven't asked but I'm sure she's a bit younger than me – maybe early twenties. Funnily enough, she has a blonde bob too but hers is much longer. She has the kind of eyes that most women would kill for; huge with long dark lashes which sweep upwards and she has these amazing bright blue irises. I'm sure one look from her could pierce the heart of any man. She has a wide, cheeky smile and a cute little nose. I quite envy people with cute little noses as mine is far from being cute, or little.

Anyway, less of the self-effacing attitude and back to the dire matter in hand. "I suppose I should ignore them," I say, as I shrug my feathery shoulders. "I've got nothing else to wear, unless I take it off..." I hesitate. "Actually, maybe not – I'm wearing my pyjama shorts and an old vest top underneath."

"Keep it on – who cares," says Jade, eyeing my orange legs and trying to conceal a grimace. "Don't show anyone that it bothers you – especially not Sarah or Jane." Jade smiles warmly and totters off into one of the toilet cubicles.

She's right you know. If Sultry Sarah or Juicy Jane think for one minute that I'm upset about this, they'll take great pleasure in mocking me for the rest of the evening. Honestly, those two women are a law unto themselves. Although, I do have to admit, from what I've seen and heard so far, that they are very professional people at work and good at their jobs. But that's the only time that the word, 'good' can be used in the same sentence as Sarah or Jane. I probably need to explain myself and tell you a little more about them.

They are both teachers. Young, gorgeous, intelligent, prosperous, fun-loving bitches. I know, that last word sounds like I'm a tad jealous...

OK, maybe I am and obviously, their names are not really, Sultry Sarah and Juicy Jane either – I made them up, but if you ever saw them, I'm sure you would agree that their descriptive, Susie-inspired forenames are extremely apt.

Sultry Sarah, who is known around the school as Miss Chambers, looks like a Swedish model who has just stepped off a catwalk. She's tall, svelte, sophisticated and elegant. Her long, baby-blonde hair swishes from side to side, in slow-motion it seems, as she glides along the corridors effortlessly. I say effortlessly, because I have absolutely no idea how she can stand up – let alone walk. How does she do it? Her perfectly matching shoes for every outfit she ever wears, are at least four inches high. How can she wear them all day?

Apart from when she's doing PE with her class and wearing trainers (still perfectly matching any sporty clothes she might be wearing that day), I would bet that she doesn't own any other flat shoes at all.

I'm trying not to be jealous. I really am. But when I look in to her wide, ice-blue eyes, expertly crafted with just a subtle hint of shimmering, aqua eyeshadow and lengthening mascara, I can't help but feel my lips tremble as I force them into a phoney smile.

As for Juicy Jane, or Miss Hodges, well... she is a curvaceous, dark-haired beauty of magnificent proportions.

Please note my magnanimous approach here – I'm trying to be kind. I really am. Jealousy is a dark, destroying emotion and I must rise above it.

However, I do have to say that she is also a bitch. Fair enough, she might be a beautiful bitch with cascading, wavy brown locks tumbling down her back and huge doe-like, brown eyes, but she's still a bitch, all the same. She wears glorious outfits which accentuate her gorgeous figure but in a respectable and appropriate way. Working in a school, I'm sure she must find it difficult to hold back from revealing her perfection any more than she does. The thing I don't get is, everyone loves her. She's fun, she's jolly and she walks around with a pretty smile on her face, all day long. I'm sure other people don't see her the same way that I do. Anyway, in comparison to her staunch friend and ally, Sarah, Jane is a bit of a mix-and-match kind of girl in the shoe department, which is very confusing, as she'll be wearing high heels in the morning and dainty dolly shoes in the afternoon. Maybe, she can't do the whole high heel thing like Sarah can for the whole day.

So, now I expect that you are wondering why they are such bitches. Well, to be honest with you, they probably aren't. Unfortunately, it is only my perception of them. Call me jealous then. OK, I probably am but they didn't have to do what they did to me, did they?

*** 2 ***

I hear the toilet flush and Jade walks out of the cubicle with a smile on her face. "You still in here," she says as she begins to rinse her hands under the gilded, mixer tap.

"Yes, I was miles away for a moment there. I'll go back in very soon." I shrug and snort. "It's going to take me ten minutes just to go for a wee though."

"Do you need a hand with anything?" Jade shakes the water from her hands and moves over to the hot-air drier.

"No, I'll be just fine," I say, a little unconvincingly. "I'll be with you all as soon as possible."

She smiles at me, turns to look in the mirror and puffs up her hair. "OK, see you in a minute," she adds, before leaving the room.

So, here I am, alone again in this posh ladies' room. The whole place is posh, in fact. I don't think I've ever been anywhere as posh as this, to be truthful. It's a magnificent hotel, set in the English countryside, on the outskirts of Hampshire. Hawksmoor Hotel is a luxurious restored, Georgian manor house, I do believe. Acres of rolling hills and picturesque gardens surround the palatial building and a white gravel drive sweeps up to and around the spectacular frontage. Yes, I can categorically say that I've never been anywhere like it before.

We're not staying here, although I think we should have. That would have been better, for me at least, if we had been staying. I could have changed my attire. I wouldn't be standing here, staring into a big mirror, feeling slightly sorry for myself. Apparently though, it was far too expensive to stay here for the night and particularly as it's the Christmas season as well. This hotel gets very busy over the holidays and has been known to be completely booked up, as much as a year in advance – and that's just for the event rooms. Weddings can be two or three years in advance. It's crazy, if you ask me.

Not that anyone *is* asking me.

Just this evening alone cost £45 per head but I suppose that did cover the cost of coach travel too. I can't moan really. I've been looking forward to tonight and was so grateful that the school could include me in the numbers and add me as a late booking.

According to Jade, the rest of the school staff arranged this Christmas work do, in January of this year. January – can you believe it? Well, I suppose there are a large number of us here. And actually, we – as in Baghurst school staff – are not alone.

You see, our school is a feeder school to the local senior school, Hightown Secondary. We have close connections with that school, which I'm slowly learning about. We share some of their facilities, like their minibuses, their expansive drama and music production stage and hall and their well-equipped sports centre and swimming pool. I've been there twice so far, as our older year groups performed their Christmas production to parents, under the stage lights, in the huge music and drama hall. I must say it was pretty impressive.

Hightown is a big school. I thought ours was big but no, Hightown is so much bigger. They have well over a thousand pupils and I can only imagine that there must be more than a hundred staff.

Tonight, the staff from both schools have joined forces and come to this Christmas work do together. It took three coaches to get us all here. To be fair, only two and a half were full but that's still a lot of people from both schools. Still a lot of people to stare and laugh at me.

I heave a sigh and waddle over to a cubicle. I squeeze myself in and around the door, before locking it. This is going to be a mammoth task in the confines of a toilet cubicle. I need to remove my feathery wings, peel off the brown body suit and perch on the toilet seat somehow.

Oh, well – here goes – wish me luck.

As I'm perched on the throne, I hear a couple of women walk into the room. They're gossiping and giggling about some other woman, called Amber, and her apparent advances on a Mr Bagshaw. Huh – not a name I've heard at our school but how funny would that be? Mr Bagshaw works at Baghurst Primary School and has a big bag. Beats Satchel any day of the week.

"She won't leave him alone." I hear one of the women say.

"I know and I really don't think he's interested in her." The other one says. "She'll end up making herself look like an idiot."

"We've got to say something to her – she's obsessed with him. It's embarrassing listening to her make suggestive remarks and sidling up to him constantly. He raised his eyebrows at me, you know – he can't get rid of her."

I hear one of the women walk into the cubicle next to mine and close the door.

"Well, you'll be the best one to tell her, she won't listen to me. I've tried but there's no getting through to her. She reckons she's going to shag him tonight if it's the last thing she does."

"I'll talk to her when we go outside for a smoke," says the woman in the cubicle next to mine. "Hello – who's that in the toilet next door?"

I freeze. Is she talking to me?

"Is that the turkey in there? Your feathers have fallen out all over the floor." She giggles.

I stand up and flush the toilet. "Yes, sorry. I..." Gathering up my costume, I pull it up and over my shoulders. "Sorry, it's a bit of a tight squeeze in here." I peer down at the gap at the bottom of the cubicle. My feathery wings are spread out under the adjoining wall.

The woman laughs. "No worries. We saw you earlier. I bet it was Sarah and Jane who put you up to this."

"Yes," I reply, while trying to zip myself up. "Apparently, it's like an initiation or so I've heard."

Both women laugh and I hear the toilet flush in the cubicle next to me. "Yes, that's right. You're new then. Teacher or TA?"

"TA at Baghurst," I say as I pick up my wings and unlock the door.

"We're TAs at Hightown," says the woman as she unlocks her cubicle door. "Nice to meet you."

I edge my way out of the cubicle and smile waveringly. "Nice to meet you too."

The woman from the cubicle is older than I expected, probably in her forties. Her big round face smiles at me. She's perspiring and her cheeks are flushed crimson. I wonder for a moment, how she managed to get in the cubicle next door as she is a very large woman with a protruding rear end.

"They've done this many times before you know," she says as she waddles over to the sink.

"Sorry?"

"Sarah and Jane. They've tricked other people as well."

"Oh, I see." I smile again. I can't show these women that I'm hurt about this.

The other woman turns from the mirror and leans back on the sink unit. "It's like it's the done-thing these days." She looks me up and down and grins. She's half the size of the other woman and I would imagine she's half her age too. "Don't worry about it, everyone knows what those two are like. Enjoy the evening anyway."

I nod and peer down at my fleece suit. "Thanks, I'll try to."

"Come on then," says the younger woman. "Let's go and sort Amber out."

The two women leave the room together and once again I'm left alone to stare at my reflection in the mirror. A turkey. Yes, that's right, I'm dressed as a flipping turkey, just in case you hadn't figured that out by now. I'm the most gullible person in the world, I'm sure I am.

Sultry Sarah was the one who came to me first. She asked me if I had an outfit for the fancy-dress Christmas do. I said that I didn't realise it was fancy dress. She then said to me that I should speak to Jane, as she had a spare outfit I could borrow. Juicy Jane said that I could borrow her turkey costume as it would complement her giant Brussels sprout outfit that she would be wearing tonight.

Let me just add at this point, Jane is wearing a beautiful silver shift dress tonight – it does not resemble a Brussels sprout in the slightest.

Stupidly, I didn't ask anyone else about the fancy-dress evening, not even Jade, as I'm quite a shy person and tend to avoid the only room in the school where normal adult conversations take place. I'm talking about our staffroom. I haven't ventured in there at break or lunchtime yet. I much prefer to sit in the classroom's conservatory and read up on the week's planning and investigate anything that I'm not sure about. Which, I must add, is quite a lot. It's not that I'm thick – far from it. I achieved three A levels at college. It's just the teaching styles that I'm getting used to, like I said before.

Anyway, back to Jane, who was *kind* enough to loan me her turkey costume. She even dropped it off to my home one night – how *super-kind* of her. Sarah was so pleased to hear the news that I had the outfit and said that we'd all go well together, as she was going as a Christmas pudding.

Trust me, she looks nothing like a Christmas pudding tonight.

So, that's how I fell for their scheming little plan to humiliate me. Of course, they apologised profusely, in between roars of laughter, as we waited together at the first of several coach pick-up points, earlier this evening. They told me how they always managed to get someone to wear it each year, whether it was someone new from our school or someone from Hightown. It was a standing joke at both schools and now it was my turn to flap about all evening in a brown and red body suit that stops at my knees, crinkly orange, fleece leggings and bright yellow, plastic turkey feet.

Deep breaths Susie Satchel, you *can* and *will* get through this. You *must* laugh it off, as if you don't care.

*** 3 ***

As I hobble out of the ladies' room, I see the two women who I spoke to a few minutes ago. They are pulling another woman towards the exit. My guess is that the other one is Amber, the one they were talking about in the toilets. She's an attractive girl with long blonde hair. She's wearing a very daring, low-cut, mini dress. I'm sure she can't possibly be wearing a bra with that dress and I only hope that she doesn't fall out of it and that she can breathe properly as the slinky red material hugs her every curve, tightly.

I peer around the expansive hall, wondering, just out of curiosity, who Mr Bagshaw might be. I remember that the women were talking about Amber as if she were a sex-mad maniac who was flaunting and flirting her way into Mr Bagshaw's pants. As my eyes flick around the sea of people in front of me, I conclude that he could be any one of the young men standing around with pint glasses in their hands.

I waddle around the back of the crowd, trying not to get noticed, as I make my way back to the group of TAs from my school. They've all been very nice to me this evening in the short amount of time that we've been here and during the coach trip too. They showed such empathy as they looked me up and down and smiled waveringly at my plight. They reminisced about the turkey victims of the past and giggled about a few. Yet, they all still love Sarah and Jane. Not one person thinks, for one minute, that the turkey victims might be completely distressed when it happens to them. None of them have any idea what it feels like, unless it's happened to them too – which isn't many of them at all. Well, *one* other TA that I know about, to be precise. So, that's not many victims, within my group of colleagues, for sure.

As I reach my group, I realise that everyone is moving forward towards the lavishly laid out tables. We're having a three-course Christmas meal before the dancing gets started.

Jade sees me and waves. I flap a feathery arm back at her as I approach.

"That looks better," she says as she greets me with a smile. "Keep it off and you'll be just fine."

I hadn't realised, but I now remember removing the crested hood from my head earlier. "But my hair..." I run my fingers through it. It's lank and has a grimy feel to it.

"It looks fine – don't worry." Jade links her arm through mine and pulls me towards the tables.

The tables are set out in long lines of about 50 places, I would guess. We walk to the furthest end of the table nearest the wall and take seats with the rest of the TAs. Thankfully, I'm sitting next to Jade.

I look up and watch as the rest of our staff fill this and the next table behind me. Suddenly, I see Sarah and Jane heading down this way. I turn to look at the empty chairs, directly behind me. Oh no. Are they going to sit there?

Yes, they are.

"Hi Susie," says Jane. "I didn't see you there – you know, just for a minute, I thought they'd brought the cooked turkey down this end to carve at the table – I didn't realise it was you sitting there." She laughs heartily and pulls out a chair.

I smile at her, while all the time, I'm controlling the murderous rage inside me. I shuffle in my seat as my tail feathers become uncomfortable to sit on.

"Thought you might have taken that off by now," says Sarah as she sits down, directly behind me. "You must be hot."

"No, it's fine. No problem. I can't take it off really, I..." I break off and pull the top half of the bodysuit over my shoulders more. "I'm wearing pyjamas underneath."

Sarah peers at me incredulously. "Pyjamas?"

I nod my head. "Yes... there's nothing like jumping straight out of a turkey suit and straight into bed."

"Ooh, who's going to be stuffing the turkey tonight then?" Jane gives me one of those looks. You must know the ones I mean. A look of hurtful sardonicism.

I pull myself up high in my chair and stare her straight in the eye. "Wouldn't you like to know."

"No, I'm not sure I would actually. I'm not into bestiality." Jane roars with laughter, followed by Sarah.

I smirk at them and turn around to face my table. Others around me are giggling at Jane's words. Even Jade is laughing. OK, I'm going to go with it too. I feign laughter, along with the rest of them. It's all I can do really. This night has got to get better – right?

Wrong.

It's not going to get any better. I've eaten my three-course meal, drunk three glasses of wine and now I'm hot. Ridiculously hot. And terribly itchy. It feels like I have an army of fleas running up and down my legs. I'm going to venture out to the ladies again – I've got to – I'm sure I have some sort of prickly heat on my legs from these stupid orange leggings. God help me. If I have got a rash, what can I do? I can hardly come back in the room in my old pyjamas.

I pull my tail feathers up from the chair, smile at Jade and mouth a, 'back in a minute' to her as I leave the table. Quite a few of our staff are drunk now. They're being very loud and silly – so maybe I would get away with coming back out wearing my tatty pyjamas.

I waddle off to the ladies' room trying to rub my legs against each other as I walk, trying desperately to stop the intense, burning itch which is getting worse by the second.

As I open the door to the ladies, I hear someone retching in one of the cubicles. "Are you OK in there?" I ask, as I see a pair of stiletto heels poking out from underneath the cubicle door. Another retch, more violent than the first. "Can I help you at all?" I'm slightly alarmed by the awful noise.

"Ugh..." The woman manages to utter before retching again.

I waddle towards the door and gently try to push it open, as it's clearly not locked. I can just see the woman, on all fours, with her head down the toilet. "Are you OK?" I say again. "Should I get you some water?" I turn to look over at the sink unit and there, on one side, is a small stack of plastic beakers. "I'll get you some water," I add before closing the door.

She retches again as I'm filling the beaker. I return to the cubicle and push the door slightly ajar again. The woman is sitting back on her heels and she's scooping her long blonde hair away from her face.

"Here," I say, passing the beaker to her.

She turns her head around and I can see that it's Amber, the girl who was dragged outside by two other women earlier. She takes the beaker from me and sips at the water.

"Thanks," she says, before coughing and spluttering. She drinks some more, turns back to the toilet and flushes it. Returning the beaker to me, she then pulls herself up from the floor. Slumping down on the toilet seat, she lowers her head.

"Do you want some more?" I say, peering into the empty beaker.

Nodding her head, she looks up and smiles waveringly. "Please."

As I walk back over to the sink, I attempt to rub my legs together again. The intense itch has come back or I just didn't notice it a minute ago, due to my unexpected nursing duties.

"Here," I say as I pass another drink to her. "Is your name Amber?"

She peers up at me with a quizzical stare. "How do you know my name?"

"Oh..."

Oh, exactly. How *do* I know her name? I can hardly say that I heard two women talking about her earlier. I can't mention that they thought she was sex-mad and trying to get into a Mr Bagshaw's pants. "I err... I thought I heard someone earlier... call out your name. Is it Amber?" I feign thoughtfulness.

She nods and sips the water again.

"Hi," I say, extending a hand. "I'm Susie. I work at Baghurst."

"Hi," she mumbles, while ignoring my offer of a handshake.

OK, maybe I shouldn't be shaking her hand anyway – she's probably got vomit all over it.

Amber pulls herself up awkwardly and bumps into the sides of the cubicle as she does so. She's obviously very drunk. I meet her eyes and grimace. "You've err... your make-up, it's smudged. Do you have any mascara with you?"

She pushes past me and staggers over to the mirror. "No, have you?"

"I'm sorry, no I don't."

"Great," she says before returning to the cubicle. She pulls at the toilet roll violently, gathering up handfuls of paper as it unrolls. "Thanks for the water," she says, upon her return to the mirror. "Never been looked after by a turkey before." She sniggers into the toilet roll, then begins to wipe streaks of black make-up from under her eyes.

"You'd be surprised what turkeys can do," I reply. "I need to get these leggings off though – they're driving me mad." I grin at her, through the mirror and waddle over to a cubicle. Once inside, I begin the painstaking task of removing the whole outfit. It's the only way I can peel off the leggings.

Relief. Well at least it's relief to get the orange fleece away from my skin. There is little respite from the insatiable desire to claw the skin from my legs as they continue to burn and itch. I'm not sure which would look better either. Crinkly orange legs or blotchy red ones? I cannot put these leggings on again. I must be allergic to the material or someone before me didn't wash them, or maybe they used a different detergent. I don't know. There's one thing I do know though – I'm not wearing them again.

So, I'll have to go back into the event room with red blotches all over my legs. Perhaps, once the music starts, the lights will dim and I can discreetly waddle back to my table and sit down for the rest of the night while my legs are recovering. Yes, that's exactly what I'll do and if anyone asks me to join them in a dance, I'll politely decline, saying something like, 'Sorry, I have a bad back'. It's that simple.

I leave Amber in the ladies, tending to her streaks and smears, and waddle back to the room. It's actually harder to walk in these plastic feet now that I've removed the leggings. I'm still very hot and my moist feet are slushing around in the huge turkey shoes.

As I walk in the room, I'm ecstatic to see that the lights have dimmed. I'm not ecstatic to see that most of the tables are being cleared away and shunted to the sides of the room. Chairs are being placed around the sides of the room and smaller tables, about knee high, are being carried in by the hotel's staff. So, that's my plan of hiding my legs under the tables, over.

As I'm watching the removals going on with a sadness in my heart, I suddenly become aware of a man standing just a metre or so away from me. I shoot a sideways glance at him before facing forwards again. Oh my God, he's looking straight at me with a big smile on his face. He's gorgeous. It's making me feel quite uncomfortable. I turn back to meet his eye and give him a quivering smile. He's more than gorgeous – he's totally perfect.

"Hi," I say and raise a hand to wave.

No... why would I wave at him?

It's too late, I've already done it. How silly of me. He smiles again and moves a little closer. Oh no – oh dear.

"I see you've changed your legs," he says, peering down.

I look down too. I'm so embarrassed by my red blotchy skin. "Yes, I..."

"Great make-up," he adds.

"Sorry?" I look at him puzzled.

"On your legs – they look like real turkey legs. They're even better than the orange ones.

I'm stunned and speechless. "Oh... err... yes." Oh my goodness, he actually thinks...

"Bet you're hot in that outfit."

"Yes, very." Oh no, why have I just told him I'm very hot? Now he's going to wonder why I don't just take it off.

"Why are you still wearing it then?" He looks me up and down with his cool-blue eyes. "Most victims would have taken it off by now."

"I... well... to be honest with you..."

"I get it," he says, eyeing me pitifully. "They tricked you into this, didn't they? And like one or two of the others, you can't take it off, can you?"

I give a joyless, little shake of my head.

"I haven't seen you before – I'm guessing you're new. Do you work at Baghurst?"

"Yes, yes I do... and yes, they did trick me. That Sultry... I mean Sarah and Jane."

The man shakes his head knowingly. "Thought so. You're not the only one who's fallen for their trick." He smiles at me.

Gosh – he's gorgeous.

"I had heard that," I say. "The thing is, I can't remove it as I... well, to be honest with you... I'm wearing pyjamas underneath."

He shakes his head and stifles a laugh. "I'm sorry – they really have done you over, haven't they?"

I nod and muster up a smile.

"My name's Ryan by the way," he says, offering a handshake.

Nervously, I reach for his hand...

"Mrrr... Baggsy-shaw... there you are... you naughty little boy..."

I drop my hand back to my side as he pulls his away too. Turning simultaneously, we both peer at...

Amber – she practically throws herself at Ryan, who I've now guessed, is the poor, pestered, Mr Bagshaw. The drunk woman leans over his shoulder and peers into his eyes. "I've been... looking for you... naughty little boy."

Ryan turns to look at me and grimaces. He attempts to shrug Amber from his shoulder but she grips on tightly. "Amber," he whispers, "go and get yourself sorted out – you look a mess."

I peer at Amber's face and realise that she has not done a very good job of dealing with the make-up mayhem spread across her cheeks. "Here," I say, "let me help you Amber. Let's go back to the ladies and get you sorted out." I smile awkwardly at Ryan and attempt to pull Amber away from him.

"No... I'm talking to Mr... Baggy-shaw." She giggles into his shoulder.

"Amber, go with this lady..." Ryan peers at me, a desperate look in his eyes. "Sorry, I don't know your name."

"Susie."

"Susie." He smiles. "Amber, go with Susie – she'll get you sorted out." Ryan steps away and manages to unlatch himself from Amber's grasp.

"Come on," I say, "let's get you tidied up." I pull her away with a mighty tug and prop her up as I lead her towards the exit. Turning my head as I go, I see Ryan staring at me. He mouths a 'thank you' to me before walking away.

"But I want to talk to..."

"We need to get your face sorted out first. You look terrible Amber, if you don't mind me saying so."

"But..."

"You're very drunk. Why don't I get you some more water to drink and we'll sort your face out? You've got black smudges all over your cheeks."

"But..."

"No, 'buts', we're going to the ladies."

*** 4 ***

Great night this is turning out to be. Not.

Here I am, dressed as a flipping hot turkey with red blotchy legs, which are still driving me insane as they continue to itch, and I'm also nursing a drunk, overly-obsessed, wanton woman. I was actually looking forward to tonight, believe it or not. I had visions that everyone would be wearing fab, Christmassy, fancy-dress outfits and the night would be amusing, to say the least. I imagined there would be a lot of funny costumes to look at and it would be a fun evening. How wrong was I?

Amber is sitting on a toilet seat, sipping cold water, while I'm leaning back on the sink feeling quite exasperated. I've had to clean her whole face. Her *whole* face, because when I removed the black smears from around her eyes and the tops of her cheeks, I'd also wiped a thick layer of foundation away. She looked two-tone, so I had to clean the rest of her face, removing all traces of the heavily applied concealing cream. How different she looks now. I think she actually looks better with less make-up, although she is a bit red and blotchy where I had to scrub her face quite hard to remove the gunk. She appears to be more innocent looking and younger. It's a shame that she has embarrassed herself tonight by being so drunk and promiscuous towards Ryan. I feel quite sorry for her really.

I look across as I hear a sob coming from the cubicle. She's crying. The small amount of make-up left on her eyes will end up on her face again.

"Amber," I say as I approach her, "are you OK?"

Obviously, she's not but what else do I say? I hardly know the poor woman, yet I seem to have been roped into looking after her. She's so vulnerable now and I can't just leave her.

Great joy.

"Huh?" She looks up at me. "I've..." She wipes her nose with a clump of toilet roll. "I've messed things up."

"No you haven't," I lie. "Look – I don't know what's going on with you and that man, Ryan, but..." I break off. Should I be sticking my nose into her business?

"He hates me."

"I'm sure he doesn't hate you."

She rolls off some more toilet roll and blows her nose. "Yes, he does."

I peer down at her, feeling really sorry for her. "Look," I say, tentatively, "can I be honest with you?"

She shrugs and heaves a heavy sigh.

"I think you'd have a much better chance with him if... well, if you backed off from him."

Peering up through watery eyes, she stares at me questioningly.

"It's none of my business really," I falter, "I'm just saying that... well, I don't think men like that kind of thing all the time."

"He hates me."

"I'm sure he doesn't hate you, Amber."

"How would you know?" she asks.

"Well, I don't know, to be honest with you. I don't know either of you. I'm new to Baghurst school – hence the turkey here." I flap my wings, trying to lighten things up.

Amber smiles and wipes her eyes again.

"Look, why don't you take all of that off?" I say, peering at the new smudges across her eyes.

She nods her head and turns her mouth down. "Might as well. I'm not going back in there." She points to the main door.

"But you can't stay in here all evening." I suddenly feel irked. I can't leave the poor girl, yet I do not want to spend my whole evening sitting in toilet cubicles with her either.

"Can," she says, stubbornly.

"Why don't we clean you up, one last time, and go back to the disco together. Everyone will be dancing now and the lights are low. It's quite dark in there..." I pause as she pulls herself up from the toilet. "No one will notice you in there."

"No – not going. I want to go home."

"You can't go home yet. The coaches aren't leaving until one o'clock," I say, feeling a little more peeved at the situation. "Trust me – I would go home now if I could. Just to get out of this silly outfit. But I can't, so I'm going to enjoy the rest of the evening the best I can."

She staggers over to the sink unit and peers in the mirror. "No way am I going back out there, looking like this."

I walk over to the mirror and look at her reflection. "You look fine. Just wipe those smudges from under your eyes. I think you look better without make-up, if I'm honest."

Amber snorts and begins to wipe the smudges away. "No way. I'm not going back. I'll wait here for the coach."

"Surely you can't..."

The main door opens and two women walk in.

"There you are Amber," says one of them. "Everyone's been looking for you." The woman turns to me and raises her eyebrows. "Our Amber is like a child – we have to keep her reins on, otherwise she disappears."

I nod my head and smile with relief. "I've been in here for a while myself – helping her out."

"Sorry," says the second woman. "We'll take care of her now, thanks."

"Thank you," I say, gratefully. "I do hope she'll be OK."

"Sure she will be – won't you Amber?" The first woman says, peering into Amber's face.

Amber is scowling into the mirror like a spoilt child.

I turn to walk away. "Remember what I said, Amber. Dignity is admirable."

"When did you say that?" she calls out.

"I didn't actually say that but that's what I meant." I smile at the other two women before leaving the room with a sigh of relief.

The event room has got darker now and coloured lights flick around the floor in time to the music. Many people have got up to dance and the disco is in full swing. I waddle around the outside of the throng of dancers, towards the area where I was sitting earlier. As I move around the crowd, I notice Ryan standing with a group of people, in front of me. He's holding a glass of drink in one hand and his other is in his pocket. He turns his head and looks at me. He's wearing black trousers, a lilac, stripped shirt and a deeper lilac tie. I hadn't noticed before how broad his shoulders are. He's so fit looking. He steps back from the group and smiles at me. I freeze and watch him approach. He's just too handsome to look at without a nervous tremble vibrating on my top lip, as I attempt a feeble smile.

"Thanks for earlier," he says, staring deep into my eyes.

"She's still in the ladies'," I reply, trying to sound cool and calm. "She's a bit of a mess, I have to say."

"Tell me about it. She's nothing but a pain when we go out." He looks down at his glass. "She pesters me every time she gets drunk."

"Oh, I see... so..."

"No, if that's what you were just about to ask? We're not a couple or anything like that."

"OK," I say, feeling a little coy.

"She's fine at school." Ryan laughs. "Well, at least she doesn't act like this, anyway."

"Does she pester you a lot then?"

He takes a long sip from his glass and I can smell the alcohol on his breath as he sighs afterwards. "I've told her I'm not interested – in the nicest way possible."

"It must be difficult for you... especially as, I take it, you're both in the same school."

Ryan nods his head. "Same department – even worse." He straightens his back and smiles. "I have to be honest though, she's not as bad as this at school. She's just a bit ditsy, that's all."

"Ditsy?"

"Yeah, a bit scatterbrained. Always got her head in the clouds."

"Oh, I see." Gosh – she sounds a bit like me.

Ryan looks across the room and his mouth drops. "Oh no, she's back. I'd better be off. Nice talking to you. Sophie isn't it?"

"Susie."

"Sorry, Susie. I'll have to catch up with you some other time. Thanks for rescuing me earlier – I really appreciate it."

Before he turns to leave, he winks at me. It's not a friendly wink, it's a slow, sexy wink. I know those kind of winks, I've seen them before. My heart flutters when it shouldn't. I'll explain why it shouldn't later, but for now I'm watching the two women from the ladies, walking around the back of the room, arm in arm with Amber. She appears to be walking much easier than she was earlier, although she's holding her head down as if in shame.

It is a shame. I'm guessing she's going to hugely regret tonight, when she wakes up tomorrow. Oh well, each to their own, I suppose. At least I'm off the hook now and don't have to be her nurse and nanny.

As I arrive at the corner of the room where most of the staff from my school are seated, I notice Sultry Sarah and Juicy Jane standing at the edge of the dance floor, chatting to a group of men. Jane is having an in-depth conversation with... Oh, it's Mr Ryan Bagshaw again. He's darting his eyes around the room as he listens to her. Now and again he smiles at her unconvincingly and then averts his gaze to the ladies' room or the exit doors. I'm sure he's keeping a watch for the return of Amber.

Suddenly, his eyes are on me. He smiles and nods his head. Jane turns around and smirks at me. Then she turns back to Ryan. She leans into him and whispers in his ear. He pulls back from her and frowns, shaking his head at the same time. I look away with the distinct impression that Jane has just said something to Ryan about me. I can't imagine she's saying anything nice about me. She's such a bitch – OK, maybe she isn't really but she most certainly is in my book. I look back and she's staring at me again. I know she's being a bitch because of the snide look on her face, every time she peers at me. I've got to ignore her – rise above it – I'm better than to get caught up in her little devious games, or Sarah's for that matter.

As I waddle off to my chair, I notice Amber coming back in from the exit doors. The two women are hurrying behind her. Amber is strutting purposefully through the room, turning her head from side to side as she goes. She doesn't appear to be drunk at all now. She spots Ryan, way before he sees her, and marches towards him.

I watch discreetly, as Amber approaches Ryan and pushes her way past Jane. Poor Ryan has a startled look on his handsome face as she appears to have some strong words with him. She's gesticulating at him and looking around the crowded room. Ryan turns to walk away, shaking his head, in what looks like disgust. Amber pulls him back by his arm and says something else to him. Then she turns to Jane and says something to her. Jane looks over to the corner of the room where I'm sitting, minding my own business, I might add. She then points in my direction.

Hang on a minute, I'm sitting against a wall here. There's no point in me turning around to see who they're both looking at now. It's me. Actually, all three of them are staring at me now.

Ryan is standing between Amber and Jane looking totally cheesed-off. He holds his hands out to his sides and shrugs as Jane beckons to me.

Stupidly, I point to myself and mouth, 'Who, me?'.

Jane nods and beckons to me again.

Oh dear, what's going on now? Am I in trouble here? I have absolutely no idea what's going on, as I drag myself up from the chair and waddle back over to the crowd.

"Ryan never told me..." says Amber, as I draw closer.

"Sorry?" I reply, searching both Jane's and Ryan's faces for clues.

"Shush, Amber," says Jane, stepping in front of the others. "Look, Susie..."

"Yes?"

"There was a little joke going around..." Jane is sounding rather awkward and won't actually meet my eye.

"Joke?" I quiz.

"Yes. Amber has got way too drunk tonight and got a bit upset – haven't you Amber?"

Amber folds her arms in front of her, snorts disdainfully at Ryan and then stomps off.

"I have absolutely no idea what's going on here," I say, a little annoyed by it all.

Ryan is standing in front of me rolling his eyes and shaking his head. He looks angry.

"Sarah has just told Amber that Ryan is going to be stuffing the turkey tonight," says Jane.

I stare, aghast.

"It's all getting a bit ridiculous if you ask me," says Ryan.

"Well you've just made it worse..." Jane breaks off and looks around at me briefly, before turning back to Ryan. "Why did you have to go and tell her that you *will* be stuffing the turkey then?"

Ryan stares at me, fearfully. "I'm so sorry," he says to me, before lowering his gaze. He then turns back to Jane. "I shouldn't have said it, I know, but I knew it would get rid of her. You know what a bloody pain she is, Jane."

"Yes, I know but you could have done it a bit more subtly. She's really hurt."

"She doesn't do subtle though, does she?" Ryan sighs heavily. "I'm sick to death of it. Every time we go out."

I still haven't said a word and continue to stare at Jane and Ryan incredulously. Who would have thought a turkey could get into so much trouble just by sitting quietly in a corner? It's ridiculous.

"Look, I'm really sorry that you've been dragged into all of this." There's a genuine tone to Ryan's voice as he looks at me, desperately. "It's the same whenever we all go out. I'm a friendly guy but Amber takes that as an invitation to swoon around me all night. And tomorrow, when she's sober, she'll be messaging me, begging for my forgiveness. And every time, I tell her that I see us as friends and nothing else. I don't know what else to do."

I nod my head at him, unable to think of anything wise to say.

"Sarah should keep her mouth shut," says Ryan, directing his words at Jane. "She's a bloody troublemaker."

"Well, it's not Sarah's fault if Amber can't take a joke." Jane peers at Ryan pompously. "I'll tell her that she's upset Amber though."

Ryan nods his head and looks back at me. "This night is not going too great for you, is it? Sorry if I've been a part of that."

"No, please, there's no need to be sorry." I smile warmly. "It's all water off a du... turkey's back."

Ryan lets out a short laugh. "I hope you'll enjoy the rest of the evening and have no fear, I'm stuffing *no* turkeys tonight."

I flush with embarrassment. "I think you should at least get permission first."

Jane glares at me, obviously shocked by my words.

"Naturally – I would always seek permission first," says Ryan, with a smirk. He winks at me again before he turns to walk away. Again, it's one of those nice winks, not just a casual one. I know it is. I know that kind of wink.

Oh God, help me. I really fancy him and that is so wrong.

Jane pats me on the shoulder, the moment Ryan has gone. "He fancies you."

"I'm sure he's not really into stuffing turkeys, Jane," I say, as I waddle away and go back to my cosy corner.

Oh gosh, does he?

*** 5 ***

Jade and I are sitting together in a dark corner. She doesn't like dancing and I'm relieved by that. The last thing I want tonight, is to be dragged on to the dance floor, just to waddle and flap through one song after another. Normally I wouldn't mind but not tonight. Not with my still raging, red legs. And certainly, not with a protruding, feathery tail stuck to my behind.

It's been interesting though – I mean sitting here and doing some people-watching. I do like to watch how people interact with each other. I try to guess what their lives are like, who they live with, if they're happy and if not, why not. I suppose that I am quite a discreet, nosey person. Luckily, Jade seems to be that type too. Either that or she's keeping still and quiet, due to her highly-inebriated state. I'm not drunk at all, although I have had several glasses of wine. Maybe it's harder to get drunk when you're a turkey – I don't really know.

Anyway, I feel I must give an update on the evening's frivolities at this point – Amber has attached herself to someone else now. Can you believe that she is standing at the side of the DJ's turntable, eyeing one of the DJs wantonly? Yes, she's all over him. I was going to say, like a rash, but when I look at my own rash, I realise that they aren't always, 'all over'. Well, anyway, that's beside the point – she is all over him and he seems to be quite taken by it. Good luck to him, I say. And her.

As for Ryan, or should I call him, Mr Bagshaw? Anyway, he's been hanging out with his friends for the last hour or so. Whenever I glance around at him, he's either at the bar drinking or he's moved to the dance floor and is giving it some, to the faster paced music. Let me rephrase that as, 'giving it some' sounds a bit crude. He's really enjoying the music and he has a great way of moving. He can dance pretty well, which surprises me a little as most men can't dance at all – can they?

Sultry-Stirrer-Sarah, (yes, I've given her a new name as she does like to stir trouble – bitch) and her accomplice, Juicy-Joker-Jane (new name too –

she thinks it's OK to back-up her mate, rightly or wrongly), have been drinking copious amounts of the wine left on the tables and I'm sure they've practically finished it all now. They've milled around the crowds during the evening, danced a bit... well, I say dance but actually, neither of them can. Whether it's the fact that they both have sky-scraper heels on or they're too drunk, I don't know but I have cringed each time they've gone on to the dance floor. I'm sure they both think that they are like heavenly goddesses, floating around the dancefloor and that every single man must be in awe of their outstanding beauty and presence – well I'm afraid that's wrong. I haven't seen one man approach them to chat them up. I believe that sometimes, a woman can be a little too beautiful and too perfect and it tends to frighten men away.

Once or twice they've peered over at me and mustered up false smiles. I know they've been talking about me to other people and don't doubt for one minute that they've been telling anyone who would care to listen, about their latest turkey-victim. Maybe they've even told people that I need stuffing. I don't know, and I don't care much either. One thing's for sure – they won't pull the turkey feathers over my eyes again. I won't fall for their tricks a second time.

***

The evening's over now. The room brightens and a sea of faces squint their eyes at the bright lights above our heads. Amber is back in the ladies. After drinking more alcohol, she turned a nasty greeny-grey colour. I mean, it *was* nasty. The last time I saw her, she was tottering as quickly as she could to the ladies, staring ahead wide-eyed with both hands cupped over her mouth. She is *so* going to regret this tomorrow.

Jade is practically asleep next to me. I'll have to rouse her in a minute and no doubt, link arms to pull her out of the hotel and on to our coach. She's a bit of a mess. I think I'm probably the only sober person here and that includes turkeys.

I heave Jade up from her chair and thrust my arm under her armpit. "Come on Jade," I say, realising she's a dead weight. "Come on – time to go home."

She opens her eyes and looks at me puzzled. "Home?"

"Yes, we've got to get back on the coach now – come on."

I pull her along and head towards the exit doors where a large gathering is forming.

"Hello again."

A voice comes from behind me. I turn my head to see Ryan smiling at me. He looks extremely drunk.

"You've been a very helpful little turkey tonight." He peers at Jade who is literally hanging from my arm.

"Yes, seems that way." I smile waveringly. He makes me feel nervous every time I see him. It's ridiculous, I know.

"Well, thanks again for saving me. Hope I'll see you again some time and hopefully, not dressed as a turkey."

"Yes, yes... I'm err... sure you will." I haul Jade upright and continue to follow the building crowd of people towards the front of the hotel.

"Maybe we should go out for a drink sometime," says Ryan, in a low voice.

Oh my goodness, he actually spoke right into my ear, from behind. I just felt his intoxicating breath on my neck. I resist the urge to shiver and grip hold of Jade tightly as she staggers along.

Oh dear, go out for a drink? I can't.

"I'm sure we will – I heard that everyone goes out at Easter," I say, politely.

"And you'll be the Easter bunny – right?"

"Absolutely not." I turn my head and look at him. We smile at each other. Oh my goodness – he's so handsome. "I... I won't fall for that next time."

"I did mean just you and me. Get a bite to eat somewhere... have a couple of drinks. What do you think?"

Oh dear Lord – no.

"Oh, right, I see what you mean," I say. My smile turns into an awkward grimace. "Err... I can't. I'm really sorry. But thank you for the invite... and... I really must get Jade on the coach now. Goodbye." With a sudden surge of energy and strength, I practically sweep Jade up, off her feet, and carry her through the crowd towards the coaches parked on the drive.

I've escaped him. Damn, damn, damn.

***

It's 2.15am and I have just got off the coach, stinking of vomit. Not mine, I must add.

Jade was sick on the way home. Fair enough, she was sick into a sick-bag. The coach company were careful to place bags into every single seat pocket. Except Jade missed the bag quite a bit, upon her first retch. All over my poor, blotchy legs it went. And worse still, she managed to aim part of her stomach's contents, directly into one of my plastic turkey feet. You do not want to know how ill I felt, having to deal with, not only her, but also the gooey mess between my toes – not to mention the plastic shoe.

Anyway, as I just said, it's very late at night... or is it very early in the morning? Whatever, the point is that the coach has arrived at its destination, on time and I'm so lucky to have a wonderful friend who is patiently waiting here at the drop-off point. I climb down from the almost empty coach, having said goodbye to those who are left and waddle and squelch my way towards Clair with a wry smirk on my face.

Clair Fowles – my flatmate and best friend. At this present moment, we go together quite nicely, what with me being dressed as a turkey and her surname. Don't worry, I'm not taking the mick, we've already done that joke.

Anyway, we have lived together for the last two years, in my small, two-bedroom flat, in the heart of town. I had said to her that I'd get a taxi home tonight but she insisted on picking me up, and said that it wasn't a problem. Bless her. I love her to bits.

"Did you have a good night?" Clair is grinning at me and I just knew that she'd come to pick me up in her pyjamas. She's standing by the front of her car with a beige coat wrapped around her and her long brown hair is tied up in pigtails. Underneath her coat, she's wearing her *Tatty Ted* pyjama bottoms and I'm guessing the top too. She's also wearing her high black boots. She's quite a picture of silliness at this early hour. Mind you, who am I to talk?

"You won't believe it..." I say, as I walk to the passenger side and open the car door. "I've been done, good and proper."

"Done?"

"Conned," I add.

Clair looks at me questioningly. "What do you mean?"

"There was no fancy dress party."

We jump into her car and she starts the engine. "Where've you been then?"

"I've been to a party at the hotel, that's for sure..." I sigh exaggeratedly, "but there was no fancy dress."

"But...?"

"I was the only one."

Clair looks at me incredulously. "Oh no, you mean you were the only one in fancy dress?"

"Oh yes – that bitch Sarah and Juicy-Flipping-Jane – they stitched me up."

Clair bites her top lip and pulls away from the lay-by.

"I hope you're not laughing," I say in jest, "It's not funny, you know."

"Sorry Suse, it is a bit funny. Actually... it's bloody hilarious."

I cross my arms around my waist and sulk as we head home.

"Did everyone laugh at you then?" Clair is trying to sound sympathetic now – I know her sympathetic voice, it goes all quiet and soft.

"Not to my face really."

"But behind your back?"

I shrug my shoulders. "I don't know. I think some people felt sorry for me. They all seemed to know about the turkey costume."

"Why?" Clair sniffs the air as she's driving along. "Eew – what's that smell?"

"My feet." I scrunch my toes up in the moist plastic shoes.

"Smells like sick!"

"It is sick. Someone threw up all down my legs, on the coach."

Clair screws her nose up. "Eew, that's gross."

"I got most of it out of the shoes but..."

"You need a shower when we get home. You stink." She opens the window slightly on her side and breathes in the cold, crisp air. "So, anyway, why did they all know about the costume?"

"It's been done before. It's like an initiation into the school apparently."

"Great."

"Yes, exactly," I say, suddenly beginning to feel extremely tired from the night's events.

"Well it's done now. Try and forget about it and enjoy the Christmas holidays. I know I'm going to."

I smile waveringly as I peer out of the windscreen. "Yeah, I suppose so."

"Suse," Clair says loudly, "You've got to enjoy the break whatever happens."

"I will – I'll try." I sigh quietly – I don't want Clair to know how worried I've been.

"You never know – it might all turn out to be all right." She shoots a concerned glance at me.

"Maybe," I say, unconvincingly. "Maybe it will be all right."

***

Considering I didn't drink that much last night; I've woken up with a banging headache. I peer over the side of the bed to see the turkey costume laying crumpled on the floor. The shoes are in the bathroom where I left them last night, filled with watered down bleach. I just hope they haven't melted away during the night and I'm going to find welded, plastic puddles in the bath. I have no idea how much turkey feet are to replace, should they have met their end.

I pull my weary self out of bed, put my dressing gown on and trudge out of the room and through to the kitchen. Clair is sitting at the small round table, ploughing her way through a mountain of cereal.

"Morning," she says cheerily, "are you OK?"

I nod my head daintily and reach for the painkillers in the tall cupboard. "Yes – OK." I grab a glass of water and throw the tablets to the back of my throat. "What time are you going?"

"I'm leaving about twelve. Should get home for four, if the traffic's OK."

I nod again and join her at the table. "All packed then?"

"Yes, I think so. I can't wait to see Mum and Dad."

I muster up a smile before sipping at my glass of water. Clair's going home to her parent's house, in Devon, for Christmas. She lives in my ground-floor flat with me because she got a job here, over two years ago, once she'd finished university here. She's a practice nurse in our local doctor's surgery. I remember how we hit it off straight away when she moved in. I'd been looking for someone to share the flat with me for months. Several people had turned up to view the accommodation but they either didn't like the flat or its situation, or I didn't like them. That was the most important criteria for being successful in getting the accommodation – I had to like the person on first impressions, as I was going to be living with them. Clair had turned up for the interview with her hair in two bunches, wearing skinny jeans and a green stripy t-shirt. I remember the day like it was yesterday. The wide smile on her pretty face was genuine and we did nothing but giggle as I showed her around the flat. So, that's how we got to know each other. We've been practically inseparable since – until now.

"I bet they can't wait to see you either."

Clair nods her head while chewing a mouthful of cereal. "Hmm."

"Send them my love, won't you?"

"Yes, of course I will. They did say…"

"I know, I could come and stay with them too."

"It's not too late." She reminds me.

"No, I'm staying here. I've got to give it a try, haven't I?" I sigh into my glass of water.

"You should, Suse. At least one more time. I'm sure he's not seeing anyone else."

"Hmm," I mumble, unconvinced by Clair's last words.

I haven't mentioned it before, where I've been so wrapped up with the stupid turkey costume, but I do have a boyfriend. Now you might understand why I said, no, to Mr Bagshaw. God, if only it had been another time, another place. He was so gorgeous. Perhaps I shouldn't be saying that but sometimes... well, there's nothing wrong with thinking things like that, is there?

I'm far too loyal, I guess. Loyal being the operative word here, as I'm convinced that this word is not in my boyfriend, Kallum's, vocabulary at all. I've been doubtful over the last month or so. I've been sneakily trying to discover whether he is being loyal to me or actually messing around with one of the numerous girls in his office. Or worse still, his PA, Tania Granger – she's just far too pretty.

Anyway, Kallum is a marketing manager for a big publishing company and he's a good-looking man with a loud, confident personality. All the girls fancy him like crazy.

I met him a couple of years ago, in a nightclub of all places and we got together. Well, he swept me off my feet entirely, to be honest. We were going to be together forever. Except we were never really together much. He makes dates with me and then drops them. He's too busy, he says. He comes here to stay for a week and then decides that he has got to get back home after two days. We make all kinds of plans and he breaks them. His phone beeps and rings constantly. It's business, he says. It's the office calling me, he says. It's a work-related message from my PA, he says.

If I'm to be completely honest with myself, I hardly know him at all. He's extremely secretive, self-important, overly-friendly with his female staff and generally evasive about anything to do with his life. In the heat of those moments in the bedroom, he promises me the world. He vows his undying love for me. He talks of the future, of children, of an idyllic country cottage with red roses growing in the front garden...

Then he disappears and I don't see or hear from him for a week or more.

I know he's been out with his PA – I saw a message on his phone one night. *Great night Kal – thanks for being you, love Tania xxxx*

Apparently, it was only a 'meet-the-client' meal and he'd offered to pay for Tania's food and drinks, and that's why she was thanking him for, 'being you'.

The other message I'd accidentally come across – OK, I sneakily and deliberately found it, was another one from Tania. *Can't get you out of my head – it was amazing! Tania xxxx*

According to Kallum, she sends kisses to everyone in her messages and the 'amazing' bit was that he'd helped to fix her car one evening and she couldn't get him out of her head because he was so helpful. Hmm, that's the one I'm really struggling with because he's also gone out and bought a whole new set of boxer shorts in the past month. I heard somewhere that that is a tell-tale sign. Isn't it?

I simply have this niggling feeling that all is not right. Our intimate times have changed recently too. He's become quite demanding and crude. The words, 'make' and 'love' seem to have disappeared from his vocabulary, along with those utterances of promising me the world. These days he much prefers to get things over with quickly and leave.

He has promised to come and spend Christmas with me. He's coming on Christmas eve and staying until the day after Boxing day. Just him and me. How lovely.

Of course, we'll go and visit my mum and dad, across town, but most of the time we will spend it here, together. Alone. Maybe this is just what we need to rekindle our slightly stale relationship.

The last time I saw him, we'd had yet another argument about Tania, who calls him at all times of the day or night. Apparently, so Kallum tells me, she's very needy and considers him to be her best friend. He says it's awkward. I say, tell her to find another friend, especially at three o'clock in the morning. Yet, every time she calls him, no matter what time of the day it is, he takes her call and slinks off to somewhere private to talk to her.

Grr. I have got to stay calm about it. I should not show any jealousy. Keep calm, stay calm. I'm probably over-thinking everything anyway.

I wave my best friend off as she leaves for Devon. I'll miss her while she's gone but I have got to make the best of this Christmas with Kallum. Maybe it will work out and he'll turn back into the man I once fell in love with. But on the other hand, maybe he won't.

Hi Kal, how did your work's do go? Mine was horrendous – explain when I see you. What time are you coming next Saturday? Thought we could go out for some Xmas eve drinks, if you fancy it? Love Suse xx

I would have liked to have seen him before next Saturday – a whole week away – but he's bogged down with tying up the marketing business before they close for a week over Christmas. Huh, he has a whole week off – well, a week and one day to be precise but he's off to London with a bunch of his mates for the New Year. I was not invited. He said it wouldn't be right if I tagged along with a whole bunch of rowdy men. I wouldn't have minded; it might have been fun, but I do see his point. Anyway, I'm not bitter and will enjoy the *three* days of Christmas that I get to spend with him. Just the two of us – heaven.

I've got a stash of decorations and a small table-top Christmas tree which I will have great pleasure in putting up this week. I also bought some ceiling decorations which will look nice above the dining table when we eat our Christmas dinner – how romantic. I'm going to spend this next week cleaning the flat from top to bottom, decorating it with lovely sparkly bits (it's been left so late because me and Clair didn't have the time to do it) and I'll also be doing some last-minute shopping. I still need to get something for my mum and dad (goodness knows what) and a couple of extra, silly bits for Kallum. Then I'm done. Come Christmas Eve, I'll be able to relax and enjoy the time with Kallum. It's going to be so cosy, quiet and sparkly. Exactly how I want it to be.

Had a good night thanks. Oh dear, that sounds ominous, tell me about it next Saturday. I'll be there around 6pm. Have a good week, Kal x

*** 6 ***

Today is Friday and I'm going into town to pick up my frozen turkey. I ordered it a couple of weeks ago, as I knew there would be a mad rush for them in the last week. It's not a huge one but I'm guessing it will take at least a day to defrost. I'm also thinking that I might brave the supermarket to get some fresh vegetables. I do have a contingency plan, should the supermarket run out of fresh produce – I've got a freezer full of frozen veg.

It's pretty chilly outside today. The sun is shining in a clear blue sky but it's still freezing. I wrap my woollen scarf around my neck, and head towards the town centre, which is only a five-minute walk away. There's absolutely no point in taking my car as it would be a nightmare trying to find somewhere to park.

As I walk down the main road towards the precinct, I note that my earlier assumption about parking was right. The two main multistorey car parks are full and the queue of waiting traffic is causing considerable congestion along the main road. Ha, maybe they should have caught a bus, or walked like me. I really don't get why everyone leaves their Christmas shopping to the last minute and then buys about two weeks' worth of food to see them over just two days of Christmas. Madness, if you ask me. Mind you, I suppose I'm not much better as I'm out shopping today too. The only difference is that I'm not planning to bulk-buy and stock-pile as if there were a nuclear war about to start. I simply need to get my turkey, a couple of carrots, a cauliflower, broccoli and maybe some parsnips. As for Brussels sprouts, I can't stand the things and I'm sure that most of the world's population must hate them too, yet we feel the need to eat them at Christmas – I just don't get it. Anyway, I will not be buying any Brussels sprouts. Yuk.

Before I pick up the heavy items (turkey and veggies), I wander around the precinct pondering over what I can get for my mum and dad. They are difficult to buy for and I usually end up buying them *M&S* vouchers. They get those for their birthdays too. However, this year I want to be a little more inventive. As it is, my mum was a bit upset that I had planned to spend Christmas at my place, with Kallum. She begged me to go to hers but I insisted that it would be just the two of us for Christmas day and then we'd visit her on Boxing day. So, when I arrive at my mum and dad's, with Kallum, on Boxing day, I want to be able to present them both with a nice gift, rather than an envelope with vouchers inside.

Maybe I'll have a quick look in *M&S* as I'm passing, as they do have some nice things in their gift section. I walk through the main doors and head for the gift department with a festive spring in my step.

Hampers. Hundreds of hampers everywhere. Why didn't I think of them before? There are food hampers, toiletry hampers, kid's hampers, men's hampers, women's hampers, grandparent's hampers and even pet hampers. Now I wish I'd brought my car. The hampers are fantastic but how do I get a hamper, a turkey and vegetables home by foot? As I peer around at the hamper displays in awe, I realise that I would like to buy two hampers. One for Mum and one for Dad. Now, the fact that I didn't bring my car is really a problem, as I want two of these big things and by the number of people swarming around them, they are going to go pretty quickly. Hence, I would not have time to rush home, get my car and then wait in the long queues for the parking. I suppose I could get a taxi home...

As I'm pondering over my dilemma, I feel a gentle tap on my shoulder and turn around startled. "Oh," I say, slapping my hand to my chest. "Hello, you made me jump."

"Hi – I think you have the same idea as we do."

"Sorry?" I say, a little flummoxed.

"Hampers, gifts."

"Oh, yes." I dart my eyes from Ryan to the pretty woman standing next to him and back again. Ryan's wearing blue jeans and a casual checked blue shirt underneath his jacket, which seems to make his clear blue eyes bluer. He has stubble on his face too, which gives him an appealing rugged look. Oh dear me, why does he have to be so handsome?

He smiles and looks down at me. "No turkey legs today then."

I feign laughter. "No, not today. I'm all done with the turkey thing."

The woman standing next to him gives a quizzical stare. She's very pretty, with long wavy brown hair. She has a long, black knitted poncho over her shoulders. "Have I missed something here?" she says in a gentle voice.

"Yes, sorry, this is... Sophie?" says Ryan, peering at her. "She works at Baghurst. Remember the turkey costume I was telling you about last year?"

"Oh, that." She looks at me pitifully. "Did you get caught with that trick?"

I nod my head. "Yes, I'm afraid so." I peer at Ryan awkwardly. "My name's Susie – not Sophie."

Ryan smacks his forehead with his hand. "Of course it is, why do I keep calling you Sophie?"

I shrug my shoulders.

"They're little buggers aren't they?" The woman shakes her head as she looks at me sympathetically.

"Sorry?" I say, totally confused.

Firstly, I'm puzzled by her words – does she know Sarah and Jane? Secondly, if Ryan has a gorgeous girlfriend like her, why did he ask me out for a drink? He's obviously a player, like I thought Kallum was before. I'm disappointed, to be honest – I don't want Ryan to be a player.

The woman smiles at me and tuts. "I know who they are – I call them Charmer-Chambers and Horny-Hodgo." She giggles into her manicured hand. "Maybe I shouldn't but..."

I laugh and peer at the woman incredulously. I feel a bit sorry for her really. After all, I'm standing next to her boyfriend and he asked me out for a drink last week. It's extremely awkward as I quite like her. "It's funny you should say that – I have names for them too."

"Oh, do you?" She giggles again. "You must tell me."

I peer at Ryan who is watching the interaction between us. "Sultry-Sarah and Juicy-Jane."

"I love it," the woman squeals. "So, we have, Sultry-Sarah-Charmer-Chambers and..."

"Juicy-Jane," I remind her.

"Juicy-Jane-Horny-Hodgo. That's fab," she shrieks.

"Rachel – keep your voice down," Ryan says in a hushed voice. He looks at me and grimaces. "Sorry, I can't take her anywhere. Maybe she should be called Roaring-Raucous-Rachel."

I grin stiffly. "Sorry, it's probably my fault too."

"Huh – he's always so bossy." Rachel eyes Ryan and smirks at him before shoving him away by his shoulder, towards the hampers. "Go on then, find the hampers you want."

Ryan turns obediently and begins to look along the shelves.

"I used to work at your school," says Rachel. "I was a TA there."

"Oh really," I reply. "Is that how you met..." I look across to Ryan who has moved further down the aisle.

"Oh God – no. I've known him for a long time" She sniggers and shakes her head. "He's my brother. We're both teachers now, but not in the same school, thank God."

I breathe a sigh of relief. "Oh – OK. I didn't realise. Sorry."

Why am I relieved? It's not like it matters that he asked me out for a drink. OK, it does matter. He is very nice. He's gorgeous actually. But I'm with someone. So that's that. I'm still relieved though. He's so nice that I didn't want him to be a two-timing player. Phew.

Ryan picks up a large blue hamper and calls out. "For Dad?"

Rachel nods her head. "Bless him, he's useless at getting presents for anyone. That's why I said I'd come shopping with him today."

"Oh, I see."

"The hampers are great aren't they?"

"Yes," I reply looking at the large double-hampers. I'm now thinking that one of those would be even nicer than two separate ones. They're very large though. "I wish I'd brought my car down here now. I've got a turkey to pick up today and wouldn't be able to carry that and a great big hamper home by foot."

"Do you live nearby?" Rachel asks.

"Yes, five minutes up the road. It won't take much to go back and get my car – I'm just worried they'll all be gone by the time I get back."

She places a hand gently on my shoulder. "I can run you home, if you want to pick one up now."

I peer at her wide-eyed. I'm taken aback to be honest. This woman has never met me before, yet she is willingly offering me a lift home. She's as lovely as her brother is. "Err... thank you, that's very kind of you but..."

"And your turkey. It's really not a problem," she adds, grinning at me.

"You're so kind – thank you. Please, let me pay your parking fee as a way of thanking you."

"Wouldn't dream of it." She smiles warmly. "Ryan – come on, hurry up and chose one. We've got a turkey to catch."

***

I've got a huge double-hamper for my mum and dad – they'll love it. It beats silly little vouchers which end up sitting in their drawer for months on end. I've also got the turkey. OK, I didn't get vegetables but then I didn't want to take advantage of Rachel's kindness to give me a lift back home. I can always venture out again tomorrow and pick them up. Gosh, going shopping on Christmas Eve – the thought alone is terrifying.

I'm making Ryan and Rachel a coffee. I felt I should invite them in as a way of saying thank you. I'm just relieved that I've spent all week cleaning and the flat looks and smells lovely. They even commented on the tabletop Christmas tree and said how delightful it is.

I carry the tray with three coffees and a plate of assorted biscuits, through to the lounge and place it on the coffee table.

"Ooh, lovely. Thank you, Susie," says Rachel. "Anytime you want a lift, just give me a shout. I'll do anything for a biscuit." She takes an oat-crunch from the plate, picks up her coffee and dunks the biscuit. "Hope you don't mind – I'm a bit of a dunker."

Ryan smiles and rolls his eyes. "Nice place you've got here. Do you live alone?"

"No," I say. "I live with my friend, Clair. She's been here with me for over two years now."

"Nice," he replies, before picking up a cup of coffee. "I want to get my own place – I live in a shared house."

"I do love it," I say, "I'm lucky to have it though. If it hadn't been for my mum and dad paying the deposit on the mortgage, I wouldn't be here now."

"Oh, you own it?" Ryan looks surprised.

"Yes," I let out a nervous laugh, "well, I will one day when the mortgage is paid."

Ryan smiles and winks at me.

Yes, another one of those bloody winks. I'm sure he knows that they are like the most heavenly winks anyone could ever wish for. Oh God. I gulp tensely. I'm finding it nerve-wracking, having him sitting in my living room, staring at me with those electric blue eyes and winking his thick, dark lashes.

"Is that why your friend lives with you? To help pay the mortgage?" Rachel peers at me. "I hope you don't think I'm being rude or too nosey."

"No, not at all," I say. "Yes, I couldn't manage without her. I don't exactly earn a huge wage as a TA."

Rachel nods her head. "Yes, I know. That's part of the reason why I moved into teaching. Don't get me wrong, I wanted to be a teacher – it wasn't just all about the money." She peers across to Ryan. "He beat me to it though, didn't you Ryan?"

Ryan nods his head and continues to sip his coffee.

"My little brother beat me to it."

"Oh, so you're older..."

"Yes, by two years. We get on really well though, don't we?" She looks at Ryan and smirks. "Sometimes, if I haven't seen him for months, we go out to town, either shopping or for a drink and people think we're a couple."

"To be honest, I thought you were when I saw you."

"Hmm," she mumbles, "fat chance of me getting a boyfriend then, if people think he's my boyfriend."

"It works the same for me," says Ryan. He looks up at me awkwardly. "You're better off being a TA, Soph... Susie. Teachers don't get much of a social life during term time... and then they have to take their sister out on the holidays." He smirks at Rachel.

"That's so not true, Ryan Bagshaw." Rachel kicks him playfully on the leg. "Come on, drink up, we've got presents to wrap."

Rachel is the first to leave. She walks down the path to her car.

Ryan stops at my front door and turns to me. "Would your reply still be the same if I asked you again, now I'm sober, to come out with me one evening over the holidays?"

Oh my goodness. I want to collapse to the floor. My face flushes and my mouth fills with a sticky saliva. "I..."

"Or anytime that suits you."

"I..." Oh no, I can't speak. I feel like I've swallowed my tongue. He's so confident. "I... can't. I'm so sorry. I would have loved to but..."

"You're not that way inclined?"

"No, no – it's not that."

"You're more into turkeys then?"

I laugh loudly. I want to cry. Oh dear me. "No... I... I'm with someone. I... have a boyfriend."

"Oh right." He pauses, looking flummoxed. "Hell, I'm so sorry. I thought..."

His eyes are darting around, avoiding meeting with mine. I can feel his embarrassment.

"No please, don't be sorry. You weren't to know," I say, trying to make him feel more comfortable.

He looks at me with a wistful smile. "OK," he says. "I do apologise. It's been very nice to meet you again, Susie. I'm sure we'll bump into each other from time to time. I hope you have a great Christmas."

"You too, Ryan."

"And just for the record..." he says as he turns away, "you were an amazing turkey."

My heart plummets. It shouldn't, I know. My Kallum is coming tomorrow night. I shouldn't feel like this. It's wrong.

Or is it OK?

They are lovely people, both Ryan and his sister. That's probably why I feel a bit sad. Yes, that's it. They've gone now and it is Christmas Eve-Eve. I'm here alone and probably just feeling sorry for myself. I'll have to keep myself busy this evening by researching how to cook a turkey. That's what I'll do. Keep smiling Susie Satchel, Christmas is nearly here.

*** 7 ***

I've sussed it out. I'm going to slow-roast it. Apparently, if I put it in the oven tonight, when we get back from our romantic evening out, it will be done by tomorrow lunchtime. Easy.

I've had a productive day today. I ventured back down to the town, on a mission to find some vegetables and was very lucky to get the last carrots on the shelf. I also struggled to reach for a cauliflower, as two women were standing in front of me arguing over the last pack of shallots on the bottom shelf (I hadn't thought about those myself, but wouldn't have wanted to get involved with the women grappling over the onions). Anyway, luckily, I just about managed to drag the cauliflower out from between them as they continued to argue over who was having the shallots. Bravely, I looked at them both and said, 'Open the bag and share them'. How cool of me was that? They both froze as they peered back at me incredulously.

Good deed done for the day, I'm thinking. I also picked up some runner beans. No broccoli though. Oh well, never mind. As for the dreaded Brussels sprouts, well they were plentiful on the three-wide shelf display – I'm guessing the shop must have ordered in extra supplies. I decided they could stay on the shelves as far as I was concerned – nasty little things. I would have happily stayed there, in the shop, and watched as they rotted away to Brussels sprout heaven or wherever it is that rejected Brussels sprouts go. Yuk.

***

It's now half past five and my tummy is filled with butterflies. I do miss Kallum when I don't see him for a while. It's been over a week now. I know he's very busy all the time, so I just put up with it, I suppose.

I'm wearing a new dress, it's a black clingy little number with a daringly low front – in fact, it's so low that it's impossible to wear a bra. I've never worn a dress like this before but I thought it would be the perfect thing for seeing Kallum again and to go out for a few drinks tonight. I've also got some gorgeous, suede, knee-length black boots which... wait for it... have got stiletto glass heels. Yes, that's right, glass heels. OK, they cost me a fortune from *HOUSE OF FRASER* but they are worth every penny – OK, every pound – all right, every hundreds of pounds then. I've got a cute little red dress for tomorrow too. I like red on Christmas day – it makes me feel more festive. So, that's my wardrobe sorted out for the next couple of days. When we visit my parents on Boxing day, I'll be wearing my new Christmas jumper which, coincidentally, matches the one I have bought for Kallum. He likes Christmas jumpers and we're going to be a pair of penguins this year. Ooh, I'm so excited about the next few days.

It's five to six now and my mobile has just tinkled. Before I even look, I've guessed that it might be Kallum saying he's running late – that's not unusual for him.

Suse, I'm a bit tied up with things here. Not going to make it until later. Sorry darling x

'Sorry darling', what's that supposed to mean? Tied up with 'things'? 'Until later'?

What 'things'? What time do you expect to get here? I'm all dressed up and waiting. Hope everything's OK. Love you xx

I wait for ten minutes before he answers. I have got to admit, I'm a little peeved.

Mum's having a last-minute panic! I'm driving her around, looking for shops that are still open!

OK, what time will you be here? Xx

Probably about 9pm x

Nine? I look down at my phone and feel like throwing it against the wall. Nine o'clock? How far is he taking his mum shopping for goodness sake? London?

Why so late?

Darling, I'm so sorry. I've promised to help mum get the last things ready for Christmas – you know what she's like! We can go out at 9pm, I promise x

Great. So now I have two choices. I can either change my clothes (temporarily) and get on with some jobs of my own or I could sit here for the next three hours and drink wine while I wait for him.

I decide to remove my glass-heeled boots (not the most comfortable of boots but worth the pain) and have a glass of wine – purely to clarify the situation.

Half an hour has drifted by as I've flicked through the TV channels aimlessly and I'm now on the second glass of wine, which I should take far slower. My thoughts drift to Kallum's mum. She's a nightmare if I'm completely frank. She's so needy, so meticulous and such a perfectionist. Don't get me wrong, I do like her. It's just that she tends to control everyone with her big puppy-dog eyes and helpless, feeble façade. Her entire family run around after her, doing whatever she asks and whenever it might be. I'm often surprised by the power she seems to have over them. It's not just Kallum who leaps into action upon her every word but his brother too. As for Kallum's dad, well he's so inadequate as a real man and such a conformist that I'm pretty sure that anyone could give him a set of instructions and he'd follow them to the letter.

My mobile tinkles again, jolting me back from my thoughts.

I will definitely be there by 9.30pm. x

Nine-flipping-thirty? Is he having a laugh? By the time we have a kiss and a cuddle, after not seeing each other for more than a week, it won't be worth going out. He lives half an hour away from me, so he's obviously helping his mum until nine and then travelling over to me. Great.

Won't be worth going out tonight by the time you get here.

Sorry darling but once I've escaped, you've got me all to yourself for three days.

OK – fair point xx

I look across the living room to my beautiful boots. Kallum hasn't seen them yet. I was looking forward to wearing them out, clicking along the pavements and showing them off as they are so sexy looking. I just don't think they'll have the same effect, scuffing along on the shag-pile carpets in my flat. What a waste my new dress has been too. It would have been such a turn-on for Kallum if we'd gone out and he'd stared at me all evening, as I practically fell out of the front of my dress. It's just not the same effect when I'm lounging back on the sofa, as my unrestrained boobs simply fall back to the sides and end up under my armpits. I have got to admit that I'm pretty disappointed really.

***

It's 9-45pm and I'm guessing that he's driving as he hasn't answered my last text message. I'm sorry but quarter to ten is really taking the piss now.

A further five minutes go by and I'm beginning to boil just as the doorbell rings.

He's here – at last. I can't say that I'm feeling ecstatic about it as I walk to the door and open it rather forcefully.

Kallum is standing there, loaded with bags in one hand and a bunch of red roses in the other. His smile wavers as he looks at me with worried eyes. "Darling, I am so sorry."

I step back, allowing him to walk through. "I thought you weren't coming for a while there."

He hands the roses to me. "So did I. Mum's such a stress-head at Christmas. She doesn't like it that I'm here for three days. She says we'll have to have another Christmas day when I get back."

I feel quite affronted – she knew, all along, that Kallum was coming to stay with me. Why does she have to make such a fuss about it now? "Well that'll be nice. Two Christmases – lucky you." I peer down at the roses and discreetly count them. A dozen – that's exactly what it should be. "Thank you for these," I say. "They're lovely."

He kisses me briefly on the lips and follows me through to the lounge. "Nice dress," he says, placing two carrier bags and his holdall on the floor. He looks me up and down and smiles.

I lay the roses across the coffee table and then pose for him. "You like it?"

"Love it," he replies. "Very sexy." He grabs me around the waist and pulls me to him. "We couldn't go out now anyway..."

"Why do you say that?"

"Because..." He kisses my mouth fervently. "Because I want to take your dress off..."

***

I'm sitting in the living room, wearing my dressing gown and sipping a hot chocolate while Kallum is in the shower. My boots are still in the corner of the room and my lovely new dress is slung on the back of an armchair.

It's creeping ever closer to midnight – Christmas day – and I'm feeling quite content. OK, so it did take Kallum ages to get here and we did miss a night out, but in the time that he has been here, we've rekindled our passion for one another and had some amazing sex.

I'm exhausted from the three glasses of wine earlier and feel quite ready to snuggle up in bed with him and drift off into a lovely sleep while Santa does his thing. Tomorrow is Christmas morning and I'm going to wake up next to Kallum, for the first time ever, on Christmas day. How lovely.

Kallum walks into the living room with a towel wrapped around his waist. He looks even more handsome when his dark, spikey hair is wet. "You haven't been peeping in those bags have you?"

I shake my head like a young child. "No, I promise."

"That's all right then. Santa asked me to look after those and hand them out tomorrow."

A new surge of excitement rushes through me – I'm such a kid. "I promise to be a good girl and not look."

He nods his head and disappears to the bedroom. I follow him in there and lean against the wardrobe as I watch him unwrap the towel, letting it drop to the floor, and pull on his boxer shorts. "Do you want hot chocolate before bed?"

"Yes, OK."

"I'll make one quickly for you," I say, eyeing his gorgeously toned body. "We've got to be in bed before midnight though – otherwise Santa won't come here."

"I'll drink it quick – we can't possibly miss a visit from him." He gives me one of those seductive winks of his before throwing a vest-style t-shirt over his head.

See what I mean? I know those winks. There's a difference between friendly or cheeky winks and slow, deliberate, sexy winks. I'm sure I must be an expert on winking, although I can't do it myself at all.

Kallum has just finished his hot chocolate and the time is 11.49pm. I grab his hand and haul him up from the sofa. "Come on – we've got to get to bed. Look at the time." I giggle like a silly child.

"I'll be there before you." He turns around and shoots out of the living room.

"Oi – wait for me."

Frantically, I whizz around the flat turning the lights off and checking the front and back doors are locked. Then I fly into the bedroom and dive on the bed. We both laugh out loud and I wish it could be like this all the time. I wish he lived with me when things are going so well. Our only problem is his unwavering commitment to his job and his workforce, because holiday times can be so special between us.

"Goodnight," I whisper to the back of his head.

"Goodnight darling. See you on Christmas day."
"Love you." I can't help saying it without a smile on my face.
"Hmm... you too," he says with a sleepy tone to his voice.

*** 8 ***

Oh dear Lord – no.

The turkey. The turkey is still in the bottom of the fridge where it should *not* be.

I'm lying in bed next to Kallum, who is still asleep, and my waking thought is not how wonderful it is to have him here. Not how perfect it is that it's Christmas day, but how bloody annoying it is that I have now got to cook a turkey at a normal oven temperature and keep an eye on it. I'm not that great a cook to be honest, so this is going to stress me out no end. I completely forgot last night while I was sitting there waiting and seething over Kallum's lateness.

Oh dear.

I leap out of bed, trudge through to the living room and turn my laptop on. I have no idea how long to cook a turkey for. Switching the Christmas tree lights on, I try to drum up some festive spirit. Then I go and make a coffee while I'm waiting for my laptop to come to life. It's getting a bit slow in its old age.

A cup of coffee in hand, I return to the laptop and search, 'How long do I cook a turkey for?'. It's a 2.5kg bird and the website I'm looking at says, cook it for two hours. Phew, that's a relief, I had visions that I'd have to cook it for something stupid like, six hours.

Now I'm happy and the festive spirit is growing. It's Christmas! I grab the bag of presents that I'd secretly stashed away in a cupboard and arrange them around the tree. Christmas spirit has arrived and I'm in full swing to start the preparations. I'm hoping that Kallum will sleep for a little longer so that I can prepare the vegetables and cook up a delicious breakfast of eggs Benedict. Gosh, he's going to be impressed with my culinary capabilities. Well, to be honest, I had practiced the eggs Benedict on Clair.

Thank goodness for Clair. I do have to say that it was getting to the point where she would screw her cute little nose up every Saturday and Sunday morning though. I had to learn how to cook the eggs Benedict to perfection. OK, so Clair was sick to death of the same breakfast every single weekend for… well, it was for about 14 weeks. But, hey, I'm now the best eggs Benedict maker you could ever meet. Unfortunately, Clair hates the stuff now, having been subjected to it for so long. However, I do think she should be grateful that I didn't make her eat turkey for breakfast every weekend. It was only the cost and the improbability of actually being able to buy one, that stopped me.

I've prepared the veggies and they are all sitting comfortably in saucepans, ready for the manic cooking marathon later. The turkey is still in the fridge and will stay there until around eleven o'clock. I'm thinking that we'll eat around two o'clock, so that gives me plenty of time to cook the turkey and 'leave to rest' – that's what the website said anyway.

"Kallum – it's Christmas – wake up." I give him a little nudge. "Happy Christmas." He stirs and opens his eyes. "I'm making eggs Benedict for breakfast – you've got half an hour."

As I go to leave the room he mumbles something.

"What was that?" I say, turning around.

"I said, happy Christmas to you too, darling."

"Oh, thanks." I turn back and exit the room. "Half an hour," I call out as I make my way back to the kitchen.

A few minutes later he appears, sleepy-eyed. He wraps his arms around my waist and kisses the back of my neck. "I love eggs Benedict."

"I know you do, that's why we're having it for breakfast."

"Can't we have a starter first?" Again, he kisses my neck, sending shivers down my spine. "I was thinking of…" He pulls my dressing gown off my shoulders and continues to kiss me.

OK, this is getting hard to resist now. "Do you want eggs Benedict or not?" I ask, trying to keep my focus.

"Yes, absolutely but…"

Oh dear, he's nibbling at my neck now and his hands have started to wander. Oh dear me…

So, over an hour of our Christmas day has passed already and we are only just cooking the eggs Benedict now, but at least we're doing it together. There's so much to do this morning, what with eating breakfast, opening presents, getting dressed (I'm determined to wear my new red dress and the glass-heeled boots, even if I am just scuffing around on the carpets) and putting the turkey on for dinner. This afternoon we've planned to go out for a little walk after dinner (not too far in my glassy boots), then chill out in front of the TV for the evening, have a couple of drinks and no doubt, have a nap too, somewhere in between.

"That was amazing," says Kallum as he wipes his hand across his mouth and stretches back in the chair. "What time did you say we're having dinner? I might have to go for a jog around the block at this rate."

I peer up at the clock on the wall. "Hmm... probably about two thirty now – three at the latest."

Kallum looks up at the clock too. "That's not too bad. This..." He pats at his tummy, "should be gone down by then."

I smile and nod my head. "Shall we do presents now?" I say eagerly.

"Yes – come on." He jumps up and takes my hand. "My turn first."

He knows me so well – and so he should, I suppose. I've got a lovely set of frilly underwear (perfect size – I'm amazed), a couple of fiction books, as I do love a good read, countless CDs and DVDs that I'd wanted to buy but didn't get around to doing, a cute little bear holding a big, red heart, a gorgeous necklace and matching earrings set (I imagine they were quite expensive) and a trendy, *Valentina,* Italian leather satchel. Yes, a satchel. It is a beautiful satchel and I actually love it. Why does it have to be called a satchel though?

Anyway, there are only two presents left to open – Kallum's penguin jumper and a box-shaped present for me.

Kallum seems very happy with the presents he got. I won't go into details as there were so many little, silly bits, that I'm sure it would bore the socks off anyone. He likes them though and that's all that counts.

"Last one," he says, handing the box to me.

I give him his squishy present and grin. "Hope you like it."

"Shall I go first?"

I nod my head and watch as he rips the paper away. He holds the jumper up in front of him and peers at the design on the front. "Cool, thanks darling – I love it." He reaches over and kisses me. "Now your turn."

I look down at the box and wonder what it could be. I'm not one of these people who frantically rips wrapping paper off presents. I like to take my time and carefully unwrap it, trying not to rip the paper. It's more fun my way – it prolongs the suspense and surprise.

As I pull the wrapping away, I see a red *Body Shop* box. It's a strawberry gift set. I look up at Kallum and smile. "Thank you – it's lovely."

"Thought you'd like that," he says. "Have a look inside."

I turn the box over and peer at the contents label. "Oh yes, I can see what's in there – how lovely."

Not.

Sorry – I don't mean to sound ungrateful. To be honest, and I couldn't possibly let Kallum know, I hate the stuff – well most of it anyway. I've had these things before and for some reason, these big companies seem to think that fruity gift-sets are the must-have items in today's society. That, on its own, would be great but why, oh why, do they have to put pips in everything? Pips and seeds, or chunks of chocolate or sparkly bits. Do they have any idea how irritating those tiny little bits can be when you've used the latest 'Body Polish' in the shower and you're in a mad rush to get to work? I spent a whole day, one time, itching and scratching in the most intimate of places because my pants were full of pips. It was embarrassing to say the least. During that dreadful day, it had been impossible to have a good old scratch and I'd scuttled around like I was walking on hot coals, rubbing the tops of my legs together and tensing my bottom cheeks to try and relieve the irritation. Never again.

"No open it," Kallum insists.

"Oh, OK." I peer at him quizzically. I pull the sticky holding tape off the sides of the box and lift the lid off. Just as expected, an assortment of body care products are neatly set out among a red satin casing. "Oh, yes – it's lovely. Thank you so much."

Kallum peers into the box and points to a smaller box, labelled 'soap'. Have a look in there," he says.

"Why?" I reply. "It's strawberry soap, isn't it?"

"Think you should check." He meets my eye and stares at me expectantly.

Oh my God.

I think I get it now. I look deep into his gorgeous brown eyes. Oh my goodness. I've got a feeling... well, I think I can sense... Oh gosh, surely not. On Christmas day? What am I going to find in the tiny soap box? My heart is galloping.

I pick up the small, scented box and shake it. Oh dear Lord – it rattles. There's no way that there is soap in the box. It's something small and hard. I shake it again and look up at Kallum as my eyes moisten. Oh my...

My heart is racing and my fingers are trembling as I try to undo the small flap at one end. Oh gosh... Is Kallum serious? Is he asking me to...?

I'm holding my breath now. I pull the flap free and tip the contents of the box into the palm of my hand.

It's a ring...

I sink down into the sofa and keep my hand clenched around it.

"Well?" says Kallum, smiling widely, "what do you think?"

I peer down at the object in my hand and turn it around. "It's... it's cool – thanks." I hold it up and look at it again. "But... I'm not a teacher."

"You teach things to kids, don't you?"

"Yes," I say, feeling somewhat disappointed.

"So, you're a kind of teacher then."

"I guess so." I look at him and try my utmost to muster up a smile. "Thank you, Kallum."

It's a ring all right – a flipping keyring, with the words, 'Best Teacher Ever' scrawled across it. A keyring. A blasted keyring. I don't mean to sound ungrateful here but... Well, surely anyone else would think the same. Why would he put it in the little soap box and create all that suspense over a stupid keyring? And where's the soap anyway? I'm being so ungrateful, I know. I really must stop it before it spoils my Christmas day.

"That's it then darling," he says with such a huge grin on his face. "I'm going to put my penguin jumper on and then I'll help you get the dinner started."

"OK, great." I grin back at him. "I've got one too, so we'll be matching... but only if you wear it to Mum and Dad's tomorrow as well. I'm keeping this new dress on today – goes with the boots."

"Cool - OK." Kallum gets up from the chair and collects his presents. He stuffs them into bags and walks out of the room.

I can't believe he hasn't mentioned my nice, new red dress – and the boots – how could he not comment on my boots? They are killer-boots. And I don't mean, 'killer' in the sense that they are killing me, I mean they are just the best boots in the whole wide world. Yet, he doesn't seem to have noticed them.

A keyring. I thought it might have been... Well, you can imagine what I thought it was going to be. I would have said yes, obviously. We've come a long way over these past two years and have only recently, acquired a mutual understanding about his overly protective and slightly too friendly approach towards his staff and particularly, his PA, Tania. It's probably me being ultra-jealous that Tania actually sees him more than I do. That wouldn't be the case if we lived together though and it is on my mind for the future – once Clair leaves.

Clair doesn't plan on staying with me forever. She's a high-flyer, ambitious and pro-active in her search for that dream-job and dream-lifestyle. And I know it will happen for her – I just know it. I don't ever want her to leave but, if and when that day does come, then I would love Kallum to move in with me.

"Did you remove the giblets before you put it in?" Kallum eyes the oven which is ticking over at 180 degrees.

"Giblets?"

"Yes, don't they usually have a bag of giblets inside them?"

I look at him incredulously. "I have no idea – do they?"

"Take it out – quick. You'd better check."

I grab the oven gloves and pull them on. Carefully I remove the heavy tray from the oven and place it on the top.

"You've stuffed it," remarks Kallum. "Were there giblets in it or not?"

"Like I said, I have no idea. I just stuffed that smelly stuff in there like it said on the packet."

Kallum eyes me with a smirk on his face. "You'll have to look if the giblets are right at the back of it."

"Can't they stay there?"

"No – they'll be in a plastic bag darling. It will melt and then we'll be eating plastic flavoured turkey."

"Oh, OK." I grab a spoon and start removing the stuffing on to a plate.

"There it is," says Kallum, peering into the back end of the turkey. "I can see the bag."

I spoon out the last bits of stuffing and put my hand into the back of the bird. Luckily, it hasn't got too hot yet. "Gosh, I can't believe I would make such a stupid mistake."

"I can," says Kallum, smirking at me. "You might be a well-educated, school-type person but you're an absolute air-head when it comes to things like this." He puts an arm round my shoulders and kisses the top of my head. "Come on, let's get this bird re-stuffed and back in the oven.

*** 9 ***

I've cooked a turkey! It's brown and crispy on the outside and white inside. Exactly how a turkey should be. It's 'resting' on the side while I roast the potatoes and cook the vegetables. I'm feeling quite proud of myself, I have got to be honest. I'm alone in the kitchen, having a cheeky glass of Baileys on ice while Kallum's setting out the dinner table. I feel so excited – it's Christmas day and we're here together and I've cooked a turkey. OK, so we didn't get engaged this morning but that doesn't matter now. I'm more than happy.

Everything is under control, either roasting, boiling or bubbling away so I leave the kitchen for a minute – it's rather hot in there, even with the back door open. I wander into the dining room where Kallum is sitting at the beautifully prepared table, thumbing through his mobile phone. He peers up at me sheepishly.

"I... err... Suse, I've got to..." he stumbles, "Darling, I've got to nip out."

"Nip out," I say, affronted. "What do you mean, 'nip out'?" My heart starts to race as I fear a return of those times when he drops everything just to attend to a work-related issue. "But it's Christmas day Kallum – what could possibly be wrong on Christmas day?" I know something's wrong by the anguished look on his face.

"It's err..." He looks up at me with a fearful look on his face. "I... I need to pop out – that's all."

"No," I've raised my voice now, "No Kallum, that's *not* all. Where are you going? Why?"

He stands up, leaving his phone on the table in his dithery state. "I need to see someone – I won't be long."

"See who?" I'm practically shouting now. "Who?"

He brushes past me. "I'm sorry Suse, I won't be long, I promise. Then I'll explain."

He leaves the room and I hear him walk across to the bedroom. He's obviously getting his shoes and coat. My heart is thudding but I'm going to do it. I'm going to look at his phone. Someone has texted him and I'm going to find out what's going on. I feel a sweat beginning to dampen my forehead as I pick his phone up and thumb through to his inbox...

I open a message from Tania...

"Suse," Kallum's voice makes me jump. "Give me my..."

My heart is thumping in my chest.

"Give it to me..." he says, reaching his hand out as he stumbles around the table.

I turn away and continue to read the message from Tania, sent at four minutes past one. Sent less than an hour ago. Kallum must have only just turned his phone on and seen it.

He snatches the phone from my hand but it's too late. I've read the short message.

He turns on his heels. "I won't be long," he says, forlornly. "I'll be back soon."

"It's too late, don't bother," I shout out, staring after him incredulously, as he leaves the flat and closes the front door behind him.

He's gone. I'm flat. No, I'm more than flat, I'm totally devastated. How can my life turn so sour in a matter of seconds? I'm absolutely stunned. Destroyed.

As if in a dream-like state, I wander through to the kitchen and turn the oven off. The roast potatoes can go to hell. I turn each of the rings on the hob off. I stare at the saucepans as the water slowly stops boiling. Reaching for the Baileys, I pour a fresh glass and gulp the whole lot down. I continue to stare, dazedly, at the now simmering water. I'm going to stay here and watch the water until it becomes completely still. That's the only thing I can think of doing... except for maybe another Baileys. A very large one.

The water is still now and so is my mind – at last.

Another large Baileys has dampened my thoughts. I've wandered back to the living room and I'm calm, but I shouldn't be. The text message had stated the facts clearly. Why am I calm? I pick the 'Best Teacher Ever' keyring up from the coffee table and sling it across the room. Another Baileys, that's what I need. Aah...

So, I'm quite sloshed now, in the privacy of my living room and everything I think about seems to be quite funny. I've got the giggles as I stagger back out to the kitchen. I open the back door and peer out. It's so quiet outside, even though it's only half past three. I imagine that people have listened to the Queen's speech and are now dozing in their armchairs with a belly full of turkey and alcohol. I love the still quietness and to top it, it's snowing.

Peering back into the kitchen, I look at the discarded saucepans, full of soggy vegetables. Kallum won't be coming back – how can he? I grin to myself and pick the cold turkey up from the tray with my bare hands. I'm wobbly on my glass heels as the alcohol swishes around my brain. I giggle again and carry the turkey, dripping with juices, to the back door.

Stepping outside, I breathe in the crisp afternoon air. Flakes of snow are falling heavily from the peach coloured sky. It's snowing on Christmas day, who would have thought it? I bet the bookies didn't, but I don't really care either way. I don't care about anything anymore.

I toss the turkey up in the air, defiantly. Without thinking it through, I kick it away as it falls back down and the whole bird flies off across the garden – minus a leg and a wing by the time it lands.

It sobers me instantly and I come to my senses.

Why did I do that? My boots – they're ruined. The turkey has landed a couple of feet away in a jellified, greasy heap. One of my boots is covered in slime and gunk. I am *so* going to regret this tomorrow. This calls for another comforting Baileys and another evaluation of the evidence I've seen. There's no way that Kallum is getting a Christmas dinner out of me now.

There is no other way of looking at it. The message was crystal clear. It said, *Lovely to see you last night but I didn't say anything to you, as I wasn't completely sure... I hope this will be a happy Christmas present for you – I'm pregnant! Can I see you again, today - urgently? T xx*

I can't tell you how utterly stunned I was, after everything that's happened between us, since Kallum arrived. It had all been so perfect. Yet, he had been deceiving me so terribly cruelly, all along. Not only did he lie about where he was last night but also – she's pregnant. Tania is pregnant. There was no other way to read the message than the fact that she's pregnant with *his* child. Kallum is having a baby with Tania. Oh my God.

The alcohol isn't having quite the same effect as it had an hour ago. I'm becoming morose, enraged and tearful. I need another drink.

It's Christmas day and the turkey is lying upside down in the garden – a sign of how life has changed for me, in one day, one hour, one second. I shudder as tears fall down my cheeks in little rivers. I'm alone, drunk and desperate. How could he have done this? I look down at my penguin jumper, which I threw on, over the top of my lovely red dress because I was chilly after the turkey tossing, and I cry even more. He's wearing the same jumper, yet he's with *her*, no doubt discussing what they should do. Whether they will keep the baby and what he's going to do about me. I suppose I have saved him a job though, as he doesn't need to break the news to me or finish with me now – I've done it for him.

However angry I feel now; I am distraught too.

The doorbell chimes and I freeze. It can only be... Surely, he hasn't come back.

Tearing myself away from the umpteenth Baileys, I stagger to the door and open it. My heart feels like it's in my throat.

"Suse," he says.

I'm shocked – it *is* Kallum. He has that fearful look on his face.

"Can I come in? I need to talk to you."

"Sure, you can," I say in a sarcastic, drunken voice. "Come and join the party."

He shoots me a quizzical stare and steps inside. "I..."

"Go through," I gesture towards the living room. "We should sit cozily around the Christmas tree while you tell me your good news."

Blimey, I seem to be taking this well. Actually, I'm not at all but I find it far easier to mock those who inflict such great pain on me and I'm totally wrecked with alcohol too. "Should we have a hot chocolate together? Get all nice and cosy?"

Kallum shakes his head worriedly. He's looking at me like I've gone stark raving mad.

Maybe I have.

"I don't know what to say," he says as he sits down. He cups his hands over his face and shakes his head again. "Suse, I..."

I take a seat on the other side of the room and perch on the edge of the chair. "Have you come back for your dinner?"

Kallum looks up at me incredulously.

"The turkey's in the garden if you want to rustle up a sandwich."

"Suse, you're drunk. I'm so sorry, this is all my fault."

"Takes two," I reply with a jovial tone.

"No, it's not your fault at all..."

"I'm not talking about me, you dimwit. It takes two to make a baby, doesn't it Kallum?" My voice is so un-jovial this time.

"Suse..."

"Stop saying 'Suse' and spit out what you have to say." I sip at yet another Baileys.

Kallum lowers his eyes. "I've made a terrible mistake..."

"So, you don't want the baby?" I feign sadness. "Ah, that's a shame. Poor baby."

"I need to tell you the truth Suse, then I'll go if that's what you want."

"Fire away." I heave a sigh, trying not to make it sound too obvious that I'm utterly deflated. OK, utterly drunk then.

"I had been seeing her – "

"Her?"

"Tania. I'd seen her a few times – "

"You see her most days Kallum. Do you mean you slept with her a few times?"

Kallum nods his head shamefully.

"You have had sex with your PA, a few times?" I glare at his lowered head. "You make me physically sick."

"I'm so..."

"Sorry?" I chime in.

I want to walk over to him and slap his face but I remain seated. I'm not a violent person... well, up until now I haven't been. Maybe I will or even, should, become violent and slap him in a minute. "Is that what you were about to say – you're *so* sorry? Did you get your leg over last night?" I pause thoughtfully. "Oh, wait – did you get your dick out twice last night? Once for her and once for me?"

Kallum shakes his head earnestly. "Suse – I went there to end it last night."

"So why did she say it was lovely to see you?"

"She's obsessed with me. She won't leave me alone. I realised a while ago how much... I love you."

"Oh dear me – please – let's not go there. You're going to be a daddy and you need to live up to your responsibilities."

"I don't want anything to do with her. I love you. I realise that now." He looks down again. "I know it's too late. I've been such an idiot."

My heart sinks. I actually believe him. He does love me. It was plainly obvious over the last 16 hours or so, even if I did only get a keyring. But I can't go back there. He's destroyed everything. I couldn't ever trust him again. This revelation is hurting even more than the first.

"Collect your stuff and go. I don't ever want to see you again."

Oh no – have I really just said that?

"But... is there no way...?" Kallum falters.

"No way, Kallum. Leave now. Collect your things and go. I'd rather go in my garden and lick the turkey's arse, than be with you," I mumble, slurring my words.

*** 10 ***

He left quickly and quietly. That was it – gone. I'm left here alone again, nursing my broken heart and a thumping head. The TV channels are bursting with fun, jovial programmes and last year's top rated films. It's Christmas day and I've eaten nothing since the eggs Benedict this morning. Griping pains of hunger and too much alcohol are tearing at my stomach so I go through to the kitchen to find something to eat. The soggy vegetables are still swimming in the saucepans and the greasy, mushy potatoes look disgusting as I remove them from the oven and place them on a top. I grab the bread and make a jam sandwich, it's all I can face at the moment.

My boots are off now. I look down at the toe of the right one and wonder how I can clean the greasy mess from it. Why did I kick the stupid turkey? What am I going to do with the bird now that it has started snowing heavily? I would normally be excited about the fact that it's snowing on Christmas day, but not today. What did kicking the turkey out of the back door achieve apart from ruining my boots? I pick my phone up and peer at the screen forlornly. There's a message from Kallum, I must have missed the notification tone while I was making a sandwich.

Suse, you wouldn't believe how truly sorry I am for messing up your Christmas? Can we talk?

'Messing up' my Christmas? Are you serious? You've done far more than that. You've destroyed my life. No, we cannot talk. I have nothing to say to you.

I love you though. I realise that more than ever now.

Good for you – shame you didn't realise it while you were giving Tania one.

Please allow us to talk, I've made a terrible mistake and I want to put it right. Please?

How on earth could you EVER put it right? We're done Kallum. Move on and have fun being a daddy. Goodbye.

Gosh, that sounded so final. Do I really mean it? I have got to mean it. There's no way back from this. Our relationship would never be the same again – especially if Tania has a baby. No, it's over – forever – no matter how much it kills me to think about it.

Hi Clair, sorry I didn't text you earlier. Had a nightmare of a day. Hope you're having a good Xmas xx

Oh no, what have you done? Burnt the turkey? Over cooked the eggs Benedict? Lol xx Happy Xmas to you both xxxx Please don't tell me you've burnt the flat down, ha ha xx

None of the above. I'm on my own. Me and Kallum have split up today – for good!

What????!!!

Tania is having his baby – how sweet for them both.

WTF! Do you want me to come home? OMG!

No, I'm OK. I'm going to Mum and Dad's tomorrow. I will get over this in time. I know I will. I'm trying not to think too much as it kills me. Going to bed early xx

OMG – are you sure you don't need me to come back? Xx

No, please, enjoy your Xmas. No point two of us being miserable xx

I'll phone you later tonight. I need to know all the details. I'm horrified Suse. I'm so sorry to hear this. Love you xx

Love you too. Yes, give me a ring when you can. Not too late though as I'll be in bed. Got a hellish hangover xx

OK hun, look after yourself. I know you're made of tough stuff xx

Am I? I don't feel like I'm tough. I want to disappear inside a hole somewhere and not come out until I can forget.

Momentarily, I think about texting my mum to forewarn her but decide not to. I don't want to spoil their Christmas day. Boxing day is going to be bad enough.

Aimlessly, I open my laptop and go to *facebook*. I'm bored with Christmas now, I'm lost in a dark void and don't want to think about anything.

I have a friend request – it's the most wonderful thing that has happened to me this Christmas afternoon. A new friend... except it's... Why?

Why would she want to be my friend? Amber Nutbrown – works at – Hightown Secondary School. *Respond to friend request.*

Do I confirm? I hardly know her and I very much doubt that she would remember me from the Christmas do. She was so recklessly drunk and ill. She must remember me though, otherwise why would she send me a friend request? I'm quite surprised that she knew how to find me. Before I press confirm, I try to look at her profile, her friends, her pictures, but they're all hidden. I will have to be her friend in order to see everything. What have I got to lose?

I click confirm and refresh the page. There she is in full glory. Scrolling down her timeline I see photos from the Christmas do. There are pictures posted to her timeline by other people too. I'm amused by the number of likes and comments from people I've either heard of or know. I never thought that so many of my colleagues would use *facebook*. Slowly, I disappear into a trail of comments, looking up people's profiles and friend lists. Amusedly, I find that Sultry Sarah and Juicy Jane have *facebook* accounts (although their privacy settings prevent me from looking at their profiles). One photograph on Amber's profile surprises me – because it's me, or should I say the back end of a turkey. There are 36 comments listed on the photo, along the lines of, 'Lol, Sarah and Jane have done it again' and 'Who stuffed the turkey?' and 'Who was the turkey this year?' It's quite apparent to me now that this really is a yearly event. I had been told this but to see the images and comments just confirms it.

My fellow TA, Jade Smith has also commented on some of the photos. I click through to her profile and hesitate as the cursor hovers over the 'Add Friend' button. Should I add her? If I do, then my profile will become more noticeable and possibly pop up in the 'People you may know' lists on other profiles. I've got nothing to hide though, so, why shouldn't I? I push my index finger down on the mouse button. 'Friend request sent'.

Jade's privacy settings are not high, I note, as I search through her friend list. I recognise so many people from both Baghurst and Hightown school.

Suddenly, my finger stops scrolling and I peer at the screen, 'Ryan Bagshaw'. It's him. As if I had peeped into his bedroom window, I hit the back button quickly and return to Jade's profile. She is friends with Ryan. I expect a lot of the others are too. I didn't hang around long enough to find out. My heart flutters with a strange excitement. It shouldn't, I know, but it does. I want to look at his profile but the strange sensation of prying, prevents me. I close the lid of my laptop and drag myself up to make a cup of much needed, sobering coffee.

I need to sort my head out before I start making new friends and doing the rounds on *facebook*. I'm sure I'm functioning on automatic pilot at the moment, which doesn't bode well for when that time does come and it suddenly smacks me in the face, exactly what Kallum has done.

***

Having chatted to Clair for about 20 minutes last night, I retired to bed early, still with the thumping head I'd had all afternoon. I don't remember much else as I must have fallen asleep pretty quickly.

I've just woken and my mind has instantly darted off to thoughts of Kallum. It's over. It really is. It's also Boxing day. I'm single. I'm seeing my parents today and they don't even know I'm single. God help me. My mum will be in tears and my dad will get into a murderous rage.

Happy Boxing Day!

Dressing in my new penguin jumper (I've got to make the effort I suppose) and a pair of jeans, I scoop my hair up into a short ponytail and put some comfortable boots on. My new ones are lying in the corner of the living room, awaiting a plan of attack... or worse, the bin. I'm distraught that I would have done something so stupid yesterday. Who goes around kicking cooked turkeys, for goodness sake? Oh wait, I do, when I'm drunk.

The small amount of snow from yesterday has completely vanished today. Maybe it's just as well, as my mum would be panicking about me driving over to see them if there was so much as a single flake on the road. Bless her, she does worry about everything.

I go into the living room and look at the beautiful wicker basket I've bought for Mum and Dad. It's a luxurious hamper filled with bottles of wine, chocolates, all the items required for an afternoon tea, nuts and nibbles and it even has a cutlery set and plates in the lid of the basket. It was quite pricey but well worth the look on their faces when I give it to them. I know it will be put to good use in the future too as my parents do like to go out on little day excursions and take a picnic with them.

Sadly, I just didn't have enough of any one type of wrapping paper to wrap the whole hamper in one go. So, I had to do it in bits. It looks original though, I'm thinking.

Once I've finished wrapping the hamper, I text my mum saying that *I* and not *we* will be round in the next half an hour. She replies with, *OK honey xx* She has obviously not picked up on the 'I' bit. It's going to come as quite a shock to Mum and Dad but I'm sure we'll get through it between us all. Wish me luck.

Suse, can we talk, please. Love Kallum

No, we can't Kallum. I have nothing to say to you. Leave me alone and get on with your new life.

But I don't want a new life – I want you. More than ever. Please?

Hi Mum, me again. Sorry, can I make that an hour? I'll be there by 11am – I promise xxxxxx

OK honey, not a problem xx

Mum still hasn't got the 'I' bit.

I'm running late now as I feel compelled to reply to Kallum's texts and get to the bottom of this break-up. It's really killing me inside but I hate what he's done and realise that I've wasted the last two years of my life with him. I've been kidding myself, that we had a great relationship, for far too long now.

Should have thought about that before. Sorry Kallum, I can't go back after what you've done. You've created an absolute mess for yourself and you need to sort it out on your own.

It's breaking my heart once again, being so cold towards him, but last night, Clair said that it's the only way to go. Easy for Clair to say, she's not the one with her heart in shreds and a mushed-up brain.

I will sort it out on my own but I still want... no I need you. I love you. I've made the biggest mistake of my life.

Yes, you have. It's over Kallum. Go and enjoy the rest of Christmas with Tania – and baby bump. Please don't keep contacting me. If you ever cared for me in the slightest, you'll leave me alone and let me move on to a happier future.

I don't want a future without you.

Too late. Goodbye.

Flipping heck, that was so hard. My heart is racing and I feel sick. It's not what I want. I don't want it to be over but Clair reminded me as well, last night, that I have got to look at the bigger picture here. The way he's been with me lately (obviously because he was sleeping with Tania) and the prospects of a future with Kallum and a baby that is not ours – it just wouldn't work. Clair made me see sense but I still don't like it. Everything is so raw and she said that it would be like that for a long time to come. Great prospects for happiness in the future – not.

Please Suse. Can we at least talk?

No Kallum. There's nothing else to say. Please respect my wishes now and leave me alone.

OK. I'm really sorry. I truly am.

There's no point in even replying to that last message. Sorry? He's sorry? What a flaming joke.

*** 11 ***

My parents live in a pretty little cul-de-sac on the outskirts of town, called Burton Grove. They live at the bottom of the road and their bungalow is central to the mini roundabout which is filled with an array of colourful flowers in the summer. Mum loves her flowers and between her and her good neighbours, on both sides, they ensure that the roundabout and their front gardens are a mass of colour and greenery. Both my mum and dad know everyone in the cul-de-sac, mind you, there are only seven houses in it, and they both love a good gossip with the neighbours about who is doing what in the area.

There's no doubt that mine and Kallum's story will be the topic of conversation one day, except it will have been embellished to the point of... Well, by the time it gets around the whole cul-de-sac, Kallum will have probably run off to the Philippines; got himself a Filipina woman; had six kids with her and then presented her and the children to me on Christmas day, asking if they could all stay in my flat.

I smile to myself as I drive the six miles to Burton Grove – at least I can joke about what Kallum has done. I'm keeping up a strong front, for the sake of my parents and more so for my mum's sake. She would not cope if she thought, for one minute, that I wasn't coping.

Pulling into the double-drive I notice the blinds twitch in the front room. They've obviously been keeping a look out for me – or should I say, for us.

The front door opens as I climb out of my car and Mum's smiley face greets me. She's wearing a snowman jumper and black jeans. Her mid-length, blonde hair is held back with an Alice band which has huge reindeer antlers sticking out of the top. Her broad beam then falters as she looks through the windscreen, searching for Kallum. She frowns.

"Where's Kallum? Sorry honey, happy Christmas – how are you?" She cups my face in her cold hands (they're always cold – she's got some sort of a circulatory problem) and kisses me on the nose. Peering around the side and back of the car she knits her eyebrows into a deeper frown. "Where's Kallum?"

"I'll explain in a minute," I say, pecking her on the cheek. "I need to get your present out of the boot first."

"I've told you not to worry about presents for me and your dad."

"It's just a little something," I say, reaching into the boot and heaving the huge wrapped gift out of the car.

"Oh my goodness." Mum stares at the box incredulously. "Is that our present?"

"Just a little one this year." I grin at her. "Could you close the boot for me?"

"But where's Kallum, honey?" Mum looks at me puzzled, "He's not in that big box, is he?"

"I'd hardly be carrying it if he were. Can we go in – this is heavy. I'll explain indoors."

"Yes, of course," says Mum, rushing past me to open the front door wide. "John..." she calls out to my dad, "Susie's here – she's got a big surprise."

That's a slight understatement. I've got two big surprises.

Dad's head appears around the kitchen door, in front of me. "Hello trouble," he says. He's wearing his favourite Santa apron. My dad loves to cook and he loves to collect aprons too. I'm sure he must now have one for every single week of the year. Some of them are quite cool but others are totally embarrassing. I mean, really embarrassing. Like his naked man one which has a turkey flapping its wings, concealing the man's nether regions or his cow one that actually has plastic udders attached to the stomach area. Not only embarrassing but ridiculous too. He has several summer barbecue ones as well but his favourite is the one that says, Mr Good-Looking is Cooking. Well, I suppose he's not bad looking for a man of his age, bearing in mind that he's my dad and I'd find it hard to look at him in any other way than just my silly old dad.

He still has a full head of hair, although it's completely grey and he insists, to this day, that flat-tops are the coolest hairstyles for men, of any age. I wouldn't know any different, I've never seen him with any other style – except when his hair is wet and stuck to his head. Now that does look odd, but kind of cute too.

"Hi Dad – look what I've got for you two."

Dad's eyes open wide. "That's a big voucher," he says, grinning widely.

I giggle as I walk towards him and peck his cheek. "Where shall I put it?"

"Through there, honey, under the tree," says Mum. She turns and looks at Dad. "Kallum's not here..."

I walk into the living room and place the box under the six-foot Christmas tree. Mum and Dad have always had a huge one. They enjoy entertaining and inviting lots of friends around to their house, hence, their preconception that everything has got to be large and impressive.

Turning around, I see Mum and Dad standing in the doorway, staring at me puzzled. "So where is Kallum?" asks Mum again, her brow still furrowed.

"He won't be coming today... in fact... not any day... ever again."

Mum gasps and places her hand over her mouth. She looks to Dad with a glazed expression.

"Why?" Dad is frowning now too.

"We've split up..." I grimace, waiting for the outburst of tears from Mum before she's even heard why. "I'm really sorry to have to tell you this today."

"When did this happen?" Mum is looking anxious now.

"Yesterday."

"Yesterday? On Christmas day?" Mum's hand is back over her mouth. "But... it's Christmas."

I nod my head and curve my mouth down. "I know. He's been seeing someone else."

"Oh no," Mum shrieks and grabs on to the side of the sofa before edging around it to collapse on the seat. "Oh no, Susie."

Dad is shaking his head from side to side with an angry expression on his face. "The little..." he sits down next to Mum and places an arm round her shoulder. "Try not to get upset Sharon, we'll talk this all through after dinner, when our guests have left – won't we Susie?"

"Yes, of course..." I hesitate momentarily. Well, I might as well get it all out in the open now and then there won't be any shocks later. "But I should tell you that the woman he's been seeing is pregnant... with his baby."

Mum gasps loudly and puts both hands to her mouth. "Oh no, how terrible. Oh honey, I'm so sorry. How awful for you. Are you... well, I know you can't be OK but..."

"I was pretty shocked – I have to say." I peer over at Mum who has tears in her eyes. "I..." Spontaneously, I burst into tears. I was not expecting it to happen.

"Come here, you," says Dad, rising from his seat and pulling me into a tight embrace. "He doesn't deserve you." He strokes at my hair. "He can go to hell as far as I'm concerned. The two-timing little bugger."

I tremble in Dad's arms and my broken heart releases all that it's been holding back. Did I really think that I could get over Kallum and what he has done, simply by drinking copious amounts of Baileys yesterday? It appears not. I am surprised by my outpouring of grief though. I thought I'd be able to stay stronger than this, especially in front of Mum and Dad.

"Oh, honey," says Mum, almost crying as much as I am, "come here." She stands up and reaches out as I step across to her and wrap my arms round her slim waist. "Oh, Susie, my precious girl. This must be so terrible for you to deal with. I cannot believe he has done this to you." She kisses the top of my head. "You have to be strong, honey. We'll get through this together – all of us."

Dad walks out of the room and then returns a moment later with a pink toilet roll. "Come on, dry your eyes, the pair of you. We are going to enjoy Boxing day without *him*. It's his loss – not ours. We'll have the last laugh and I'll be having his bloody Christmas jumper too."

Both me and Mum reel off some tissue and blow our noses. Then we peer at each other and burst into hysterical, tearful laughter.

The tears have ended and Dad is busily preparing the dinner. Mum went and reapplied the little amount of make-up that she ever wears and I have been setting out the table for five people.

"Ooh, it looks lovely," says Mum, entering the dining room with her freshly mascaraed eyes and a wide grin. "Are you sure you don't mind Doreen and Malcolm joining us for dinner?"

"No, not at all. I'm fine Mum, really I am." I place the last of the cutlery down and look up. "The more the merrier."

"I thought you'd think that... well, before you told me the awful news today." Mum sniffs and rubs a finger under her nose.

"Let's not start that again," I say, feeling the urge to gulp. "I want to try and forget about him and what he's done."

Mum nods her head feverishly. "Yes, of course, honey. He's not worth thinking about." She forces a smile and claps her hands together. "Right – shall we put the crackers out? I bought some expensive ones this year but don't tell your father. They've got really sweet little gifts in them."

I nod and smile back at her. "Yes, OK... and my lips are sealed, although Dad's bound to know that they're expensive when he sees the gifts – surely?"

"Special offer," says Mum, winking at me. "That's what I'll say – I got them at a discounted price of 20 little pounds."

I peer at her incredulously. "Twenty pounds? How many have you got?"

"Just the six." She grins conceitedly.

"Six? Six crackers? They cost you 20 quid?"

Mum shakes her head. "No," she whispers, "they cost £55."

"Fifty-five? What have they got in them – gold?"

She places a finger over her lips. "Shh, remember, they were twenty – not fifty-five."

The phone rings in the hallway and Mum gives me a puzzled look before turning on her heels to go and answer it.

"Hello," I hear her say.

I hold my breath for a second. Who would be phoning Mum's house on Boxing day? I hope to God it's not Kallum. I couldn't bear it if he phoned here. My dad would grab the phone anyway and give him a real piece of his mind. And that would not be good for Kallum, trust me. But then, why should I be worrying about what's good for Kallum? I should be hoping that he'll rot in hell – I'm just too nice for my own good sometimes.

"Yes, of course, that's absolutely fine Doreen. Yes, of course he can." She pauses. "I'm quite sure. No, no, they would love to see him. It's been a very long time – how exciting." Mum peers through the living room door at me, raises her shoulders and smiles. "Yes, same time. Dinner at two o'clock – is that OK?" She nods her head. "Hmm, OK – see you at 1.30."

"Oh wow – I'm guessing that's Jett who is coming?" I ask, as Mum breezes into the room.

"Yes – how exciting. He turned up unexpectedly, this morning. Doreen wanted to check that it was OK for him to join us."

"Cool, that will make a nice round six of us then." I return to the dresser in the dining room and begin to set another place on the table.

"My goodness, how long is it since you've seen him?"

I pause and look up. "Must be 15 years or more."

"Yes, it must be. I bet he's grown."

I giggle and look at her incredulously. "I would think so Mum. He'll be at least 26 now – he's two years younger than me. I'd imagine he has definitely grown a bit."

"So, we haven't seen him since he was ten or eleven." Mum claps her hands together excitedly as she walks back to the hallway. "John – honey – you'll never guess who's coming to dinner. We need some extra roasties doing..."

*** 12 ***

Jett Wilson – he's the grandson of Doreen and Malcolm. We grew up together. We spent many a sunny day squabbling over toys or fighting over who was going on the swing in his back garden first. I was the oldest, by two years, and felt that he should rise to my every command – and I was a girl anyway, which automatically gave me the right to go first on everything – didn't it? We were like a brother and sister except we lived in different houses. It was only when I started to 'develop' and mature that my parents and his grandparents decided that we were getting too old to have sleep-overs at each other's houses on the weekends.

Then he left. Practically overnight, he went to join his mum in Spain, where she lived. His grandparents had brought him up for nearly all his life, as his mum had chosen a career in Flamenco dancing when he was only a year old. She hadn't been able to take him with her but vowed that the time would come when she would be settled enough to have her own place. Then she would take Jett over to live with her.

Initially, her plan had been to settle within her first year but it was more like nine years before she was ready. She had seen Jett over that time though. She returned to the UK three times a year for holidays, just to see her son and her parents.

As for Jett's dad – well, no one ever knew who he was. His mum, Sasha, had had a string of one-night stands during a rebellious period in her life and she didn't even know that she was pregnant until she was almost seven months gone.

Of course, all of this has been very hard on both Doreen and Malcolm over the years. They're in their seventies now, although you would never believe it. I've never know such a fit, fun and bubbly couple. They gave Jett a wonderful childhood and taught him good manners and politeness – except when it came to the swing in their back garden, of course.

I remember Jett being a lovely looking boy with bright blue eyes and dark, almost black hair which was quite an unusual combination. He was shorter than me, obviously, as he was younger, so it's going to be very strange to see him today. He quite possibly will be taller than me now.

At least there is no swing to argue over anymore.

"How come he's turned up at his grandparents' house unexpectedly?" I ask, curiously.

"Well... it's quite a long story, I'll tell you everything later. I need to keep my head straight and get the table finished first," says Mum, as she carefully places the lavish crackers around the table. "I'm glad I bought these now though."

"OK," I say, as I peer at the cracker box and read the contents label. "Blimey, there are nice gifts inside."

Each cracker contains a different gift. There's a smart looking mini compass on a keyring; an elegant, silver-plated bottle stopper; a silver-plated, embossed bookmark; a cute compact-mirror in a leather case; a cylindrical leather container with four stainless steel shot glasses inside and a pretty, jeweled handbag charm.

"I know," Mum whispers, "that's why I bought them." She gives a little cheerful shrug and starts fussing over the minor details of straightening every knife, fork and spoon and carefully folding napkins in a way that has always amazed me.

"I still don't get how you make those."

"Come on, I'll show you again," she says as she starts to turn the second red napkin into a delicate rose.

I did it. I made a rose from one of the spare napkins. OK, it's not a perfect rose, in fact Dad thought it looked more like a withered tulip, but hey, at least I had a go.

I'm getting quite nervous at the prospect of seeing Jett after so many years. Apparently, according to what Mum was telling me earlier, Jett has been living back in the UK for over a year now.

I can't believe she'd never told me.

He'd met an English girl online and moved back to be with her. The most bizarre thing is that he lives about three miles away from me in a rented room and I knew nothing about it. My mum can be quite scatty-brained sometimes, she does like a good gossip but when it comes to the important bits of her over-the-fence chit-chats, she forgets to tell me.

As for my dad, he doesn't care one way or another and couldn't be bothered to tell anyone anything. When it comes to the gossiping in the cul-de-sac, he listens and nods his head but doesn't really take anything in. As long as the neighbours attend his summer barbecues he's quite happy. Any excuse for a new apron, I suppose.

Back to Jett and it turns out that he split up with the girl he was seeing, just a week ago and decided to turn up at his grandparent's house unannounced, last night. He had planned to travel to the girlfriend's home for Christmas but it had panned out that she wasn't quite what he thought she was, a year into their relationship. She had introduced her *close* girlfriend to him and asked if they could both share him and all live together as a threesome. What man wouldn't want to do that? Jett, it seems, didn't want to. I can't blame him though. I've heard that those sorts of set-ups never work out anyway. Not that I would ever entertain anything like that either. One to one is enough for me. Well, it *was* anyway.

I keep forgetting that I'm single now and when the little tormenting memory comes to mind, my mood plummets into an abyss of fiery anger and downright desolation.

Deep breaths, keep calm, I will get through this.

The doorbell rings and I freeze. Mum is scurrying to the door in a bit of a flap. She gets nervous when people come to her home. She likes everything to be nice – to be perfect in fact. She has spent the last half an hour going around each room on the ground floor checking for dust and bits of muck on the carpets. I knew there was not much point, but I did say to her to chill out as it wasn't the Queen coming round for dinner. She just huffed at me and said that she liked things to be clean and tidy. Then she rushed off to squirt toilet cleaner around the bowl in the downstairs toilet.

Honestly, I don't think you'd find a cleaner house in the whole of the UK. Her spring-cleaning regime goes from the beginning of March until the end of February of the next year and then she starts all over again.

I hear Doreen's high-pitched, jolly voice, followed by Malcolm's more reserved low tones. Then there's another voice. One I haven't heard before, or at least not in its maturity. Oh my Goodness, Jett sounds like a man. Well, of course he's going to sound like a man – he is one.

I peer at myself in Mum's mirror above her fireplace and puff up my crinkly bob haircut. I say crinkly because I decided to remove the pathetic little ponytail earlier, and now I have an unruly kink in my hair. I don't know why I'm fretting so much about my appearance. OK... I do know why. I haven't seen Jett for so long and I want to make a good first impression. He will think that I've grown up a lot. Oh dear, now I feel like the Queen *is* coming to dinner. I check my mascara in the mirror, take a deep breath and walk towards the living room door.

Doreen is practically on top of me as I open the door. She must have just been about to walk in the room. "Darling, Susie, happy Christmas my little sugar-plum. Oh, it's so lovely to see you." She throws her arms round me and hugs me tightly.

Peering over her shoulder, I see a tall man standing just behind Malcolm. Oh... my... goodness... I smile and pull away from Doreen. "Happy Christmas to you too," I say, grinning at her. She moves to one side as Malcolm approaches me in a much more relaxed manner.

"Good to see you Susie. How's everything going?"

"Good, thanks," I say, politely.

Then my eyes meet Jett's. Oh... my...

I smile nervously.

Oh... good... grief.

"Look at you," Jett says in his deep voice. He steps towards me as Malcolm moves out of the way and opens his arms. "You've grown up a bit."

"So have you," I say, shyly.

He wraps his arms round my shoulders and I tentatively place mine round his waist. He smells gorgeous. Oh dear me. He is like a Greek God. He is totally, amazingly gorgeous. He's perfection. I swallow hard, he's making me feel so terribly coy and flustered. What is going on with me?

"It's really good to see you again. How long is it?" he asks, as he pulls away and looks down at me.

Oh dear, I'm not even sure I can talk to him in coherent sentences. His eyes are incredible. His dark hair is... well, when it's the backdrop to those ice-blue eyes, he looks unreal. His chiselled features and the curvature of his lips are just too much to cope with. "Fifteen?" I swallow again. "Must be..." Come on Susie, get your act together, you've known this fella since the beginning of time.

"Fifteen years – wow. How time flies."

"Hmm..." I give him a twitchy smile. Are my teeth clean? God, I hope so. "Hmm..." Oh dear, I need to say more than, 'hmm'. "Hmm..."

"How are you? What's been going on in the last 15 years?"

"Err... hmm..." I turn around and look at the others. They're all watching us lovingly like we're the long-lost brother and sister who are having a reunion after so many years. Well, I suppose it is like that really. So why am I now making myself look like a complete and utter twerp by repeating the same pathetic mumbling sound every time he says something. Come on

Susie, get a grip. "Shall we..." I usher everyone into the living room, it gives me time to compose myself and breathe.

Why is it that I get jittery when a handsome man walks into a room? He's like a brother to me, yet I'm like a star-struck wreck as I sit down.

"I'll put the kettle on," says Mum, clasping her hands together nervously. "Then we can have a lovely catch-up with you, Jett. You're looking fabulous."

"Thanks," he replies. "You're looking as lovely as ever yourself."

"Oh bless you, Jett. Thank you." Mum gives a cute little coy grin.

Jett sits on the sofa next to me and I can already feel my cheeks filling with red-hot blood. I pull myself up so that I can sit in the most elegant way, bearing in mind that Mum and Dad's sofa is the most luxurious, encompassing sofa ever. You could lay on it without consciously doing so, as it sinks into a heavenly enveloping softness of comfort and ease.

Jett smiles at my mum politely. "You're welcome," he says, before turning to peer at me again. "Come on then..." His voice has lowered to a gentle tone. "You sounded a bit tongue-tied a minute ago. So, what have you been up to?"

"Err... nothing much. You?"

He laughs and puts an arm round my shoulder, pulling me closer to him. "I've missed you, all these years. Wanna go, play on the swing?" He then withdraws his arm and stares at me.

"It's not there anymore, is it?" I avoid his gaze for fear of turning into a blubbering mess again. I peer down at his thickset legs and imagine, just for a moment, how muscular they probably are underneath his jeans. He's broad shouldered too, I noticed that at the front door. He's in perfect proportions all the way down to his tan boots, to be honest. Oh dear, he's like the brother I never had, for goodness sake.

Stop it. I know I sound like a sex-starved nymphomaniac but that couldn't be any further from the truth.

"We could make a rope-swing from Nan's tree."

"Too cold out there," I reply, hoping that the words I'm actually saying are the ones I'm thinking I am saying.

"Is Kallum here, Susie dear?" Doreen looks at me expectantly. "I was telling Jett about you and him."

"Err..." I shuffle on the sofa uncomfortably.

Dad gives me an awkward look.

"No, he's not. I'm afraid we're not together anymore."

"But..." Doreen looks to Malcolm. "I thought he was coming for dinner today. Your mum said only yesterday..."

"He was," I reply and give Jett a sheepish grin. "We split up yesterday."

"On Christmas day?" Doreen stares wide-eyed. "Surely not on Christmas day."

I nod my head and turn the corners of my mouth down.

"Sorry to hear that," says Jett, mirroring my downturned mouth expression. "If it's any consolation, I'm in the same boat."

"Yes, I heard. Sorry to hear about yours too."

The atmosphere in the room is turning gloomy. We're like two heartbroken rejects, captivating our audience in a bereaved hush.

"Right," says Dad, clapping his hands together and pulling himself up from the chair. "I'd better check on those roasties."

"Need a hand?" I ask, which is quite unusual for me but I'm in an unusual kind of mood.

"No, you stay here and catch up with Jett. I'm sure you've both got loads to talk about." Dad gives me an odd, puzzled look, because I offered to help, and leaves the room.

"Come on Malcolm," says Doreen, slapping his back. "Let's go and see if we can do anything in the kitchen and leave these two to have a natter."

Oh my goodness – really? We're going to be in the room on our own now. That means we will have to talk, which isn't a problem for Jett but it seems to be for me at the moment.

"So," says Jett, the second the living room door closes. "The last time I saw you, I think you must have been about 12 or 13, so what have you been up to since then?

He's like a brother. It's that simple. Keep calm and talk to him. He's just like a brother. I've known him for years and years. The fact that he has turned out to be the most handsome man I have ever set my eyes upon is neither here nor there.

I'm supposed to be a downhearted, rejected woman anyway, so I shouldn't be thinking the way I am. I should be in that, 'I hate all men' phase, shouldn't I? Not fancying the first man who walks into my life the very next day.

*** 13 ***

Actually, he's not like a brother. You don't gaze into a brother's eyes and want to kiss his lips or remove his clothes so that you can stroke his warm body. You don't get excitable rushes of sexual desire when you're sat next to your brother, so no, he's not like a brother.

The thing is, I get the distinct feeling that he doesn't see me as, just like a sister, either. He showed signs of more than a little admiration for me. He was quite flirtatious when we chatted in the living room. He also got a bit tongue-tied from time to time and I'm quite sure that his eyes undressed me on several occasions. Awkward. That's a slight understatement. Very awkward – but quite nice too.

Anyway, I'm fluttering back down to earth at this present time and we are all sat at the table with steaming hot plates filled with turkey, roasties, vegetables and stuffing balls (my first Christmas dinner!). Mum is passing the gravy boat around the table and everyone is chatting about me and Jett, funnily enough.

"It's strange how you two have ended up being single in the same week," says Doreen as she passes the gravy boat to Malcolm.

I nod and smile waveringly.

"Perhaps it's a sign." Jett looks across the table at me and winks his eye.

Oh dear, he is another one of those men who ask you to sleep with them when they wink their eye. I can't cope with men winking like that.

"Ooh, young Jett – are you making a proposition to our little girl," says Mum with a giggly tone in her voice.

"Mum..." I gasp.

"I'm joking honey. Don't take everything so seriously."

Me? Take things seriously? I'm pretty sure I don't take things like that seriously. I mean, when you've been dressed up as a turkey and made to look a complete idiot and then your boyfriend of two years makes you look like even more of a complete idiot, I'm thinking that I'm not doing too bad here. "I'm not really Mum. Maybe Jett is right..." I shoot a cursory glance at him, "maybe it's meant to be and a sign that we can help each other and struggle through our break-ups together – you know, support each other."

"Exactly," says Jett. "I'm definitely here for you if you need a shoulder to cry on."

"Thanks," I say, "but I don't need a shoulder to cry on – I'm over him. He's the one that will lose out, not me."

"Good girl," says Doreen. "You have got to keep strong – and you too, Jett."

"Nan, I'm cool, no need to worry about me." He looks over at me and winks again.

God, I wish he'd stop that. "So... shall we change the subject to something more interesting?" I suggest.

Everyone looks around at each other like I've just announced that I am the virgin Mary and bearing a child. I'm sure they don't know what to talk about apart from me and Jett.

"This looks good," says Malcolm, shaking pepper over his potatoes. "You've done a good job, John."

Dad nods his head. "Cheers, Malc, I do rustle up a good roast spud now and again."

"Yes, thank you to both of you. The table looks magnificent too." Doreen picks up the cracker in front of her. "Are we going to pull these?"

"Oh yes, please go ahead." Mum grins at Dad and passes one end of her cracker to him.

"These look expensive," he says.

"I got them on offer – a real bargain."

Bang!

Everyone is pulling and making cracking noises with the crackers, including me. I open one cracker with Jett and one with Doreen. They both win their half but Jett passes his gift to me. It's the compact mirror.

"Not the sort of thing I'd use," he says with a smile. Then he winks his eye again.

Stop it please. Stop, stop, stop. I need to eat my meal in front of him without dribbling it down the corners of my mouth or without choking. Worst case scenario would be to miss my mouth completely while I'm taking sneaky looks at him and end up with food all down my new penguin jumper. Incidentally, although I do like it, why did I have to go and wear a silly penguin jumper today? I should be wearing a sexy outfit... hmm... OK, maybe I shouldn't. He's supposed to be like my brother.

Dad had once again trumped it. The dinner and his homemade Christmas pudding were delicious. Now Mum and Doreen are in the kitchen tidying up and Dad and Malcolm are sitting in front of the TV, staring at the screen with droopy eyelids. As for me and Jett, well, we haven't moved from the table yet. He's been telling me about his life in Spain, which sounds very interesting and, also, perpetually sunny, in an odd kind of way. My childhood and adolescent years were much cloudier. Don't get me wrong, my parents were and still are the best parents anyone could ever wish for but my life, so far, has been pretty bog-standard compared to Jett's.

"Do you want to go for a walk?" Jett has suddenly changed the subject entirely. "Work off some of that Christmas pudding."

"Yes, sure, why not. I could do with some fresh air," I lie, but I guess it beats sitting around all afternoon waiting for Mum to get the Monopoly out and Dad to wake up from his guaranteed snooze, which I predict will start in about three minutes flat.

We both stand up at the same time and almost bump heads. "Go on, you first," says Jett, allowing me to get through the narrow gap at the end of the table.

"I'll get my coat – looks a bit snowy out there."

Jett nods and follows me out to the hallway.

"Mum – me and Jett are going out for a little walk – won't be too long," I call out.

"OK honey – have fun."

Have fun? What does she mean by, 'have fun'? What does she think we're going to get up to? "We'll have fun if we can find a swing," I reply.

Jett laughs and pulls his padded jacket over his shoulders as I do the same. Gosh, he looks even more hunky now, with his jacket on. He then offers me his arm.

"Shall we go madam?"

Coyly, I link arms with him and we shuffle out of the front door.

"Where should we go?" Jett asks as we reach the end of the drive.

I pull my arm away from his and he frowns at me. "Err... we could walk down towards Grimly Park if you like."

"Come on then." He offers his arm again. "Don't want you slipping up – it looks a bit icy."

Again, I link arms with him and we stroll towards the park.

If Kallum could see me now, he would fall over with shock. He knows about a boy called Jett but he wouldn't know that this man, I'm linking arms with, is that boy from my past. Jett's striking features would make any woman or man look twice and the fact that I'm linked up to him makes it appear like we're a couple. I actually wish that Kallum *would* turn up to my parent's house and see me with Jett. That would shock him, just like he did to me yesterday.

I'm sure I should be more upset than I am but all I feel is hatred and pity. Yes, I actually feel sorry for him because he's in this terrible mess that he created all by himself. Stupid idiot. Oh, now I do feel sad again. I must stop thinking about him.

"Are you OK?"

I snap out of my deep thoughts and turn my head to smile. "Yes, sorry. I was miles away for a minute there."

"I could see that." Jett raises his eyebrows and grins. "I just said, did you fancy a drink at the pub?"

"At the George Inn?"

"Yes, that's the one. I couldn't remember the name of it."

"I don't have any money on me." I stuff my free hand into my pockets, checking for change.

"I've got some."

"OK, I'll owe you one," I say.

"One – I was thinking of several." Jett laughs and winks his eye.

"I can't have several, I'm driving home tonight."

He squeezes my arm with his and grins at me again. "I could always ask my nan if you could stay at hers for a sleepover with me."

I look up at him wide-eyed. "Jett Wilson – we were banned from doing that years ago."

"But we're adults now..."

"Exactly," I jump in, "That would be even worse."

He stops and turns around to meet my eye. "And what do you mean by that Miss Satchel?"

I shrug and give a short nervous laugh. "Adults of different sex don't usually have sleepovers together unless they're..." I break off, feeling the heat in my cheeks.

"Unless they're what?" he asks teasingly. The glint in his eye suggests he's playing with me.

"Sleeping together – "

"There's no harm in snuggling up to someone to go to sleep together." He grins cheekily.

"Suppose not, if you look at it that way" I say, shyly. "Come on, let's get to the pub for that drink. And it will be only one drink OK?"

Jett nods his head obediently and sets off walking again. I'm still linked up to him and funnily enough it feels perfectly natural.

OK, maybe two drinks will be all right.

Three? Probably not but I'm past caring now. I'll have to stay at Mum's tonight – simple. She'll lend me some of her pyjamas and I can go home in the morning. It's not like I've got anything planned for tomorrow… or the day after… or the day after that. Kallum has put a stop to any of that.

"Go on then, I'm guessing I'll be staying at Mum and Dad's tonight. They won't mind though."

"It's all for a good cause," says Jett, pulling his wallet from his pocket.

"Good cause?"

"Yes, we're drowning our sorrows, aren't we?" He grins before walking away to the empty bar.

I don't know why the pub has even bothered opening today, to be honest. They have about six customers in at the moment, and two of those are us. The other four are all elderly men. It's quite sad really that they would rather sit in a pub drinking all afternoon than be at home with their families. Maybe they haven't got any family. Each one of them looks like your typical, ruddy-faced, red-nosed alcoholic whether they've got family or not. It's so sad.

I haven't been able to suggest leaving the pub as I've been enthralled by Jett's stories about his life, his now ex-girlfriend, his job and everything else about him. He's just a bag full of entertainment. His ex-girlfriend was a freelance fashion model – a fashion model, can you believe it? I'm not surprised really. I mean, look at him, he could be a model in his own right, so why wouldn't he date gorgeous women? As he was telling me about her, I could feel myself sinking lower and lower into my chair. I am so not in touch with fashion models or any kind of models to be honest. They are so above me. The only thing I'd be any good at modeling would be a nice cosy winter knit for penguins of the world.

As for Jett, well he left a brilliant job in Spain. He worked as an architect. An architect, can you believe? He'd only had the job for a year before he returned to England. He spent six years studying at *Universidad Europea de Madrid*. Trust me, I sank even further in my chair as he was telling me about this. I'm sure that a qualified European architect and a budding teaching assistant are worlds apart. Jett must have fallen deeply in love to have left his amazing job for a woman in the UK.

He currently works for a large estate agent, as a sales rep. His job mainly consists of the usual negotiating of sales, securing valuations, arranging viewings and keeping on top of administration. He works in the town where we both live – how weird. He's been right under my nose all this time.

Just four then – no more.

Are you OK honey? Did you find a swing? We're having a buffet around 7pm. Hope to see you back by then. Love Mummsie xxxx

We've been here for over two hours and I haven't once thought about contacting Mum to let her know we're OK. She's probably privately pulling her hair out with worry.

Sorry Mum. We ended up in the George. We'll be back very soon xx

OK honey, that's fine. See you soon xxxx

Yes – be back very soon. Could I stay tonight? I've had a few drinks xx

Yes, of course you can, honey. You don't need to ask. You are a silly billy xxxx

'Silly billy', honestly, who calls their grown-up daughter a silly billy? My mum does. I've just shown Jett her message and he found it incredibly funny. I'm guessing they don't have 'silly billies' in Spain.

I'm giggly-drunk now and Jett appears to be amorously tipsy. He keeps putting his arm round me, pulling me close to him and squeezing me. He smells so good. The amorous bit came a moment ago when he took my hand, looked deep into my eyes and said that he was so happy to have met up with me again after all these years. He then kissed the back of my hand softly and sensually, like he was kissing a lover's lips. It made me shiver with excitement, to be honest.

It's driving me mad. *He's* driving me mad. Crazy in fact. I shouldn't fancy the pants off him but I do. It's just not right. There's a static electrical charge between us. Yet, it seems that we're both trying to ignore it. Maybe it's just the alcohol and the fact that we're both on the rebound from our last relationships.

"We should go. Your mum and my nan – they'll be talking about us again." Jett rises from the chair and takes my hand.

I hope to God he's not going to kiss it like before. I couldn't possibly cope. "Yes, let's go. I feel quite drunk. It's all your fault." I giggle as he pulls me up and then he holds my coat up for me. He pulls it over the back of my shoulders and before I know it, he has pecked me on the cheek, from behind. I turn around instantly and our eyes meet. We stare at each other intently. I tear my eyes away from his and brush a hand across my cheek.

"Sorry about that, I just wanted to say thank you." Jett looks slightly worried.

"Thank you? For what?" I smile reassuringly. "It's OK."

"For helping me to move on. Your friendship is important to me but you've also made me realise what a real, beautiful woman should be like. Beauty on the inside as well as the outside."

Oh my goodness. I immediately blush from one ear to the other. "Ah, that's sweet of you to say – thank you Jett. You're a pretty sound guy yourself." That sounded quite cool but inside I'm flitting about in a million pieces. Oh dear, please someone, help me...

This sounds absolutely terrible, but it has literally, just happened as we've been walking back to Mum's house. The dark icy streets are eerily quiet as families are probably sitting in their warm homes feeling stuffed out from the festive food and alcohol. Anyway, somehow, I managed to slip up as we giddily walked along and Jett did the proverbial, knight in shining armour bit and rescued me before I hit the ground. Pulling me up towards him he hugged me tightly. Then we gazed into each other's eyes and that's when it happened, accidentally. Well, I say accidentally but...

Pulling away from my mouth, Jett peers into my eyes. "I'm sorry – I didn't mean to do that," he whispers.

"It's OK," I reply. I'm stunned, even though my alcohol addled mind has removed my inhibitions. I'm actually stupefied to be honest. He just kissed me. I mean, he really kissed me. Full on the lips. At first it was with closed mouths but as I willingly pushed against his lips, they opened. It was purely sensational – I'm talking the most amazing kiss I have ever experienced.

But now what?

"No, I shouldn't have done that." He looks mortified.

"It's done – don't worry." I gather my feet, having nearly done a triple somersault only moments ago and we continue to walk along the street towards Burton Grove. He's got his arm round my shoulders now. I'm not sure whether it is to prevent me from slipping up again or a beautiful, fond embrace.

"I shouldn't have..." Jett repeats himself.

"I'm fine with it, Jett. Please don't feel worried. It's OK."

Surprisingly, he stops and turns to face me. "No, it's not OK." His eyes scan my face. "Because..."

"Because?" I search his face for clues. "Because what?" My breath is shallow and rapid.

"I liked it too much." He averts his gaze and peers down at the ground.

Instinctively, I raise my hand to his head and stroke his hair. "It's OK, really it is... and I did, too."

Snatching me into his arms, he kisses me again. This time there is intense passion radiating from his warm, moist mouth. I let it happen. Rightly or wrongly, I can't stop it. I don't want to stop it. We're standing just around the corner from Burton Grove, snogging each other's faces off. It's insane. It feels so right. Yet it should be so wrong.

"Hi – sorry we're so late back," I say as I walk through the door, guiltily. "Hope we haven't missed the buffet."

Dad peers around the kitchen door and smiles. "Had a good time?"

"Yes, we did. Had a few too many though," says Jett as he removes his coat.

"Oh, there you are. I was beginning to wonder if you two had eloped." Mum gives us a big cheesy grin as she walks out of the kitchen with a plate of sausage rolls. "Only joking, honey." She brushes past me and gives a little smiley shrug.

Jett has gone very quiet and simply smiles sheepishly at everyone. I know how he's feeling. I'm putting on a brave front, feigning a normal response to everyone, it's so un-normal though. The electrical charge between us has magnified, yet, no one else can see or feel it.

What am I going to do? How can this have happened? Only yesterday, I was with Kallum, before he shattered my heart and my life. Shouldn't I be a blubbering mess today? No, it seems I only needed a few drinks before I willingly, opened my mouth to Jett's demands. I really don't know how to feel about it all, now that we're back at my mum and dad's house and it's just a 'normal' kind of Boxing day. I need enlightenment from some higher being above, to get me through this.

*** 14 ***

Well that was yesterday. Maybe I should try and forget it happened.

Doreen, Malcolm and Jett left at about 9.30pm. Jett asked for my mobile number before they left, which both Mum and Doreen thought was so sweet. They commented on how lovely it was that we could keep in contact now. Gosh, if only they knew.

I went to bed, in my old room, soon after they'd gone and didn't hear anything from Jett. Maybe I should have taken his number too but I didn't want to appear too keen in front of everyone else. Damn, I wish I had.

I've woken up with a bit of a dull head this morning, because we ended up having more drinks last night, during and after the buffet. I, for one, was pretty drunk by the time they left and I'd imagine that Jett was too. He was very quiet for the rest of the evening and kept glancing at me and smiling nervously while we all had a game of Monopoly.

I drag myself out of bed and plod through to the bathroom. Gosh, I look a mess this morning. My hair is in clumps and my eyes are puffy and smeared with black mascara. I really need a shower and then maybe I could borrow Mum's make-up and do my hair. Although I love my new hairstyle, I'm finding that a shorter cut is harder to deal with in the mornings. When my hair was longer it seemed to look OK when I got up and I simply brushed it through and scooped it all up into a ponytail or a bun. Now I've got a proper hairstyle, I have got to reshape it, dampen down little areas and make it look like that proper hairstyle every morning. Maybe I'll go back to long hair.

The tinkling of my phone pulls me from my muse. I grab it from the pocket of Mum's old dressing gown, which I'm wearing, and look at the screen. It's a message from an unknown number. Oh gosh, is it Jett?

Morning Susie. Hope you're OK. I was wondering if you'd like to meet up later today. We could go for a bite to eat somewhere. What do you think?

Totally understand if you don't want to. Sorry again about what happened yesterday. J x

I quickly save his number to my contacts. I need to read the message again – well, maybe several times – before I reply and I don't want to appear too keen, do I?

Saved. Now I've got his number. Oh gosh.

Morning. I'm good... apart from a thick head, but some would say that's normal for me, lol. Yes, that sounds good. I'm not doing anything else today...

No, that sounds like he's the only option I have left. I delete the last few words.

... I would really like that, thanks. I need to pop home this morning but let me know when you want to meet up. Suse x

I could pick you up from your place if you want me to? X

Yes, sure – what time? X

Does 3pm sound OK? X

Sounds fine. I'll see you then x

Just one thing...

Yes?

Where do you live? Lol x

Mum kept asking me if I was all right, all morning. By the time I left, showered *and* styled I must add, she was driving me crazy. She thought I was dealing with the break-up with Kallum remarkably well and she feared I would come crashing down at some point. She kept telling me that she was always there for me if I needed her. I kept saying that I knew she was, but I was feeling fine. Her look of puzzlement was awkward to deal with. I couldn't have told her about what happened last night. I just couldn't. It wouldn't have been right and she would have stressed out about it anyway. She would worry about what Doreen and Malcolm would say and she would be uptight about what the neighbours would say, once they found out. And they would find out sooner or later. No, it's best that she knows nothing. For now, at least.

I'm back in my flat and I can't seem to get Kallum out of my mind. It's like he's left a ghost here. I feel hugely guilty about kissing Jett, now I'm back home. I suppose it didn't feel real when we were out last night. The darkness and copious amounts of alcohol can be clever at shielding true feelings but now I'm home, it feels really real. And really wrong. Don't get me wrong, it's not like I want Kallum back but...

OK, I'm back to the 'brother' thing. Jett is supposed to be like my brother. Here I go again. We grew up together, we fought, we played, we argued, we cared. Now look at the mess we're in. He wants to see me again today and I have an unnerving feeling that there could be a repeat of last night. I could be wrong but somehow, I think I'm not.

Hi gorgeous lady, hope you've had a fab Xmas. You'll never guess who I saw yesterday, love Suse xxxx

I smile to myself as I press the send button. Clair knows all about my childhood and the boy I grew up with, who vanished overnight.

Hi Suse, yes had a lovely one thanks. Did you see Kallum? Have you sorted things out with him? Xxx

No, not him. He's beyond sorting out. Someone turned up at Mum and Dad's for dinner yesterday. Came with Doreen and Malcolm xxxx

Jeez – do you mean the boy you grew up with? Xxx

Yes, Jett, remember? Haven't seen him for about 15 years. God, he's turned into a right good-looking young man. Xxx

Ah, that's so nice. Is he single? Lol xxx

Yes, just split up with his girlfriend. What a coincidence. Xxxx

Send a picture to me, I want to see how good-looking he is xxx

I'm meeting up with him later, for a meal, so I'll try and get a picture of him xxxx

OK, if he's that good-looking don't let him get away again until I get home. Love ya Suse, xxx

Love you too, bye xxxx

Oh dear, that's going to be awkward. Poor Clair hasn't had much luck with the opposite sex but then she does spend so much time working. She has definitely lost the gist of that work/life balance we're all supposed to have. How can I introduce him to her when I'm not sure that I don't want him for myself?

He's like a brother. Just like a brother.

I'm pacing the living room carpet nervously. Every two lengths of the room, I veer off to the window, which looks out on to the street. There's a parking spot right outside my flat so I'm guessing he'll pull up there. Gosh, I'm shaky with apprehension. I peer into the mirror on the wall, checking my appearance for the umpteenth time. I didn't have a clue what to wear so decided to go for something smart but casual. I've got my favourite white, skinny jeans on and a gorgeous pink, paisley blouse. My poor glass-heeled boots are still sitting in the corner of the room feeling sorry for themselves. I haven't worked out what to do with them yet so I'm wearing a pair of more conventional, beige knee-highs which have a much smaller heel, At least that way, I shouldn't go slipping up and have to be rescued by Jett again... or do I want him to rescue me?

As I'm looking out of the window Jett's car pulls up. I know it's him because I saw his car on Doreen and Malcolm's drive yesterday. Oh gosh, here I go.

He's pulled into the space and I can see him looking at the building. I pull back the blind and wave at him.

He's seen me. OK, deep breaths. I grab my coat and bag – off I go.

He kissed me on the cheek as soon as I got in the car and commented on how nice I looked. Then he apologised for kissing me on the cheek and tried to explain that it was just a show of friendliness. Of course, I said he didn't need to apologise for doing it and that I was more than happy.

Awkward start.

He looks so hunky in his jeans and a different shirt to the one he had on yesterday. He's like a sex-magnet, I want to touch him and feel the strength in his arms. I want to stroke his solid legs. Oh dear.

We travel to the outskirts of town and then turn into the countryside. We haven't said much between us except to briefly discuss the puerile arguments that my dad and Doreen were having over the Monopoly last night. It was pretty amusing and funny, especially as we were all intoxicated – some more than others, namely, myself and Jett, I might add.

"Where are we going?" I say as we weave through the country lanes. The sky is that strange orangey colour again. I'm sure it's a sign that there could be more snow. "Looks like it could snow – hope we don't get snowed in somewhere. These roads might be bad if it does."

"That's my plan..."

"What?" I'm taken aback.

"Joke – it's just around the next bend. Nearly there."

"Phew – you had me worried for a minute then – I didn't bring my pyjamas."

Jett laughs. "You wouldn't need pyjamas with me – skin to skin is much warmer." He turns his head briefly and winks. "Sorry, I'm joking again. I like to see your face when I say something like that."

I can imagine he does because I'm sure I must look like a prudish Victorian who has just been insulted. It's not the shock value of his jokes that stupefies me but the wanton desire I ashamedly feel.

"Here we are," he says, pulling into a large gravel car park. "It's a Michelin Star restaurant."

"Wow – looks fab." I peer up at the old building in awe.

"Sixteenth century, I believe. They do amazing food here. Hope you're hungry."

I smile and nod my head. "Yes, I am. Thanks for bringing me here – I love historical places like this."

"You're welcome and it's all on me, OK?"

Again, I nod. "Guess I'll have to owe you one then."

"You're on," says Jett as he climbs out of the car.

I'm relieved that I wore flatter boots as I try to navigate the gravel car park and walk around the side of Jett's car. He's waiting for me on the other side and as I near him, he offers me his arm to link up to. I willingly take it and we walk into the woody smelling, quaint little restaurant together.

I don't think I've ever had Michelin Star food before – it's amazing. Jett and I have ploughed our way through three courses and had such a giggle along the way. We've been reminiscing about the past, about the swing and about the times when we played with my dolls and gave them all a tea party. Of course, Jett hated playing those games but he had nothing else to do, so he tended to follow my lead. After all, I was the eldest and I was in charge. How things have turned around. I now feel like he's the one in charge and I'm the one who looks up to *him*. Admiringly, I have got to add.

"Thank you – that was totally amazing," I say, placing the spoon on the side of the plate. I've just eaten the most exquisite warm chocolate mousse with cookie dough.

"You're welcome. Thought you'd like it." He wipes his mouth with a serviette and smiles at me. "So, what's next?"

I give him a quizzical look. "Next?"

"Do you want to go anywhere else? A drive in the countryside? Shopping? I know you ladies like to shop. Coffee somewhere?" He pauses. "I wondered if you wanted to do something else, you know, instead of us going our separate ways."

"Oh, I see." I laugh nervously.

I'd like to go to bed with you actually.

"Err... I'm really not fussed, what would you like to do?" I ask.

Jett shrugs his shoulders. "Back to yours for a coffee? I'd love to see your flat. I share a place with two other guys – you would not want to go there."

"Yes, sure, why not. It's a bit untidy but you're more than welcome to come to mine. Clair's away at the moment so it's fine."

"Would it not be fine if Clair was at home? I'm only coming in for a coffee."

"Err... yes, of course it would, I..." I stumble, "I mean, we'll have the place to ourselves. You can put your feet up and watch a bit of TV as well as coffee – whatever you want to do."

Jett laughs. "You're so funny. I'm only coming round for coffee and a quick look at your flat. I'm not planning on whisking you off to your bedroom or moving in."

"I know." God, why do I sound so stupid sometimes.

"Let's have a quick coffee here and then we'll go. I'm looking forward to seeing the place where my childhood, best friend lives."

"It's a mess, I've pre-warned you."

*** 15 ***

"Nice little place," says Jett as we enter the flat.

"It's not bad. It's big enough for me and Clair." I usher him towards the coat hooks by the door and he removes his jacket and hangs it up.

"Coffee then?"

"Yes – please."

He follows me through to the kitchen and props himself against a worktop while I make the coffee. There's a highly-charged atmosphere emanating from both of us, I'm sure of it.

"Cool, you've got your own little garden as well," He steps towards the back door and peers through the window. "What..." He breaks off and looks closer. "Did you know you've got a turkey on the lawn?"

"A what?" I reply, feigning surprise. "A turkey?"

Why have I just said that? Why have I made out that I don't know why a turkey is laying in my garden?

"A real one?" I quiz.

"No," says Jett, incredulously. "A cooked one."

I laugh uncomfortably although it is quite funny the way he said, 'a cooked one'. "Oh, that one." I walk over to the door and peer over his shoulder. "Oh... that turkey."

He turns and gives me a puzzled frown. "Why's it in your garden? You'll get rats coming in."

"I err..."

God, how stupid is this going to sound. "Well... err... when I split up with Kallum, I was... err... cooking the turkey at the time."

"OK," says Jett, patiently. He's eyeing me with a slight smirk on his face.

"Well, I got annoyed about everything and quite drunk after he'd gone and I..."

"Yes..."

"Well, I thought to myself, stuff the turkey, and then I kicked it out of the back door."

Jett's expression turns from a smirk, to a puzzled frown and then into incredulous laughter. "I'm sorry but... that's so funny," he splutters. "Just one thing though, Susie..."

Now I'm frowning in puzzlement. Why's it so funny? "What?" I reply as I watch him chuckle so much that he has got to hold his stomach.

"Was it already stuffed before you stuffed it?" He lets out a roar of laughter and shakes his head from side to side as he peers at me through watery eyes.

"Eventually... yes." I'm beginning to find it all quite hilarious now.

"Eventually? What – please don't tell me you stuffed it once it was in the garden?" He bends over as his fit of laughter continues.

"No – not when it was out there," I say, pointing to the garden. "When I was cooking it, I had to take it back out of the oven to remove the stuffing because I'd forgotten to take the giblets out. Then I re-stuffed it."

Jett is leaning over the worktop, practically in tears. "You stuffed it with the giblets in..."

"Yes." I giggle and turn back to finish making the coffee.

"So, you stuffed it twice – no, three times?"

I've really picked up on his sense of humour now and he is managing to make the whole thing sound absolutely crazy. "Yes – I suppose I did do it three times."

"Oh dear – come here," he says, moving across the room and pulling me round by the shoulder. "You are so funny, you make me laugh..." He wraps his arms round me and hugs me tightly, while he continues to chuckle.

I can smell his fragrant woody cologne and I want to stay here, in his arms, until I can't stand up anymore.

He stops laughing and pulls away from our embrace, just enough to look down at my face. He peers deeply into my eyes. We're both sober – surely, it's not going to happen again...

Mind-blowing. It did happen and I'm sorry if 'mind-blowing' is a pathetic cliché but it was.

OK, let's try this again. He kissed me. It was a lingering, slow to end, sensual kiss. Each time he tried to pull away and stop, he was drawn back like a magnet, to my lips. And every time, I welcomed him back. Oh my goodness, it was too good.

Where do we go from here? There is an overriding, powerful attraction between us, no matter how wrong it might feel afterwards.

Eventually, he steps back and stands there staring at me, speechless. It's all so intense that I have got to turn around and try to get to grips with finishing off the coffee.

"I'm sorry Susie." His voice is low and husky now.

"We're back to where we were last night. You don't have to be sorry," I say, boiling the kettle again without turning around. I daren't look at him – it could happen again and I fear where it could end up. I felt the urge and I'm sure he did too.

I finish making the coffee and turn to look at him. He's gone awfully quiet as he continues to prop himself against the worktop on the other side of the kitchen. It's almost like he's too scared to come near me again. "Sugar?" I say, a little croakily, before I clear my throat.

"Two please."

I add the sugar and pick the two mugs up. "Do you want to come through?" I beckon to him to follow me through to the living room.

"Nice," he says as he enters the room. "No turkeys laying around in here then?"

"Not that I know of." I giggle and place the two mugs on the coffee table. "Just my turkey infested boots." I point to my once beautiful glass heels.

Jett crosses the room and picks them up. "These are pretty classy."

"Were..." I say.

He gives my boots a closer inspection. "You 'stuffed the turkey', as you say, and kicked it while wearing these?"

I nod, regretfully. "Yes – I know – stupid."

"Have you got any cornflour and talc?"

I peer at him and frown. "I don't know – why?"

"It could take a while but I might be able to get this cleaned up for you." He takes my one soiled boot and sits down in the armchair opposite me. "It's been left for a couple of days so you'll need the cornflour and talc to purge out the stain."

I stare at him incredulously. "How do you know that?"

He shrugs his shoulders and turns the boot around in his hand, eyeing the glass heel and then the great big greasy stain on the toe. "Don't know really. I think my mum must have used it at some point and I just remembered."

I'm stunned. He's not only a total pleasure to feast my eyes upon, charming, kind, generous, sexy and funny but he's also domesticated too. I'm sorry, but forget the 'brother' bit, he's too much of a catch for me to worry about the guilty feelings I keep getting.

"I think I might have both – I'll go and look." Before I leave the room, I turn to face him. "Thanks Jett – you're amazing."

He smiles back at me and then comes that damned wink. I wish he'd stop doing that. It's so dangerous.

My boot is standing on a plastic carrier bag, smothered in a mixture of talc and cornflour around the toe area. Jett says it will have to stay on overnight, in the hope that it will soak up the grease. I really hope it works as I don't want to lose my beautiful boots. I blame Kallum entirely for this.

"Have you got a suede brush?" Jett asks.

"Yes," I say, proudly, "Funnily enough, I got one with the boots – now where did I put it?" I think for a moment and then remember. "Ah, I'm sure it's in the bedroom. I'll be back in a minute."

Returning to the living where Jett is relaxing back in the armchair and flicking through the TV channels, I hold up the suede brush and grin. "Good job I bought it when I got the boots – I wasn't going to at first but the sales woman kept going on about how expensive the boots were and how I should look after them properly. I'm so relieved I listened to her now."

"Well, you just never know when you're going to kick a turkey and get them covered in grease." Jett shakes his head despairingly. "Do you want me to put the turkey in the bin for you?"

"No, I'll do it tomorrow, no worries." Gosh, I feel stupid – who kicks a turkey out of their back door? Oh wait – I do. "So, what do I do with the boot tomorrow?" I ask.

"You'll need to brush off most of the powder with your suede brush and if it looks OK, clean off the rest with a damp cloth."

"It's that simple?"

"I'm not saying it's going to work, and you might even have to do it twice, but it could work."

"Thank you so much Jett, I don't know what I would have done without you. I'd probably have stuck them in the back of my wardrobe and never worn them again."

"Well I'm guessing they were *more* than expensive, so it's worth giving it a try."

He smiles at me so sweetly that I want to give him a big hug but something holds me back. I think it's the fear of what could happen again.

Oh well, I simply cannot resist his smile and I am hugely grateful for his help – I'm going in...

"Thank you so much," I say as I approach him with open arms. I lean over him and wrap my arms round his shoulders. "I really do appreciate it." I kiss the side of his head and he pulls me down on to his lap. I'm now straddling him on the chair.

"If you're going to cuddle me, then cuddle me." He laughs and wraps his arms round my waist.

It's happening again. We're peering into each other's eyes with a desperate longing...

"What am I going to do about you," he whispers.

Our heads are moving closer.

"I can't help being drawn to you..." he adds.

Our lips meet again. Hot and urgent, our mouths open and join into one...

It's different this time. It's prolonged and it's creating a heated sexual desire. "You can't help it?" I reply in a breath.

"No," he whispers back. "I can't help it." He runs his fingers down my back, causing me to shudder.

I am stunned by his strength as he rises from the chair, still kissing me and holding me up at the same time. I wrap my legs round his waist – I've no idea where we're going but I'm past caring. It will be the sofa or the bedroom, if he can find his way. It really doesn't matter which now...

We're lying on the floor between the coffee table and the sofa, it's very cosy as there's barely enough room for two. Jett has just rolled off me and is laying on his back breathing heavily. He turns his head to look at me, beads of sweat dotting his forehead.

"How did that happen?" he says in a low, husky voice. He rests one arm on the top of his forehead and continues to look at me with searching eyes. His glistening naked chest rises and falls as his heavy breath begins to slow.

I'm lying next to him semi-naked, and suddenly I feel vulnerable and exposed. "I have no idea how it happened," I whisper back. "Could you pass my clothes over?"

He reaches over to get them and I immediately put my underwear on. He watches my every move.

"You're so beautiful," he says. "I'm sorry... are you feeling OK?" He pulls himself up from the floor, puts his boxer shorts and jeans on and sits in the armchair.

"I don't know," I say, truthfully. "How are you feeling?"

"Tired – and thirsty." He smiles warmly.

That's a typical response from a man I suppose. Their first thoughts are always physical needs and then the emotional stuff comes later.

"I'll make a coffee," I say, gathering up the rest of my clothes.

"I'll help you." He pulls himself up, moves across the room, towards me, and puts his arms round me. "I hope you're OK..." He kisses me tenderly on the lips.

"Yes, I think I am. Hope you are too."

He nods his head.

"I'll get tidied up and meet you in the kitchen."

We just had some hot, passionate sex – trust me, it was amazing. He was amazing. He wrapped his legs round mine while we were joined together and his movements were incredibly fast at times and then so excitingly slow and teasing at others. He pinned me down with his legs at some points and then suddenly let me go, so that I didn't have a clue what was coming next. I've never had sex like it. At one point, I even wondered if he was some sort of secret porn-star, he was that good. Yet, there is such an awkward atmosphere between us now. I'm sure that he is feeling as guilty as I am. Why should we though?

As I enter the kitchen I'm amazed to see Jett outside, in the garden, wearing just his jeans. It's freezing out there. He picks up the turkey gingerly and carries it over to the dustbin. Then he stops in his tracks and peers down at the lidded bin. He places the bird on the ground again and lifts the bin lid. Then he picks up the turkey and lowers it into the bin.

Gone. The end of my Christmas. The end of Kallum. Jett has just done something that was so significant and a symbol of my miserable Christmas, until today. A rush of emotions fills me and tears prick at my eyes.

As he enters the kitchen, he looks at me surprised. "Are you OK?"

That's enough for me to burst into real tears.

Hurriedly, he washes his hands off and dries them. "What's the matter?" he says as he pulls me into a hug.

"Oh, nothing. I'm being silly."

"Have I...?"

"No, it's not you – it's just the turk..."

"The turkey?"

I nod my head, still buried in his arms.

"Did you still want it?"

I look up at him with wet eyes and he's peering back at me incredulously. "No." I laugh. "It's just..."

"What?"

"I'm just being silly and sentimental."

"Over a turkey?" He searches my eyes in puzzlement.

"No." I begin to laugh more. I'm not sure if I want to continue laughing or cry some more. "Sorry – it was just what it symbolised."

"Christmas dinner?" Jett is smiling and trying to make me laugh more. "Should I have removed the stuffing first?"

"No." I laugh heartily. "I'm over it now. It just reminded me of what's happened over Christmas."

The smile falls from Jett's face. "Oh, I'm sorry – I can see now. I'm so sorry Susie." He releases me from his arms and steps back, still peering into my eyes deeply. "Do you want me to go?"

"No, I don't. It's only been two days but I am so over, Kallum. I want you to stay."

"Are you sure I'm not making things worse?"

I nod my head and smile. "I'm sure, in fact you've made things better. My Christmas has turned out far nicer than I thought it would."

*** 16 ***

I'm lying in bed, wide awake, reliving last night. He stayed. He's lying next to me, still sleeping. Jett is still here.

After the turkey episode and my little tearful moment, we had another coffee and then later, a sandwich. I'm sure there must have been something in the ham as, no sooner had we eaten our sandwiches than we were removing each other's clothes again. That time, however, we made it to the bedroom in a frenzied, groping surge of entwined bodies. I led him there and I'm so glad I did as I fear the living room, and all its furniture, would not have stood up to the vigorous, multi-positioned intimacy which took place. Again, it was incredible. He's incredible. He actually makes Kallum look lame and there was me, thinking that sex with Kallum was great. I obviously haven't ever lived.

I slip out of bed, trying not to wake Jett, and waddle through to the kitchen. I say waddle because I'm almost at a point of not being able to walk. I think I've used muscles I didn't even know I had. Don't get me wrong, Jett is not a brutal lover, far from it, but I have now done things in a way that I had never done before. Amazing. No, more than amazing – indescribable.

Jett's prodigious appetite for great sex and attention to detail is second to none and I realise now that Kallum was nothing more than a 'wham-bam-thank-you-ma'am' kind of guy who was only interested in meeting his own needs. Gosh, I'm 28 years old and I feel pretty naïve in comparison to Jett. How can he be such an expert at such a tender age? He's younger than me – OK, only by two years but, even so, how does he know so much?

I flick the kettle on and stare out of the back door. There's a stained patch on the grass, where the turkey was. I smile to myself as I think about the conversation we had. Jett makes me laugh a lot and he nearly makes me cry when the overwhelming emotions of love-making come to a crescendo. I've fallen for him so quickly that just for a fleeting moment, I wonder if it's wise. I'm sure we must both be on the rebound. What else can it be?

"Morning my little sex-kitten," says Jett, as he staggers into the kitchen looking cute with his hair stuck up on end. "Are you OK?" He approaches me, puts his arms round my waist and rests his chin over the back of my shoulder. "Are you missing the turkey?"

I turn to face him, giggling my head off. "No, I'm not missing it. I'm glad the damn thing has gone."

"Good," he says and peers around at the kettle. "Any chance I could have one?"

"Yes, of course."

"I've got to go into work today." He pulls the corners of his mouth down. "Wish I didn't have to – we could have gone out for the day or something."

"Aah, that's a shame. You know what – I haven't got a clue what day of the week it is – I've lost all track of time."

"Wednesday."

I nod my head. "Ah, OK. That means Clair isn't back for another six days yet."

"Are you here on your own over the New Year?" He takes over the making of the coffee.

"No – I am going to the most prestigious New Year's Eve party you could ever imagine. And... wait for it... I might even stay over, at the swanky little hotel next door."

"Really?" He looks at me a little disappointed. "Where are you going?"

"To your nan's."

Momentarily it doesn't register and then he laughs. "You're going to my nan's house for New Year's Eve?"

"I turned down all the other offers," I say with a smirk on my face.

Jett shakes his head as a grin appears on his face.

"Well, to be honest, I didn't have any other offers at the time. Kallum had told me he was going on a lad's weekend to London so I knew I wouldn't be spending it with him. So, when I asked Mum what they were doing, she said I could go round to your nan's with them."

"OK, cool."

"So, what are you doing?" I'm wondering if I really want to hear his answer. I'm a little bit star-struck by him and would love to spend more time with him – particularly a time like New Year's Eve.

"Funnily enough, I'm going somewhere prestigious too. Somewhere renowned for its respected event listings and impeccable service..."

"Oh really?" My heart plummets.

"Yes, I'm going to my nan's too."

Tiny tears prick at my eyes but I instantly blink them away. "Really?"

"Well, I'm pretty much in the same boat as you. I had plans, before *we*, me and Crystal, split up."

"Ah, OK." I try to look sympathetic but inside I'm screeching, yay! Is that selfish of me? "Well, it could be a good night. I think all the residents of the grove are going."

Jett nods his head. "I'll ask Nan if I can go, today."

"Cool. That makes me feel a bit better. At least I won't be the only one under the age of 50."

He laughs before handing me a steaming hot mug of coffee. "OK, so the main age bracket for this rave-up will be, 50 to 80, I'm guessing, if all the neighbours are going."

"Yes." I giggle. "Should be a good night."

Jett laughs again and looks at me with his clear blue eyes. "We'll make it a good night." He winks an eye in that sultry way that he always does and I get a rush of excitement that fizzes inside me. "Right," he says, pulling himself up from his slouched position against the worktop, "I'll finish this coffee and then I should have just enough time to sort your boot out, before I go."

***

He's gone. He's left me with a perfectly clean boot though. I'm so chuffed. I'm sitting on the sofa, mindlessly flicking through the channels. I'm not even dressed yet and it's approaching twelve o'clock. Oh well, maybe I should have a pyjama day, I've nothing better to do.

Suddenly my mobile rings and makes me jump. I peer at the screen to see that it's Kallum. Kallum – who's he? I've *so* moved on from him. "Hello?" I say in the most nonchalant tone possible.

"Suse, it's me, Kallum."

"Oh right..."

"Yeah, I was... Can I come..."

"To see me?" I chime in.

There's a slight pause before he says, "Yes."

"No, you can't."

Silence.

"Ok? Did you hear me?" I ask, just to make sure he's still there.

"Yes, I heard you. Can we meet somewhere then?"

"No," I repeat. "No, we can't meet somewhere."

"Why?"

"Because it's finished Kallum. I'm..." I break off, thoughtfully. I need to be careful here. I do not want him to know anything about Jett. "I'm moving on and so should you."

"I'm not with Tania, if that's what you're thinking."

"I'm not thinking anything, Kallum. What's going to happen with the baby then?"

Silence.

"Well?" I say, impatiently.

"I don't know," he replies, eventually.

"Well you ought to know. That's a little human being's life you're both playing with."

"Do you have to say it like that?" Kallum's tone of voice has changed.

"Hmm... sounds more real doesn't it. You need to be responsible, Kallum. You need to face up to your responsibilities and commit."

Whoa - I'm starting to sound like my mother here.

"You sound like your mum," he says.

"Excuse me?" I say.

"Doesn't matter. Are you sure I can't come round or meet you somewhere?"

"I'm sure," I say, adamantly. "I don't want to see you ever again. You're the one who did this, Kallum – not me. Go back to Tania and learn how to be a responsible da..."

I hear a click and realise he's put the phone down on me. How rude. It's a real shame that I have wasted the last two years with him. It's strange but when I was speaking to him, I felt no sadness or longing. It's over, not only physically but in my heart and head too.

***

Two days have passed and I haven't seen Jett. I can't get him out of my head. He has called me on both evenings, just to catch up and tell me about his day's work but it has not been the same as getting my paws on him. However, it's New Year's Eve today, so I will get to see him tonight, thankfully. The only problem is that we'll be in the company of my parents and his grandparents and they don't know anything. Jett thinks it's not a problem to let them know but I, on the other hand, don't feel ready to reveal all. I'm sure that both my parents and Doreen and Malcolm would be thrilled that we were together but it just doesn't seem right to me. Not yet anyway.

I went out shopping yesterday, which was more to do with relieving the boredom, rather than actually needing anything, but I'm so glad I did. I know we're only going to a house-party, and an antique one at that, but I need to look good, especially as Jett said we should nip into the local pub before we turn up at the house. I said that I supposed it wouldn't look suspicious if we turned up together – he's like my brother, right?

So, anyway, while I was out, I spotted this dress. It's not my normal kind of style but I loved the look of it and decided that it couldn't hurt to try it on. Oh my goodness, it just goes to show, doesn't it? I'm very set in my ways when it comes to style. I'm quite plain and simple and never follow the fashion trends. Yet, when I peered into the changing room mirror, I was quite taken aback. I'm not sure what my parents will say when they see it – or Jett for that matter, but for some strange reason, it looks amazing on me, even if I do say so myself. Coupled with my *clean* glass-heeled boots, the outfit will be pretty stunning, extremely provocative and will probably have Jett's eyes popping out on stalks. Mission accomplished.

I do a quick re-run by putting the dress on again. It's a sexy little mini dress, which has a fitted bodice. Black lace covers the dress in an overlay and it has a nude under dress. The hemline is made from black ruffled lace and it has two cross straps at the back, as it is backless right down to where my bottom starts. At the front, it's more of a waistline than a neckline, it's that low. I actually thought it was nightwear at first, as it is so daringly sexy but it was definitely hanging among the glitzy, party wear and had a label saying, *Nightlife-Party*.

I feel quite nervous now that I'm wearing it again. It hugs my figure so tightly and accentuates every curve perfectly. I'm now wondering if it's appropriate for an OAP house party. Maybe it's not, but my excuse will be that we've been out beforehand. I just hope that Jett has managed to get tickets for the George Inn's event night, like he said he would.

I apply a second coat and hold the mirror further away. Wow, this new mascara is great. Four times longer, thicker lashes, it says. It works. I look like a *Barbie* doll. I seriously need to go out to a nightclub or some sort of big event with Jett tonight. Not down to the local pub and then on to a hoary house party. That's being very unkind and ungrateful though. The party alone, would have been a welcoming event if it hadn't been for me meeting Jett again and suddenly becoming a wanton, well-dressed wench. I should be thankful for the kind offer though and anyway, it means I get to spend some much-loved time with my parents, who I adore to the moon and back, millions of times over. I'll have the best of both worlds with Jett by my side too.

I'm barely wearing underwear, as this dress does not allow for much of that. I've got a tiny thong on, and that's about it. I think about Jett and imagine us in the throes of a passionate session. At least it won't take much to get *me* naked.

I've got my beautiful, glass-heeled boots on and I also managed to find a cute little black handbag in the bottom of my wardrobe. I stare at the long mirror opposite me and hold my phone out, ready to take a photograph. I have got to send one to Clair – she'll love this new look of mine.

She texted me the other day asking where the picture of Jett was and I had to tell her I didn't have one yet (I suppose I could have sent her a naked one – not). Anyway, I said I would get one tonight, as I was meeting up with him again at the house party. OK, so that's a little lie but little white lies are acceptable sometimes when the happiness of others depend on them. I haven't yet, worked out what I'm going to say to her when she comes home on Tuesday. That can wait though, I have far more pressing issues to deal with at the moment, like, what is Jett going to think of my outfit, never mind Clair?

Wow!!! You look stunning Suse – I LOVE IT!!! Bet Jett will love it too – you STILL HAVEN'T sent me a picture of him yet!!!!!!! Mwahahaha... there could be a new romance on the horizon with you two. Have a great night, love ya xxx

I'm quite surprised that she sounds like she's encouraging *me* to have a relationship with Jett now. I thought she wanted him for herself.

Thanks Clair and I doubt it – romance, I mean. I hope you have a fun time with everyone there too. See you on Tuesday xx

Can't wait to see you, I've really missed you and our cosy little flat xxx

I should think so, lol. Will send piccie pronto! xx

I'm pacing the carpet, backwards and forwards, peering out of the window and scanning myself in the mirror as I pass by. I'm hot with nerves. Jett has arranged to pick me up in a taxi. He also got tickets for tonight's New Year's Eve event at the George Inn. So, it's all go.

Mum knows we're going to Doreen and Malcolm's party, together, later. I told her we'd be there about eleven so that we can see the new year in with them. She was quite surprised to hear that I was going out with Jett, but also, she was happy to hear that we were looking after each other, just like a real brother and sister would. Oh dear.

It's here. I can see Jett sitting in the back of the taxi, peering through the window. I wave a hand against the glass, take a deep breath and head towards the door. Here goes...

Jett jumps out of the back of the taxi as I approach, and runs around to open the door for me. His gorgeous eyes scan the length of me and his jaw drops.

"Wow – you look amazing," he says. He kisses me briefly on the lips and watches as I climb into the back seat.

The taxi driver even turns his head around and smiles at me. I'm beginning to feel a bit like a movie star.

As Jett clambers in, on the other side, he peers at me incredulously. "I mean it – you look totally stunning."

"Thanks," I say, coyly and tug at the hem of my dress, pulling it down a little. "You look pretty awesome too."

He's wearing a pair of black trousers and a pink and cream, striped shirt underneath his black jacket. His cropped, dark hair is spiked up on top, giving him a boyish look. He's remarkably handsome and just as he can't stop looking at me, I can't take my eyes off him either. As the taxi pulls away, he takes my hand in his and smiles. Then comes that incredible, enticing wink.

We're in the George Inn and it's heaving. There's a live band on tonight, hence the requirement of tickets. We make our way through the crowds of people, towards the bar. As we're waiting to be served, Jett places an arm round my waist. "How can I be falling in love with you so soon?" he says in my ear.

It takes my breath away. He's falling in love with me? So soon? OK, If I'm honest, I am falling for him too. How could I not? He's perfect, in every sense of the word. "Let me know if you find the answer... because I am too."

"I've missed you," he says, pulling me even closer.

I look deep into his eyes. "I've missed you too." Oh God, why don't we just go back to my place and get it over with. I want him so much.

"I want you."

There, you see, it's not just a one-way thing. "I know," I whisper into his ear. "I want you too."

God, this is starting to sound like an epic romance film but it's just like that – honestly. It's ridiculous after just a few days, I know, but that's just how it is.

Finally, we get served and collect our drinks. We ordered two rounds of doubles as the bar is so busy that we'd spend most of the evening waiting to be served if we had singles. We inch our way out of the crowded bar area and walk towards the back of the room where it seems to be a little less congested. In the far corner, I spot a vacant table.

"Shall we sit over there for a while? At least until I've finished one of these." I hold up one of the glasses and grin.

"Sure, come on, I've got my hands full here."

We place the glasses on the small round table and peer around the pub, before sitting down.

"I can't believe how busy it is in here," I say, nervously taking a sip from my drink.

"A stark contrast to Boxing day."

"Hmm," I mumble, sipping the drink again.

"You look incredible in that dress," he says, eyeing me adoringly. "I'm proud to be here with you."

"Ah, that's nice, thank you."

"I mean it – I've never seen anyone look as beautiful as you do."

I blush and smile. "Oh, that reminds me..." I thrust my hand into my handbag and pull out my phone, "Clair has been pestering me about a photo. Would you mind if we did a selfie, then I could send it to her?"

"Of course I don't mind." Jett shuffles his chair next to mine and we huddle together.

We pose and wait for the timer to count down. Click. I check the picture but Jett has his eyes closed. I giggle.

"Can we try again, you look like you're asleep?" Click. Again, I check the picture. "That's better." I peer long and hard at the photo of us both smiling and looking happy together. Our heads are touching and Jett has his arm round the back of my chair. I love it and I think Clair will too. "Right, I'm just going to send it to her and then she'll stop pestering me."

"Does she know about us?" He stumbles, "I mean... well, you know."

"No, I haven't told her."

He nods his head. "Fair enough – it's early days, I suppose. I meant what I said earlier though..."

I look at him with a quizzical stare.

"How I feel about you."

"Oh, that. Yes, I know. I'm the same – it's mad, isn't it?"

"Do you think we should tell them at the party?"

"Who – my mum and dad and your grandparents?"

He nods his head before taking a long sip from his drink. "Why not?"

"I think it's a bit soon. My mum would be so shocked – what with Kallum only just off the scene."

Jett nods again. "Yes, you're right. I'll have to rein it in while we're there then."

"Rein what in?" I look at him and laugh.

"How I'm falling in love with you. It could show, and my nan is clever when it comes to sussing things out. It's so strong a feeling that I'm sure I must have a flashing neon sign above my head constantly."

I giggle, as Jett places a hand on the top of his head and open and closes it in quick succession, indicating a flashing light.

"And what does the sign say?"

"It says... I love Susie Satchel, of course." He leans over and kisses my lips tenderly. "I know it's crazy and it's all happened so soon but I really do love you," he breathes on to my lips.

Oh gosh, I think I really do love him too. Should I say it? I shake my head and peer at him desperately. "I... I shouldn't because it's been such a short time but..."

"You love me too?"

I nod. "Yes, I do."

Does it sound insane? I can't help it – I really do.

*** 17 ***

It's been an amazing night so far. The live band are pretty good and very interactive with the crowd. They've been taking requests, from the mass of onlookers, for any music between the 60s and 70s. Surprisingly, they've met each request with a fantastic rendition of that particular song. Their talents, I feel, are a little wasted in this small pub, they should be playing a gig somewhere bigger, where they could get noticed more.

Jett has had me laughing until my tummy hurt on many occasions. He's so adorable. I *do* love him. How could I not? Whether it's because we've simply fallen in love at first sight, as they say, or it's something deeper because we grew up together, I really don't know. I just know it feels great, it feels different to what I've known before and it feels right.

He's kissed me so many times tonight. They seem to be coming thick and fast now. Just discreet little pecks here and there or his lips brushing on mine briefly, but they are enough to excite me and increase my desire for him. I want him so badly and I know he wants me too.

We've danced together and I have got to say that he's an amazing little mover, although I was not surprised, to be honest. We've smooched to a couple of the slower songs too. He had his hands placed around my back at the lowest point where the backless part of my dress ends. As we danced together, his fingers lightly caressed the skin of my lower back, causing me to shudder and tingle. This was when his lips kept brushing mine. It has been so erotic to smooch with him on the makeshift dancefloor and now and again, his hands moved to the tops of my hips and he pulled me closer to him. He pushed at my hips to move them from side to side as his moved in unison. It was like we were making love with our clothes on. Wow.

"We'll have to go soon," says Jett, peering down at his watch. "Better see the new year in with our families."

"Yes – definitely." I pick up my third double of the night and drain the glass. "I'm ready when you are."

Jett does the same with his drink. "I'll go out and see if we can grab one of the taxis outside. Wait here a minute."

I nod and smile at him before he disappears through the crowds. Slowly, I follow behind him, towards the main doors, as I feel the vibration of my mobile phone. A moment later I see Jett's face peering through the doors. He spots me and beckons to me.

"Got one," he says and holds the door open for me as I peer at my phone.

OMG! He's gorgeous, Suse! You'd make an amazing couple – you look so great together. Work on it girl. Anyway, might not get chance later so, HAPPY NEW YEAR! Here's to a new year and a new start for BOTH of us! Explain my new start later. Love ya, hugs and kisses, from Clair xxxx p.s. I really mean it – the photo is gorgeous – you look like you were made for each other xxx

I follow Jett, with a big smile on my face, to the second taxi along the street and he opens the back door for me. He's such a perfect gentleman. Perhaps Clair is right and the new year will be a new start for me – I'm just a little curious about what her 'new start' is.

Ushering me into the car, Jett bends over and kisses me tenderly before closing the door. He smiles through the window and then walks around the back of the taxi and opens the other side...

I hear a loud, penetrating screech of rubber tyres on tarmac. I grimace. Peering up, I see Jett through the opened door. His head is turned around, towards the terribly loud, screeching sound...

I blink, as if in slow-motion. I turn my head to the back window to see what Jett is looking at. An indescribable cracking, smashing sound tears through my ears. I'm instantly catapulted forward and sideways, hitting my head on the frame surrounding the side window.

I blink.

I wince.

The stench of burning rubber sears my nose.

Slumping back in the seat, I stare ahead.

I'm in a daze...

Then I turn to look...

He's gone. The door's gone. My head begins to thump. The central framework of the taxi is buckled and twisted.

He has gone. The door has gone, I note again.

I hear screeching tyres – further away this time. The violent revving of an engine. A woman's fearful scream.

The taxi driver turns around to peer at me in dismay. I blink the irritation from my eyes. Warm liquid is seeping into my eyes. I blink it away again.

Time has slowed – everything is happening like a slow-motion replay.

A man's voice, out on the street, shouts words I cannot comprehend. All I know is...

He's gone. Jett's not there on the other side of the car. I can't see where he's gone.

I try to open my door. It's stiff, like it is wedged in. Giving it an almighty push, I manage to clamber out of the car. People are in front of me. They're flowing out from the pub. Why are they leaving the pub so soon? It'll be midnight soon.

I peer over the top of the taxi. Where is Jett?

Several people, including the taxi driver, are rushing towards something lying in the road, some 50 metres away. I blink and wipe the annoying irritation away from my eyes. It's wet, it's warm.

Someone puts an arm round my shoulders, making me jump.

It's Jett...

It's not Jett. A woman is trying to drag me back towards the pub. I shrug her off, blinking away the blurriness in my eyes. I can feel my heart beating in my head. It's so painful. I try to focus...

Through the forest of legs, gathered in the road ahead, I can see metal. It's the taxi's door...

Another heap, close by.

There are so many people in the road now. Several are crouched down around the heap...

"Please, come into the pub – an ambulance is on its way." The same woman tries to pull me back by my arm.

Again, I shrug her off and frown at her. It hurts to frown. I walk away with a wobbly stride. Stepping down from the pavement, I move towards the group of people, gathered in the middle of the road. Someone is lying on the ground. Oh God – has someone been run over?

The screeching car. It makes sense now.

Where's Jett? Is he helping them?

As I weave and push my way through the group of people, I hear a siren in the distance. It's getting ever closer.

I look down...

On the road, lies a body. It's a man. He's wearing the same clothes as...

Why is he there? What's he doing? He's not moving.

Slowly, I push my way through and lower myself to the ground.

A man, kneeling beside me, turns Jett's head forward.

Now Jett is peering up to the starry sky. What is he doing? I blink as a tear falls. He does not blink. I crouch down, right beside him, gulping back the sickness rising in my throat. He still doesn't blink. He's looking upwards but he won't blink.

I lean right over him to get in his eye line. He's *my* Jett. His beautiful eyes are shining but he's looking straight through me. Why can't he see me? I stroke his wet cheek. He's bleeding. I wipe the blood from my hand, on to my dress. Turning my head, I look up at the people above me and the two men to the side of me. They are shaking their heads...

No. No. Why are they shaking their heads? Who do they think they are? How dare they shake their heads at me...

Two paramedics push through the crowd.

I'm holding Jett's cold hand. He needs to blink – his eyes must be stinging. I stroke his wet hair. More blood. I must tell the paramedics they need to put a bandage on his head. I wipe my hand on my dress again.

The uniformed men talk to me. I don't know what they're saying. My head is buzzing. I feel strange and fuzzy.

All I know, is that the paramedics need to make Jett blink before his eyes get sore...

The buzzing sound is getting louder in my head...

"Jett," I whisper, as one of the paramedics holds two fingers on his neck. "Jett, please blink." I squeeze his limp hand. "Or just wink... please wink for me..."

I sway on my bended legs.

Buzzing...

Fuzzy...

I'm travelling in an ambulance, lying on a stretcher, facing up towards the roof of the vehicle. I turn my head to see if Jett is there. A woman is by my side – she's a paramedic. She's holding my wrist and smiling at me. I lift my head and my throat fills with vomit. Holding a large cardboard kidney dish underneath my chin, she places a hand on my back and turns me over to one side. I'm violently sick...

I'm so tired. My head hurts. I don't know what's going on. I need to see Jett...

I recall being pulled about for a while. I could hear several unknown voices speaking above me. I couldn't see them and I didn't understand what they were saying. I know there were machines all around me, making bleeping and whirring noises.

I was too tired to wake up properly. I still felt sick and my head was thumping, in rhythm, to every beat of my heart.

Then I slept...

I'm waking up properly now. I've been so tired. So terribly sick.

It's warm and cosy here. There is a lovely softness underneath me.

My hand is being held...

It's Jett's hand, so big and strong...

I open my eyes to the glare of bright lights above me. I wince and feel something stuck to my forehead.

I see, through squinted eyes, that my dad is holding my hand...

It's not Jett.

Dad is sitting next to me. I'm lying in a hospital bed.

"Susie," he says, rising to his feet. He looks tearful. "Can you hear me, love?"

I nod my head and a dull ache throbs momentarily. "What...?" I try to pull myself up.

"Stay there," says Dad, placing a hand on my shoulder. "Don't move."

"Where...?" I struggle to pull myself up again, even under Dad's protest. "Where's...?"

"Mum's with Doreen and Malcolm. She'll be here in a minute."

"No – I mean, Jett. Where's Jett? I need to see him."

Dad shakes his head at me and a deep frown darkens his face.

"Dad?"

"He's... he's gone, love. Jett's gone."

"Where?" My stomach is tightening into knots. I shrug dad's hand from my shoulder and pull myself up. "Dad?" He has a look on his face that I've never seen before. I don't like it. He avoids meeting my eye. "Dad?"

"He didn't make it love." Dad shakes his head slowly.

"What are you talking about, Dad?" I frown at him, even though it's painful to do so.

"He's gone, love."

I place a hand up to my head and feel a large bandage going halfway across my forehead.

"You banged your head and cut it quite badly. You've got stitches," says Dad. "They said you've got concussion and you'll have to stay in overnight, so they can keep an eye on you."

"But..." I'm so confused. "We were just on our way to come and see you..." I peer at my dad incredulously. "Where's Jett gone to? We were just on our way..."

Dad lowers his gaze. "I know," he says with a quiver in his voice. "He's... he's dead, Susie."

"No," I say and laugh out hysterically, which sends stabbing pains to my head. "No, he's not..." I feel the burning pain of sour vomit rise in my throat and try to gulp it back. "He's not, Dad – you've got it wrong. I saw him. He was looking at me." Tears prick at my eyes painfully.

Dad shakes his head slowly. "Your mum's here but she's with Doreen and Malcolm. She'll be in to see you again soon."

"Why are they here? No... he's not dead, Dad. What do you know, for God's sake? You weren't there, how can you know anything? Go away and leave me alone." I snarl at him.

He reaches for my hand and squeezes it. "He's gone, love. I'm so sorry."

"No... no, no..."

***

Nothing matters anymore. I'm in a nightmare. I must wake up from it soon. I'm aware of my drooping, expressionless face. I'm numb except for the ache in my chest – my heart isn't beating the same, it hurts with every pulsating jab. Nothing matters anymore.

***

I open my eyes and stare out of a large window. Flurries of light snow sweep across the glass. I'm in a small room, alone. I don't know where anyone is. I'm not sure what day it is. I'm not sure that any of this is real.

My dad – did I dream that I saw him? Why did he say those nasty things to me? Where is my mum? Where is Jett? Why has everyone left me alone here...?

***

"Good morning, Susie," A nurse has walked into the room. She's middle-aged and has her greying hair tied up in a neat bun. "You should be able to go home later today."

I stare at her, speechless.

"How are you feeling this morn..." She breaks off and peers at me pitifully. "In yourself, I mean."

I shrug my aching shoulders but no words leave my mouth.

"Do you feel sick?"

I shake my head very slightly, so as not to feel any more pain.

"That's good. You can have some breakfast and we'll see how you go from there. OK?" She picks up a clipboard from the end of the bed and scribbles something on to a sheet. "Now then, I'm just going to take your blood pressure and... pop this in your mouth." She pushes a thermometer into my mouth and grins at me.

Again, the nurse scribbles on the sheet and then removes the pressure pad from my aching arm. "That's all looking good," she says with a jovial tone. "Breakfast will be here shortly and I believe your parents will be back soon too." She collects up her things and walks towards the door. "Is there anything I can help you with?"

I try to say no, but nothing comes out, so I shake my head very slightly.

She pauses and points to a door in front of the bed. "Oh, while I think of it, the toilet is in there, if you need it. Do you need help with that?"

I shake my head again.

She gives me one last smile and then she's gone.

I turn my head back to the window and slowly close my eyes. Visions of Jett's unblinking eyes, the distorted taxi, lots of people milling around, blood, screeching tyres and ambulances, whirl around in my mind. My dad's voice keeps echoing in my ears. What was he talking about? Has he gone mad? What does he know? It's all making me feel sad, worried and sick. I've had some terrible dreams. Maybe another little sleep will help me feel better and then I can get out of here... and find Jett.

I ache everywhere – surely sleep will make it all go away.

"Susie?"

It's my mum's voice.

"Honey?"

I hear her again.

"You've got some breakfast here, honey."

I open my eyes to see both my mum and dad peering over me. They look pale and tired. A worried, fearful gaze taints their eyes. I pull myself up and rest back on the pillows. I still ache everywhere.

"How are you feeling, honey?" says Mum, leaning over to kiss my cheek.

Dad does the same, and as I gaze into his eyes, I realise it wasn't a dream. "Dad..." I break off. I don't want to hear him say the same thing again.

He nods his head deliberately, his mouth a downturned, sorrowful reminder of his words the last time he spoke to me. "You're coming home today, with us," he says, adamantly.

Mum nods her head in agreement. "Yes, honey, come and stay with us for a few days. Your dad can collect some things from your flat, for you."

I want to ask... but I can't. If they tell me it's true, then it will be real.

"Doreen and Malcolm would like to see you, if you feel up to it," says Mum in a hushed voice. "When you're ready, of course."

A tear falls from my eye and I brush it away. "Is it... true?" I've got to ask because the torment is killing me inside.

"Do you mean... Jett, honey?" Mum reaches for my hand and holds it tightly.

I stare at her face fixedly, without uttering a word.

"Yes, honey. He's..." She sniffs and wipes under her nose with a screwed-up tissue from her free hand. "He... he has gone, honey."

It's like I'm frozen. My expressionless face doesn't change, my shallow breath slows and my eyes stare hard as I watch my mum begin to cry. Dad puts an arm round her back and pats her gently. He's looking straight at me. Am I supposed to break down in tears? I can't – I'm frozen.

"He's dead?" I ask, as the ache in my chest returns. "Is he?" I peer questioningly at Dad.

He nods slowly.

"How can he be dead? How...?"

Mum sniffs again and blows her nose. "You need to eat some breakfast, honey." She stuffs the tissue into her coat pocket. "The doctor will be here soon and then you can come home." She runs her fingers underneath her eyes. "You'll have to eat something first, before they'll let you go – please, honey."

I peer into Mum's eyes. "He's dead?"

She nods and her bottom lip begins to tremble. "Yes honey, Jett died instantly."

"But... he was looking at me..."

Mum shakes her head, as another round of tears fall. "The paramedic said..." She retrieves her tissue from her pocket again.

"Said what?"

"He was gone, honey. When you were talking to him, he was already gone."

"No... he just needed to blin..."

"No, honey... he died straight away. He knew nothing about it, which is some comfort to Dor..." Mum breaks off and buries her face in her hands.

I've never had this feeling before. My breath is so shallow and it's like my lungs are pushing out every last ounce of breath until I'm giddy. Then I inhale the next small breath, just to exhale it all until my lungs are tightening and squeezing themselves completely empty. Is this what it's like to have that empty feeling? Is this how it feels to be heartbroken? It's horrible. I've turned inward and all I can feel is this empty breathless void and an ache in my heart. I can't even cry.

*** 18 ***

Doreen and Malcolm have the same gaunt look on their faces. They both hug me, tearfully, when they walk into Mum's living room. Doreen peers into my eyes, searching for something. She utters a few wavering words about how lucky I am and how relieved she is that I'm OK. She says that we were like a brother and sister and she's sure that I must feel like I've lost a family member too. I stare back at her, unable to think of anything to say.

I haven't said much since I've been back at Mum and Dad's house. It's supposed to be New Year's Day. It's the day when people make plans for the future, start afresh and hold high hopes for the year ahead. I still can't believe this is all real, apart from the wound on my forehead which, apparently, has four stitches in it. I'm aching all over, which, according to the doctor, was caused by the force of the impact, thrusting me against the inside of the car. I hadn't even put my seatbelt on, as we'd only just... as *I* had only just got in the taxi.

Mum and Dad have told me that the police are coming *back* to see me this evening. They'd tried once, last night at the hospital, or should I say, in the early hours of the morning, but I had concussion and they were not able to talk to me.

It's almost six o'clock and Mum is rustling up some sandwiches and sausage rolls for everyone. Doreen and Malcolm went straight through to the kitchen, once they'd hugged me and told me how lucky I was.

Lucky? Jett has died, just like that, he's gone forever. I wish I were dead too at this present moment. He was a young, fit man. Handsome, sexy, fun-loving, kind – how can he be dead? Why would someone like him die? He had everything to live for. He had a future, he was falling in love with me – he *was* in love with me and I was in love with him – how could he just die? I'm still in love with him – he's got to come back. We haven't finished yet. He's not like a brother, I haven't lost a family member – I've lost the love of my life. I've lost my soul mate. I've lost a part of me. It might have been less than a week, but it was real, it was intense, it was already built to last.

***

They asked a thousand questions and requoted me constantly, as the second officer wrote everything down. My breathing was shallow again. I felt sick. My heart raced as the officers spoke to me and told me things. My mum added to the story with further details from time to time – things she'd heard from the hospital. My heart slowed to a mournful beat when no words were spoken and the officers simply went through their notebook. I sat on the sofa with my hands clasped together tightly, in my lap. I didn't want to know. I didn't want to hear. Yet, I needed to know... I needed to have the truth clarified.

The car had hit him, straight on. It knocked him down the road ahead, along with the crumpled door. Then the speeding car went over Jett's chest before it sped away. The man driving the car was drunk. He was angry. He'd had a row with his girlfriend and taken her car. He killed Jett instantly, as he drove over him in his maniacal attempt to get away. He was caught by the police, less than a mile away. I didn't want to know all the details, just enough to clarify the truth, but they told me anyway.

It's now dawning on me. Jett couldn't blink because he was already gone. He couldn't see me leaning over him. He could never wink at me again. It hurts me to think that the last time I saw him alive, he had just tucked me safely into the taxi, kissed me tenderly on the lips and smiled at me, before moving around to the other side of the car. I felt his love at that moment. I knew he loved me.

Right, piss-head! It's now 8pm on New Year's Day and I haven't had a 'Happy New Year' from you. You're either recovering from the BIGGEST HANGOVER IN THE WORLD... or... you shagged that gorgeous hunk senseless last night, or this morning, or this afternoon or all the aforementioned, lol. Hope you had a great night – I certainly did – speak to you soon. Happy New Year, love Clair xxxx

I read the message again and tears fall down my cheeks. She doesn't know anything. Why would she? The last communication from me was the picture I sent to her of...

I'd forgotten about the picture. I want to look at it but...

I have got to look. There are two of them. The first one was when he had his eyes closed. I smile at it, as I recall the fun we had. That was only last night. I can't believe it was only last night. My smile quivers and without warning, I break down. I've never cried like this before, certainly not since I was a child. I didn't have this many tears when Kallum left.

I'm sitting on the bed in my old bedroom, at Mum and Dad's house. I managed to eat a sausage roll earlier but that was it, nothing else. I told them that I was going for a bath, but I haven't quite managed that yet. I'm still crying profoundly, as I peer at the second picture. Clair was right, we do... we did look like a lovely couple. Somehow, we just seemed to go together.

I've stopped crying now and the bath is running. I'm exhausted and my aching body is worsening. The doctor at the hospital said it would get worse before it got better. The impact jolted me with such a force that I'm sure that every muscle I own, is crying out for a warm relaxing bath. I peer down at my mobile phone, in my hand, and wonder what I can say to Clair. How can I tell her in a text message? I don't feel like talking much, but I know she would be straight on to the phone, calling me, if I told her in a text message.

Happy New Year – I'll talk to you on Tuesday x

Is that it? Love from sad Clair xx PS at least tell me if you shagged him, lol xxxx

It's enough to bring back those burning tears. I undress in a daze and step into the bath.

He's gone Clair. Can I talk to you on Tuesday when you're home? X

Gone? Where? Thought you might have got it together xxxx

He's gone forever x

My phone vibrates and starts to ring. It's Clair – I knew it would be.

"What do you mean he's gone?" Clair's voice sounds puzzled.

I sniff as tears begin again.

"Suse?"

I can't say anything as I cry down the phone.

"Suse? Are you crying?"

"Uh-huh..." I manage to splutter.

"Babe – why?"

I still can't talk. I'm sobbing heavily into the phone.

"You fancied him, didn't you? Has he gone back to Spain?"

"No," I whimper.

"Where's he gone then? Or is it that arsehole Kallum?"

"No..." I say with a trembling voice, "it's not Kallum."

"What then? Tell me – it's driving me insane."

Clair doesn't have much patience when it comes to wanting to know something. I know that if I don't explain now, she will jump straight in her car and head home at breakneck speed. She's quite protective of me and cares a lot.

"He's..." I'm not sure I can say it. "He's not here anymore, Clair. There was an acci..."

"What? An accident?" Her tone has turned deadly serious.

I nod, and then realise she can't see me. "Yes..."

"What kind of an accident? What do you mean, he's gone?" She pauses and I can picture her face. Her expression will be deadpan. "I hope you don't mean he's..."

I muster up the will to say it. "Dead..."

There's a momentary silence and then Clair's voice speaks in a softened whisper. "Suse – oh my God. He's dead?"

"Yes."

"Jeeze... Suse..." Her words are broken. "I... How? Are *you* hurt...?"

"I'm OK." I say and sniff again.

"I'm coming home..."

No, please... Don't do that Clair. I'm at Mum and Dad's. I'm staying here. I'll see you on Tuesday."

"Are you sure? Oh my God – what happened, Suse?" She pauses and sighs. "I can't believe this... you only just sent me a picture... He's dead?"

"Can I tell you everything on Tuesday?" I sniff again. "I need time..."

"Yes – of course. God, I'm so sorry, Suse – I feel like crying myself."

I hear a sniff down the phone line and it makes me cry more. She's in tears too. "Clair?"

"Sorry, Suse. I don't know why..."

"It's OK," I say. "I know."

"How did he...?"

"Car crash."

"Oh God – no. Was you in the car? Are you sure you're not hurt?"

I hear her blow her nose, as I wipe my own with the sopping wet flannel from the bath water.

"Are you sure you don't want me... to come home?"

"Yes," I say. "I'm sure." I heave a sigh. "I'm in the bath – can I talk to you on Tuesday?"

"Yes, sure, no worries. I'll get off the phone but, Suse?"

"Yes?"

"Call me if you need me to come home."

"I will, thank you." I pull the phone from my ear and press, 'end call'. Lying back in the bath I close my eyes. I'm so tired, so pained, both physically and mentally. I want to sleep so this misery will end.

Love you lots Suse. Remember – if there's anything I can do, or if you want me to come back early, I'm here for you. Whatever you want. I'm utterly stunned by what you've said, even though I don't really know what's happened. Keep strong and I'll see you on Tuesday (if not before). Love ya, Clair xxxx

***

Jett's mum is travelling back to England this morning. Understandably, she was heartbroken when she heard the terrible news. She arranged to get on the first flight back to the UK. She needs to see her little boy, one last time. Her words made everyone cry even more than they had before. Somehow, today, it seems even more real. Jett was my waking thought, a lingering nightmare that won't go away. Our relationship was so brief but so powerful and all encompassing. The saddest part for me is that no one knows what had happened between us. They don't have a clue what we felt for each other. They think my erratic outbursts of tears are because he was my long-lost friend, just like a brother, not because we had fallen in love so desperately quickly.

"Mum, can I talk to you?"

She's tidying up the house, in case the police come round again or Doreen and Malcolm bring Jett's mum, Sasha over, later this afternoon. Sasha's due to arrive back in England at 12.20pm.

"Yes, what is it, honey?" She pops the duster on the mantelpiece and joins me on the sofa.

"I want to tell you... about Jett."

"Oh – go on then. What do you want to tell me?" She places her hands in her lap and listens attentively.

"We were more than just good friends."

"I know, honey." She nods her head, sympathetically. "I understand how you feel."

"No, I mean, we had grown much closer..."

"He was like your brother – I know, honey. It's all so terrible." She grabs hold of my hand and squeezes it. "I know how difficult this is for you. We all feel it, honey. I feel like he was a step-son to me."

"No, you don't understand, Mum." I pull my hand away from hers. "It was more than that."

"Oh?" she says, frowning at the withdrawal of my hand. "What do you mean?"

"We... we'd been seeing each other."

"You mean, like girlfriend and boyfriend?"

I nod and peer at her apprehensively. I'm not sure how she will take it but it's too late now, I've told her.

"But... it's only been a week."

"I know," I say. "It happened very quickly."

"How did that happen? Do you mean you were dating him?"

I nod again. "Yes – it started on Boxing day."

"On Boxing day?" Mum repeats, incredulously. "But... what about Kallum?"

I look down at the floor – I know it all sounds a bit crazy. "What about Kallum? That was over the second he left my flat, Mum."

She shakes her head. "You do make life difficult for yourself, honey." She clasps her hands together, in her lap again. "So how do you mean it 'started' on Boxing day?"

"When we went to the pub... well, on the way back. We both liked each other – a lot." I meet Mum's eye sheepishly. "He came to stay at my flat in the week."

Her eyes widen and her jaw drops. "You mean you were a *proper* girlfriend and boyfriend?"

"Yes," I say. "He told me he loved me on..." I pause, remembering our last moments together. "that night... we were coming to tell you all." I blink away welling tears. "I loved him too."

"Oh Susie... honey. I know you are distraught by what happened but..."

"But what?" I jump in.

"But... well, surely you couldn't have loved each other in less than a week, honey."

"It's true Mum. It was like love at first sight. They say that can happen to people. It happened to us."

Mum shakes her head again and sighs.

"I lost him, Mum. We had fallen in love and now... he's gone."

"Oh, honey, come here." Mum throws her arms round me, hugging me tightly while she rocks us both from side to side. "Oh, Susie – my beautiful girl – this is terrible. It's awful. I'm so sorry for you." She sniffs and I wonder if she's crying too, as I can't see her face while I'm buried under her arms. "You've had a terrible, terrible Christmas. Me and your dad are here for you – that's all I can say – we're here for you, honey. Oh dear, oh dear."

She rocks me from side to side until I feel like I want to go to sleep again. Back to that place where I don't have to think, I don't have to remember, I don't have to know.

*** 19 ***

Sasha arrived several hours ago. Doreen and Malcolm brought her round to Mum and Dad's house and everyone spent the afternoon crying again. She had wanted to see me particularly, as I was the last person to see Jett alive. She wanted to know if he was happy that evening and did he have fun. Seeing Jett's mum made me feel closer to him in some sort of strange way. I wanted to talk to her about him and I wanted to hear everything that she had to say about him. The sad part about the conversations was that Mum had told me not to mention the fact that me and Jett had become a couple in such a short time. Mum was worried that they either wouldn't believe it or they would think it very odd that I should declare this information, after his death and particularly when we had only seen each other for six days. Mum didn't want them thinking that I was either a floozy – having only just split up with Kallum – or a delusional, slightly sadistic attention seeker. I could see her point – it had all happened quickly and it was quite incredible. So, as a result, I kept shtum about it.

Doreen, Malcolm and Sasha are visiting the chapel of rest tomorrow. Sasha wants to see her little boy... I want to see him too. I want to say goodbye to him properly, instead of moaning at him about not blinking or giving me a wink. I want to see his gorgeous face one more time and touch his soft hair.

"I really don't think it's a good idea for you to ask if you can go," says Mum as we sit around the dining table, still eating half of the leftovers from the party food. "What do you think, John?"

Dad hasn't been paying too much attention as he's looking over Mum's shoulder at the darts match on the TV. "What was that, love?"

"I said... I don't think it's a good idea – do you?"

"What's not a good idea?" quizzes Dad.

Mum tuts and rolls her eyes. "Your daughter wants to go and see Jett. She wants to ask Doreen if she can go with them."

"Not a good idea. Not with them anyway. Let them have their own time with him. They're his family, after all." Dad grins, without taking his eyes off the TV. "But there's nothing to say that you can't go and see him at another time, love."

Whenever my dad speaks on any subject, it seems that his word is final. Yet, he's so nonchalant about everything – including the fact that he knows about me and Jett now, as Mum told him. He simply wanders through life aimlessly, dishing out good advice at totally unexpected moments. Or so it appears to others. I know that deep inside that flat-top of his, he knows exactly what's going on around him and chooses not to get involved until it comes to the crunch. Then he's right there, giving out the best possible solution to anyone who cares to listen.

"I wouldn't recommend it though, love," he continues. "You'd be better off remembering him how he was."

"I never said goodbye to him, Dad."

He averts his eyes from the TV and meets mine briefly. "If you really want to see him, I'll take you... but after tomorrow."

***

According to Doreen, Sasha has been in a terrible state since she saw 'her little boy'. Apparently, she hadn't believed it to be real until she saw him. Doreen isn't much better, as in 'terrible state' wise, but she's trying to hold things together for her daughter's sake.

As for me, I'm going home today, against Mum's wishes. She even said that Clair could stay at hers, as well as me. I think she was trying to entice me to stay longer, for two reasons. Firstly, she worries way too much about me and secondly, she likes nothing more than to look after people, whether they be ill or grieving or simply just in need of a little bit of nurturing. Whatever it might be, 'Mum' really is the word.

Clair's coming home today – already. The week has gone by so quickly, it's all been a bit of a blur. I'm looking forward to seeing her though. I'm looking forward to going home to my own place and wearing my own clothes, rather than Mum's. I do love my mum dearly, but she can be quite needy herself, sometimes. Either that, or she worries over me and pampers me far too much, which has only been heightened since Jett's death.

I can say those two words now. 'Jett's death' – it still cuts through me like a red-hot knife but I've accepted that it happened now. I feel like the last week's 'whirlwind romance' – yes, there goes another cliché – was all just a dream or a fantasy. It's like it wasn't real. At one point, last night, I was almost grateful that it had happened now and not six months down the line, when we could have been completely in love and making plans for a future. OK, I know, I should never be grateful that it happened now and not later. I should only be grateful to be alive myself but, in an ideal world, none of it would have happened… or ever happen in the future either. But we don't live in an ideal world, do we?

Dad's taking me to the chapel of rest tomorrow. Again, he said that his best advice was that I should remember Jett how he was. He told me that seeing him could make me feel worse. Against his best advice, I still want to go and Dad has already phoned them for me and made an appointment.

"Are you ready to go home, love?" he calls up the stairs.

"Coming," I say. I pick up the hospital carrier bag, which has my blood-stained dress in and my glass-heeled boots. Mum had offered to wash the dress for me, to see if the stains would come out but I told her not to bother as I could never wear it again. There are too many painful memories attached to it.

I descend the stairs carefully, wearing a pair of Mum's jeans, an old jumper and her old trainers – thank goodness we're both the same size. I'm going carefully down the stairs because I still ache, although the pain is beginning to wear off just a little now. I have got to go to my doctors next week to have a check-up and the stitches removed from my head. I'm guessing that I will have a small scar, but luckily, it will be just under my fringe. Apparently, my condition has got to be logged with my doctor as well as the hospital, in case of an injury claim. To be honest, I can't be bothered with all that kind of stuff and the last thing I want, is to gain compensation money at Jett's expense. No way.

I give my mum a big hug and a kiss and climb into Dad's car. She looks tearful as we pull out of the drive. She waves to me continuously, until I can no longer see her, as we pull out on to the main road and head for home. My home.

***

The flat is eerily quiet. The last time I was here, I was waiting for Jett to pick me up in a taxi. That seems like such a long time ago, yet it was only three days ago. I walk through to the kitchen and am instantly reminded of Jett's kind act to dispose of the turkey, lying in the garden, and the funny conversation we had about it. I suddenly feel lonely. Christmas and the New Year went by in a daze and only the middle bit of it was good. I could never have imagined, on Christmas eve, while I waited for Kallum to arrive, that by the following week, I would have been through so much heartache.

It's true what they say, you never know what's around the next corner. When I think about it, over the last week I've had two boyfriends, two lovers in fact and now I'm single. I know, it sounds absolutely terrible – two men in one week – but I now feel like an empty widow.

"Suse – I'm home."

I heard the front door open seconds ago and waited momentarily for the familiar call out. She's back. My best friend is home and I just know that as soon as I set eyes on her, I'm going to burst into tears. Even the thought of it has made me well up, during the course of the afternoon. "In here," I call from the living room.

She opens the door and stops in the doorway. "Are you..."

I stand up and go to hug her. Already, the tears have started. She hugs me back and begins to cry herself. We look at each other's tearful faces and laugh hysterically.

We're still crying but we're laughing too.

"I'm OK," I say, wiping my face on my sleeves. "I'm going to see him tomorrow..."

"Him?" says Clair, puzzled.

"Jett – at the chapel of rest."

"Oh God, are you?"

I nod and sit back down on the sofa. "I need to say goodbye to him."

"OK – I get that."

"Are you OK?" I realise that mine and Clair's relationship has been all about me over the last couple of days and I have a vague memory that she had something to tell me about her New Year. "How did everything go with your family – your Christmas?"

"Oh, never mind about that for now. I want to talk about you. I need to know that you're coping with this, Suse. I saw..." She breaks off and peers over at the coffee table. "I saw it... on the local paper's website."

I nod and sigh heavily. "Yes, I saw it too. Someone called Mum's house – a reporter wanted to interview me – but Dad wasn't having any of it and told them not to call again, as I would not be giving any interviews to anyone."

"Good old Dad – eh?"

"Yes, good old Dad."

"Is your head OK?" She points to the wide plaster across my forehead.

"Yes – fine. I'll be having the stitches out next week." I run my fingers over the area where my forehead was cut. It's still tender to touch but upon my last inspection, it looks neat and clean which is the important thing.

"You've been through so much lately..."

I nod and smile weakly. "Yes – I just want to get back to work now – be normal."

"Well..." Clair gives me a cheeky grin, "as normal as possible – eh?"

I smirk at her. It's so good to have her back. She brightens up the flat. She has a positive outlook on life and if there are times where there are no positives, she finds some. She believes in waking up every morning and thanking the universe for her existence. She thanks flowers for looking so pretty or smelling so nice, she thanks the cows for bringing her milk for her cereal in the mornings, she thanks the local shop for running out of eggs at the weekends – just so that she doesn't have to eat any more eggs Benedict. She's a beautiful, kind-hearted person and I don't think I've ever met anyone else who is so aware and grateful of their possessions and surroundings as she is.

"So," she says, kicking her shoes off, "tell me about Jett – are you OK to talk about him?"

I nod my head positively. I want to tell her. I need to tell her how it was with him. I know she'll understand my pain then.

"Suse..." She shakes her head slowly and thoughtfully. "It couldn't have been any worse... I'm so sorry for you, babe."

"I know... He was snatched away from me so cruelly. So suddenly. I don't know what might have happened in the future but..." I break off and swallow hard. "Well, it was the present that counted, wasn't it?"

Clair nods agreeably. She gives a long sigh and stands up. "Do you fancy a coffee? I'm gasping for one but please, keep talking about Jett if that's what you want to do."

"Yes, coffee, why not. I'll make it, if you want to get your bags into your room. There's nothing else I can say about Jett really. I've told you everything." I suddenly realise that the more I talk to people about him, the more final it becomes. There is no more to tell.

"OK – I'll put this lot away and join you in a minute." She picks her bags up from the hallway and trundles off to her bedroom, looking as cheerful as always.

Before I make the coffee, I look at my phone messages. I'm sure that Clair said something about her new year being special – I need to check what she said before I ask her about it again. I find the message and read through it with sadness. It's the one she sent me after she'd seen the picture. The one where she said we'd make an amazing couple. I try to shrug off the haunting memories. She also said that she was going to explain her 'new start' later. I knew there was something.

Clair arrives in the living room with a packet of chocolate fingers and grins. "I've learnt a new trick with these," she says, waving the packet in the air. "You have just got to try it out."

I peer at her curiously. "OK, show me."

"Here," she says, passing me a finger, "Nibble both ends off first. Not too much – just the very end bits."

I watch as she bites the ends off her biscuit and then I do the same.

"Now it's a straw," she says, beaming at me like she's just revealed a world-class innovative design.

"A straw," I say, holding mine up for her to inspect.

"Good," she says, "now you need to suck your coffee up through it."

"Really?"

"Yes – watch." Placing the end of her chocolate finger in her hot coffee, Clair begins to suck it hard. "You've got to suck it really hard," she says, before returning her mouth to the biscuit. "Until you can feel hot coffee coming through."

I watch her in amusement.

"Then eat the finger." She pops the whole thing into her mouth. "Hmm... yummy," she mumbles.

"You're mad," I say, grinning at her.

"Try it – don't knock it until you've tried it. Go on." She picks up another finger and repeats the process.

Following her lead, I do the same. She's right – it's absolutely amazing. The inside of the finger melts to a gooey mush of biscuit and chocolate, so I have got to have another one, just to perfect the art. And maybe just one or two more.

"Good, aren't they? You can do it with *Twix* bars as well, but I forgot to pick some up. *Twix* are the best."

"Incredible," I say. "Best start to the new year so far."

She shrugs and picks up another finger.

"Talking of new starts..." I take one more finger-straw and begin to nibble the ends off. "You said in one of your messages that you were going to tell me about your new start."

She peers up at me as she's sucking the coffee through her biscuit. "Umm..." Then she pops it in her mouth. "I... well, I didn't want to say anything... not just yet... what with everything that's been going on with you."

"Oh?"

"It's not really important right now."

"No, please tell me."

She hesitates, reaches for another finger and nibbles the ends off. "I saw Archie."

"Did you? How's he doing?"

"Yeah... he's good."

She avoids my eye and I know there is more to it. Clair's always had a thing for Archie. He was in the year above her at school and he was her childhood crush. They became good friends as they grew up, even though there was a year's age gap, which, when you're young, seems bigger. They lived in the same road but once they both left school, they went their separate ways and didn't see each other anymore.

"What's he doing these days?" There's more to this – I know it.

"He works in a warehouse, near where we lived. He drives a forklift."

"So where did you see him?"

"I bumped into him in the town. I went out with some of the old uni-crew the first night I got there." She gives me an uncomfortable smile.

"Go on then – spit it out. There's more to this," I say, trying to ease her awkwardness. I practically know what she's going to say next anyway.

"I couldn't believe how grown up he was, Suse. He's turned into a really nice man." She pauses thoughtfully. "We worked out that we hadn't seen each other for about seven years. Seven years – where did that time go?"

"Do you still fancy him?"

"Are you kidding? He's even more gorgeous than he was before." She gives a little smirk. "OK – I might as well tell you."

"You're seeing him?"

She nods her head like she's being apologetic.

"What's wrong with that? It's good, isn't it? I'm really pleased for you."

"Yes, it is... I just feel guilty because you had such a horrible Christmas and New Year and I... well, I had the best time of my life."

"I'm really pleased for you," I say, and I genuinely mean it, I am really happy for her. It's about time she had a new boyfriend and hopefully, he'll help her sort her work/life balance out in his favour. "So... how far has this new relationship gone?" I ask, curiously. Although Clair wouldn't believe it, it actually makes me feel better listening to her happy story, instead of feeling remorseful that I haven't got a 'happily ever after'.

"It all happened quickly, a bit like you and..." She falters and looks at me with pitying eyes. "Well... I mean, we're definitely an item now. I stayed round his flat a few times over Christmas."

"I'm so happy for you – really, I am."

She peers at me sheepishly. "I was going to ask a favour actually – but, what with everything that's happened..."

"Stop worrying about that. Please, ask away."

"Well..." She picks her coffee cup up and peers into it. "Obviously, we're a long way from each other and..."

"You want him to come here to stay, maybe at the weekends..."

She eyes me amusedly. "How did you guess?"

"It's obvious, isn't it."

"Is it?" She looks surprised.

"How else could you see him? I don't suppose you can keep driving back to Devon every weekend."

"Well, I could but..."

I smile warmly because I know she's getting anxious. "That would be too much, Clair. You'd need to take turns, surely – alternate weekends." I watch her face change from a worried gaze to a look of pleasant relief.

"You know me too well – that's exactly what I was going to suggest. Are you sure it would be OK?"

"Of course it's OK. I used to have Kallum stay sometimes, didn't I?"

"Yes, I know, but it's your flat."

"*Our* flat as far as I'm concerned." I grin at her just before she shocks me by slamming her mug on the table, leaping across the room and flinging her arms round my neck.

"Oh, Suse, thank you, thank you, thank you." She kisses the top of my head with a loud and expressive, mwah, mwah, mwah. "I'm going back this weekend, so I'll tell him he can come on the following one. Thank you so much – you're the best."

*** 20 ***

My heart is racing so much. It takes my breath away as I tentatively reach over and touch his ice-cold hand. His eyes are tightly closed – I wait expectantly for them to open. Just one last wink – please. He looks perfect. He seems peaceful. Happy even. I feel like I didn't really know him now that I'm peering into his face. I whisper, 'goodbye' as a tear falls from my eye. 'You were amazing'. I withdraw my hand from his and continue to stare at his pale face. How can he be so perfect and not wake up?

It's eerily still in this room, the faint sound of soothing music can just be heard coming from above my head somewhere. I look around at the majestic jardinières, filled with colourful arrays of flowers and the plush, maroon drapes hanging from the window. It's nice in here. A lovely place for Jett to be. Why did he have to go though? He was so young and fit. How can young, fit people die?

'Goodbye... I love you... I'll never forget you...'

I leave the room and him, so sorrowfully. I'm empty. I've come to realise the finality of it all.

My dad has been sitting in the waiting room. He jumps up and puts his arms round me and hugs me tightly. I cry like a child. It's the end. Finished. Gone.

Dad had asked me before I went in, if I was sure I wanted to do it. I'd said I wasn't sure at all but felt compelled to say goodbye to Jett. In a way, I'm happy that I did, but in another way, it's made me think deeply of my own mortality. I'm more aware of life and how none of us could ever know what might happen next. It's suddenly made me realise how precious my family and friends are and how time should be made for those I love. Jett's death has taught me a great deal, although it's been an extremely tough lesson to learn.

His funeral has been arranged for a week's time, which I will attend, alongside Mum and Dad. They are my pillars of strength and I am indebted to them for their endless support and love. I owe them so much, yet they wouldn't agree.

I'm going to hold on to those precious memories of my time with Jett. I'm so lucky to have known him, to have spent time with him, to have loved him. He'll be in my heart forever – a symbol of the greatest of human nature.

***

I'm due back to school tomorrow which fills me with dread. So much has happened over the holidays, so much has changed. Momentarily, I think back to the last time I saw most of my colleagues – I was dressed as a turkey. I know there will be giggles and sniggers going on behind my back, or in Sultry Sarah or Juicy Jane's cases, they'll be laughing in my face. I'll have to laugh along with them all, as I don't know any of them well enough to divulge my terrible Christmas holidays to. It's probably better that way anyway. The last thing I want is to have sympathetic comments which could make me burst into tears at any given moment. What they don't know, won't hurt me. It's simple.

The back-to-work mindset has made me think more about Kallum too, for some strange reason. The last time I was at school, I had a long-term partner – now I'm single. Now I've experienced a loved one's death, first-hand. Now I've been a turkey for everyone to see and laugh at. I feel like a different person to the one who walked out of school at the end of term, with such high hopes – I'm now a lonely, sad person with no expectations of the future. No high hopes anymore.

I gather my clothes together, ready for the morning's rush. I like to prepare the night before so I don't get in a fluster about what to wear to work. Although, Clair and I do have a ritual on work mornings. I use the bathroom first, then she uses it while I make us coffee and toast, then I get dressed while she clears up, then she gets dressed while I tidy around the living room. We both like to come home, after a hard day's work, to a tidy flat. After the ritual, we usually leave the flat together and then go our separate ways. We make a good pair of flatmates and I really couldn't see anyone else fitting in so well, should Clair ever decide to leave… And that has played on my mind a tad since she told me about Archie. It's early days though, anything could happen. God forbid nothing so terrible should happen like my nightmarish story.

Everything's done now. I've got my clothes ironed and hanging over the wardrobe door, my school bag is filled with my 'Grammar Book for Idiots', a shapes dictionary, my pencil case, my spare trainers (should we suddenly go out on an unexpected trek), spare socks (to go with the trainers) an empty water bottle with 'Miss Satchel' written in capital letters, two boxes of golden vegetable *Cup-a-Soups* (should I forget my lunch one day), a hairbrush and some spare hairbands. I have my own locker at school, where I keep all my home-from-home things. Which reminds me – I will have to remove the small picture of Kallum which is stuck to the inside of my locker door with *Blu-Tack*. Yes, I know, I'm quite sad, as I really do make the interior of my locker look like it's a little piece of home. As long as it doesn't now turn into a memorial shrine (although, I do only have one picture of Jett anyway), I can consider myself to be still reasonably sane. Heartbroken but sane.

***

This morning's ritual didn't quite go so smoothly as it used to. It's probably because Clair went back to work yesterday and got up on her own, hence, she did everything on her own. I'd stayed in bed, listening to her pottering about and wondering how I was going to deal with seeing Jett and what he'd look like. I'd never seen a dead person before. Anyway, I digress – so, this morning was like the first day that we *both* went to work.

All in all, myself and Clair made it out of the flat on time and said our goodbyes for the day. So, here I am now, at school, and the usual surge of children are coming into the school, telling each other big, exaggerated stories of what they got for Christmas and what they did over the holidays. It can be anything from receiving a real, live horse from their great aunt, on Christmas day (which they are keeping in the garden), to travelling to Africa to ride giant elephants and then nipping up to Lapland to visit Santa. Bless them – they have great imaginations, well, most of them anyway.

I came straight into the classroom after I'd filled my locker with my bag's contents (including my lovingly-prepared-by-Clair lunch) and ripped Kallum's photo from the locker door. I stuffed the photo in my bag, not daring to throw it in a bin in case the caretaker or a cleaner found it and pinned it to the staffroom notice board with a sign saying, 'Who does this belong to – found in the bin?'.

Our staff notice board has all sorts of funny little messages on it like, 'Where's the Spectrum Math – Grade 2 book? Someone must have it – I've searched the whole school', or 'Can someone please remove the crystal gardens from the fridge – they look nasty', and another one we had was, 'There's dog poo all over the field – please check your children's shoes, until it has all been removed, as it got walked into the hall this morning and Mr Crabb had to clean the floor twice' or 'Who hasn't yet paid their coffee-club money? There will be a name and shame list going on the board again – very soon'. And there really are name and shame lists on the notice board from time to time, so everyone tries their hardest to remember to pay up for things like the 'staff-fund', the staff night's out, dinner money and of course, the coffee-club.

I'm settling back in nicely. The teacher I work with (Mrs Pearson) is very organised and gives me clear, daily instructions on what I need to do. She's a fairly old woman – I'm guessing, near to sixty-ish? She has white hair which is neatly styled into a very short bob and she wears long, flowery skirts every day.

Not that I have much experience in these matters, but I think she's a very good, patient and kind teacher. She cares about her pupils and she certainly looks after me.

"Morning, Miss Satchel," says Jade Smith.

It's funny how we all call each other by our surnames at school, even when the children are not within earshot.

"Did you have a good Christmas?" Jade has popped into our empty classroom to drop off some paperwork for Mrs Pearson. It's break time and the children have gone out to play for 15 minutes.

"Not too bad, thanks. You?"

"Yeah, good. Went far too quick though." She places the papers on to Mrs Pearson's desk and peers at me. "Are you coming to the staffroom – there are 'welcome back to school' cakes on the table."

"I might do later – I've got a few things I want to catch up with here," I lie. "Thanks anyway."

"OK – might see you at lunchtime then."

"Yes, of course." I smile at her, willing her to leave. I'm really not in the mood for chit-chat with anyone and besides, I need to go to the Head's office and write my name on the sign on his door. It's a way of getting to see him as soon as he is available. He will come and find me as soon as he is free.

As I'm walking back from the Head's (Mr Reynolds) office, I peer down the long corridor, towards the upper-school area. Gliding effortlessly towards me, wearing a cream jumper-dress and knee-high, black stiletto boots, is Miss Chambers (Sultry Sarah). She's waving a hand at me.

"Yoo-hoo, Miss Satchel. How are you? Did you have a good Christmas?" She approaches me and grins as she looks me up and down.

"Yes – OK. Did you?"

"Bit boring really, apart from the actual Christmas day and Boxing day." She grins again. "You were a good sport."

"You mean the turkey?"

"Yes." She giggles and peers down at her arm, picking fluff from her jumper-dress. "It suited you actually. You make a great turkey."

"Thanks for that."

"Have you been in the staffroom...?"

"Cakes? No, I haven't." I feel that the conversation between us is somewhat stifled. She's done the, 'you look great as a turkey' bit, so we could probably move on now and go our separate ways.

"No, I meant the 'wear red' day – I don't do cakes, they're full of unneeded carbs you know. Not good for your hips." She looks down at my hips and I notice just the faintest curl of her top lip.

"What's the 'wear red' day then? I haven't looked."

"It's fundraising for our orchestra – run by the 'All Reds' parent's committee." She gives me a contemptuous look. "You should check the events in the staffroom – especially when you first come back to school. I thought you might have known that by now."

I nod my head agreeably. "I will – thanks."

"Must dash," says Sarah, as she spots Jane walking away from us, along the corridor. "Don't work too hard and stay away from those carbs. Think hips, Susie, think hips." She glides away with her head held high and a flirtatious wiggle of her perfectly sized hips.

Bitch. Patronising bitch. She always manages to annoy me. I should rise above it – I'm better than that and the things that I have been through lately should make me a stronger person. But I don't feel strong, I feel out of touch with everything, with everyone. I'm in a huge school, surrounded by children and adults and wish I could disappear. Don't get me wrong – I love my job. I enjoy teaching the small groups of children in my care and I do like most of the adults – I just think that maybe I'm not as ready for this again as I thought I was. I've got to try and stay strong, move on and keep my nose down until I feel more able to cope with the likes of Miss-Bloody-Sultry-Sarah-Chambers. As for Juicy Jane, well I haven't had the honour of speaking to her yet. That's to come, I'm sure.

As I look down the corridor, I can see them both whispering and giggling. Jane looks towards me and waves. I wave back and force a smile before returning to my classroom – my sanctuary at this moment.

Get through the day, Susie Satchel – you can do it, I keep repeating to myself.

Mr Reynolds appears at the classroom door and beckons to me.

Excusing myself, to Mrs Pearson, I walk towards the door, my heart beating heavily in my chest.

"Can you come to my office at twelve?" he says.

I nod. "Yes – err, thank you." I always feel nervous when I see him. He reminds me of a bird, with his hooked nose and pointed chin. He has balding, grey hair and mean-looking, beady electric-blue eyes, which I'm sure, could bore holes through my skin.

He looks down his nose at me, kinks his lip into a brief smile and then turns on his heels.

I return to the table where I was sitting with a group of children, shrugging my shoulders and grinning sheepishly at Mrs Pearson as I go. She gives me an odd look and I realise that I will also have to speak to her too. Not now though. I will speak to her once I've seen Mr Reynolds.

It's twelve o'clock, lunchtime, and I walk towards Mr Reynolds' office nervously. I tap on his door lightly and wait.

"Come in," he says from the other side of the door.

I open the door slowly and walk in. I've never seen inside the Head's office before. It's airy and bright. He has two large windows in front of his long desk, overlooking the school's entrance gates and there are ceiling-height palm trees in giant pots, in three corners of the room.

"Have a seat," he says, ushering me to a curved sofa along the back wall. He's sitting on a brown, leather office swivel chair which he deliberately tilts backwards and forwards as I sit down.

"Thanks," I say anxiously.

"Job going OK?"

"Yes – really well, thanks. I'm enjoying it."

"Good," he says, stroking his fingers across the top of his lip thoughtfully. "So, what brings you here today?"

"I wondered if it would be OK to have a day off... next Wednesday... I have a... a funeral to go to."

"Sorry to hear that," he says. "A family member?"

"No... well... not really. He was a close friend..."

"I can only give you a full day off for family funerals." Mr Reynolds looks at me nonchalantly.

"I... I grew up with him. He was just like my brother." I feel a stab of pain in my chest. Am I really going to have to beg for a day off? Jett was like my brother.

"What time is the funeral?" Mr Reynolds hasn't shown any empathy to my cause.

"It's at ten o'clock."

He turns his chair around to his desk and taps something on his computer. Then he peers at a list of class timetables. "If you could come back in the afternoon, I can give you the morning off."

"Come back?" I say, incredulously. "I don't think..."

He turns back round to face me and places his hands in his lap. "That's the best I can offer you. Particularly as it's only someone who is *like* a brother, as you say."

I meet his eye. My own fill with tears. Oh no, I didn't want this to happen. I'm crying.

Mr Reynolds grabs a box of tissues from the end of his desk and passes them to me, indifferently. "All I can suggest..." he says, sounding like he's going to backtrack, "...is that you take the afternoon unpaid."

"Yes." I nod my head and sniff into a tissue. "Thank you, that's fine."

Unpaid? Frigging unpaid? The man I had fallen in love with, practically died in my arms and I'm not even allowed to have one afternoon off without it being unpaid? I try not to stare at Mr Reynolds aghast.

"I will expect the morning to be made up at some point."

I look up at him, utterly amazed by his complete lack of empathy. "Yes, of course." I wipe my nose and screw the tissue into a ball, gripping it tightly in my hand.

"Maybe an after-school club or you could help out with a couple of lunchtime clubs."

"Yes, I will. Thank you."

"Can you let Mrs Pearson know."

"Yes – I will."

"That will be all then," he says, waving his hand away, indicating that I should go.

I rise from the sofa and smile falteringly. "Thank you, Mr Reynolds. I appreciate it." I walk out of the room, close the door behind me and rush off to the toilets before anyone can see me.

And that's where I have spent my whole lunchtime – in a toilet cubicle. Crying. Each time I heard someone come in, I tried not to sniff or make any noise until they had left. I didn't eat my lunch which made me cry even more because it was a lovingly-prepared-by-Clair lunch, and I know it would have been good. I miss my flatmate desperately and wish I could go home now. But then she wouldn't be there anyway. Life really sucks sometimes.

It's approaching one o'clock and I realise that I need to gather myself together, ready for the afternoon's lessons. I think about Mr Reynolds and how unsympathetic he was. It makes me angry enough to stop the tears. I've decided that the Head is a horrible, uncaring, shallow man and that's enough for me to drag my sorry self, up from the toilet seat, and go out to the washbasins to give my face a splash before returning to work.

I'll get through this – I know I will. Somehow.

*** 21 ***

First day back at work and I've spent it either, in tears, in dismay or in denial. When I arrived home this evening, I spent a few more hours in tears as I wept on Clair's shoulder. The fact that I hadn't even eaten her lovingly-prepared-lunch, made me cry even more. Silly, I know.

"It will keep until tomorrow Suse. Is it back in the fridge?"

I nod my head sorrowfully.

"Good – so take it tomorrow and go and sit in the staffroom and talk to people while you're eating it. You won't be able to hide away forever." She peers at me worriedly.

"I might do," I say, unconvincingly.

"No, you *will* – you *must*. Suse, I think Jett's... well, I think it's only hitting you now. You're back to work and everything's supposed to be normal but..." She breaks off and I can see that she's thinking carefully. "Everything is so un-normal for you, isn't it?"

I nod and a single tear drops from one eye.

"You've been through so much over Christmas, what with Kallum and..." She breaks off again and looks at me. "I've been thinking..."

"Oh?"

"About staying at home this weekend – I'm not sure that I want you to be on your own here – unless you'll go to your Mum and Dad's."

"I'll be fine," I say, wiping my nose for the umpteenth time. "I'll chill out and get my head straight. Please, go back home to see Archie."

"Are you sure?"

"Yes, I'm sure," I reply forcefully. "I need some time on my own to... to think and to focus on the important things in life."

"Like?" Clair still has that worried expression on her face.

"Well, like my family, friends, my job and this flat. You never know – I might even decorate."

"That might be a good thing. They say a change is as good as a rest. You should do it. Fresh coat of paint on the walls – fresh start."

"Exactly," I say, realising I've just given myself a huge task for the weekend. But then again, what else have I got to look forward to? "Thanks Clair, I don't know what I'd do without you sometimes."

She smiles and gives me a hug. "You'd do just fine without me, Suse. You'll have to manage without me now because I'm going for a bath. Cope with it because you're not getting in there with me." She pecks me on the forehead, giggles and walks out of the living room.

***

My lunch was fine the following day but, despite Clair's good advice, I didn't sit in the staffroom. I'm just not ready to chat to people. Luckily, no one could have read the local paper over Christmas and they seem to be none the wiser to the unfortunate event. Or they did see it but didn't connect it to me, or they're just not saying anything about it. I've been luckier still because we've had gorgeous sunny weather with only a slight breeze, although it's still very cold, but it means that when I've been out on the playground, no one has noticed the scar on my forehead either. It's pretty well hidden under my fringe. When I think about my scar, it makes me feel guilty for being so vain and worrying whether it can be seen or not. I shouldn't be so worried about it, after all, I could have been dead.

To be honest though, there have been times, in the middle of the night (which is when I do most of my crying now), when I've wished I were dead. I know that's a terrible thing to say but there comes a dreadful feeling of self-condemnation when you're the survivor. I lie in bed thinking, if it hadn't been for this or we hadn't done that, he would still be here. I know that these thoughts are bad for me and it's pointless to think about how things could have been different, as it wouldn't change anything now, but I can't help it. I wonder if it's a part of the grieving process and my soul-destroying thoughts will slowly begin to disappear over time. I do hope so.

***

It's Friday already. I can't believe how quickly those first few days back at school, went. On my way home tonight, I popped into the local DIY store and picked up some cream paint, a brush, a roller, a large, cream plant pot and an indoor plant. The plant has some ridiculous name to it but resembles a palm tree. I thought it looked nice, so I bought it. Knowing my luck, it probably grows to eight feet high with a width of the same. Oh well, it'll look nice for now, in the empty corner of the living room, next to the sofa. I have a pale blue settee suite so I thought that the cream would go nice with it. My mum has a lovely cream and pale blue, decorated conservatory so my living room might even feel like home from home once I've finished decorating.

Shopping has made me feel so much better. Those who say that shopping is retail therapy, are right. Once I'd dropped off the paint stuff and the plant, I nipped to the supermarket and stocked up on pizza, chocolate, cracker-crisps and wine. I'm going to have a work-hard–stuff-myself, kind of a weekend. Alone. But that's not a problem either. I've planned to watch some films in the evenings while I stuff all the goodies and sniff the paint fumes. Weekend sorted.

Clair comes into the living room, wearing her coat. "I'll be going now. Are you sure you're going to be OK?"

"Yes, I'll be fine – honestly. I've got my whole weekend planned out."

"OK, I'll be back on Sunday night. I'm looking forward to seeing the new-look living room." She smiles and peers around the room. "You never know – I might even get inspired to decorate my bedroom."

"Maybe you should, I'll help you. You could have it looking like new before Archie comes to stay."

"OK," she says, joyfully. "If you're going to help me – it's a deal and then I'll help you do yours."

I smile at her falteringly. I don't mean to but, well, there's not much point in doing mine. I've hardly got anyone to invite into it, have I? Perhaps I'm just being overly negative and should just decorate it anyway. It might even cheer me up to wake up in a pretty room and I have seen some very nice wallpaper which I would love to have on the wall opposite my bed. Maybe my dad would even hang the paper for me, if I ask him nicely. He could even wear one of his aprons while he's doing it. Funnily enough, I'm feeling just a little more positive now at the thought of a pastel pink and blue, floral, ditsy print wallpaper in my bedroom.

Clair approaches me, leans over and gives me a hug. "Call me if you're feeling fed up at all."

"I will. Have a great weekend."

I watch as she leaves the room and listen to the front door closing. She's gone. I'm alone. I can do this. Keep positive.

***

It looks fab. Even though I do say so myself. Clair will love it. I had to give the walls two coats to cover the deep pink paint that was there before but I've just about finished it and Clair won't be home until later tonight. The room looks bigger and brighter and somehow, it instills a positive outlook in me.

I'm going to try and eat less today, after my binge evening last night. I watched a couple of films and stuffed my face stupidly, so I'm feeling the bloated tummy today. I'm also feeling something else creeping up on me. Loneliness – I've evaded it all weekend, but now I've finished decorating and there's not much else to do, I'm starting to think back to Christmas again.

I open my laptop to have a look on *facebook*. I don't go on it that much but when I'm bored I have a little look – just to see who is doing what, in their lives. There are two messages and twelve notifications. The messages are from Kallum (who I should have deleted from my friends list) and Amber Nutbrown. Curiously, I open the one from Amber.

Hi there, thanks for adding me. I remember you from the Christmas do. You were the one wearing the turkey outfit, lol. I was a bit pissed that night – oops sorry. Hope I wasn't too much of a pain. Ryan, the love-pest in my life, said I was. Oh well, he's always nagging at me – he's like my bloody dad! Anyway, hope you had a good few days back at school. Lol, I won't recognise you if I see you again, unless you're wearing a turkey outfit!

Ryan the love-pest? Is she serious? I got the distinct impression that *she* was the love-pest, not Ryan. I have got to be tactful as I reply to her.

Thanks for adding me Amber. Ha ha, you were a bit drunk that night. But the turkey came to your rescue! Yes, thanks, school was OK. The holidays went far too quickly though. Still, only seven weeks and we'll be having half-term... not that I'm counting the weeks down... much!

I click on the message from Kallum.

How are you doing? Susie, please forgive me, I miss you like crazy.

Oh, God. Do I miss him too? Or am I just vulnerable at the moment and craving anyone's company? I picture me back with him but it makes me cringe. No, I decide, I'm simply craving *anyone's* company.

Don't think we need to be friends on here anymore. Hope Tania and the baby are doing well. Good luck to you all.

I go to Kallum's profile, which he never hardly uses anyway, and remove him as a friend. I don't block him, just so that he can still send messages to me. I don't know why, but I've left that little window open, just so he can message me back if he feels he needs to. Besides, he has my phone number anyway, so he can text me. I admit, I'm craving attention – whoever it's from – but I do not want a relationship with Kallum again. It is most definitely over.

***

She loved it, just as I thought she would. Clair was in high spirits when she returned home. She'd had an amazing weekend with Archie and eventually told me that she felt quite strongly about him. It had taken me all night to get every little detail out of her, as she said she didn't want to upset me by telling me about her wonderful, new love life, when I didn't have one. I explained that I was fine with it.

That was last night but now, I'm walking into school and it's suddenly struck me. Every single child who has walked past me towards the playgrounds, where they line up to start their school day, is wearing red. Bright red, dark red, light red, maroon, deep pink, spotty red, stripy red... Red – everywhere. Oh dear.

I live in my own world, where the only vision I have, is through a long dark tunnel with no light at the end. Every single staff member I see, is wearing red. Sultry Sarah told me about this day but I didn't trust her, and therefore, I didn't take that much notice of what she said. The girls from the office peer through the door at me and either smile or gesticulate to their own clothing. I shrug my shoulders at them and mouth, 'I forgot'.

"Miss Satchel..."

Great – I've just bumped into Juicy Jane as I turned the corner to enter the corridor. She's wearing a gorgeous, fitted red dress which I would say is a little too low, around the neckline, for school.

She peers at me disappointedly, "Where are your red clothes?"

"I completely forgot," I say, shrugging my shoulders. I'm wearing black trousers and a deep blue blouse today – I couldn't be any further away from red if I had tried.

"You'll stick out like a sore thumb today, but I guess you're used to that anyway." She laughs at me. "You would have been better off coming as a turkey – at least you would have had a red crest."

"Ha ha," I say sarcastically, "very funny."

"No, seriously," says Jane. "I do have a red scarf you could borrow. It's a chunky knit but you're welcome to use it."

A chunky knit. As if I'm going to wear that around school all day. It's hot enough in this school as it is. The radiators, all along the corridors and in each classroom, belt out a whopping great amount of heat all day – they're almost a safety hazard, they're so hot. "Thanks, but no, I'll have to admit to failure this time."

"I hope Mr Reynolds doesn't point you out in assembly."

"So do I."

Jane shakes her head. "He's done that kind of thing before, you know."

"Oh really?"

"Yes- I'd try and hide at the back if I were you."

"Thanks," I say. "I'll do that."

"You all look marvelous," says Mr Reynolds.

He's standing proudly, at the front of the hall, surveying the sea of red in front of him. He is wearing a red tracksuit which looks absolutely awful and I dread to think if it is actually one of his 'at home' outfits.

"We have raised over £650 today for the orchestra and it's all down to you."

There's a united gasp from the children, then they begin chattering.

"Thank you, children." Mr Reynolds holds his hand up and the din stops. "I'd like to thank, practically the entire staff..." He peers directly at me with a steely look in his eyes, "...for dressing up so well today too. Let's give your teachers a round of applause."

Cheering and clapping resonates around the large hall as almost 700 children congratulate the staff enthusiastically.

"Miss Satchel forgot." A boy, from my class shouts out, as the clapping comes to an end. He's one of our more difficult children. He's loud, far too opinionated for a seven-year-old and gets angry very quickly.

A sea of faces turn to stare at me. My face flushes red. The staff, seated around the outside edge of the hall, peer over at me. I shrug my shoulders and feel my cheeks burning. I point to my face, 'Red face – see?' I mouth to as many people as I can, trying to salvage my dignity.

Mr Reynolds stares at me disdainfully and then claps his hands once and everyone turns their heads back, instantly, to the front of the hall. "It saddens me to see that not all of our staff have made the effort but when so many of you have, the clear majority far outweighs the odd straggler."

I cringe and wish I could disappear into a hole somewhere. I hate Mr Reynolds – I really do hate him.

He then continues with the rest of the assembly, while peering across the hall to me, now and again. I know he is deliberately trying to make me feel uncomfortable. And it's working, to be honest.

I've been completely humiliated by a seven-year-old. I'm demoralised by the evil stare of Mr Reynolds, over and over again. I'm sure he is revelling in making me feel uneasy. His constant glare, in my direction, makes other members of staff stare at me too, although not in the same malevolent way as Mr Reynolds does. I clasp my hands together tightly, in my lap, and peer straight ahead. I want to cry. I want to run from the hall. I want to...

No, I don't want to die. I should never think like that, ever...

OK... at this moment, I *do* want to shrivel up and die. Sorry, but I can't help the way I feel.

*** 22 ***

Clair is being so ultra-supportive at the moment – I really don't know what I'd do without her. She thought that Mr Reynolds was 'out of order' to allow a 'little brat', as she calls them, to shout out something like that, in an assembly. She was so angry about it that she wanted to go down to the school and speak to Mr Reynolds. She said he was unprofessional to keep glaring at me across the hall too. Of course, I said there was no way she could go and speak to him. Thankfully, she listened to me and calmed down about it.

I'm not going to work today. I waved Clair off earlier, after she'd given me the biggest hug ever, and now I'm dressing in my black clothing. It's what Jett's mum wants. She's requested that everyone wear black or dark clothing today.

I'm feeling numb this morning. I don't have any inclination to cry, smile, be sad, be happy or anything. I'm emotionless, if there is such a feeling. I'm on automatic pilot as I drift around the flat getting ready. I've got to be at Mum and Dad's by about nine o'clock as we're following behind the procession of hearses and limousines, when they leave.

Apparently, it's not going to be a big event. Jett didn't have a big family and all his friends are in Spain, although two of them have flown over for his funeral. A couple of people will be attending from his work place and one of the men who he shared a house with. His ex-girlfriend is going too, surprisingly. According to Mum, she was very upset when she heard the news and requested that she come to the actual funeral, although she wouldn't attend the wake afterwards, which is being held back at Doreen and Malcolm's. I'm relieved that she's not going to the wake as I can't help thinking that if she hadn't been a complete weirdo and asked Jett to 'share' their relationship, he'd still be with her and still be alive.

I've kept in contact with Mum this week, or to be more exact, she has been texting or phoning me every day since I returned home. She keeps me updated on who's going or who's not going to the funeral and gives me a daily run-down on how Doreen, Malcolm and Sasha are. Which, by all accounts, is not good. Understandably so though. She also keeps asking me if I'm OK and tells me that my old bedroom is always there if I want to go back and stay for a few days or over the weekend. I thank her kindly for her concern and have got to insist, each day, that I stay at my flat as I'm fine and I have Clair here anyway. I didn't dare tell her that Clair wasn't here last weekend as she would have come over, packed my bags for me and made me go back to hers.

There's a strange sullen atmosphere at Mum and Dad's house. I was expecting it to be sullen but not strange. Mum and Dad are both speaking in hushed, low tones, as if the funeral is being held in their house. They are also walking around with their heads bowed, which is most bizarre.

Like me, they are both dressed in black and Mum has a single black rose clip in her hair. It's a bit antiquated but that's my mum for you. She does like to wear things in her hair.

"The hearse will be here in 20 minutes," Mum whispers, as she peers in the long mirror, in the hallway.

"Mum, why are you whispering?" I say, and I have got to admit, I ask in a hushed voice as well. Maybe it's catching.

"It's a mark of respect, honey." She adjusts the rose in her hair and pulls at her black jacket, swivelling it around and down over her hips.

"But we're not at the funeral yet."

She stops fiddling and looks at me. "I know but... I don't want Doreen hearing us, next door."

"Have the walls turned to paper then?"

Mum huffs and walks past me to the kitchen.

"Don't you feel morose today, honey – I know that I do."

"Yes, of course I do. I just wondered why you were whispering."

"I don't know really. It just feels right."

I nod my head and go into the living room and peer out of the window. Nothing feels right to me today. Whispering, shouting, screaming, crying, talking – nothing feels right.

It's here. Slowly, it pulls up next door. A limousine pulls up behind it. Flowers fill the inside of the hearse, so much so, that I can hardly see the...

I gulp and put my hands up to cover my face as unexpected tears fall from my eyes.

One of the larger flower arrangements says 'son'.

Jett's in there. He really is. He's dead and this is the end of his life story today. I turn away from the window and slump down into a chair, as I sob profoundly.

Mum enters the room. "Oh, honey – come here." She kneels by my side and hugs me. "He's going to get a good send off today – he would be proud."

I dry my eyes and look up at her. "I know... it's just... seeing the..."

"I know, honey. It's so hard. A funeral makes it all seem so final. He'll always be in your heart though – you'll keep the memories of him forever."

I nod and reach for the tissue in my pocket.

"You have some very precious memories of him, honey. Hold on to those as they are very special."

"I will," I say and sigh deeply.

"Come on, wipe your eyes. We'll all get through this together." She strokes my hair and kisses me on the top of my head. "It's a bright day – do you want to borrow a pair of my sunglasses?"

"Yes... please."

"It helps if you can hide behind sunglasses sometimes."

"Thanks Mum." She's so right. That's exactly what I want to do – wear sunglasses. How is it that Mums always seem to know what is the best thing to do? Sunglasses always seem to give me more confidence – they're like a veil of certainty to hide behind. I pull myself up from the chair and shoot a cursory glance out of the window. I can do this. I must do this. For Jett's sake.

***

It was the worst experience of my life. I don't really know what I was expecting but... Well, it was harder than I thought it would be. I flick my thoughts back to the day I was sat in Mr Reynolds' office. He had wanted me to go back to work this afternoon. Was he serious? Has he ever been to a funeral? Does he have any idea how people feel after attending such a lugubrious, mournful ceremony? No, I doubt he does.

We're travelling back to Doreen and Malcolm's house and I'm sitting in the back of Mum and Dad's car consumed by an emptiness, I never thought I could feel. None of us have spoken since we got in the car and there is a deathly silence as we travel along because Mum had insisted that the car's radio be turned off, as we travelled to the funeral, and it's remained off on our journey back.

I remove Mum's sunglasses and peer out of the window. The brightness of earlier has turned to a gloomy, grey – almost in time to reflect the hearts and minds of everyone who was at Jett's funeral.

I saw his ex-girlfriend briefly. She came with another woman, who I'm guessing, might have been her, 'friend' – *the* friend. The one who wanted to share Jett. They were linked arm in arm throughout the whole funeral service and seated to the right of us. She didn't speak to anyone, not even Doreen or Malcolm, who she must have known, and she stayed at the back all the time. She cried quite a lot, which surprised me and made me feel quite angry. If only she hadn't... Anyway, it's too late now to blame others or reflect on what could have been different. He's gone and no amount of yearning will bring him back.

***

The wake was a small affair. Malcolm and an incredibly tearful Sasha welcomed people in and directed them towards the dining room where there was a table filled with triangle sandwiches, sausage rolls and other nibbles. Doreen had busied herself in her kitchen by making teas and coffees. She looked tired and pained. Everyone talked about Jett and reminisced about their own memories of him. As for me, well I didn't say too much because, apart from my childhood memories, my greatest recollection of him was, and still is, shrouded in secrecy.

Now we're back home, at Mum and Dad's house. It's only four o'clock but we all feel utterly drained. I, for one, have spent the best part of the day in tears. Whether my tears hid underneath the sunglasses or not, as I did remove them at the wake, there have been an awful lot of them. It was like I only had to look at someone else who was crying and it started me off. And then there was just the thought of people crying that made me cry. It makes you feel so utterly tired.

"I'm going home in a minute, Mum."

"OK honey, but are you sure you don't want to stay for some tea later?"

"No, I'm so tired to be honest but thanks all the same."

"Yes, we're tired too – aren't we John?"

My dad nods his head and turns back to the TV. He's got his slippers on already and I don't think it will be long before he's snoring.

"I wasn't going to cook anything actually..." She smirks at me. "I'm going to order a takeaway. Are you quite sure you won't...?"

"No, I need to get home, have a bath and an early night."

"OK, honey. I'll text you later... just to make sure you're all right." She glances at me with a worried look in her eyes.

"I'll be fine Mum. No need to text me. I might even be in bed, asleep."

"OK... are you coming over at the weekend?"

I shrug. "I might pop in. Clair has got Archie staying for the weekend so I may well come over, just so they can have some peace."

Mum grins at me. "Come over Saturday and we'll go into town for a coffee."

"I will." I grab my coat from the hallway and return to the living room to kiss my dad on the cheek. He's completely unaware that I've said goodbye to him because he's already sound asleep and grunting under his breath.

"Call me if you need a chat," says Mum, cupping my face in her hands. "Things will get easier, honey. Give it time."

"I know," I say, giving her a warm hug. "I know it will."

Once again, Clair has been brilliant. She made me another packed lunch for tomorrow, while I soaked away my sorrowful existence in the bath. She also cooked a gorgeous chilli, which we had with crusty bread, while watching the *Great British Bake Off*. It was a really nice, cosy ending to a dreadful day.

Now I'm lying in bed, watching the minutes of my digital alarm clock tick by. I can't sleep, yet I'm stupidly tired. My brain is whirring round and round with thoughts of today, the last couple of weeks, my life as a whole and what the future might hold. I'm 28 years old and apart from a flat of my own, a stable job and a reasonably nice car, what do I have? Will I ever be like my mum and dad? A house, a marriage, a family? Can I ever be really happy or fall in love again? I doubt it. Jett left a legacy of pure love, kindness, compassion and an understanding of the depth of a beautiful human soul. And he managed to do all of that in just under a week.

I turn over, on to my side and peer into the darkness. I need to sleep.

***

Archie has come to stay for the weekend. He's tall, lean and smartly dressed as he enters the living room to meet me. He's wearing black jeans and a crisp white polo neck t-shirt. His brown hair is neatly cropped around his rather handsome face. He's very nice. Different to what I'd expected. I don't really know what I was expecting but he surpasses any preconceptions I did have about him. For some reason, I wasn't expecting him to be so good-looking either. I don't know why but I just wasn't. He smiles at me and extends a hand.

"Nice to meet you Susie." He takes my hand and shakes it gently. "I've heard a lot about you."

This all feels very formal and Clair is standing behind him with a grimacing grin on her face.

"I hope it's all good," I reply. "If there's anything bad, don't believe her."

Archie shakes his head and laughs. "No, nothing bad. Thanks for letting me stay here this weekend."

"Oh, it's no problem – you're very welcome."

"Right," says Clair, stepping forward. "Shall we get your stuff put away in the bedroom.

Archie turns to her. "Sure and then we'll..."

"Oh, I haven't told Suse that yet."

I look at her expectantly. "What's that?" I ask.

"Archie has offered to take us for a get-to-know-you meal, wherever you choose."

"Oh – really? That sounds nice. Thank you."

Clair grins at me. "You could come out with us tomorrow if you'd like, as well. I'm taking Arch around the town – you know, show him where I live and all that kind of stuff."

"No, that's fine. You two go off and have a nice day together – you don't want me tagging along with you, and besides, I promised Mum I'd go for a coffee with her, in town. You never know, we might even bump into each other anyway."

"OK," says Clair, looking a little calmer than she had a minute ago. "I didn't want you sitting in the flat, alone, while we're out gallivanting around town."

"I'll be fine, honestly. You enjoy yourselves over the weekend and don't worry about me." I smile at Clair and Archie. "Now, I suppose I'd better get changed if we're going out for a meal. To be honest, I really quite fancy that – thank you."

Do you know who he reminds me of? He's funny, he's highly entertaining and he has all those endearing qualities that you don't always find in men – well, at least the types of men who have come into my life in the past (excluding Jett). He's considerate, caring and also, he's extremely generous. He wouldn't let Clair or I buy a single drink – and trust me, we've had a fair few. Yes, he reminds me of Jett, which saddens me a great deal because I can picture the four of us going out together and having a great time.

Clair is completely taken by him – it's quite amusing to watch her. I don't think she has taken her eyes off him once during the evening and I swear her pupils have turned into heart shapes. It's like she should have little hearts and butterflies and tiny cupids and sparkly bits floating around her head. I can also see that Archie has a strong affection for her. He's a very tactile person with her and spent most of the evening with his arm round her back, rubbing or stroking her shoulder. Yet, neither of them made me feel like I was the gooseberry. We've had a fun evening of conversation and lots of laughter and it's just what I needed.

*** 23 ***

The weekend has flown by and I got through it with very little self-pitying or sorrowful moments. I went for a coffee with Mum yesterday and we did a bit of shopping. I was incredibly surprised to see Mum buying Dad a new apron from the market – she always moans about all his aprons. She said she hadn't seen one like it before and that Dad would love it. She also said that it would be the last one he ever got from her. OK, so it was a funny apron but I'm sure Dad has got similar ones. It's a picture of a naked, muscle-bound man, crossing his hands in front of him, obscuring his lower regions and the text across the chest says, 'Women want me – men hate me – cows fear me'.

As for me, well, I went all-out and bought a couple of polo t-shirts and two pairs of jogging bottoms. I'll be wearing them to work soon as we will be starting the weekly trek, with 30 children, to Hightown Secondary, for their swimming sessions. Great joy.

Archie cooked an amazing chicken curry for us all last night and we had two bottles of wine to wash it down. Again, I didn't feel like the odd one out and we all had a fun evening watching the TV and chatting about stupid things.

Today has been a quieter day as Clair and Archie went out earlier, on a visit to the local museum. They asked me if I wanted to go with them but I declined their kind offer, saying that they should spend some time on their own, especially as Archie had to travel back home this afternoon.

"So, what do you think of him?" asks Clair as she enters the living room, beaming from ear to ear, having just spent about 35 minutes saying goodbye to Archie, at the front door.

"He's really nice – I like him. You're so suited to each other."

Clair swoons as she sits down next to me. "He said he loved me last night, when we went to bed."

Where are those cupids and the sparkly bits? They should be swimming around her head. I suppose I must have been like that when I was with Jett.

"Wow – serious stuff then?"

She nods her head while her eyes are gazing upwards to the ceiling.

"Yeah..."

"I'm really happy for you," I say. "He's a very nice man."

"Yeah... we just need to find you a very nice man now..." She peers at me and I detect just a hint of pity in her eyes.

"Oh no... I would much rather be on my own now, thanks."

"But you can't be on your own, Suse."

"Yes I can... I'm going to concentrate on my new job, decorate some more of the flat and..."

"And what?"

"Well... I don't know, but I'll find things to do."

"As long as you're happy, that's all that matters." She leans over and gives me a squeeze. "I want you to be as happy as I am."

"I will be – give me time."

***

We're going to be taking them swimming on Thursdays – it's all been sorted out. So, I'm going to be praying that it doesn't rain ever again, on a Thursday. It is only a 15-minute walk to Hightown, from our school, but when you've got 30 children to chivvy along, that 15 minutes can feel like an hour.

It's been a pretty quiet week, both at school and at home. Clair has floated around the flat each evening with a permanent grin etched on her face. At precisely nine o'clock, every night, she hurries into her bedroom and takes a call from Archie. Then, about an hour later, she comes back out of her bedroom with an even wider grin on her face. He phones her religiously, same time, every night. It's so sweet really. By now, I'm thinking she should have a whole crowd of cupids floating around her head, along with several butterflies and of course, the sparkly bits, just to add flare.

I go to my bedroom to try on the new polo shirts and tracksuit bottoms, which I bought last weekend. I'll be wearing them tomorrow for the children's first swimming session. It'll be pretty boring for me, I imagine, as I will be looking after part of the class while the others are in the pool. Mrs Pearson will be on poolside, with the instructor and I have a terrible feeling that she will be donning a swimming costume, which will be a sight to see.

Apparently, there's a nice room, with large windows, overlooking the pool, where we will be able to sit and watch the other swimmers. The children also have a workbook to do while they're waiting to go in or once they've been in, so I'm hoping it will keep them amused and most importantly, quiet. I'll also be on toilet duty and chivvying the children along in the changing rooms. Such joy.

My new clothes fit – I look quite sporty actually. So, I'm all kitted-out for the expedition tomorrow. I'm a little nervous as it's all new to me but I'm sure I'll get through it. At least I don't have to don a costume and get in the pool with Mrs Pearson. That would be totally horrendous.

According to Mrs Pearson, Jade Smith will be coming along with us next week because Mrs Pearson *really* needs me to help out *in* the pool as we have a lot more non-swimmers than first expected...

What? I'm sure my face must look utterly horrified because she just asked me if I could assist *in* the water.

"But... I'm not qualified..." I mutter, absolutely mortified by Mrs Pearson's request.

The swimming instructor, whose name is, Steve – I know because he's wearing a name badge – smiles at me. "You'd only be in the shallow end, helping to organise the children and give them the kickboards and the swim-noodles, while myself and Mrs Pearson instruct the others."

I hesitate before asking, in a pathetically weak voice, "Could I... could I not stay on the side of the pool?"

"I need you in there really, Miss...?"

"Satchel," I say as my heart plummets. "Miss Satchel."

"The children are messing around while they're waiting, so I could do with you being in there with them. So... you can start from next week, yes?"

How can I say, no? Although it's not in my contract to wear a swimming costume and get in the pool...

"It will really help us to get the children swimming," says Mrs Pearson, eyeing me expectantly. "But if you really don't want..."

Oh dear. If I refuse to do it, that won't look good for my career, will it? "No, it's OK – I'll do it." I sigh.

Oh no, did I really just say that? Now I have got to buy a swimming costume.

Then it suddenly dawns on me and I fill with even more dread – I'm going to get wet. My hair is going to get wet. I'm going to have wet hair and I do not see there being any time to wash, blow-dry, straighten and style my hair after each session. I'm going to be a chlorine-infused-fuzz-ball.

What am I doing?

Oh God – I have got to get IN the pool next week!!! Yes, IN!! Do you have a swimming costume I can borrow?

That will be great, honey. Think of the experience you'll be getting. Yes, I've got a nice navy-blue one that would be very apt for school.

But my hair will look awful if I don't blow-dry it. I'm dreading it, Mum.

I've got an old swim cap somewhere – you could borrow that too x

I'm mortified, Mum. I'll come round at the weekend and try the costume on... not sure about the cap though as no one has seen my scar at work. Don't want all the questions – especially from nosey kids x

OK honey, see you at the weekend. Love you xx

Love you too and thanks, Mum xx

***

Clair practically skipped out of the flat last night, swinging her weekend bag as she went. As for me, I spent the evening watching TV and worrying about the week ahead. I don't know why I've got myself in such a state over getting into a warm pool of water and supervising about eight children at any one time – *and* getting paid to do it. I'm sure anyone else would jump at the chance. I'm guessing a lot of my colleagues would say that it beats classroom lessons. Hmm... I think I'll have to be the judge of that.

I'm off to Mum's this morning, firstly, to try on her swimming costume and secondly, just to have some company. I said it wouldn't happen and I'd keep myself busy but... I actually feel quite lonely today.

"Morning honey," says Mum, in a chirpy voice, as I walk through the front door. "Are you OK?"

"Yes, fine – why do you ask?"

"Oh, just checking, you know... what with everything."

"I'm OK, really I am. As for the swimming, well, I'll just have to wait and see how it goes."

Mum peers at me thoughtfully, then changes the subject completely. "Sasha flew back to Spain yesterday."

"Oh, did she? I hope she'll be OK." It all floods back to me momentarily.

"Yes, so do we. She lost over half a stone in weight while she was here. Poor thing – there was nothing of her as it was."

"I know."

There's an awkward silence for a minute and then Mum rushes towards me and flings her arms round me. "Come here, honey – give me a hug," she says.

I don't know why, but my mum hugging me, brings an unexpected tear to my eye, which I blink away quickly.

"Come in the living room, honey. I've got a couple of old costumes for you to try on and the swim cap. Then I'll make us a nice cup of coffee."

I ended up staying at Mum's all day. I had some tea there as well. As for the costumes – well, it definitely had to be the navy-blue one. The other two were a little too revealing to wear in front of a bunch of children. The swim cap fitted too but I declined the offer of taking it as, when I put it on and tried to cover over the scar on my forehead, which is still very red and tender to touch, the tightness of the cap made my head hurt. I will have to try my best to keep my head well above the water and make sure that none of the children splash me because there's no way I'm removing any of my make-up either.

Now I'm back at home, on a Saturday evening and the loneliness that I had vowed I would avoid, has set in. The TV is on, in the background, but I'm not watching it. It's on more for the sound of people talking and the movement it creates. For some reason, this weekend is the first one that I have felt miserable and lonely and I hope that there won't be too many of these. Maybe it's to do with the fact that Sasha has flown home. Perhaps I feel that her departure was the final act in the story of Jett's life. Gone forever.

***

Thursday morning has come around far too quickly. I've been dreading it all week. And to make matters worse, I spoke to Jade the other day, only to find out that I'm the second option. Like I wasn't good enough to be asked first hand.

Jade had been approached first. Mrs Pearson had asked her if she would be prepared to get in the pool with the children. Her instant reply had been, 'No way'. Jade laughed at me when I told her I was going to be doing it, against my better judgement. She said that I should have refused – it's not in my contract. Too late for that now. I'm all kitted-out and ready to take the plunge... I think.

Ok, so it wasn't so bad in the water, to be honest. I slipped in, almost unnoticed and the children didn't take any notice of me anyway. They were too ecstatic about being in the water themselves.

Jade watched me from the poolside room and now and again, she waved to me or gave me a thumbs-up and a cheesy grin. I know that she was laughing at me really, but I don't mind.

I managed to get showered, dried off and dressed quite quickly, in the confines of one of the private cubicles and now I'm peering into a mirror forlornly. The young girls are still getting dressed around me but I take no notice as I look at my bedraggled hair and grimace. I know I said I wasn't going to get it wet but when you have got to be in water with some of the boys in our class, 'No splashing' does not come into the equation.

"Your hair looks nice, Miss Satchel," says one of our more confident girls from the class.

"Thank you," I reply, sarcastically. "It'll look even better when it's dry." I shoot a wry smile at her, through the mirror. "Come on, hurry up please girls. We'll be going back to school in 15 minutes."

I resign myself to the fact that I am going to look like a frizz-ball every Thursday and walk out of the changing rooms, carrying my sports bag. I take a sharp breath in and freeze on the spot.

"Hello – how are you?"

Oh God, it's Mr Bagshaw – Ryan Bagshaw. He's smiling at me as he draws nearer.

"Been swimming?"

I nod my head and grin at him pathetically.

"So, you're a duck now – not a turkey."

I laugh nervously as he stands in front of me. What's he doing here? He's wearing the same as me – a polo shirt, tracksuit bottoms and trainers. I suddenly remember that he's a PE teacher and we are in the sports department – duh.

"Did you have a good Christmas?"

"OK," I lie, "You?"

He nods his head. "Yeah – OK, I guess. My sister... you met her, didn't you?"

"Yes, she's very nice."

"She's moving to this school at Easter."

"Oh..."

I manage to meet Ryan's eye briefly but soon avert my gaze. He's just as handsome as I remember. I can only look at him for bouts of a millisecond before I feel the flush rising in my cheeks.

"Yes – I reckon she's only moving here so she can keep an eye on me." He lets out a little laugh.

"Oh, I see." I peer into the poolside room and can see Jade watching me and smiling. Then I turn back to Ryan and notice his gaze has lowered to my chest...

Oh my God, what a bloody cheek – how dare he be so obvious. How dare he be ogling my chest so fixedly. I peer at him affronted.

He looks up at me. "You err..." He looks more embarrassed than I do. "Your..." He waves a finger at my chest and looks down at it again.

I'm absolutely horrified at his sheer audacity.

"Sorry... your..." He points at me again. His eyes are darting around like he can't look at my chest again. Obviously, because he's been caught out, I'm thinking. What a pervert he is.

I peer down at myself, wondering why he keeps pointing to my breasts. I have got to say, I'm somewhat shocked at his sheer nerve...

Oh God – No. Oh no.

I clap my hand to my chest, desperately trying to conceal the...

"Thanks... err..." I splutter, gripping my t-shirt tightly around my chest area. "I'd... err... better... go back." I point a shaky finger behind me, indicating to the changing room from where I have just left.

Oh no – how did that happen without me noticing it?

"Sorry, err... goodbye," I mumble.

With that, I scarper back into the changing rooms, leaving Ryan standing there, looking perplexed.

Oh dear, how did I not notice it when I was getting dressed or when I was peering in the mirror? Probably because I was so busy worrying about my stupid hair.

The wire from my bra has worked its way right out and gone through my t-shirt. It must have been sticking out when I put my bra on. It's poking right out between two buttons of my new white polo shirt...

I can never ever look at Ryan again, let alone speak to him. There was me thinking that he was taking a quick peep at my chest, when, in reality, he was trying to help me by telling me the wire was protruding. How embarrassing. I must have looked an utter mess, what with my lank hair and underwear which would appear to be falling apart.

Once I've calmed down, I leave the cubicle and go back to the mirror above the sinks. All the girls have left the changing room now and I'm on my own, thankfully. I've removed the wire, for fear of it making another appearance this afternoon and some child reaching out and grabbing it, saying, 'What's this Miss Satchel?' That would be just as cringeworthy as Ryan seeing it.

I tut at my reflection, realising that I now look lop-sided. Apart from one boob looking higher up than the other, it also looks bigger. Great – it's going to be difficult to disguise this all afternoon, while wearing a brilliant white t-shirt which seems to accentuate the problem. I guess I will have to walk around with my arms folded or stay seated for the whole of the afternoon. And heaven help me if Sultry Sarah or Juicy Jane get wind of it – then I'd be doomed.

Bravely, I leave the changing rooms and go back to the poolside room. Ryan is nowhere to be seen and I sigh with relief. As I approach Jade, who is helping Mrs Pearson to get the children lined up, ready for our walk back, she leans over and whispers to me. "He fancies you."

"Hmm," I reply, still in shock from my most embarrassing moment ever.

"Why did you run off, back to the changing room, like that?"

As we start to move out of the sports department and head towards the school exit gates, I walk alongside Jade at the back of the line. "My bra..." I whisper. "The wire – it was poking right out of my t-shirt."

Jade bursts into laughter and the last four children in the line, turn and look at us puzzled.

"Carry on," I say to the curious little faces, peering at Miss Smith as she continues to giggle. "Keep up with the others please." The children run ahead and get back in the two by two line.

"Did Mr Bagshaw notice it?"

"Yes," I say in a hushed voice as we desperately try to keep up with the others.

For her age, Mrs Pearson has an energetic gait and us adults struggle to keep up with her, never mind the children with their half-size legs.

"He was the one who told me it was sticking out."

"Oh no." Jade covers her mouth with her hand and stares at me with laughter in her eyes. "How embarrassing."

I nod. "I know – I'll never be able to look at him again."

"That's a shame," says Jade, "because I reckon he really does fancy you."

"I doubt it – I told him I had a boyfriend, at the Christmas do."

"Oh, do you? I'm sorry – you should have said."

"It's OK, I don't have a boyfriend anymore."

"Oh, awkward... sorry."

"No need to be sorry," I say. "His leaving me was the best thing that could have happened... well, sort of."

I'm aware that I need to keep my voice low as we walk along the streets, back to our school. I would not want the children to hear anything I've got to say, and for some strange reason, I suddenly feel compelled to tell Jade everything about my Christmas.

*** 24 ***

Jade was really shocked by my sorrowful little story. She said that she had noticed the scar on my head but didn't like to ask about it. So maybe I should stop worrying about it, as I expect that other people have seen it too, and not said anything. I've been a bit overly-obsessed about hiding the scar but I guess it's because it has such a poignant memory attached to it. It is slightly comforting though, to know that I don't have to repeat my story to everyone and that they simply accept me with a scar and not comment on it. Maybe I've been avoiding talking to people at school unnecessarily and perhaps I over-think everything way too much.

Jade said that she knew I'd gone to a funeral last week too – blimey, news travels fast around school – but she assumed it might be family and again, didn't mention it. She was also gobsmacked by the Head's lack of empathy, when I told her about it, but in his defense, she said that he hadn't been told the whole story so he wouldn't have realised how important it was to me. Fair point, I suppose.

You know, after our little chat today, I kind of like Jade a lot, she's actually very nice. I'm sure that if I invited her round one evening for a girlie night, Clair would like her too. Maybe that's what I should do – have a girlie night. That might make me feel better about the mundane existence I've recently come to find myself in.

***

As I'm preparing to leave work tonight, I ponder over how quickly the time has gone by. It's six weeks since Jett's... well, you know what I mean. Time seems to go much quicker, when working in a school as the year is broken up into little sections, with breaks in between. It will soon be half-term and that means a week's holiday which I'm quite looking forward to. I plan to do some more decorating in the flat and spend more time with my parents, when they're free.

As for the swimming sessions, well, thankfully, they've finished. I've been fortunate enough not to bump into Ryan again, which I dreaded every week. Although, I did see Amber one week. She was overly friendly towards me, expressing her pleasure in seeing me again and how different I looked without a turkey tail. I'm really not sure if I like her or not. There's something about her, I just can't put my finger on. It's like she has an underlying deceitfulness but I can't quite fathom it out. Oh well, I don't know why I should worry as I will hardly ever see her anyway.

As for Kallum, well I haven't heard from him for weeks but, according to Clair, he is still with Tania. She went into the doctor's surgery where Clair works, to have her pregnancy confirmed by her doctor and guess who went along with her, dutifully holding her hand? Apparently, he completely blanked Clair, when he saw her, and even had the cheek to give her a scornful look. He's just a disgustingly rude and shallow man and I can only wish Tania good luck with him. I sound so mean and nasty but it does still hurt, you know.

I'm wandering along the school corridor, daydreaming, when I suddenly see Sarah and Jane – they are always together, always whispering and giggling and especially once all the children have left school. I'm trying desperately to like them and to chat to them whenever I can. I'm even putting a lot of effort into not calling them Sultry Sarah and Juicy Jane either – it's hardly fair, is it? Although, they have absolutely no idea what I call them behind their backs, thank goodness. Anyway, they are walking along the corridor, towards me, chattering away and giggling as usual. I suppose that they have got that Friday feeling, like I used to have.

If I'm completely honest with myself, I don't get that anymore. My alternate Fridays are filled with dread as the pending loneliness creeps in, the moment Clair leaves the flat. On the other Fridays, I'm not quite so bad but it's still kind of a lonely place to be when I see Clair and Archie together, having fun, laughing a lot and going out to all sorts of wonderful places over their weekends together.

"It's Miss Satchel," says Jane, eyeing me contemptuously as we meet in the corridor. "Got yourself a satchel yet?" She looks at Sarah and giggles. "I've just bought a new one – it's so nice. It's leather patchwork – you've seen it, haven't you?" She glances at Sarah again and grins.

"Yes – very lovely. Come on Jane, we've got to go," says Sarah, tugging at her arm. She turns and looks at me. "We're away for the weekend – a trip to London. Doing the theatre, nightlife, the lot, aren't we, Jane?"

Jane nods conceitedly. "Might even be able to pick up stuff for our costumes for Monday."

"Costumes?" Sarah peers at her puzzled.

"You're as bad as Miss Satchel here." Jane looks at me and grins before turning back to Sarah. "Dress up day? Have you forgotten?"

Sarah shakes her head frantically. "No, I haven't forgotten." She looks around at me. "Hope you've remembered this time."

I do not have a clue what they're talking about. How have I missed this again? It's easy I suppose, when I go around school with my head in the clouds half the time. The only time I'm actually on planet earth these days is when I'm teaching the children. The rest of the time, I seem to drift through the day with tunnel-vision, tunnel-sound and tunnel-sense and anything else that can be restricted to a tunnel. "I... err... what was it again? Could you remind me?"

Jane tuts and shakes her head at me desparingly. "Clown-day, remember? You've got to dress up as a clown, on Monday. You must have heard old Reynolds talking about it in assembly this week? Don't let him catch you out again." She grabs hold of Sarah's arm and pulls at her. "Come on – we've got to go or we'll miss our train. Have a nice weekend, Miss Satchel – bye."

Mum – help!! I've got to be a clown by Monday morning!

I've rushed home from work and texted Mum straight away – she'll know what to do. Although Clair is home this weekend, I really don't want to burden her with my dilemma. She'll be busy entertaining Archie or they'll be out most of the time. Their relationship is still very sweet and fresh.

A clown? Why?

Not just any clown, Mum. I have got to be the biggest, best clown in town.

That'll show them. I am going to town, on being a clown this time. I will not stick out in the assembly and be humiliated again by Mr Reynolds or anyone else for that matter. I'll show Sultry Sarah and Juicy Jane (yes, I know, I'm back to their pet-names) that I can play the game.

Don't think I've got anything clown-ish, honey

Would you come shopping with me tomorrow then? Pleaseee Mummy xx

Yes, of course I will. Why don't you try the fancy dress shop on East Street? You could hire one rather than buy one. It's not often you're going to want to wear a clown outfit in the future, honey.

Good idea – thanks Mum. See you tomorrow, love you lots xx

Love you too, honey xx

OK, I'm being spoilt now. I did mention it to Clair in the end, and she has offered to do my make-up on Monday morning, as long as I get up an hour earlier. I was a bit hesitant at first – do I really want to leave the flat with a clown face on Monday morning? But like Clair said, before she went out with Archie, all I'm going to do is get in the car, drive to work and go into school. I suppose she's right and I wouldn't be able to do it myself once I'm at work anyway. I'm so excited and I feel like I'm starting to become a real team-player at the school. Go me!

My mum, bless her, took me to lunch today. We went to a cute little café in the heart of the precinct and had hot sausage rolls, followed by fresh cream scones. Then we went to East Street and I managed to find the perfect clown outfit for Monday. As long as I return it by Wednesday, it will only cost £25 to hire – sorted. What a bargain.

I'm staying at Mum and Dad's tonight for two reasons: number one, Dad is cooking his famous risotto, while wearing his Italian Stallion apron and number two, Clair and Archie are having a quiet night in and I thought it would be nice for them if I wasn't around. Clair had said it was fine but she'd say that anyway. Whether it was or not.

The smell of Dad's cooking wafts up our noses as me and Mum sit down at the dining table.

"Umm... it's making me hungry," says Mum, patting her tummy and grinning at me.

"Me too."

"You are going to look fabulous on Monday – that outfit quite suits you, honey."

"Thanks Mum. So, you're saying I look good dressed as a clown," I tease.

"Yes, you do actually." She giggles. "Put it on for your dad, after tea – see what he thinks."

"OK," I say, resignedly. "I will."

If I'm honest, it does suit me. Maybe it's the bright, colourful material. I'm wearing a bright red, spotty jumpsuit, which has three huge, fluffy pom-pom style buttons down the front, a matching hat, a crazy, multi-coloured wig, a white neck ruffle, which is enormous, white gloves and a pair of plastic, blue clown-shoes, which are quite difficult to walk in. They would be impossible to drive in so I'll have to take them to school and put them on there. I'm sure that once Clair does my face (I bought some face paints from the fancy-dress shop) I will look like an amazing clown.

"What do you think then, Dad?" I say, opening the living room door in a 'ta-da' kind of way.

He looks at me aghast. "It's all a bit... big, isn't it?"

"Yes, big and bright. That's what clowns are like."

"I know that, love but..."

"But what?" I frown at him, feeling a little upset that he doesn't seem to approve.

"Isn't it a bit OTT?"

"No, not at all. It's school, Dad – the kids will love it. Everyone dresses up – even Mr Reynolds."

He nods nonchalantly. "Then it's a fine clown outfit. Well done."

"Thanks, Dad. I'll leave you in peace to watch your TV now. Great risotto – thanks again."

"You're welcome love, any time."

***

I'm sorry but I am so excited. Sooo excited. Clair has just finished painting my mouth. I'm sure no one will recognise me – I hardly know myself. I've got a typical Auguste-style, circus clown look. Clair has been so patient while applying the face paints, as I got an itchy nose, an itchy eye, an itchy chin, in fact, I got itchy everything. She did say to me at one point, 'I hope you're not allergic to face paints, Suse'.

How would I know? I don't think I've ever had my face painted before. Yes, it seems I've led quite a sheltered life. No, I think the itchiness was more to do with the fact that Clair kept tickling my face with the brush – I had to make a conscious effort not to keep giggling. But now it's done and I'm gazing in the mirror at someone else – I actually feel like someone else. I feel silly, I want to be silly. I'm a clown after all, aren't I?

"I'm going to have to shoot off now Suse – look at the time."

"Oh gosh," I say, looking up at the kitchen clock, "I didn't realise it was so late. I'd better get going too." I take one last look in the mirror and grin. I bet I'll be one of the best clowns at school today.

I pick up my size 20, blue shoes (I'm guessing they must be about a size 20), put my packed lunch in my school bag – which hasn't been lovingly-made by Clair today as she wouldn't have had time this morning, so I did them last night – and let out a long sigh. "Thank you so much, Clair. I don't know how I could have done this without you. You're really good at face-painting. Maybe you should take it up as a side-line."

She smirks at me. "No thanks – once is enough. I'm just relieved that you won't be dressing as a clown too often." She picks up her bag and lunchbox. "Have a fun day – I'll see you tonight."

"I'll try to – bye." I waddle through to the hall and collect my coat as Clair leaves the flat. Then I hang it back on its peg. How can I wear my coat over this lot? It won't fit. Resigning myself to the fact that I am just going to have to bear the cold, I open the front door, check no one is around, lock the door behind me and skitter across the pavement to my car.

I drive to work feeling quite amused by the looks I am getting by pedestrians and other drivers in the morning's heavy traffic. Most people smile at me but one or two do a double-take and frown. I peer at the clock in the car, willing the time to slow as I'm running very late for work. Mind you, I'd imagine that once people see me at school, they won't worry about the fact that I might be a little late. They'll be so bowled over by my efforts for clown day. Suddenly, I wonder what clown day is for – it hadn't occurred to me to ask. I wouldn't have asked Sarah or Jane anyway, fearing that they would laugh in my face for being so useless and not knowing what events go on at school.

I park in the school car park and notice the time – I'm over ten minutes late. The children have gone into school already and just a few parents are left on the playgrounds, huddled in groups and having a natter. I climb out of my car, awkwardly, and grab my super-size shoes and my bag. I'm excited but nervous as I begin to walk towards the school.

As I pass by the parents, I hear them giggle and whisper. I expect that they think I look pretty cool in my outfit – I know *I* do. As I walk towards the front office, I can see two of the office girls peering out of the window. They're frowning, like they're puzzled. I'd imagine they do not recognise me at all. I snigger to myself. I'm not sure I would recognise myself either – I look that good. I hold a gloved hand up and wave at them. One of the girls' beckons to someone else and then there's three of them peering out. I wave again as I get closer and watch in amusement, as I see Karen (I think that's her name – I haven't had many dealing with the office staff to date) shaking her head at the others.

Then I disappear from their view, as I enter the reception and punch in the code to open the inner door.

Karen comes out to the reception desk. "Hello, can I help you?" she says, in a formal tone.

"It's me," I say, leaning over the desk. "Miss Satchel."

Karen looks taken aback. "Miss Satchel?"

"Yes, I'm a bit late. I'd better dash – I need to get my shoes on." I hold up the blue shoes and grin proudly at her. I'm sure her look of amazement is due to the outfit... or it might even be my expertly-applied, made up face. She certainly didn't recognise me, which I find highly amusing.

Karen nods slowly, her face ashen with shock. Her mouth is ajar and I want to tell her to close it before she catches a fly but I don't know her well enough, so I just waddle off down the corridor. I need to get my shoes on quickly before I head off to the hall where everyone will be joining in the Monday morning singing assembly.

I've put the silly shoes on now and I really can't walk in them – it's worse than when I was at Mum's house, trying them out. But then, I suppose I wasn't exactly walking far, going from one side of Mum's living room to the other. I have now got to make a conscious effort to carefully place one foot in front of the other as I walk down the corridor towards the hall. OK, I know I'm a clown but I don't want to act like one, by tripping over and falling flat on my face, straight into the hall. What an entrance that would be.

My heart beats nervously as I hear Mr Reynolds talking loudly in the hall. He's saying something about a cross-country racing event – another event? Then, just as I open the wide, hall door, I hear Mr Reynolds say, 'Mr Bagshaw, from Hightown'...

Suddenly, I trip over my feet and stumble into the hall, having misjudged my footing upon hearing the name, Bagshaw. I practically land right on top of one of the teachers, sitting at the front of the hall. "Oops – sorry," I whisper, trying to regain my footing without giggling...

A unified gasp resonates around the hall, so loudly, it stuns me.

A cacophony of children's voices, giggling, laughing and even some screaming, fills my ears as I look up across the sea of faces...

They are all staring straight at me...

They are all wearing school uniform...

Not a clown in sight...

Teachers, around the edge of the hall, have their faces either buried in their hands while they're shuddering with laughter, or they're gawping at me incredulously...

At the front of the hall, Mr Reynolds is standing with his arms crossed in front of him, deep furrows distorting his brow...

Mr Bagshaw... Amber... Two other men, who I don't know, but I have seen before in the Hightown sports department – they are all staring at me fixedly with their mouths wide open. They're all wearing shorts, t-shirts and... running shoes...

'Cross-country racing event.' Mr Reynolds' words are going over in my mind, again and again. 'Cross-country racing event'.

I'm frozen to the spot as hundreds of faces stare and gape at me. I feel like I can't move – I daren't move for fear of tripping over my feet again. I can hardly breath as my mind tries to make sense of everything.

Ryan Bagshaw hasn't taken his eyes off me yet, his mouth is still ajar.

The realisation of it all hurts, like a knife has been plunged into my chest. My eyes fill as panic rises in me. Swiftly, I turn around, feeling so terribly sick. So mortified.

I kick off the stupid clown shoes, snatch them up and wrench the hall door open...

I run...

I cry...

I wish I could die...

*** 25 ***

As I head away, as fast as I can, bearing in mind the ridiculous outfit I'm wearing, I hear Mr Reynolds' loud voice ordering the children to calm down and to be silent. I gather speed and run straight past the office towards the toilets, sobbing as I go. Darting into the first cubicle, I slam the door behind me and sink down on to the toilet. Oh my God. I can't believe that has just happened. I'm heartbroken. I hate my job. I hate this school. I hate everyone in this school. I hate clowns.

I want my mum...

I whip the clown hat from my head and throw it on the floor. Then I remove the thousands of hairgrips from around the wig (OK, not thousands but it feels like thousands). I tuck them in the pocket of the jumpsuit and snatch the multi-coloured mop from my head. That goes on the floor too. I blow my nose, take a deep breath and try to stop the tears but they keep on falling. I can't face anyone ever again. Sarah and Jane have completely humiliated me. I should be angry but all I can feel is a deep, empty sorrow. How could they do this to me? How could they be so cruel? This has affected, not only me, but my mum and Clair too, once they find out. Mum and Clair gave their time for me – they helped me. What will *they* say? I have so many thoughts going around in my mind that it's hard to concentrate on any one thing...

I hear the main toilet door open and then the click, click of footsteps – high-heeled footsteps.

"Susie? Is that you in there?"

Oh God, it's Sarah. How can she...?

"Susie? It's Sarah... I... I don't know what to say."

I sniff and wipe toilet paper under my nose. Peering down at it, I see smears of white and red paint. I imagine my face looks a complete mess. I just want to go home now.

"I want to go home," I say, with a wobbly voice. "Can I go home?"

"Can I talk to you first?"

The main door opens again. More footsteps. "Susie – are you in here?" It's Jade's voice.

"Yes, she is," says Sarah. "I need to talk to her... then she can go home if she wants to."

"Go home?" quizzes Jade.

"Yes," Sarah replies, snappily "She *wants* to go home."

"Susie – are you OK in there?" Jade calls out. "Come out and talk to me – I know exactly what's happened here..."

"I didn't think she'd really..." Sarah has an unusual tone in her voice now. I haven't heard her speak like this before. She sounds nervous.

"Well, she has," says Jade in an equally unusual voice. "I can't believe you'd..."

"Hang on a minute..." says Sarah.

The main toilet door opens again and I hear a third set of footsteps.

I can hear whispers but I can't make out what they're saying.

"Mr Reynolds wants to see you, Susie. I think he's going to let you go home to get... changed." It's Jane – she's in here as well now.

"Can't she just go straight away?" Jade's voice speaks out.

"Mr Reynolds wants to see her," Jane reiterates. "Me and Sarah will go with her – you can go back to the hall now. We'll sort it out from here, thanks."

"I want to know that Susie is OK first. Susie?"

"I'm OK," I call out in a rather squeaky voice. "Please tell Mrs Pearson I'm going home and... I'm sorry."

"Don't worry about that, Jade. We'll sort everything out. You go back to the hall now." Sarah's voice suddenly sounds authoritative, which is in stark contrast to her timorous tone a few minutes ago.

"Susie – I'll catch up with you later. Oh, and Susie?" says Jade.

"Yes?"

"Accept my friend request on *facebook*. Then we can talk."

"OK," I say and listen to footsteps walking away towards the main door.

"Are you coming out now?" asks Jane.

"In a minute," I say, forcefully as the anger begins to build in me. "You can both go now. I'm sure you got what you wanted. I need to wash my face and then I might see Mr Reynolds."

"We're going with you," says Sarah. "We need to explain this to him as well."

"I don't want you to go with me. I'm quite capable of going on my own. Worried now, are you?" I say.

"No – we just need to tell him what a mix-up this has been." Sarah's voice has changed again. She's gone all wobbly.

"No mix-up," I say, adamantly. "You deliberately did this."

"Susie?" Jane has joined in again.

"What?"

"We were joking," she says, sternly.

"Yeah – we didn't think you were going to take us seriously. Who would?" Sarah is backing up her colleague now. "We thought you would check it out, at least – just to make sure."

"Well, I didn't... because I believed you. Especially after the 'red day'."

"We are really sorry Susie," says Jane. "We were as shocked as everyone else when we saw you – we had no idea that you would really do it and we'd completely forgotten about it to be honest with you."

"Yes," adds Sarah, "so you can imagine how shocked we were to see you looking like..."

"An idiot," I say. "Looking like a complete idiot."

"No... you don't look like an idiot, Susie. You look simply amazing actually. I didn't recognise you at first – I don't think anyone did."

I quite believe what Sarah is saying – I did look amazing – if only I'd been in the right environment.

I unlock the cubicle door and inch my way out with my head held down. I shoot a cursory glare at Sarah and Jane as I pass them, and note their worried expressions. "I'm cleaning this off," I say, pointing to my face, "then I'm going home."

"What about Mr Reynolds?" asks Jane, tensely.

"Tell him I'll talk to him tomorrow."

"But..." Sarah splutters.

"I don't care about your 'buts', I'm going home," I say, quite angrily.

"Come on," says Sarah, tugging at Jane's arm, "We'll talk to him now and Susie can go straight home."

I turn around, suddenly realising that I have got bare feet. "Could you do me one favour before you go? I think you owe me that at the least." I peer at their pretty faces. They both nod their heads, expectantly. "Could one of you get my bag and trainers from my classroom please."

"Yes, of course," says Sarah. "I suppose you can't drive home in those super-duper whoppers, can you?" She points to the blue shoes, still lying on the floor in the cubicle, alongside the hat, the wig and the gloves.

"No, I can't," I say with a deadpan expression on my messy face. I really don't find Sarah's pointless little comments amusing at all.

"You might get home quicker if you 'step on it' wearing those though." Jane giggles briefly and then straightens her face in an attempt to look serious.

I just know that, as soon as I'm out of earshot, they are going to laugh their heads off at this and so are most of the school, I would imagine. It angers me further. "Bye then – the shows over," I say, sarcastically and wave them away.

The pair of them turn on their heels and march out of the room, leaving me to stare at my messed-up face in the mirror. It's still hurting, the humiliation, I mean. I'm totally gutted that my efforts have been a farce. I know my mum and Clair will be really angry when I tell them. As for my dad, well, I won't mention it to him as I'm sure he would come down to the school and give Sarah and Jane a piece of his mind and that would really not be a good thing. When my dad blows – he really blows.

It takes me a good while to literally scrape the paint from my face. Without any cream to remove the remnants, I am having to use damp paper towels to continuously wipe at my face. My skin is at the point of being incredibly sore. I've got red blotches on my cheeks and my chin and I can still see a faint outline of the black, which Clair used to outline my Auguste features. I've had enough of the scrubbing though. I'm just going to walk straight out of school, without looking back, and go home.

Jane brought my bag and trainers along, a while ago, with a sheepish grin on her face, so I'm ready to make a quick exit now, even though I'm still wearing the stupid jumpsuit. I don't really have much choice but to wear it, as I only have underwear on underneath. Huh – maybe I should walk out in just that. That would give them all something else to snigger about, wouldn't it? I'm sorry but I can't help feeling bitter about this and the worst bit is... the whole of bloody Hightown Secondary will get to hear about it too, because Amber and Ryan saw the whole thing. I feel I'm doomed to a lifetime of ridicule from here on in. God help me.

"Miss Satchel – "

I freeze right by the exit door.

"Can I have a word with you, in my office please."

Oh no. I can't do it – not now. Instinctively, my hand reaches for the code panel and I punch in the number, not daring to breath.

"Miss Satchel – "

He's getting closer. I wrench at the door handle as I hear the click of it opening.

"Miss Satchel – "

Closer still.

I pretend not to hear him and dart out of the door, through the reception area and out of the main door. The chilly air hits my tender face and I know I've escaped. I'm free. Free to run to the car park, jump in my car and head for home as fast as I can.

"Did you get home early?" Clair looks me up and down with a puzzled stare. "I was expecting to come home to a clown."

I'm sitting at the kitchen table in my pyjamas, sipping a mug of hot chocolate. "Yes... I got home early and jumped straight in the bath."

"How did it go?" She drops her bag on the floor and proceeds to make a hot drink herself.

"Yeah..." I mumble, over the top of my mug, "...really good."

Why have I just said that? Why?

"Did you win a prize for being the best clown in school?"

I laugh off her comment. "No... but I *was* the best dressed clown I reckon."

Well, that's not a lie, is it? I was... because there weren't any others to compare myself against, so I was the best.

"Cool," she says and smiles warmly. "Glad you had a good day – hopefully you've now redeemed yourself after the 'red day'.

"Oh yes, I've certainly done that."

Just as Clair is about to sit at the table with me, my phone rings and vibrates across the table top. I peer at the caller and freeze.

Oh no, it's Baghurst School. Oh God, it could be Mr Reynolds. School's over now and I can just imagine Mr Reynolds sitting in his big, swanky swivel chair, waiting to talk to me on the phone. I shudder at the thought of it.

"Are you going to answer it then?" says Clair, eyeing me with questioning eyes.

"Yes, of course... yes..." I stall for time, hoping the phone will stop ringing. Then I pick my mobile up and discreetly end the call, just before I place the phone to my ear. "Hello? Oh, too late, I missed it," I say, rolling my eyes upwards and tutting. "They'll phone back if it's important."

"Who was it?"

I peer at my phone as if I'm searching the missed calls. "Oh – it was only Jade. I'll call her later... something to do with the plans for tomorrow, I expect."

Why am I not telling her the truth? I've now made things difficult for myself. Why am I covering it up? How stupid of me.

"What are you up to tomorrow? Don't tell me you're dressing up as a pantomime horse."

I laugh and shake my head. "No, we've got a... a cross-country race... or something like that."

"Oh, OK. Look, while I think about it, do you want me to drop your clown costume back to the shop tomorrow? I'm going into town at lunch time."

"Yes please, that would be really helpful – thanks Clair."

"Pack it up ready for me to take in the morning then."

I nod and smile gratefully. "Thank you for everything you've done Clair. I don't know what I'd do without you."

"No worries – what else are best friends for." She winks at me. "I'm going for a quick bath, then we could do some tea together, if you like."

"That sounds perfect, thank you."

And it is perfect. She is my best friend. I like nothing more than rustling up a bit of dinner together and sitting down to eat with her in the evenings. But particularly this evening as I've been feeling so low all afternoon. So why didn't I just tell her what happened? I think it's probably because she might see me as the stupid one for not having checked Sarah and Jane's story first, or for not being a little more aware of the goings-on at my place of work. Clair has said to me a few times, that I live on a different planet and more so since the passing of Jett. I think she is absolutely right. So, I really can't tell her how absolutely wrong I've been today.

Hi honey, how did your clown day go? Xxx

Oh, it was amazing, thanks Mum. I was the best one there! Xxx

Pleased to hear it, honey. Have a wonderful week xx

I will, thanks Mum. Love you xxx

Love you too, honey xx

Oh no, I hate lying to my mum. It makes me want to cry.

I'm sitting here, still in the kitchen, listening to the bath water running and worrying about who was calling me from school. Maybe I should call them back – get it out of the way.

OK, I'm going to do it. I need to be more pro-active and more aware. Susie Satchel – you can do this – call the school back now.

"Hello, is that Karen?"

"Yes, it is."

"Oh, hi, it's... Susie Satchel."

"Hello Susie, are you OK my love?"

"Yes – thanks. Someone from school called me about 20 minutes ago. I was just wondering who it was."

"I think that was Mr Reynolds – would you like me to put you through to his office?"

I gulp. "Err... yes. Thank you." I feel sick with nerves as I hear the phone click off, but I guess it could be worse. I could actually be sitting in Mr Reynolds' office waiting for him to grill me.

I hear the phone click again. "Putting you through now..." says Karen.

"Hello Susie, Mr Reynolds here. Thank you for getting back to us."

"Hello," I say in a tiny voice. "I... I'm sorry I had to leave..."

"I would like you to come to my office, first thing tomorrow. I have spoken to Miss Chambers and Miss Hodges and would like to speak to you too."

"Yes... of course... at lunchtime?"

"No, I want you here at eight fifteen please?"

"Err... yes. OK." Eight fifteen? Half an hour earlier than normal? What a cheek.

"That way, Miss Satchel, you won't miss any further teaching time."

"Yes – of course. I am sorry."

"Thank you," says Mr Reynolds in his usual dispassionate tone. "See you promptly, in the morning."

"O..." The line goes silent. He's put the phone down – just like that. Great, now I've got to go into work early tomorrow. Oh dear – am I in trouble? Why didn't I just tell Clair and my mum the truth?

*** 26 ***

"Ah, Miss Satchel – do come in."

Nervously, I walk into the room and sit down where Mr Reynolds' finger is pointing to.

"Now, it appears to me that you have a bit of an issue with the events we have going on in the school." He sits back in his lavish chair, eyeing me contemptuously while he taps a pen on his chin. "This surprises me somewhat – I have to say. I would like to think that you've been with us long enough now, to know the school, know the schedule of events and all that these opportunities have to offer our school."

I lower my head shamefully. "It's my fault, I know, I've been very lapse and I apologise."

"Lapse, Miss satchel? I would say it's a little more than a brief 'lapse' of concentration. Would you not agree?"

I peer up at him, sitting there all high and mighty on his throne. "I've… I've had a lot going on since…"

"We all have influences, good or bad, to deal with outside the workplace Miss Satchel."

"Yes, I understand that but…"

"Miss Satchel…"

"Yes?"

"You would do well to pay more attention to your work environment. We are a busy school with a lot of events and activities taking place on a regular basis. I need a workforce I can depend upon – do you understand?"

I nod my head agreeably but inside I'm thinking, what an absolute insensitive arsehole he is. "Yes," I say, forcing a smile.

He points a finger towards a pile of papers, lying on the coffee table in front of me. "There on the table…" he says, still waving his finger about, "…is the school's calendar for your inspection. Also, I have included the term-by-term, whole-school planning for your guidance. I would expect each and every member of my staff to know what is going on from one week to the next, in this school, Miss Satchel."

"Yes – of course. I'm sorry."

"Too late for 'sorry', Miss Satchel. I'm afraid that you have some work to do now to regain your credibility here."

What? Did I just hear him right? I meet his eye and feign sincerity as I nod at him. "Yes, of course."

"As a part of our team, Miss Satchel, I would expect you to participate in the school's rich environment of both indoor and outdoor activities and events in a dignified, well-informed manner. I hope you won't be repeating the tomfoolery of yesterday, again."

Tomfoolery? Tom-frigging-foolery? What an absolute arsehole he is. I actually hate Mr Reynolds. I hate him, I hate him. I want to cry. I will not cry. Not in front of him anyway. "No, I can promise you I will not. It will never happen again."

He gives one single nod of his sovereign head and shoos me out of his office.

I head straight to the toilets. It's time to start work but I don't care. I'm an emotional mess again, I just can't help it. I feel just as humiliated as I did yesterday, but in a different kind of way. Tomfoolery. Credibility. Who does he think he is? OK, he's the Head, I know, but still, how dare he be such a cruel, degrading man. Does he not understand how Sarah and Jane tricked me? Does he even know that? I'm wondering what exactly, those two scheming bitches said to him yesterday. I've got to accept responsibility for this and not try to pass the blame on to others. I will never listen to Sarah and Jane again. I will rise above this. I will.

A fail, and that's before I've even started. Luckily, Mrs Pearson was very sympathetic to my needs, eventually, but I didn't manage to get into class until 9-20am, which was rather late, as she stated at first.

I explained the situation to her and tried to gain some credibility in the classroom but I spent most of the morning in a dizzy day-mare (a nightmare daydream, in my eyes) which did my integrity no good whatsoever. Hence, I see today as nothing more than a complete fail, although, Mrs Pearson came round to my way of thinking in the end and said it wasn't as bad as I was seeing it.

I briefly saw sultry bitch and juicy bitch (Yes, I can't even bring myself to say their real names anymore) at lunchtime and they couldn't apologise enough and constantly offered me help with keeping up with the school's events. They were a little patronising, to be honest, but I wouldn't expect anything less from them. I currently hate working at the school and feel like the odd one out. Throughout the whole day, I have been subjected to some odd looks, one snigger and several quizzical stares – I might as well have been a proboscis monkey and got my money's worth today really. Honestly, some people just don't have a life if all they can do is gawk at me all day. OK, maybe that's me as well (I don't have a life) but still, they shouldn't be so rude, staring at me all day.

***

It has got easier as the non-eventful week has unfolded and finally come to an end. Note the word, 'non-eventful' because I have checked the school calendar religiously this week. Several people at school, spoke to me in great depth about the 'incident', as some of them described it. The overriding consensus was that Sarah and Jane were very cruel and their bullish behaviour would have been better suited to someone who wasn't quite so new to the school. Huh – I don't think they should be allowed to get away with their little games with anyone, however long they've worked there. Yet, it seems, they do get away with it. I'm sure it must be because they are so perfect in every other way conceivable. Bitches.

I've been quite amused during the week to see Sarah and Jane being so creepy towards me actually – like I give a damn. 'Good morning Miss Satchel', 'You look nice today, Miss Satchel', 'Have a lovely evening Susie', 'Have a great weekend, Susie', 'Blah, blah, blah'. What a load of old twaddle, if you ask me.

It's Friday night and I'm sitting in the living room with my feet up on the coffee table, staring at the TV mindlessly.

"What are you doing this weekend?" Clair is packing her rucksack, ready for her fortnightly jaunt to Devon. "Going to your Mum's?"

"Haven't planned to, why?"

"Oh, I just wondered..." she pauses and peers at me. "You haven't been yourself this week – and before you say anything, I know, I've noticed, so don't try to deny it. You're a bit down aren't you?"

"No... I'm OK. Really I am."

"You've been quiet and you've had early nights all week. I know you Suse, you're not right. You're feeling down, aren't you?"

"Well... maybe a little bit." I smile waveringly. "I'll be fine over the weekend. I might even go over to Mum's at some point."

"You do that," says Clair, turning back to her rucksack and checking through the items in it. "I don't want to find out you've been moping around the flat on your own, when I get back."

"I won't, I promise... or if I do... I'll have a paint brush in my hand – would that be OK?"

She nods and smiles at me. "I'm just worried about you, that's all."

"I know, but you don't need to be. I've just had a bit of a rubbish week at work, that's all."

"Oh?" She stops again.

"Oh, it was nothing really."

"I thought you had a fab day on Monday – what with the clown thing. So, what's gone wrong since?"

"Oh... nothing really... it's just been one of those tricky weeks... you know, kids and stuff." God, I hate lying to Clair. I'm so stupid sometimes and create more of a problem than there really needs to be. Damn.

"Well, as long as you're all right, I'm happy to leave... and Suse?"

"Yes?" I look at her expectantly. Is she going to ask, 'Do you want to come with me?'. Is she going to say that she's changed her mind and she's staying at home this weekend?

"Don't sit around doing nothing. Go and see your mum. Paint. Get drunk. Anything but nothing – OK?"

"OK, I promise – go on then, off you go. And say hello to Archie for me."

She grins at the mention of Archie's name. Shoving the last bits into her rucksack, she comes over to me and gives me a peck on the cheek and a big hug. "See you Sunday night."

Once again, I have a lonely, miserable weekend to look forward to. It seems even worse than the last few because it's pouring down outside and the weather reports are for much of the same, all weekend. My positive outlook has dwindled away recently and I really can't be bothered to do anything over the weekend. I should be getting excited as there is only one week left at school before the half-term break but I'm not in the slightest.

I flip open my laptop and turn it on. I still haven't accepted Jade's friend request and at this very moment, I need another friend...

Done. Curiously, I search through Jade's profile and then her friend list. She has a lot of friends from Hightown Secondary, including...

Gosh, what must he think of me? The first time he met me, I was dressed as a turkey. OK, fair enough, I did meet him and his sister in town after that, and they came back to mine for a coffee – which was very nice but, as of late, I've looked like a complete imbecile each time I've seen him.

What does he think of me? Why would it matter anyway? As I peer at his profile picture, I feel a little flutter in my chest. It does matter what he thinks of me, because I like him. And he liked me too – he must have done, as he asked me out twice. Unfortunately, I blew any chance with him by telling him I already had a boyfriend – how life sucks sometimes.

Hi Jade, thanks for adding me...

I don't know what else to write. I can't just leave it at that as it sounds a bit... well, abrupt, I'm thinking.

Thanks for giving me support when I've needed it. To be honest, I haven't had a great start to the new year at all and my stupidity and lack of foresight have got me into a couple of embarrassing situations. Thanks for being there for me.

I can't believe that I am now hovering the cursor over the 'add friend' button on Ryan's profile. I'm completely sober, what am I doing? I'm trembling and my mind is in a yes/no battle. Do I, or don't I? A picture of Jett flashes through my mind. It's the one of the two of us together on New Year's Eve. It's enough to make me move the cursor away from the button and right across the screen to the red cross. I close the laptop down, snap the lid shut and slump back on the sofa. Shit.

***

I was only going to apologise for my hurried escape the other week when my bra wire was sticking out of my t-shirt. That would have been an acceptable reason to contact him, wouldn't it? I'm on the half-term holidays and it's only day two. I'm bored out of my skull.

I went on *facebook* again while Clair and Archie were out on Saturday night – they are such a loved-up pair, I must tell you. It's quite sweet but also painful for me to see them so happy together. That sounds pretty selfish but there are two reasons why it's painful. The first is, I miss having a loving relationship – when I look back at how me and Kallum were, I realise that it had been a one-sided, loving relationship for quite a while. The only real love I think I've experienced, was... well, you know. My second reason is that I worry (and this is actually a very selfish reason) that Clair will move back to Devon, or leave the flat to go and live with Archie somewhere else. Yes, it's completely selfish. I can't help it.

Anyway, back to *facebook* and I keep being compelled to go to Ryan's profile page. I haven't yet, but I always linger over that blasted 'add friend' button. It's driving me insane. All I can see, when I think about adding him though, is the look on his face the day, Clown-Susie fell into the school hall. He looked horrified, embarrassed and dare I say it... ashamed. Surprisingly, I've heard nothing from Amber. I half expected her to message me, asking what on earth I was doing that day, but nothing. On the flip-side, I haven't messaged her either, even if it was just to try and redeem myself and my actions. On the upside, I did get a message back from Jade this morning – it only took her eight days to reply. I'm not complaining though.

It said: *No worries, it's understandable after what you've been through. What are you up to this week?*

So now I'm going to reply to her on messenger, that way I can avoid *facebook* altogether and its magical, magnetic powers which draw me to a particular profile page to gaze dreamily at the photo of a handsome man.

Absolutely nothing. Bored to be honest, my flatmate is working all week. Going to see my mum tomorrow, but that's it. You?

Ha, ha, me too. Bored I mean – not going to see your mum, lol. Do you want to go out clubbing Friday night with me and my mates?

Do I want to go out clubbing? Do I want to go out on Friday night? Is she insane? Of course, I do.

Sounds like fun, I'd love to, thanks.

Woohoo – I'm going to have a life after all. Go me! Susie Satchel bounces back.

*** 27 ***

OK, so Jade and her mates are all considered to be in their 'early twenties', whereas I would be labelled, 'late twenties'. There's a marked difference you know. Especially when most of the men, swarming around us, like flies around... Well, you know the saying, but anyway, these men are barely out of school. Bless them – they are all very young. Half of them look inexperienced in the art of chatting up girls and the other half don't know what to do once they have chatted a girl up.

Jade's friends are lovely actually, which is a relief because I was feeling very nervous earlier. I didn't want to go over the top tonight but I've ended up wearing a pair of black, shimmery skinny trousers, a white, halter-neck, wrap-around top, which does not leave much to the imagination, and a pair of black stilettos. I puffed my hair out with a bit of back-combing and I even rushed out at the last minute today, to get some false eyelashes. Yes, false eyelashes – I've never worn them before and I'm really not sure why I went out and bought them but I did. Don't get me wrong, they are not super long ones, so I don't look like I've got a pair of spiders sitting on my eyelids – they look quite natural actually. But when I looked in a mirror earlier, I realised that maybe my intention to, 'not go over the top tonight' has probably failed miserably.

So, we're in a bar called, The Stage, and it is heaving. I mean, really heaving. It took at least 20 minutes to get served at the bar and we all opted for triples in the end as the waiting time can only get worse, judging by the number of people pouring in through the doors. I feel a bit old as I watch the long-legged teenage girls coming in, with skirts up to their waists and breasts hanging out all over the place. Why they bothered wearing clothes, I really don't know. Now that does sound like a statement an older person would make.

"Hey – Susie."

I turn my head, startled by the loud mention of my name.

"You're miles away," shouts Jade.

I smile at her and her friends. "Sorry – what were you saying?"

"We're going upstairs – it'll be less crowded up there."

"OK – coming." I follow the girls up the wide, elegant staircase and we manage to find a free table and chairs.

"We'll have these and then go on to Jemma's," says Jade. "That OK with you?"

"Who's Jemma?"

The girls giggle around me.

"The new nightclub, Jemma's, we can all pole-dance there – have you not heard about it?"

"No, I haven't."

Gosh, I'm so out of touch. Did she just say pole-dance?

"Is it good?" I ask, nervously, trying to look totally unfazed by the mention of pole-dancing.

The girls nod their heads and grin cunningly.

"Fab – let's do it." I give them a determined thumbs-up and try to look super cool and hip. I need my drink. I need to get drunk. Pole-dancing? I've never pole-danced in my life...

I can do this. I will do this...

OK, maybe I won't be able to do this. I haven't tried yet but just watching makes me feel dizzy and sick.

We ended up having two rounds of triples before we came here – big mistake on my part. I'm sure that Jade and her friends are hardened drinkers by the speed that they gulped down their drinks. I managed to keep up with them but since walking here, to Jemma's, I've become incredibly drunk.

There are poles everywhere and warning signs too. The poles are raised up on low stages and there are thin, soft mats underneath them. It appears to me that the consensus here is that the women swing around the poles, in the most attractive way possible, while the men gather around and watch. Hmm – not really my thing but I'm being young, cool and hip remember? I have got to go along with it.

We've just found a free pole and Jade and her friends are so excited to get on it. I am amazed as I watch each one of them swing around it, in turn.

"Your go," says Jade, pushing me towards the pole. "Go on, try it. Take your shoes off."

So – all they did was grab the pole and swing themselves around. How hard can it be? "OK," I say, brightly, feigning a cool sober composure. "Here goes..."

I lunge at the pole, grab hold of it with both hands and swing myself round....

I did it. I actually did it. I'm a pole-dancer.

Returning to the group, I watch as Jade and her friends have another go.

Oh dear me. This time they are jumping on to the pole, in a most elegant way of course, wrapping their legs around it and sliding down slowly.

OK, I can do that too.

Jade and her friend, Terry, have gone off to the bar to get triples for everyone. I'm left with the other three girls and we are really getting into this pole-dancing stuff, so much so that we have been awarded our own little group of onlookers. It's quite nerve-wracking now that we have an audience – even if it is only three men, but that's not the point.

The youngest looking of the girls, steps up to the pole, leaps on to it and winds her slender legs around it. Then she leans her body out and releases one hand. The other girls clap before she twists her body around and ends up hanging upside down. Oh God, that's not quite the same as swinging round the pole. But I should have a go, shouldn't I?

There was me, thinking that the younger girl had done some amazing acrobats on the pole – until I watched the other two. They are professionals – they must be. My heart is racing – our audience is waiting expectantly. Oh no, how can I do anything even half as good as they did?

I pace up and down the stage, my heart beating so rapidly, I think I might die. I can do this. I can do this.

Without warning, I find my legs moving rapidly towards the pole. I leap up and grab it. Twisting round, I wrap my legs around the pole. I let go with one hand and slide down to the bottom. OK, it wasn't the greatest manoeuvre ever but I did it and the three men smiled at me. Yes – I'm nearly an accomplished pole-dancer – who would have thought it?

We've been swinging and sliding for at least an hour. The three men have even had a go. Everyone is merry and drunk and there is a nice, friendly and fun atmosphere. Jade is getting on particularly well with one of the men and the two younger girls are chatting with the other two male onlookers. It just leaves me and Terry to do our thing on the pole.

Terry is very experienced and she is giving me some instruction, which is so cool. I've learnt a few moves already but I had to roll my trousers up as far as I could, to be able to grip the pole comfortably. I'm incredibly drunk and have no inhibitions left, whatsoever. I'm cool and hip – I rock.

I'm going to do the pike spin now. I'll be sliding down the pole, with two hands and my legs will be stretched out in front of me at 90 degrees. I'm aching a bit after several goes at the less demanding moves, but I have got to attempt this final manoeuvre, then I really will be accomplished. It all looks so elegant and quite sexy too.

I grip the pole as high as possible with one hand, start walking around it and then grab a hold with my other hand, lifting myself off the floor. I pull my legs up, in front of me and slowly slide down the pole, twirling as I go.

I did it. I actually did it. Everyone claps and whistles at me. I'm a pole-dancing queen. I've got to have one more go before I drink the rest of my third triple, but this time, I'm going higher. I'll have to do a little run and jump-up to reach higher but I'm feeling ultra-confident. After all, I'm a professional pole-dancer now.

I step away from the pole, bracing myself for the burst of exertion I'll need to get up higher. Several more men are approaching but I don't look at them – it might make me nervous and I don't want to look like a novice, now that I've put so much hard work into this. I take a deep breath and peer up at the pole ahead of me. OK, Susie Satchel – you've done it once, you can do it again. It's just a little higher...

I take a short run up to the pole...

"Well, well – look who it is, Miss Satchel..."

My heart skips a beat but I reach out to grab the pole as high as I can. I'm searching for the owner of the voice as I go...

I shoot straight past the pole, missing it by millimetres. With my arms flailing and my legs following, I glide through the air on a rapid descent, past the top of the stage and down to the floor below. I hear a discordant mixture of gasps, exclamations and shrieks...

Thud.

Amazingly, I'm OK. I've landed on my front with my chin inches away from the floor – that was so lucky. A curtain of legs and feet surround me and I try to lift myself up, before realising that someone else is helping me. As I stagger on to my feet, I look around for the voice. It was the voice that threw me off track. If it hadn't been for that voice I would have...

"Oh dear, Miss Satchel."

A man lifted me to my feet but it's not his voice I heard. I turn my head to the right in search of the familiar man's voice. Oh God – why? Not now. Not here. My ears did not deceive me...

I dust myself off and assure the onlookers that I really am OK. Jade and her friends have come rushing down from the stage in a desperate bid to rescue me. They are all flapping about, checking me over and questioning me, all at once.
"I'm fine," I call out. "Really I'm fine – the show's over."
"You're certainly a bag full of tricks, Miss Satchel."
Jade spins on her heels as soon as she hears the voice. She peers, incredulously, at the man standing just behind her.
"I hope *you* haven't tried anything like this, Miss Smith."
Jade shakes her head from side to side as if in slow-motion. "No... I..."
"What's so wrong with us doing this then?" I say, knowing full well that my gritty response is due to an alcohol-fueled mind.
"Nothing at all – I was purely suggesting that Miss Smith should not try and follow your failure of a routine. You're getting quite good at the 'failure' aspect of things, aren't you?"
Failure? How dare he? Who does he think he is? We're not at school now.
"It was your fault that I fell off anyway," I bite back.
Mr Reynolds is not going to inflict his high and mighty pompousness on me tonight. Not here. Not at the weekend. How dare he?
"You should accept responsibility for your own actions, Miss Satchel. Haven't I told you that before? And you should certainly not encourage my staff to do such irresponsible, dangerous things. I do not want the children's learning to be impaired by staff members with broken arms and legs. That's all I'm trying to say to you."
"That's all... Who do you...?"
Jade grabs me by the arm and drags me away. "Susie – shush – come on."
"Get off me, Jade. Who the hell does he think he is, talking to me like that?"
"Come and sit down Susie. You've had a lot to drink." She pushes me into a chair and I flop down.
"But..." I break off. Mr Reynolds is walking away, through the crowds, along with two other men. "Who the hell..."
"Susie – calm yourself down," says Jade. "He's gone now – just leave it. Please."

"But..."

"No 'buts', leave it."

I take a deep breath and blow it out slowly. "He can't talk to me like that – I'm not at school. How can he?"

"Because he's an arsehole." Jade pulls up a chair next to me and tentatively puts an arm round my shoulder. "And arseholes think they can."

"What's he doing in here anyway? He's got to be about a hundred years old. What's he doing in a place like this?" The adrenaline that was racing around my veins a moment ago, is subsiding and I'm beginning to feel quite exhausted and headachy.

"Divide that by two," says Jade, grinning at me. "He's 50 actually. I only know that because we all did a birthday party for him, last July. I don't know why he's hanging out in here though."

"It's disgusting," I say, screwing my nose up. "He's a dirty, old pervert."

"I'm sure he's not really," says Jade. "But I did hear that he split up with his wife of 30 years, over Christmas – maybe he's having a midlife crisis."

"Oh no," I say, suddenly feeling a bit overly hateful towards him. He's had a bad Christmas just like me. But why does he have to be such a pompous arse? Maybe his wife left him because of the way he is. I'm beginning to feel like a good Samaritan – I want to go and tell him exactly where he's going wrong and how he makes people feel. That way, he could make amends with his wife and have good relations with his staff. Yes, I should make that my mission in life – save Mr Reynolds from himself.

"Susie?"

"Yes?" I say, returning sharply from my epiphany.

"Are you OK? You went off into a daydream."

"Yes, sorry. I was just thinking... oh never mind. Let's have another drink, I'm so done with pole-dancing."

I'm going to do it. I'm going to do it right now...

I snuck in at 2.15am, having shared a taxi home with Jade and her friends... well, not all of them as one of them, Casey, went off with some fella and texted Jade to say she was making her own way home. Anyway, I've just made myself an extra strong coffee as I know that once I get in my bed, the room will start spinning. I hate that feeling and I'm hoping that staying up for another half an hour, to drink a strong coffee, will help. So now, I'm going to do it...

I will...

OK, I will... in just a minute.

I *am* going to do it...

Just bear with me because...
I will...

Oh dear me, I don't think I can.

If I do, I will wake up tomorrow and think, oh no, what have I done?

No, I won't. Why should I? It's not as if I'm asking him to marry me by requesting to be his friend, is it? I hover over the 'add friend' button, willing my finger to press the mouse as my heart beats fast. Just do it Susie Satchel – the worst thing that can happen is, he won't accept. Simple.

Before my muddled mind has had time to think it through further, my finger does an involuntary press. I freeze. Oh my God, I've just done it. There's no turning back. 'Friend request sent'.

Wait a minute – I can cancel the request.

Hang on a minute, aren't I being a bit childish about all of this? It's a friend request for goodness sake, that's all. I'll simply send an explanatory message, along with the request and then it will be fine.

Hello Ryan... or should I call you Mr Bagshaw? I hope you don't mind me adding you as a friend. I just wanted to apologise for my quick exit, that day at the pool. I was a bit embarrassed, to be honest. Oops – sorry. And what you must think of me after the clown day, which turned out to NOT be a clown day after all and was in fact, a cross-country day. Well, I can't imagine what you must think about that. My entrance wasn't exactly graceful and I had got it all completely wrong. Oops – sorry again. I don't mean to keep saying sorry but I just don't want you to think that I'm some sort of a weirdo. From a nursing-turkey to a wired-chest to a clumsy clown, I couldn't blame you if you didn't want to accept my friend request.

I take a sip of my coffee, smile at my laptop and continue, feverishly.

I'm a bit drunk tonight (well, a lot actually) as I've been out pole-dancing with friends. Mr Reynolds hates me even more now than he did before half-term because he was at the club tonight when I fell off the stage. He saw everything and he now thinks that I am a bad influence on the rest of his staff. He can go and get stuffed (by the cruelest means possible) as far as I'm concerned. I wanted to die actually, lol. Talking of dying – my boyfriend died at Christmas, well, not the one I was with when I spoke to you, I mean another one, ha ha. The one I was with when we had the Christmas do, left me because he got someone else pregnant. He walked out on me on Christmas day – can you believe it? Of all the days to dump someone, he chooses Christmas day! And my other boyfriend died on New Year's Eve. That sounds terrible because it sounds like I had two boyfriends in one week, ha ha. Well, I did really but it wasn't like it sounds, ha ha. I'm not a floozy or anything like that, ha ha.

I sip at the coffee again but it's not helping my swirly, fuzzy head. I'm struggling to concentrate on what I'm writing but it feels good to talk because I feel like I'm actually having a one-sided conversation with Ryan.

It changed the world for me when Jett (boyfriend no.2) died. I feel like it was all my fault but please don't think that I killed him because I didn't. However, I've come to realise how short life can be now and I need to make the most of it. Have you got a girlfriend yet? Not that I'm asking you out or anything like that but it's just nice to chat. I hope I'm not waffling on too much but then you have got a choice of whether to accept my request or not. Ha ha – you really must think I'm a weirdo. OK, maybe I am. Maybe I'm a lonely weirdo, ha ha. Sorry. I'm going now because I've written loads and I can't even see properly now because I'm too drunk, ha ha. Lonely, drunk weirdo, ha ha. Goodbye, hope to hear back from you but if you decide not to, then I totally understand. After all, who would really want to be acquainted with a weirdo-freaky-turkey-clown with metal tits who has two boyfriends in one week and one of them ends up dead? Ha ha ha. Kindest regards, Susie Satchel.

I'm actually laughing under my breath. I realise that it's early in the morning and I don't want to wake Clair and Archie (I'm not that drunk that I don't have a conscience) but I'm pretty amused by my little message and just a little bit too giggly. So much so that I accidentally press the enter button...

The little box marked, 'press enter to send' is ticked.

Oops – I've sent it. Oops, I'd better go to bed now, as I feel even more drunk since coming into the warm flat and drinking coffee. How can that be? Oops...

*** 28 ***

I open my eyes and squint at the clock. It's 1.20pm. I become aware of my thick head and aching body. Have I been in another car crash?

It starts to dawn on me. Pole-dancing. Drinking too much. Mr Reynolds. Oh no, Mr Reynolds. Friend request. Oh dear Lord – no. I sent a friend request. Oh dear.

I gasp and hold my breath, wracking my brain for some clarity. Did I send a message to Ryan? I remember writing something and giggling about it. What did I write? Hopefully, whatever it was, I didn't send it.

I drag myself from the bed and feel the bruised pain in my arms and legs. Oh no, did I actually send a message? It's slowly coming back to me...

"Afternoon."

As I walk into the kitchen, I see Archie and Clair sitting at the table, eating, what smells like, bacon sandwiches. It turns my stomach. I nod my head at them and wish I hadn't as my brain rattles around my skull.

"Did you have a good night?" asks Clair.

I raise a hand up and shake my head once. "No." Grabbing a glass of water, I slouch off to the living room. The smell of the bacon is too much and I desperately need to open my laptop.

I did send a friend request. Oh no. Oh my God – and a message. I sip at my water and read the message through. A flush of dread burns at my cheeks. Oh dear Lord – what have I written? I've got to delete it before he sees it.

'Actions' – 'Delete conversation'.

'Cancel request'.

Phew. That was close. If Ryan had seen that, I would have been mortified. How embarrassing would that have been? I've also cancelled the friend request.

I slump back in the chair and heave a huge sigh of relief. That was so close. I would have made myself look like a complete idiot. What was I thinking, for goodness sake? OK, I was totally pissed – I must have been to write such a stupid message.

"Are you OK, Suse?"

"Oh – you made me jump."

"What are you doing?" Clair is peering at me with that grown-up worried look.

"I... I was... really drunk last night."

"And...?"

"I sent a friend request to one of the teachers at Hightown... he's quite nice."

"What's wrong with that?"

"Nothing really but..." I break off and sip my water again. "I sent a really stupid message as well. One that would have made me look like a complete freak."

"Oh, Susie – really?"

"It's OK – I've deleted it now."

"Did you actually send it?"

"Yes – but it's gone now."

"Only from yours..." says Clair, gravely.

"What do you mean, only from mine?"

"The message will still be on his *facebook* messages."

I've just swallowed another mouthful of water but it goes down the wrong way and I begin to choke and retch. Clair rushes over and pats my back forcefully.

"Suse – are you OK?"

I nod as I begin to recover. "It will still be there?" I splutter.

"Yes, it will still be in his messages – I'm sure of it."

"No..." I put the glass of water down and bury my face in my hands. "He can't see it..."

Clair sits down next to me and puts an arm round me. "It can't be that bad, surely."

"It is," I cry. "Oh Clair – what have I done?"

"What did it say?"

"Oh my God – he can't see it. It's terrible."

Clair rubs my back and I feel the bruised pain in my shoulders. "It can't be that terrible, Suse."

"It is – it really is. I can't ever see him again. I can't ever go to that school again." I burst into uncontrollable tears. "I'm doomed. My life might as well be over. I'll have to leave school – I'll have to move away."

"Suse, come on, get a grip. It can't be that bad. You're over-reacting." She hugs me and pats at my arm. "Let me go and check with Archie about deleting it – I might be wrong."

A moment later she's back. I peer up at her through watery eyes, desperately hoping she was wrong.

"No, sorry Suse, it will still be in his messages."

"What am I going to do?"

Archie walks into the room with a look of awkwardness. "Are you friends with him on *facebook*?"

"No, I'm not – why?" I sit up straight, wondering if there is a glimmer of hope in all this despair.

"If you're not friends, the message should have gone straight to his, 'filtered messages' folder, which means he might not see it."

"But it will still be there?" I ask.

"Yes, I'm afraid so." Archie curves his mouth down sympathetically. "I don't think there's any way you can get it removed."

My tears have stopped now but I stare out of the window vacantly. What an idiot I've been. The message sounded absolutely awful. I can only hope to God that he never ever sees it.

"Do you want a bacon sandwich?" asks Clair, cutting through the silence. "Something to eat might make you feel a bit better."

I shake my head and screw my nose up. "No thanks – I couldn't face anything at the moment."

"OK... well, me and Arch are going to town today. Do you want to come with us? It might help take your mind off things."

Again, I shake my head. "No – I feel rubbish. You two should go on your own. I wouldn't be good company for anyone today. I think I might actually go back to bed."

***

So, I'm going to sneak into his house and find his phone or a laptop or a computer that might belong to him. He's bound to have the *facebook* app or it will be on a favourites bar and he'll probably be already logged in so I won't have to worry about retrieving those details. If I do have to retrieve his log-in details, I've got my password-decoding gadget which I can insert into any device, via a headphone jack.

I'm wearing a black balaclava, black trousers and a black, padded jacket. I can do this.

I've got a roll of *DUCK TAPE*, a small hammer and a bag of dog treats with me too. I'm going to sneak around the back of the house, find a small window (not too small – I need to be able to fit through it) and tape it up. Then, when I hit it with the hammer, apparently, it won't make too much noise. I saw it on TV once. And, if he's got a dog, I'll have my bag of treats ready to befriend the animal. It's so easy really. Once I'm in – I will be able to delete the message and he will never know any different. Simple.

As I approach the side gate of Ryan's house, I check for a lock. Luckily there isn't one – I'm going in. The gate creaks as I push it open. It's so dark down the side of the house that I have got to blink several times, until my vision adjusts to the caliginous alleyway. I really should have brought my night-vision goggles with me too – maybe I didn't think this through properly.

A figure is crouching at the end of the alley. A dog? No, it would have come forward, surely. A man or woman?

As I draw closer, I see it's a... dustbin. Phew, my heart is thumping in my chest...

But there's something else behind the dustbin...

The figure of a man...

Crouching awkwardly...

Piercing blue eyes glint at me through the darkness...

It's... it's Mr Reynolds...

I open my eyes with a start. I must have been dreaming but my heart is still racing. I'm in bed and dusk is already setting in at the window. I can't hear any noise in the flat so I'm guessing that Clair and Archie are still out. I've wasted a whole day in bed. With a despondent sigh, I drag myself out from under the duvet and pad through to the kitchen while re-running the dream through my mind. If only I could...

***

It doesn't matter which way I look at it – there is no way that I can get hold of Ryan's mobile, or his laptop (that's even if he has one – how would I know?). If only dreams could come true. If only I could really pull it off, by breaking into his house (I don't even know where he lives) and deleting the message before he has chance to read it. I know it's impossible, but by the time I had spent the rest of the weekend trying to think up ways to do it, I had become a neurotic sociopath by last night, I'm sure of it.

I'm back at school today and so far, things are running smoothly. I've even checked the school calendar and filled in some important dates in my diary. Look at me.

I'm trying to have a positive start to the second half-term and do my best in everything. I haven't seen Mr Reynolds yet, but then I didn't go into the morning assembly, as Mrs Pearson asked me to do some photocopying for her. I've decided to say nothing to him about last Friday night (I had been thinking of apologizing to him, but, why should I? I've done nothing wrong), and will simply smile and say good morning, should I bump into him.

I've decided that I'm going to keep my head down, get on with my job, do it well and go home each evening feeling happy with my achievements. That's how my life is going to be from now on. I've made mistakes, I can't change anything, so there's no point in wallowing in the past. I need to move on in my life. It's that simple.

Except... to be completely honest... I still wish I could delete that message from Ryan's account. Life would be perfect then. I can't even remember what it said exactly now, but I know it was horrendously awful. I remember that much.

I must keep focused on work, family and friends. I need to keep my mind on the positives and not descend into the negative traits of my life. Onwards and upwards, Susie Satchel. Onwards and upwards.

Incidentally, speaking of onwards and upwards, I forgot to mention that my mum and dad went to court on Friday with Doreen and Malcolm. I was supposed to go along with them but, when it came to it, I couldn't go through with it. I didn't want to be dragged back to that terrible night on New Year's Eve. I'm sure that it explains why I got so mindlessly drunk on Friday night and made a complete fool of myself, in more ways than one.

Anyway, the taxi driver was a witness, along with the woman who was outside the pub that night, and who kept trying to drag me back into the pub. So, luckily, I didn't have to be too involved in it all.

As for the man who had been driving the car, he was sentenced to the maximum of 14 years, for causing death by dangerous driving. According to my dad, he was very remorseful which kind of makes me feel a bit sorry for him. I mean, we are all capable of doing bad or silly things in the heat of the moment – particularly when drunk. And I can understand how anger can cause people to do terrible things which they could genuinely regret afterwards. Anyway, what's done is done. There's no turning the clock back now.

"Susie – hello. Are you OK after your..." Jade breaks off and smiles at me, "...fall?"

"A bit achy but getting better."

"I sent you a message on *facebook*, asking if you were OK."

"Oh, sorry. I hardly ever use it. Just now and again really," I say, nonchalantly, but secretly, I feel sick at the mention of any type of social media. It can be a very dangerous, destructive thing. Especially if you're pissed out of your brains.

"Have you seen Reynolds?"

"No – have you?"

Jade looks at me worriedly and shakes her head. "No – don't think I want to either."

"He can hardly say anything to us, can he? I mean, he was in the club too. What was he doing in a young person's club – and a pole-dancing club at that?"

She shrugs her shoulders at me. "I suppose you're right. It was a good night though, wasn't it? Well, apart from when..."

"Yes, it was. I got a bit too drunk though," I say.

Huh – that's an understatement.

"Do you fancy going again sometime?" Jade is standing with her hands behind her back, grinning at me, stiffly.

"Sure – why not. I might even be able to stay on the pole next time." I laugh.

"Cool." Her face relaxes. "We're hoping to go once a month – what do you think?"

"Sounds fine by me. Thanks."

"You're welcome. It's good to get out and have fun."

"Absolutely," I say. "You can never have enough fun."

This conversation has lifted my spirits. I've got friends. I've got a life to look forward to. I'm going to have fun.

I am most certainly going to lock my laptop away somewhere though, when I do go out. And I'll probably give the key to Clair.

*** 29 ***

I've been out twice now with Jade and Terry. The other three girls dropped out of the group, due to having new boyfriends. So, it seems that there are just three of us singletons left. You know, I do feel like a bit of a leftover sometimes, especially when I see Clair and Archie together or when me, Jade and Terry go out and they get most of the attention. It must be an age thing. I probably look more mature and more accustomed to the one-liners, than Jade and Terry do. I'm a seasoned 'has-been' but it really doesn't matter too much because I have a lot of fun when I go out.

Most importantly, I don't get quite so drunk that I'm creeping into Clair's bedroom (if she's home) or calling her mobile (if she's not home), begging for the key or for her to tell me where the key is, so I can unlock my laptop. And I really do get Clair to lock it away, each time I go out. When she's going away for the weekend, I have got to go without my laptop until Sunday mornings. She then texts me to tell me where the key to the cupboard is.

I've had little conversations with my other self where one side of me says that it would be a good idea to message Ryan again and apologise for the last one and the other side says, no way – stay clear of any sort of message to him. I've never heard anything back from the message so I'm assuming he hasn't seen it or like Archie said, he hasn't found it. I have got to admit that it is a bit like a cloak of doom hanging over me though and I do dread the day that he does find it.

We have been to Hightown school once, since I wrote that message. We had a swimming gala to attend but I kept a low profile for the whole day and avoided the corridors outside the poolside rooms. I was pretty nervous all day as I haven't seen him since the day I was a stupid clown. We are going back there at the end of May for a sports fun-day but again, I will keep low (look at me, knowing all about these events in advance). My diary is full with entries for this and that and even Sarah and Jane have been kind to me and checked that I know what is going on and when. I'm seriously considering removing their pet names as they've been so helpful...

Well, maybe not just yet. I don't trust them fully.

I've been feeling a bit selfishly sad today as Clair has got a week off, once she finishes work tonight.

OK, I know that I've had lots of time off, including two weeks for Easter, which was a couple of weeks ago, but I can't help working in a school. I didn't ask the government to give school holidays every six or seven weeks, did I? Oh, and while I think of it, there was supposed to be another work's do over Easter but everyone decided to go out in separate groups for a change, so me and Jade went clubbing on our own. I have got to admit that I was slightly relieved to not be going to another joint work do with Hightown school.

Anyway, getting back to Clair, I'm selfishly sad because she is going back to Devon, to stay with Archie for the whole week and I will miss her madly. Her and Archie are almost inseparable these days. I don't know how she manages to get through, from Monday morning to Friday night each week, without shedding a tear. He still calls her every evening at 9pm, on the dot, and they talk for hours. I often hear her giggling in her bedroom and sometimes she comes out of her room with a flushed face and she can't look at me without chuckling to herself. Honestly, they are so in love it's ridiculous.

I'm worried because, just recently, Clair has been saying that she's fed up with her job in the surgery and is thinking of getting work in a hospital.

Which one? That's what I want to know. Does she mean a Devon hospital? I haven't dared ask because I don't think I want to hear the answer.

"Have you packed everything?" I ask, trying to sound helpful.

"Think so." Clair has her hands on her hips and she's peering around her bedroom thoughtfully. "Yes, I have."

"Good," I say. "I hope you're going to have a lovely time... I'll miss you though."

"Ah, come here..." she says, holding her arms open.

I walk around her bed and hug her. She doesn't really know how much I am going to miss her. I know we only see each other for a couple of hours in the evenings and a whistle-stop hour in the mornings but the place won't be the same without her. A lonely person and a lonely flat are not a good combination.

"You should invite Jade round one evening. Get a pizza, watch a movie, something like we used to do," she says.

'Used to do', exactly. Don't get me wrong, I'm not bitter, in fact, I couldn't be happier for Clair but I do miss the old days.

"Yes, maybe I will. Don't worry about me though, I'll be fine. You concentrate on having a good time."

She smiles at me, picks up her suitcase and carries it through to the hallway. "Time for one quick coffee and then I'll be off."

"OK, I'll make it. Biscuits?"

***

<u>My list for the following week so I don't miss Clair too much.</u>
This weekend – cleaning and painting (Boring).
Monday night – pop in to see Mum and Dad (Yay).
Tuesday night – washing and ironing (Boring again, but needs must).
Wednesday night – Jade? Pizza? Movie (All three – hope so)?
Thursday night – *Poldark* – say no more (Best night of the week).
Friday night – Err… (Err, exactly!)

I've been keeping myself busy today, cleaning the flat, catching up with washing and ironing and writing a list to get me through next week. I sent a message to Jade, via *facebook*, to ask if she fancied coming round one evening next week (I can always shuffle my jobs around, during the week, if Wednesday is not good for her but Thursday is a no-no, unfortunately).

Tomorrow, I will be painting the bathroom. There's only one small area of untiled wall to do, so it won't take too long. I'm doing quite well with all the decorating, to date. Over the Easter holidays (when I wasn't being torturously bored), I painted the hallway, the kitchen walls and the back door. Go me. The flat is looking lovely and fresh and clean and I've decided that I will do something in my tiny garden as well – obviously not paint it.

I've been looking at the plants at school, in our outdoor-learning area and I keep asking our environmental teacher, Miss Hoskins, what they all are. I know, I know, it's amazing but I really do appear to be getting my life together even though there are still a lot of ups and downs… well, more downs than ups, to be honest. But I'm not bitter. I'm getting on with it – making the best out of any poor situation.

As I look back over my list, I try to think of something to do next Friday evening – we're not due for another clubbing session for a couple of weeks. I need something to do, which will take my mind off the pending weekend. I don't like the weekends too much, especially when Clair is in Devon. As I'm pondering over next Friday evening, my phone tinkles. I pick it up and see a message from my mum.

Hi honey, me and your dad have decided to have a weekend break next week – wondered if you'd like to come along with us? Love Mum xx

Wow! Really? Where to and yes, I'd love to. I was just sitting here wondering what on earth I was going to do next weekend as Clair is away on holiday. How weird. xx

We're only nipping down to Helen and Tim's holiday home. They had a spare weekend available and said if we could use it, it was ours. Weather is supposed to be nice xx

Ooh, yes please Mum. Thank you, I'd love to come. How much is it?

Don't worry about that honey, it will be our treat. We'd like to get away by 4pm, on Friday, if you can manage that? Xx

Yes, no problem. I'll do all my packing beforehand and come straight from work. Thanks Mum – you've saved me from a lonely weekend xx

I've told you lots of times, honey. If you're feeling lonely any time, come round to us xx

I know, thanks Mum. Love you both tons xxxx

Love you too xx

Well that's that sorted then. I don't need to worry about next Friday night now, or the weekend – woohoo. I'm going on a mini-holiday.

Helen and Tim are Mum's neighbours on the left side. They own a holiday-home in Hayling Island (near Portsmouth) and they often loan it out to friends, family and neighbours. I remember when I was young and we used to go there for a week or even two sometimes, almost every summer. Mum doesn't like flying so we never had any holidays abroad. But I didn't mind because what you've never had, you don't miss.

To date, I still have never been abroad and find it quite a curious thing to think of people on the other side of the world. For years and years – OK, until just a couple of years ago – I wondered if they breathed the same sort of air as we do, in other countries and if they had the same sky as us. I know, it's shameful, but I really have led quite a sheltered life.

When I was with Kallum we talked of going for a holiday abroad but somehow never quite got around to doing it. I even applied for my first passport on the promise of a short trip to Europe. But no, it never happened. Me and Clair have spoken about it in the past too but what with paying the bills for the flat and one thing or another, that never happened either. And I can see now that the only holidays Clair will be taking in the future, will be with Archie. Who can blame her?

Anyway, that's me sorted for the next week – I feel happy again.

***

Jade's only free evening this week was Friday, so I scrubbed that idea off my list and used the time to pack a small holdall for the weekend. I'm way too excited about going away for the weekend, to a caravan park, with my parents – what's that all about?

It will be the usual kind of caravan holiday that we've always had, except it will be squeezed into a shorter timeframe. Mum will cook us a huge, English breakfast each morning, then we'll go for a swim in one of the pools (Dad will stay at the caravan as he doesn't like to go swimming), then we'll wander around the holiday park and do whatever takes our fancy for the afternoon. To be honest, there is a lot to do, or see, or buy there.

After that, we'll go back to the caravan, where Dad will be sitting outside sunbathing, on a deckchair (obviously, he won't be doing that if it's raining). He'll then make a pretty good meal, considering the small hob and oven, which we'll eat *al fresco* (again, weather permitting).

Finally, we'll get dressed up and head over to the owner's club (Helen and Tim get special passes made for us) and drink copious amounts of alcohol.

Please don't get me wrong, things were slightly different when I was younger – I didn't drink copious amounts of alcohol and stagger home at 11pm when I was twelve. That's more of a recent thing for me.

***

Oh my goodness. So we're here, it's 8pm on Friday and we jumped straight into the getting dressed up bit and came to the club about 20 minutes ago. Oh my goodness indeed. Who has just walked into the owner's club, with an older man and woman (who I assume could be her parents) and a younger man? What the hell is *she* doing here?

It's Amber. Amber Nutbrown – the girl who dotes on Ryan Bagshaw and especially when she's pissed out of her brains. She's wearing a low-cut, summery dress which is covered in a ditsy print. It's just the kind of print I want for my bedroom wallpaper actually. Obviously, I won't tell her that though. Or should I?

What is she doing here? And who is that rather nice looking man with her?

I watch her and her group walk over to the bar and order drinks. She hasn't spotted me yet but I'm sure she will, in a minute. Then it hits me, oh dear. The last time she saw me, I fell into the school hall, just as a clown would do. And I *was* a clown – doing what clowns do best. Will she remember that? Of course she will – who could forget it?

As they are standing at the bar, I see the young man slip a hand round Amber's back and squeeze her. She looks at him and smiles. Then she kisses him on the nose. It's a kind of eureka moment for me – she obviously has a boyfriend now. I bet Ryan is relieved about that.

"I know her," I whisper to Mum. "She works at Hightown Secondary."

"Why don't you go and say hello, honey? Beats sitting here with your parents."

"I don't know, she's with other people."

"I'm sure you could just go over and say a quick hello."

"I might... later."

Oh no, they're coming over this way, laden with glasses and bottles on trays. There's a spare table behind us and I just know they are going to sit there.

"Hello," says Amber, as she approaches me. "You're..." she breaks off, looking thoughtful. "Susie – Susie Satchel. I thought I recognised you."

The group move around our table and put their trays on the table behind.

"Who would have thought I'd bump into you here..." she adds.

"Hello Amber – yes, small world, isn't it?"

She smirks at me and pulls a chair out, directly behind me. "Are you here on holiday?" She peers at my mum and dad.

"Just for the weekend. This is my mum and dad."

Mum gives a little wave of her fingers and Dad nods his head in acknowledgement.

"Hello," says Mum, "pleased to meet you."

Amber grins at her. "Your daughter is so funny. She made us laugh so much." She flicks a cursory glance at me and turns back to my mum.

"Oh?" says Mum. "Why is that?"

The rest of Amber's group have sat down at the table now and are talking amongst themselves.

"Rob – you remember me telling you, don't you?"

The young man turns around and the older couple peer across the table too.

Oh no – is she going to tell them about the clown?

"The turkey?" Amber reminds him. "My turkey-minder for the night?"

Mum giggles into her hand. "Oh yes, Susie did tell us about that. She can laugh about it now – can't you honey?"

Mum looks at me and I give her a fleeting, sarcastic smile.

The young man, called Rob, peers at me vacantly.

"Sorry, let me introduce you. This is my boyfriend, Rob." Amber puts a hand on his shoulder and gazes down at him. "And his mum and dad – Gracie and Reg."

I nod my head to them and smile politely, as do my mum and dad. God, I hope we're not going to spend the whole evening with them. Gracie seems OK – she has short, greying hair, a round, smiley face and she's wearing red-rimmed glasses, which are a bit garish against her pale skin, but she looks nice enough. As for Reg, well, he looks like he's just stepped off the *Godfather* movie set. He's a large, partially bald man with big rosy cheeks. He's wearing black trousers, a white shirt and a narrow black tie. There's an air of importance about him. I'd noticed the staff behind the bar earlier, regarding and responding to him like he was some sort of eminent personality. His manner is polite but his eyes are sharp and somewhat shifty.

"Pleased to meet you," says my mum, politely. "I think Susie was a little tricked into the turkey costume."

"Apparently so," says Amber.

It's suddenly occurs to me that Amber has a loud, booming voice and I'd quite like her to go and sit down with her cosy little boyfriend and his family and leave us alone. I do not want her to mention the clown.

"The clown was the best though..." she says with a giggle.

"Oh, did you like it?" Mum has perked up and is grinning at Amber. "She looked fabulous... although I never got to see any pictures of her once her face was made up." She turns back to meet my eye. "Did you ever take any photos, honey?"

Oh dear Lord. How have we got on to this subject? "No – no pictures."

"It was so funny when she fell into the hall..." Amber giggles.

I glare at her, attempting to send amnesia brainwaves to her so she'll suddenly forget.

"The best bit was the kid's faces – and you should have seen old Reynolds face, he was so shocked. You did a good job there, Susie."

Gracie, Reg and Rob are all staring at me now. I wonder if they know this story. Whether they do or don't – my parents *do not* know. I just couldn't bring myself to tell them at the time. They were so proud of me for participating in school events so wholeheartedly – how could I have told them?

"Oh?" says Mum. "Why were they so shocked?" She turns to look at me again. "You never mentioned that they were so shocked by your brilliant costume. Well done, honey."

Amber lets out a loud burst of laughter. "No, they were shocked because..." She's laughing more now. So much so that she bends over and holds on to her tummy. Luckily, she can't speak at the moment.

Both my mum and dad are staring at Amber puzzled. Then Rob and his parents begin to laugh too.

"Sorry – I don't know what we're laughing at but it's funny just to see Amber laughing like this," says Rob, apologetically.

I lower my forehead and rest it in the palm of my hands. Oh dear me.

"Haven't we got to be getting back now?" I say to Mum, eyeing her desperately.

"We've not been here long, honey. Why the rush?"

"No – don't go yet," says Amber, composing herself. "I haven't finished telling you..."

"Did you fall into the hall on purpose, honey? Was it part of your act?"

"No," I say, shaking my head. "It was an accident..."

"But you pulled it off because you were a funny clown?" Mum giggles to herself. "That's my girl."

I think Mum is trying to defend me but she's totally rubbish at it. But then again, she doesn't know the real, humiliating story, does she?

Yet...

Amber is still laughing and Gracie and Reg are shaking their heads with laughter as they watch Amber.

"Haven't you told your parents?" Amber suddenly stops laughing and looks at me, surprised.

"No – I have not," I reply, glaring at her.

"Oh... sorry. I thought they knew."

"Easy enough mistake to make," comes Reg's deep voice, out of the blue. "Easy enough..."

Mum and Dad turn around and peer at him.

"What happened, honey?" asks Mum, turning back to me. She's more than curious now.

"You've got to explain yourself now, Amber," says Rob. "You can't tell us half a story and keep that laugh of yours to yourself."

"Well, it's not for me to say... if Susie's parents don't know. Sorry Susie." I sneer at her.

"I'm sorry – how was I supposed to know? It's obviously upset you a lot – why don't you just chill out? It was a mistake. Everyone makes mistakes... some are just bigger than others." Amber holds her hands up in the air. "Sorry, sorry, sorry. We'll leave it at that, shall we?" She pulls her chair away and turns her back to us. "I'll say no more."

I glare at her back and watch as she leans right over her table and begins to whisper to her boyfriend's parents.

"I'm going back to the caravan – stay here and enjoy yourselves," I say, peering at Mum and Dad.

"But..." says Mum.

"I'm fine Mum – don't worry about me. I need an early night. I'll leave the door unlocked for you. I'll explain later..."

Mum peers at me worriedly but nods her head and mouths, 'OK, honey'. Dad winks at me and I know that he understands that I'm feeling awkward.

"Nice to meet you all and... see you around sometime, Amber," I call out, as I rise from my chair.

Amber and the others say an awkward goodbye to me and I walk out of the club with my head held as high as possible.

What a loud-mouth cow she is.

*** 30 ***

Mum and Dad came back less than an hour later, declaring that they too, needed an early night. Yet, we stayed up until the early hours as I filled in the gaps, in my defense. Amber had told them everything about my clown day, because she knew a lot more than I thought she knew.

Thanks to Sultry-Slapper-Sarah and Juicy-Jumped-Up-Jane (note their new names – and there was me thinking that I'd remove their pet names – well, never, I'm afraid), Amber had been given every minute detail of my school life and how terrible I was at keeping up with events and how I shouldn't really be working in a school if I was so slack and incompetent.

Apparently, Sarah and Jane are *sooo* worried about me and my job. Bless them. And Amber felt she needed to express all these concerns to my parents – bless her too.

Bitch.

Mum's a bit upset to be honest. She was shocked and embarrassed to hear all this news about her daughter, while being on a supposedly, chilled-out weekend break away. She was upset that I'd lied to her about the clown and she didn't appreciate Amber's comments and opinions, which were passed around both tables. And she definitely did not like Reg's hard words about how some people just aren't cut out for it. Of course, Mum and Dad then defended me by telling them what a tough time I'd been through – which included two boyfriends in one week. Mum said that Amber was very sympathetic and shocked by the story.

To be honest, I had to hold my tongue, as I don't want to upset my parents, but do they realise that the whole of Hightown will now know about my private life, and probably Baghurst too?

I suppose I can't blame Mum and Dad for trying to defend me and they were very upset that I hadn't told them the truth. Mum can't understand why I would feel so ashamed of making such a big mistake. She said I should have told them about it. After all, it sounded to Mum like it was an easy trap to fall into. And those two 'irresponsible teachers', as she put it, should have known better.

On the upside – I don't think I need to worry about the message I sent to Ryan now. I'm sure Amber will revel in telling him everything, even if she has got a new boyfriend.

***

The rest of our short break was relatively quiet, in comparison to the first night. Thankfully, we did not see Amber or her boyfriend, or his parents again and spent Saturday and Sunday having a chilled out, fun time while the sun shone brightly. It was really nice to be fair... considering.

I'm back at the flat now and I'm waiting for Clair to arrive home. I've missed her this week and cannot wait to see her. Mum and Dad were unanimous in their view that I should tell Clair about the clown episode as she would also be upset if she found out from someone else. I tried to argue the point by saying that she would never find out – how would she? But Mum is worried that she may accidentally say something one day and she doesn't want to be responsible for something like that. To be honest, I think she has a fair point there as she does come out with some very random things sometimes. So, I guess that I may have to tell Clair, especially as she was the one who put the most effort into my appearance on that day.

If you ask me though – I think this has all been blown out of proportion. I made a mistake of going to school as a clown for Pete's sake. It's not as if I went to school naked, is it? However, I'm now thinking that I might as well have done that because, by the time Amber has finished telling her tales, I'm sure the Chinese whispers will eventually end up that way.

I'm sitting in the living room when I hear the front door open. She's home, at last.

"How was your week?" I ask, as she walks through the door.

Clair is beaming and she has a nice little tan across the bridge of her nose and the tops of her cheekbones. "Oh, Suse – I've had an amazing week." She falls back into the sofa and peers at me with that dreamy look in her eyes. "Have you had a good week?"

"Yeah... not too bad really. I ended up going to Helen and Tim's caravan with Mum and Dad, this weekend. I've only been back an hour or so."

"Oh good, I'm so glad you had a nice weekend." Her beaming smile begins to falter.

"Are you OK?" I ask, noticing her slight preoccupation.

"Yes... yes. I'm fine. Shall we have a coffee?"

"I'll make it," I say, jumping up from the chair. "You get sorted out and unpacked and I'll do the coffee. I think we've even got some chocolate biscuits in the cupboard."

"Ooh goody, I'm a bit peckish. I'll be less than ten minutes." She gives me an unnatural grin before heading to her bedroom with her suitcase. "If you've been good – I might even have a little present for you," she calls out. "Only if you've been good though."

"I have. I promise... well, kind of... no, yes, I have been good. There is something I need to tell you though..."

"I'll be done in ten. Get those biscuits out. I've got something to tell you too," she shouts out from behind her bedroom door.

By the time I reach the kitchen, my heart has plummeted. I don't think I like the sound of Clair's last few words. She had an odd look on her face after the initial greeting too. She looked happy enough but I could see there was something underlying in the way her lips quivered in and out of a forced smile. I have a feeling I'm going to need more than coffee and chocolate biscuits here.

"Oh my God, Suse. I can't believe you never told me. Surely that's a form of bullying. Why didn't Sarah and Jane get in trouble?" Clair is sitting, cross-legged on the floor, directly in front of the tin of biscuits, which are on the coffee table. She's wearing her owl onesie, which is about three sizes too big but thankfully the extra material makes a nice little tray in her lap for all the biscuit crumbs she's been dropping. I know she's nervous because she's eaten about eight biscuits (not that I'm counting) and has enough crumbs to make another one.

"I have no idea what was said to them but they did go to Mr Reynolds' office."

She shakes her head disgustedly. "What a pair of bitches, and that Amber doesn't sound any better."

I shrug at her. "Well, what can I do? It's done as far as I'm concerned. I just want to move on."

"And so you should. If they've got nothing better to do than to discuss your life, then they haven't got lives of their own." She screws her face up and clenches her fists. "Ooh, it makes me angry. I want to... I want to..."

"Smack them one?"

"Yes – exactly that."

"Well I... or we, can't do that, so I'll have to live with it." I shrug my shoulders exaggeratedly and smile. "Anyway... enough about me and my folly, what is it you were going to tell me?"

Clair's face drops and I know instantly that I'm not going to like it. "You're leaving me, aren't you?" She's like a rabbit in the headlights. I can see straight through her eyes and into her whirring mind. "You are, aren't you?" I repeat.

"It's not a hundred percent yet..."

"But almost?"

She nods her head in tiny movements as if she doesn't really want to nod her head at all. "This has been so hard for me Suse..."

"You're leaving?"

"I've... I've applied for a job in a local hospital in Devon."

"What if you don't get..."

"I've been for an interview this week – it all happened very quickly." She shakes her head slowly. Her mouth is downturned and I can feel her sadness.

"Interview? Already?"

"Yes – I'm so sorry Suse. I didn't go on holiday with the intention of getting a job but... well, the opportunity came up and I..."

"You don't need to explain yourself. I do understand. I know you want to be closer to Archie."

"I'm so sorry Suse. I feel bad..."

"You shouldn't feel bad. You've got to live your life fully and happily. You must do whatever that takes." Hark at me sounding all altruistic, when, in reality, I'm tearing up inside.

"They said..." she breaks off thoughtfully. "I mean, at the hospital – the interviewers – they said I'd hear from them by Wednesday." She looks down at the crumbs in her lap and begins to scoop them up, into her hand.

"How do you think it went?"

"The interview?"

"Yes." I'm hoping she's going to tell me it was awful. She failed miserably to answer any of their questions. She was so nervous that she trembled all the way through and got tongue-tied. She got it all wrong and thought she had to dress up as a clown for the interview and stumbled into the room and fell flat on her face, at their feet...

"It went really well. I think they liked me," she says, almost apologetically.

"Good..." I mutter. Damn. "I'm really happy for you."

"Thank you Suse. I was dreading telling you. I know how you're feeling and I'm so sorry. Do you fancy another coffee and we could talk about it more, if you like?" She's holding her cupped hand out, full of biscuit crumbs, as she gets up.

"Yes please. Don't be sorry, Clair. You've got to do what's right for you." I follow her through to the kitchen. "So... when do you think you'll go, if you get the job?"

"I have to give a month's notice, so it would be at least a month – that's if I get the job."

"I'm sure you will," I say. "I just know it."

She turns around from the kettle and leans back on the worktop with her arms folded. "If I do... well, if I do, it doesn't stop me worrying about you, Suse."

"Why should you worry about me? I'm absolutely fine – really I am."

She peers at me and shakes her head. "You're not the same old Suse you used to be."

I shrug at her. "I'm OK though."

What else can I say? She's probably right – I'm not the same, but don't people change as life experiences challenge them? Sure they do.

"I've had quite a year so far. I expect that's why I'm not the same. But you don't need to worry about me."

"OK," says Clair, turning back to the kettle. "I may not even get the job and you'll have to carry on putting up with me anyway."

She will. I just know she will.

***

She got the job. It was a no-brainer. She was going to get it all along. Of course she was. It was quite amusing to see her face twist and contort as she tried to tell me in a 'sorry' kind of way, when really, she was screaming with joy inside. Who can blame her? I certainly don't. However, it has made me more miserable over the last few weeks. I've tried my very best not to show it though.

I've decided to leave it for a few weeks before I advertise for a new flatmate. I can't bring myself to even think about someone new in the flat. They will never match-up to Clair and things will never be the same again.

Don't get me wrong, I'm really happy for her and excited to watch the development between her and Archie. Who knows – there might even be wedding bells in the future. That would be so sweet. And then there might even be miniature Clairs and Archies running around all over the place – that would be totally amazing. I'm so happy for her – she so deserves this.

Today is the sports fun-day at Hightown Secondary. I discovered that there will be no possibility of hiding away from a certain person today – he's running the whole damn thing. So, I've made sure that my bra wires are securely tucked in, where they should be, I'm not dressed like a clown and hopefully, I do not resemble a turkey in the slightest. As for being a two-boyfriend-one-died slapper, I have no idea whether that is common knowledge or not. I think I'd rather be a turkey to be honest. Oh well.

Mrs Pearson is being very jolly today. She's leading our class into Hightown Secondary with a skip and a bouncy trot. The sun is shining and a warm breeze is blowing, just enough to keep us from getting too hot. It's a perfect day for a sports fun-day. It's just a shame that Ryan Bagshaw is running it.

I lower my head as we arrive at the sports field. I'm at the back of the line and I can just see Ryan, Amber and several other staff members, as I peer out from under my fringe. They are all dressed in bright orange t-shirts and navy blue shorts. Mrs Pearson is talking to Ryan and he is pointing a finger towards one of the large tent-like structures over on the far side of the field. The children are all very excited, so I can't hear what is being said, over the din. Then Ryan turns to our class and holds up his hand.

Instantly, the noise stops and 30 little faces peer up at him expectantly. Well, 31 actually, although I'm still trying to hide under my fringe a little.

"Good morning children," says Ryan. "In case you have forgotten, my name is Mr Bagshaw."

Amber and the other teachers have gone off to greet the other classes coming from our school.

"Good-morn-ing-mist-er-bag-shaw." The children drone as they follow Mrs Pearson's lips as she mouths the greeting.

Ryan smiles at them and I can't help but smile back at him. I wish there wasn't so much bad history between us – all created by me.

He then speaks to Mrs Pearson again before turning back to the children. "Now, children. We have lots of fun activities for you to do today but things will only go to plan if you follow instructions and listen when you should. Myself and the other team members want you to enjoy the day, and of course, win some prizes."

There's an uproar of cheering and chattering and Ryan has got to raise his hand in the air again. The noise from the children stops so quickly that

I'm quite impressed by his presence and authority. Well, he is a teacher, I suppose.

Mrs Pearson begins to lead our class towards the tents and, as I pass by Ryan, I keep my head lowered.

He turns and starts to follow us.

"Good morning Miss Satchel. Are you avoiding me?"

I look up, through my fringe. "Morning – no, I wasn't. Sorry."

"How are you?"

I hear a hint of mocking in his voice which annoys me. "Fine thanks."

"Nice to see you wearing... err... normal stuff today."

He *is* mocking me. I look up again and sneer at him. "Ha ha – very funny."

"Sorry – I'm only joking."

"Not a problem," I mumble.

"So... how are things with you?"

"Fine thanks. You?"

"Yes, OK – I can't grumble. Well... except for my sister, Rachel, you've met her before, haven't you? Well, she works here now. She didn't like her last school and managed to bag a subject leader position here."

"That's really good. She's nice – I liked her."

"She liked you too." Ryan smiles at me. "Mind you – she's never seen you as a clown."

Again, I sneer at him.

"Sorry, sorry – I'm joking. It was hilarious though – you must see that."

I shrug at him. "Suppose so."

We're half way across the field now and I can see, in the distance, that the tents have a few chairs scattered around and matting on the floor, which I assume is for the children to sit on. There are numerous pieces of equipment, markers and other sports paraphernalia scattered about the field, which indicate the different sporting activities for the children.

"So... how's your flat?" Ryan has his hands in his pockets and is peering down at the ground.

"It's feeling very well thank you – had a bout of flu a while back, but that's all cleared up now."

He laughs and meets my eye. "You or the flat?"

"You asked me how the flat was."

"So your flat had flu?"

I smirk at him. God, he's so gorgeous. He has a tan already and it's only the end of May. I'm guessing he works outside a lot as he's the PE leader.

"Boyfriend OK?"

I avert my gaze from him. Oh no, does he know? Has he read the message on *facebook*? Is he fishing for more information? "It ended."

"Oh – I'm sorry to hear that."

We continue to walk across the field, in silence. As we reach the tent, Mrs Pearson instructs the children to sit on the matting and get their water bottles out. I stay at the entrance as Ryan goes in and squats on the ground in front of the class.

"OK, children, you can have a quick drink now and then you will be leaving your bags here. We will come back to this tent for a break later and then lunch."

A boy puts his hand up politely.

"Yes, young man."

"Where are the toilets, Mr Bagshaw?"

Ryan looks across at me and smiles. "I'm sure, when you've all had a drink, Miss Satchel will take you to the toilets." He looks over at me again and nods.

I nod back and smile. Oh gosh – which toilets? Where? The ones near the swimming pool? I don't want to appear incompetent or stupid again.

"You can go straight to the ones by the pool room, Miss Satchel." Ryan is walking back towards me with a smile on his face.

Did he read my mind?

"Go straight across the field, there." He comes up alongside me and points to a building on the left.

"Oh, OK. Thanks." I get a waft of musky cologne and suck it up my nose. He smells good. "I can see I'll be on toilet duty most of the day with this lot."

He rolls his eyes and looks at me pityingly. "If I thought I could get away with it, I'd send Mrs Pearson to do the toilet runs," he whispers.

I giggle into my hand before he strolls away to the front of the class and begins chatting to Mrs Pearson again.

I'm sure he doesn't know about... I believe Amber hasn't said anything to him about my boyfriend situation last Christmas – she can't have. Either that, or he's very clever in hiding the fact that he knows. I actually do care what he thinks about me. Firstly, because he's a highly-respected teacher and secondly, and most importantly, because I fancy him stupidly. I'm sorry, I just can't help it.

*** 31 ***

It really has been a fun day... for the children anyway. As predicted, I did spend most of my day, chivvying children backwards and forwards across the field, to the toilets. And not just our class. Between me and two other TAs, we did toilet runs for the whole year group.

My skin feels like it's burning, I just hope that I don't look like a lobster. Although, that's one look I haven't tried out yet and I'm sure it would add to Ryan's amusement, in regards to me. I haven't had a chance to talk to him anymore today as he's been busy with the activities but I did see him look around at me a couple of times. Each time he smiled at me and I smiled back which was kind of sweet.

Amber has avoided any sort of eye contact with me today. I don't know whether it's because she's ashamed of the things she said or whether she point blankly does not like me. Either way, I don't really care.

It's almost time for us to leave and head back to school. We've gathered back in the tent and Ryan and Mrs Pearson, who *is* beginning to resemble a lobster, are standing in front of the class.

"Have you enjoyed yourselves?" Ryan shouts out.

A roar of 'yes' cries out around the tent and then the children chatter wildly.

Ryan puts his hand up and the din dies down. "So have we. You have all been a perfect example to your school and you should feel very proud of yourselves. Give yourselves a pat on the back."

The children pat themselves, awkwardly, on their backs and beam up at him.

"I will be talking to Mr Reynolds about your exemplary behaviour today. I'm sure he will be very proud of you too."

The children sit in silence, peering up at Ryan like they're in awe of him.

"Thank you to your nice teachers for bringing you here today. I hope we will see you all again, very soon."

Teachers? Oh, bless him – he's referring to me as a teacher as well – that's nice.

Mrs Pearson says thank you to Ryan and instructs the children to collect their bags and line up, which they do pretty quietly and orderly. I have got to say that I'm quite proud of them too, as I wait for them to move out of the tent, so that I can walk at the back of the line.

Surprisingly, Ryan joins me and we walk out of the tent and begin to traverse the field together.

"So... getting back to our conversation earlier..." Ryan grins at me.

"Which bit?"

"I was curious about the boyfriend bit."

"Oh? Which bit?" Oh no – he does know. He's going to humiliate me, just as we're leaving. I suppose I should be grateful that he's going to do it now and he hasn't made me suffer it all day long.

"Whether you still have one..."

"No... I don't."

"Oh, I'm sorry to hear that."

"Oh, don't be sorry, I'm better off without one – nothing but trouble."

Did I just say that? Why?

"Oh really." Ryan looks a little disappointed. "I'm guessing you haven't had much luck with men."

"Could say that."

"Please – tell me if I'm sticking my nose in where it's not wanted."

"You're sticking your nose in where it's not wanted."

Ryan stares at me surprised. "I..."

"I'm joking." I smile reassuringly. "Sorry."

He laughs and meets my eye for a bit too long, bearing in mind we are walking across a field. Two of the children in front of us have stopped as one of the boys has crouched down to tie his shoelace. Ryan manages to sidestep around him but I go tumbling straight over the top of him in a sort of slow-motion dive. As I hit the grass, I hear gasps coming from the children and several giggles. Quickly, I pull myself up and dust off my clothes, feeling embarrassed. Mrs Pearson, alerted by the children's gasps, has stopped up ahead, and is asking if I'm OK. I nod my head at her and straighten my t-shirt.

Ryan looks like he's frozen to the spot and stares at me incredulously. Then his straight face turns into a smile... and then a discreet laugh...

"Are you OK," he says, with a glint of laughter in his eyes.

We have moved off again and I'm feeling completely stupid now. I nod my head at him and then look down at my grass-stained knees.

"Can't believe you fell for me like that."

"Who wouldn't," I say, and smirk. But inside, I'm totally annoyed at myself. Why do I always seem to be the clown – especially when I see Ryan?

"Seriously, are you OK?"

"Yes, fine," I say, feeling a little twinge of pain in my knee.

"Miss Satchel..."

"Yes?" I peer at him, questioningly.

"Come out with me some time," he says, in a hushed voice.

"Children – can we say a big thank-you to Mr Bagshaw."

Mrs Pearson and the children have arrived at the end of the field. The children shout out, 'Thank you Mr Bagshaw' in unison.

I'm flummoxed and stop still at the end of the line speechless.

"You're very welcome – and thank you all for being such perfect pupils," Ryan replies.

Mrs Pearson turns and leaves, followed by the line of children, walking along in pairs.

"I..." I stumble. "Sorry, I've got to go..." I walk off, trying to gather my erratic thoughts. I turn my head and glance at him. Why do we have to leave now? And so hurriedly too. OK, I know we have got to get the children back to school in time for their parents to pick them up but...

"What is the answer Miss Satchel?" Ryan calls out as we exit the field.

"Sorry?" I call back, sheepishly. I can't do this. I can't shout out 'yes – I'll go out with you'. Not in front of the children. Not in front of the whole year group.

"The mathematical equation, I just asked you about. Was it positive or negative?" Ryan is standing by the field gate, watching us get further and further away.

I hold my hands up in an exaggerated shrug. It's too late. He's too far away for me to reply and he keeps being distracted by children waving at him and the other teachers thanking him as they pass by.

I can't scream, 'Positive' to him now.

Damn.

***

I've been helping Clair to pack this week. She's been dithering around for days. She can't pack this – she can't pack that yet.

The staff at the surgery where she works, have insisted that she has a proper send off and they've arranged a leaving do for her on Friday night. She can't decide what to wear, hence, her whole wardrobe remains... in the wardrobe. I had mentioned to her that she's hardly going to be wearing her pyjamas or shorts or t-shirts or winter coats to her do, but she still hasn't packed any of those either.

So, you must be wondering what exactly I've helped her to pack. Well, there was her colouring books (adult ones of course), her countless packs of pens and pencils, her books (and she has hundreds of those), her memorabilia boxes, her pictures, her ornaments, her bedding, her towels (I was surprised how many of those she has and I'm now wondering if I actually ever owned any of my own), her kitchen gadgets (OK, so now I need to get my own food mixer and a coffee maker), her cushions and throws, and her toiletries (I now have two empty bathroom cabinets – except for a crinkled up toothpaste tube and a soggy, old toothbrush).

My flat is starting to look pretty sparse and I realise how little I actually own and how much Clair had contributed to the cosy feel of our home. It's not cosy or homely anymore. As each day has gone by and the stack of boxes at the front door has grown, my spirit has crumbled away, bit by bit. It's really hitting me now that she will be leaving on Sunday morning and I don't like it one little bit.

I still haven't put an advert in the paper or contacted the local estate agents. I can't bring myself to do it while Clair is still here. It's like I'm holding on desperately, in the hope that she might end up staying here. Of course, that's not going to happen but... well... you never know.

I haven't heard anything from Ryan – but then again, how would I? It's not like he has my number, it's not like we're friends on *facebook* (I did check to see if he'd added me but was quite relieved to find that he hadn't. He would see the message for sure, if he did). So, I continue to live a pretty mundane existence, which is only going to get worse once Clair goes.

I should count myself lucky that I still have the monthly jaunts to the pole-dancing club with Jade and Terry – I've become a bit of a pro at swinging around the poles like a chimpanzee. I love it – it's great fun and although I get plenty of offers from doting men, each time we go out, none of them quite hit the spot. I'm not that desperate, honestly. I can well do without a hormonal young man or a lecherous older man, slathering all over me, offering me the world if they can have a snog, and no doubt, a shag. No thank you.

***

"That's everything," says Clair, returning from her fifth trip to the car. "I'm ready."

I notice a wetness in her eyes and turn away as she passes me. "Another drink before you go?"

She nods. "Yes, OK."

I follow her to the kitchen and without warning, I burst into tears. I wasn't expecting to cry like this.

Without saying a word, Clair spins me around and hugs me. I look at her and she is crying too.

"What a silly pair we are," I say, trying to be brave. I wipe my eyes and sniff. "I'm sorry – I don't know where that came from."

"I'm going to miss you, Suse. We've come such a long way together."

"I know, I'll miss you too."

"Come to Devon in your summer holidays…"

"Really?" I say, pulling away from her embrace and switching the kettle on.

"Yes, absolutely. Come and stay and even if I can't get any time off, you could do your own thing. It would be a nice change of scenery."

"It would," I agree. "I'd really like that."

"Then we'll arrange it for a week in August." Clair pulls a tissue from her sleeve and wipes her nose. "You know, we might be a distance away from each other but I'll always keep in contact and come to see you when I can."

I smile at her. "I know… it won't be the same though. I'm going to miss our slob-out-in-front-of-the-telly nights, our routine in the mornings and your lovingly-packed lunchboxes."

"And our choccie-biscuit-pyjama-movies."

"Yes, all of it." We're both crying again but laughing at the same time.

"You will find someone else though," says Clair, trying to reassure me.

"I know I will… it will never be the same though. No one could be as good a friend as you've been."

"Not 'been', 'are'."

"Are then." I try to make the coffees through blurry eyes. A dark cloud is looming over me, even though Clair is trying her best to convince me that things won't change that much. It's very different for her. Don't get me wrong, I'm not bitter about it. It's just that she is going off to start a new and exciting job and life with Archie, whereas I am left here, in the same job (OK, I don't mind it too much), in the same life and the same lonely little flat. So maybe that does sound like I'm bitter but I don't mean it to. I really shouldn't be feeling sorry for myself and I should be grateful for what I do have. I've got a job and my own flat for goodness sake – some people don't have either.

I put the coffees on the table and sit down, opposite Clair. We're both still blurry-eyed but each time we look at each other we burst into laughter and then start crying again. What a pair we are. What a pair we're not going to be anymore.

"I'll text you when I get there," says Clair, sniffing and wiping her reddening nose. "And there's a lovingly-made-by-me packed lunch in the fridge, for tomorrow – it's a special one. Don't peep until tomorrow though – promise?"

"I promise."

Well that's it. I'm a complete sobbing mess now and a dull headache is beginning to form. This is it. She's really going. My life will never be the same. So much has happened and changed this year and we're not even half way through it. I have never felt so miserable in my... well, except when Jett... well, you know all that already.

***

I've struggled through this week. I've had to rush off to the shops every lunchtime (apart from Monday) to get something to eat as there have been no more lovingly-made-by...

The lunchbox on Monday contained all the usual things that I like to eat, but also, a tiny teddy on a keyring (which made me have watery eyes but luckily, I was sitting in the class conservatory and not the staffroom) which said 'Best Friends' and a note which read:

Susie satchel you're the best
In comparison to the rest
You're loving and kind
And really don't mind
When I get things wrong
Or make an unusual pong
You've been there for me
And this I can see
You're a treasure
And it's been my pleasure

To know you
To love you
Like a best friend should
Like only you would
Life will not be the same
It is a great shame
My heart is broken
So here's a small token
Of our everlasting friendship
A teddy to accompany every trip

Lots of love, Clair xxxx

And that really made me cry.

***

I've been wondering if I could put, must-make-packed-lunches, down as one of the requirements for a new flatmate. And maybe even, must-wear-pyjamas-while-watching-TV and must-eat-chocolate-biscuits, or must-create-an-awful-smell-in-the-toilet-after-a-curry-night. No, maybe that last one can be left out – I don't exactly miss the toilet pongs and am more than capable of making my own.

I've been quite lonely in the flat this week. Each night, I've come home from work, wandered around not knowing what to do and spent most of the evenings staring mindlessly at the TV. I know Clair has been on holidays before and not been here for a week or even two on some occasions, but this is entirely different. She's gone and she's never coming back. I hate it.

She has texted me most evenings, just to let me know how she's settled into Archie's flat and how her job is going (she totally loves it). But it's not the same as having her here and the pair of us curling up on the sofa, in our pyjamas and giggling about everything.

She said that time heals and once I get a new flatmate things will be better but I don't want a new flatmate at the moment – I just can't bring myself to do it. They could never compare to her. Yet, I have worked out that I can only manage financially for about three months before I will need to have someone else sharing the expenses of the mortgage and bills. So, I've decided to give myself a month's grace before I advertise and hopefully, by then, I'll feel a little less dejected.

*** 32 ***

So, it's Friday night and I now have a whole weekend to look forward to – not. I've just sat down with a bowl of curry noodles which look more like a bowl of soggy, brown worms. So unappetising.

There's not much on the TV unless I can convince myself to take up an interest in golf, football, mysteries of the universe or river monster fishing. It's no use, I can't convince myself, so I mindlessly flick to the news channel and begin to slurp my way through the mushy noodles.

I freeze, midway between shoving another mouthful of worms into my mouth. The doorbell has just rung. Who could it be at half past nine at night? Has Clair fallen out with Archie and she wants to come home?

I place the bowl of worms on the coffee table and pad through to the hallway. I can see a tall, dark figure fidgeting on the other side. I'm nervous. Who is it? What do they want? I'm alone in here. I've got no flatmate anymore. Does that make me vulnerable? I approach the door and hook the security latch across. It suddenly dawns on me that I'm wearing my scruffiest, Eeyore onesie and oversized MONSTERS, INC. slippers. I open the door slowly and peer through the gap, trying to conceal my hideous attire...

"Hi, sorry it's late but..."

Oh my God. My heart has leapt up to my throat. I unlatch the door and open it slightly wider, while trying to hide my feet behind the door – the slippers are far worse than the onesie. I peer around the door, clutching on to it as my body tilts at an awkward angle.

"I was just passing... and wondered..." He's jittering from one foot to the other, nervously.

"Hello, yes?" I say, still gripping on to the door.

"I just wondered – like I said, I was passing – if you..."

"Yes?" The moment I say yes, I lose my grip on the door and fall sideways, into the doorframe opposite, cracking my head on the side. The door opens further and I'm left standing by the side of the frame, rubbing my head.

"Are you OK?"

"Yes, sorry, I slipped."

No, actually – I've just smacked my head on the doorframe and now the door is open wider and my MONSTERS, INC. slippers are on full view. I'm not OK.

I watch Ryan's eyes, fleetingly, look me up and down and then his gaze lands on my chest. Haven't we been here before? I haven't even got a bra on underneath my thick onesie so it can't be another free-roaming wire.

"You've err..." he falters, "Is that a... a worm?" He points directly to my chest.

I peer down to see a lengthy curry noodle snuggled up by the zip of my onesie. "Oh God, no... it's a... oops, sorry, I was just eating my tea... noodles. Ghastly things really but I haven't done any shopping this week."

"Sorry, I thought for a moment, it was a..."

I pick the noodle off my onesie and look at it. Do I eat it? Do I flick it out of the door? What is the etiquette supposed to be when you've had to remove a soggy noodle from your chest while welcoming a potential guest and trying to appear demure at the same time? I have no idea.

I decide to hold it between my thumb and finger, in the most dainty, feminine way possible.

Ryan is looking at me in a kind of bewildered way.

I force a sincere smile at him. "Sorry about that – you were saying?"

"I was just passing and... well... I was wondering what you were doing tomorrow night." He's twitching erratically from one foot to the other, while his hands are in his pockets. "Sorry it's so late but... I didn't get an answer and... I just wondered what it was."

"You do a lot of wondering," I say, without thinking. I don't mean to sound abrupt, it just slipped out. Ryan looks at me expectantly. "Err... do you want to come in at all?" I add.

Please say no, please say no, please say no. I've got a bowl of worms on the coffee table, a week's worth of my old, wet knickers hanging on a clothes horse, drying next to the TV and the toenail clippers and corn plasters are on the sofa. Yes, I do get the odd corn – especially when I wear certain shoes. As for the kitchen – there is a whole week's worth of washing up in the sink and the floor is sticky. Please don't get me wrong – I'm not a slob – well, not usually anyway. It's just been a miserable, lonely week and

I've tended to wallow in self-pity every night and not do a single ounce of housework. The place is an absolute mess and I can't exactly invite him into the bathroom (which is fairly tidy), can I? And the only other option would be one of the bedrooms and that would look so wrong.

"No – but thank you anyway. I'm on my way home from work and just thought I'd..."

Phew.

Hang on a minute – he's on his way home from work? At this time? A quick calculation would mean that he took a detour of about four miles if he's on his way home from work and passed by here. I remember his sister telling me that he lived out in the sticks, on the other side of town, so he's travelled in the wrong direction, completely, if he's on his way home. I'm beginning to think this was a bit more deliberate.

"I'm not doing anything tomorrow – why?" I say in a most demure, unexpecting way. God, is he asking me out again?

Ryan looks down at his feet and I feel relieved that it's his feet he's looking at and not mine. "Would you come out for a drink with me?" He looks up and his cheeks have flushed and he looks quite boyish and sweet.

"Err..." I hesitate and try to appear thoughtful. "Yes, OK. Why not."

I can see the sigh of relief in his shoulders as they drop and relax. "Cool, shall I pick you up at say... eight?"

"Eight sounds OK with me. Where are we going?"

"Err... to be honest, I haven't thought that far ahead. What do you like? Town? Country?"

"Either, I don't mind."

"OK," says Ryan, looking a little less stressed. "I'll think of something and see you at eight then."

"OK – great – thanks. Yes, eight o'clock it is then."

He raises a hand in a goodbye gesture, smiles and then turns around. "See you at eight then," he says, turning back round and holding a hand up again.

"Yes – eight – see you then. Bye."

"Bye – eight o'clock then – bye."

I close the front door and scowl at the noodle, still squished between my fingers. Yuk. I've suddenly lost my appetite and will have to throw the whole bowl of cold, soggy noodles in the bin. Yuk.

My heart is jumping about in my chest as it suddenly hits me – Ryan Bagshaw has just asked me to go out with him. He came out of his way to ask me. I'm going out with him tomorrow night. Oh my goodness – I've done it. I've said yes. A rush of fluttery excitement surges through me. Oh gosh. Oh golly gosh.

***

The first thing I thought of, when I woke up this morning, was, oh my goodness – I'm going out for a drink with Ryan tonight – what on earth do I wear? Since then, I've spent the rest of the day trying on every single item in my wardrobe – some things twice. I don't want to appear too sexy, too reserved, too bright, too dull, too long, too short, too skimpy, too heavy or too unworthy of his admiring eye. Why do us ladies get in such a flap about what to wear on a date? Oh my goodness – a date. That's actually what it is, isn't it? A date. A real date...

Is it a date or is it just a friendly drink? I don't really know – whatever will be will be, I suppose.

I think I've found something now. Casual but smart – I'm sure that will be OK. So, I'm going to wear my trusted, old white jeans (it's a lovely summery evening), a flowing, floral, see-through blouse (obviously, I'll be wearing a camisole top underneath) and a pair of heeled sandals – sorted. Off to do my hair and make-up now which will take a good hour.

I'm relaxed at the moment, which is surprising. I've spent the whole day flapping about, cleaning the flat (just in case he does come in later) and emptying my wardrobe. But now I'm ready – I think.

Oh gosh – it's just hit me again – I am truly nervous now. It's quarter to eight and I'm standing in front of the wardrobe mirror. I look quite nice actually. My hair has been kind and done what it's supposed to do, I've got just the right amount of make-up on (not too much, just a subtle look), I don't look like a turkey, or a clown, or have bra wires sticking out, or even worms on my chest. I think Ryan will be quite pleasantly surprised that I can look normal and nice.

The doorbell rings and I hold my breath. He's here. Oh gosh – now my heart is pounding. I go to the door and open it. "Hi," I say, grabbing my handbag from the coat hook.

He looks totally gorgeous, dressed in a pair of black jeans and a short-sleeved, green, checked shirt.

"You look amazing," he says.

I can see a look of sheer surprise on his face. What did he expect? Did he think I'd be wearing my onesie or have more curry noodles stuck to my chest? "Thanks," I say, shyly. He offers his arm, which shocks me somewhat, I thought Jett was the only one who did that. I link up with him and walk along the pavement to his car.

"Thought we'd go to a nice little country pub – you OK with that?"

"Yes – I like the country."

"Have you eaten?"

"No, I haven't actually," I say.

To be honest, I did have a sandwich about an hour ago, but that was just a precautionary measure to, A) prevent any alcohol from rushing straight to my head and B) to move along any flatulence I might have as I can't bear the discomfort of having trapped wind and having to hold it in all night.

"Cool – I was thinking maybe you would like to have a meal?"

"Yes, why not. I'd like that."

We get to Ryan's car and I'm surprised to see how posh looking it is. I don't know what it is as I'm not really into cars and just think of them as either nice or not nice. The colour has a lot to do with it, for me. Ryan's is a lime green one and I love it.

"Jump in," he says, politely holding the door open for me.

I have got to try my hardest to not think about the last time a handsome young man did this for me. "Thanks," I say and give him a fleeting smile.

"You really do look amazing," he says as he climbs in beside me.

I blush and peer at him coyly. "I don't always look like a turkey or a clown you know."

"Or have things stuck to your chest... or even poking out of your chest..."

We both laugh as Ryan pulls away. I'm thinking to myself – well, he's seen me at my worst, so now I want him to see me at my best. I'm going to enjoy this evening, whatever it takes. It's about time I had a bit of fun and some nice male company.

*** 33 ***

It's a lovely little restaurant. Out in the middle of nowhere, yet pretty packed considering we had to travel down long, windy roads to get here. We had a couple of drinks before we sat down for our meal and now we've just had the first course. There's been no stilted conversation as we have covered every topic from school... through to school. OK, we've only talked about school stuff but it's been funny and interesting. OK, so the funny bits were the turkey, the bra wire, my clown day and me falling over on the field.

I like Ryan a lot. He's a real gentleman and has impeccable manners. He's also incredibly sexy, strong-looking and handsome. I don't mean to, but I keep watching his lips more than I should do, when he talks. He's got a cute little kink in his top lip, which I had never noticed before, and it's very sexy when he speaks. He stares deep into my eyes when we talk and it makes me feel quite shy and nervy.

"Will you excuse me," he says, touching my hand, "I must go to the gents – those cokes have gone straight through me."

"Yes, of course," I say, trying to be as polite as he is.

As he walks away, I peer down at the table. His phone is there.

Oh my God – his phone. I bet he's got the *facebook messenger* app on there...

The terrible message...

If I could just...

As soon as he is out of sight, I instinctively snatch up the phone and hold it under the table. My heart is beating rapidly and I feel slightly sweaty and sick. I've got his phone – now what? Without moving my head, I strain my eyes to peer downwards and under the table. I'm shaking sporadically. I touch the screen and the phone lights up. Flicking my gaze upwards, I scan the restaurant, before looking back down again. Wow – this is scary – I feel like a criminal. Does it make me a criminal just to have a little look? If I could just get into his apps, I could find *facebook messenger* and...

His phone isn't locked. A wallpaper appears – it's a picture of a red sports car. Hmm... it's OK I suppose. I prefer flowers or waterfalls myself. I dart my eyes upwards again to check the scene and then look back at the phone. My hands are clammy and I wipe each one in turn on the plush seat of my chair...

Oh my God – footsteps – he's coming back. It's too late to return the phone to the tabletop. Oh God. I look up and greet him with a warm smile as I shakily clutch his phone under the table.

"I think our main is on the way," he says.

"Oh... good... yummy. I mean... good, I'm hungry... in my big tummy."

Really? Why have I just said all of that? Ryan is now looking at me a little perplexed. I'm still clutching the phone in my sweaty palms and worrying that it might slip from my hands. "Oh – look," I call out, using my eyes to indicate behind him. "Dinner's coming... goody." As soon as he turns his head I quickly shove the phone in my back pocket. "You know... I think I'd better nip to the ladies before I eat – I'm bursting too," I whisper as the waiter arrives with our meals. I stand up and casually push the phone further into my pocket as Ryan is being distracted by the waiter. "Back in a minute," I say, before walking off quickly.

I've almost given myself a headache, trying to be an undercover detective. I can imagine it's a very hard job to do on a daily basis. I'm heading towards the toilets. My heart is still racing and I have no idea what I'm going to do.

Toilets. That's it. That's exactly what a detective would do. I can't exactly place Ryan's phone back on the table, in front of him and say, 'Oops – sorry, I don't know how that fell into my pocket!'. No, I'll have to put it in the men's toilets and he'll think he left it there when he used the gents.

What else can I do? He will notice that his phone has gone sooner or later. Oh dear, what a bit of a mess this is. I've got to do it though – there's no way I can let him find out that I have got his phone. I'm sure he thinks I'm weird enough without him discovering that as well.

As I reach the toilet doors, I casually glance around and then dart into the gents.

I'm so fortunate that no one is in here – although I did have a backup plan if there was. I was going to say that I'd accidentally walked into the wrong one.

There are three cubicles on one side and the usual, smelly trough type thing (OK – I forgot for a moment but I've just remembered it's called a urinal) where men stand in a line. Yuk – I don't know how they can do that and not be embarrassed. There's no way I would want to lob my genitalia out in front of others and stand there holding it for everyone to see.

There's a strong smell of urine in here which is making me feel quite queasy and my nerves are in shreds as well. What am I doing in here? What if someone comes in? How do I always manage to get myself in difficult situations?

Quickly, I scuttle across the floor and into a cubicle. I lock the door behind me, sit down on the toilet and lift my legs up, just in case someone comes in. There's a huge gap under the door and it would look quite odd if some man saw a pair of women's sandals poking out the bottom. I pull Ryan's phone from my pocket and peer at it. God, I feel guilty now. What am I doing?

Just as I'm about to touch the screen, I hear the main door open. I freeze and begin to do shallow, silent breathing. Footsteps walk across the floor and then I hear the sound of a zip. Then the flow. Quite a long, gushy flow to be honest.

How long is the man going to pee for? I'm sure he's done enough to fill two buckets by now. On and on it goes – is there something wrong with him? Does he have some sort of affliction where he's got an oversized bladder... or maybe even two?

Suddenly the flow stops and I hear a zip sound again. Phew – he's finished. Then I hear running water briefly and the scrunching sounds of paper towel.

As I hear the door close, I stare at the phone again. I've stupidly got myself in a ridiculous situation here but if I could just get rid of the *facebook* message, everything will be OK. I touch the screen and see the icon for apps. As I press it, the door goes again. Oh God.

Footsteps come closer towards my cubicle and then I see and hear the paper-thin walls rattle as the cubicle door next to mine, closes with a bang. I can hear a rustle of clothing and then a loud, grunting sigh as the man sits down (I can only assume it's a man, as I'm guessing that no other woman would be doing what I'm doing).

Plop... splash... and two more... then a warm, foul smell wafts into my cubicle and I place a hand over my nose and mouth. More splashing sounds but this time continuous. Can they do both at once? A rustling sound and then the flush of the toilet.

He's finished – thank goodness. That must have taken about ten minutes – I bet he's one of those men who takes a book or a paper with them to the toilet. Why they feel the need to sit in a toilet for so long is beyond me. I suddenly get an image of my dad, and yes, he's the same. He has a cook book in the bathroom cupboard just for the daily occurrence of having a poo.

I hear the tap run and then paper towels being pulled from the dispenser.

Hurry up and go – please.

The door opens again but it can't be the man using the paper towels. Oh no – someone else is in here now. What am I going to do? It's like all the men in the restaurant are having a toilet break at the same time.

My hands are so sweaty and my legs are beginning to ache as they are scrunched up on the edge of the toilet seat. I can't stay in here much longer – Ryan will wonder where I am and my meal will be getting cold. I'm sure I must have been gone for at least 15 minutes now. I try to adjust my position as silently as possible, because perching on top of a toilet is not comfortable –

Clatter – splash...

"Argh... Shit!" I groan and grunt, out loud, before smacking a hand to my mouth to silence myself.

Oh no – oh God no – no, no, no.

I jump to the floor, clicking my heels on the tiles, and bump into the side walls, creating a scuffle of commotion in the cubicle. Thrusting my hand down the toilet pan, I snatch the phone up. It drips in my hand. Yuk. Now what?

"Hello?" a man's voice comes from the other side of the door. "You OK in there, mate?"

I open my mouth to speak...

I can't speak – I don't have a man's voice.

"Hmm," I mumble in a deep throaty growl.

"You OK?"

"Hmm..." I growl louder.

"Do you need help mate?"

"No." My voice crackles and grunts in a low tone.

I hear the footsteps move away as I hold my breath in fear. Please leave me alone. Please go. Please let me escape from here. I pull several pieces of toilet paper from the roll and dry Ryan's phone. It looks OK and luckily, the screen is not smashed.

I've now gone off the idea of being a detective completely...

I hear the main door open. Has the man who spoke to me, left now?

No. More footsteps. More gushing watery sounds. Why do so many men need a wee all at once? I want to get out of here...

He's gone too. That was a quick one and the filthy bugger didn't wash his hands after holding his... well, you know what I mean.

I peer down at the phone again and want to cry. Why did I take it? A droplet of water seeps out from one edge of the phone and I reel off more paper to dry it.

I've got to get out of here. Twenty minutes must have gone by now – Ryan will think I've left. And what a waste of 20 minutes it's been. I could have deleted the message by now but I've spent more time mopping up the droplets of water and patting the phone dry than I have looking through his apps.

Hesitantly, I unlock the cubicle door.

The main door opens again and footsteps stride in at a pace. They head straight for my cubicle door and I instantly flip the lock back on.

"Excuse me sir – are you alright in there? One of our customers informed me that you might be ill. You've been in here for some time now."

I roll my eyes and peer up at the ceiling. Heaven help me.

A knock on the door makes me jump. "Sir – do you need any help at all?"

"No," I growl, which makes my throat sore. "Go away."

"OK, just checking sir," comes the cheery voice and then I hear the footsteps walk away and the main door closes.

I unlock my door again and open it slightly, so I can peer out. There's no one there. I've got to make a run for it before someone else comes in.

Without another thought, I charge to the main door, open it just enough to be able to see through the gap, and freeze.

Ryan is standing directly opposite the door, talking to a waiter. He's gesticulating and I just catch the end of what he's saying. "...check the ladies. She's disappeared..." Slowly, I close the door again and tiptoe back to the same cubicle. Oh no – what am I going to do now?

I hear a door opening in the distance and the muffled sound of a man's voice calling out. "Hello – anyone in here?" The waiter must be in the ladies next door. Oh no, Ryan thinks I've gone missing and he's sending out a search party. How am I going to talk my way out of this one?

I sit on the toilet for several more minutes, pondering over my dilemma. I can either sit it out and hope to God that Ryan doesn't leave without me or I could...

My heart races again at the thought of the other option. I could casually walk out of the gents, bump into Ryan and say, 'Oops – I went in the wrong door'. I'm not sure which is the best option as I've been gone a while now. It's going to look very odd.

Suddenly, the gents' door opens. "Hello – anyone in here?" Footsteps get closer. "Hello – may I ask who's in there?"

"No."

"Is that the same person as before?"

"No." God this makes my throat hurt. I'm not designed to have a deep, gravelly voice.

"Sir – are you in any difficulty?"

"No." I hear a ruffling sound and then see a hand on the floor.

"Excuse me, is that a...?"

Shit – my feet are on the ground. I snatch them up from the floor and hug my knees.

"...a woman?"

The hand disappears and I hear more rustling noises. Then the footsteps move away to the door. "Sir?"

More footsteps, two sets of feet.

"Susie... is that you in there?"

Oh God, it's Ryan. Oh no. Heaven help me.

"Susie?"

"Yes?" I squeak, ready to burst into tears. I can't cope with this detective stuff – I want out.

"Susie – what are you doing in there?"

"Oh no... oh no... Ryan... you've..." I force the emerging tears to fall. "...you've saved me..." I drop my feet to the floor, check the phone is stuffed deep in my pocket and unlock the door. "You've saved me..." I say again, rushing out of the cubicle and into his arms. "Thank you, thank you, thank you..."

Ryan is staring at me incredulously as I look up at him. I then step away from him and drop my arms from around his neck. I wipe tears from my face.

"You saved me... I didn't know how long I was going to be stuck in here... Thank you, thank you."

He hasn't blinked yet and his eyes are wide open, as is his mouth.

"I went in the wrong... oh, how silly of me. I've been stuck in here. I've been panicking. Oh, silly, silly me. Thank you for rescuing me..."

Ryan still says nothing. He looks dumbfounded. I think he's overreacting, to be honest. After all, anyone could make that mistake, couldn't they?

"Why didn't you..." Ryan has found his voice again.

"Walk back out?" I finish his sentence.

Ryan nods his head slowly.

The waiter is gawping at me which is quite annoying. Fair enough, he was probably the one who was asking me if I was OK. I can understand that he might be a little bemused by my man-voice, earlier, but he doesn't have to stare at me like that.

"I couldn't," I say, peering at Ryan with the saddest look I can possibly do. "Other men were coming in."

Ryan snaps out of his stupor and offers his arm to me. "Do you need to use the ladies?"

"No... it's OK. I did it in there," I say, pointing to the cubicle.

"Come on then, let's get back to the table – your dinner will be cold."

"We can warm your meal through, madam. Shall I take it back?" Although he's being very kind and polite, the waiter is still giving me an odd look.

"Yes please," I say, peering at him through narrowed eyes.

I walk out of the gents, holding on to Ryan's arm. As we traverse the restaurant, several people, sitting nearest to the toilets, give me strange looks. I don't care. I'm never going to see them again. They can stare at me as much as they like.

Ryan pulls my chair out for me and I sit down. Phew – I've almost got away with it. I just need to put his phone back on the table. My plan didn't work unfortunately, as I couldn't leave it in the gents. Somehow, I will get rid of that message though. There's got to be some way.

Putting his hands up to his mouth, Ryan shakes his head. Then he bursts into laughter. "You got stuck in the gents – Susie Satchel – you do make me laugh. You never cease to amaze me."

I smirk at him and then pull my compact mirror from my bag to check my eyes. I look OK. I had to put on a flood of tears to make the situation seem all that more dramatic. It worked though – I got away with it.

"I'm quite shocked by it all," I say. "I can't believe I made such a mistake – how silly of me."

Ryan continues to laugh at me. "Do you want a drink? I can get you another one straight from the bar."

"Oh – yes please. That's just what I need."

"Same again?"

I nod and smile at him, keeping that sad, vulnerable look on my face. He gets up, checks his pocket and then walks away to the bar. As soon as his back is turned, I grab his phone from my pocket, place it back in the middle of the table and casually drape my serviette over the top of it.

Done. Phew.

My dinner returns and it looks steaming hot. I pick up my serviette and place it into my lap. "This is awkward," I say, giving Ryan a wry smile. "Eating on my own."

"I couldn't fit another one in." He laughs and then peers down at his phone. "That's odd," he says, picking it up. "I was looking for this a while ago – thought I'd left it in the car."

I shrug my shoulders at him and start to eat the food around the edge of the plate – it's way too hot in the middle.

He screws his nose up and tilts the phone up and down, examining it. Then he shakes it and to my horror, another droplet of water falls out.

"It's wet," he exclaims. "How...?"

"Wet?" I say, feigning surprise. "How can it be wet? Have you spilt something on it?"

"No..." He shakes it again and another droplet falls. Then he touches the screen. "It's... it's not working. It's wet. What's happened?"

"I have no idea," I lie. "Maybe the waiter spilt something on it."

While I struggle to eat my meal, Ryan continues to fiddle around with his phone. He wipes the water from it with another serviette and tries to turn it on again.

I have got to say here that it was working when I dried it off – I'm sure it was.

"I have no idea what's happened here but it seems that it's soaking wet and broken."

"Oh no. How on earth could that have happened?"

"I don't know but I'm going to ask. Do you mind?"

"Of course not – you go and get it sorted out. Looks like an expensive phone."

"It is... or it was."

With that, he walks off to the bar again, with his phone, while I watch from the table. I'm struggling to swallow my food as a raging guilt tears at me. How awful have I been? I feel really bad but don't quite know how to redeem myself. If he finds out – I've blown it.

*** 34 ***

Ryan was not able to get to the bottom of the mysterious wet phone incident. He was pretty annoyed when we left the restaurant and said to the waiter that he wouldn't be returning in a hurry. The waiter gave me a strange look of suspicion. How dare he? He couldn't have known it was me. Could he?

We've just pulled up outside my flat. "Thank you for a lovely evening," I say.

"An interesting one..."

Oh no, he doesn't ever want to see me again. He thinks I'm an absolute weirdo. To be honest, I haven't exactly got a good track record whenever I see him. Oh dear – I feel sad.

"We'll have to do it again sometime."

I'm shocked. No, really, I'm shocked.

"Yes, we should. Apart from the toilet incident and your poor phone, I've really enjoyed myself." I break off and peer down at my lap for a moment. "Do you... want to come in for a coffee?"

"If you're sure..." Ryan turns the engine off.

"Yes, I'm sure. It's a nice way to round the evening off."

"Will your flatmate mind?"

"I haven't told you – she left last week. I'm on my own for a while now."

"A while?" Ryan looks puzzled.

"Yes, until I get a new one."

"Oh, I see."

I smile before climbing out of the car, then Ryan follows me to the door.

An hour and a half has flown by and we've had two cups of coffee each. I don't know where the time has gone to be honest.

"I'll have to be going now," says Ryan, stretching his arms above his head. "I'm coaching a kid's football team in the morning."

"Oh gosh – what time?"

"In about eight hours." He looks at me and winks. "I need to get my beauty sleep in."

"You don't need any beauty sleep... not like I do anyway."

"I wouldn't say you need any at all."

I blush and smile at him.

"Right –" He jumps up from the sofa and tugs his shirt down. "I'd better go. Thanks for the coffees."

I follow him to the front door and he grabs his jacket from a hook. I open the door and he steps outside and turns around. "Are you doing anything... next weekend?" he asks, hesitantly.

"Err... no... not really."

"Shall we do it again? Except we'll go somewhere different." He laughs. "I can't afford to lose another phone."

"Yes – that would be nice."

"You've made my evening Susie. You're funny, sweet, amusing and..."

"And?"

He scuffs his shoe, backwards and forwards on the ground. "And beautiful." He meets my eye and smiles as he steps closer.

Oh God, is he going to...?

He leans in and kisses my cheek before I've had time to think. I stare at him, not knowing what to say.

He's drawing closer again. He touches my lips with his. I allow him to kiss me. Softly, with mouths closed. He slides an arm round my waist and kisses me again. This time he pushes harder against my lips, opening my mouth with his.

Oh my goodness – we are full on now.

Wow.

"I really have to go," he says, pulling away from me. "Can I see you next Saturday?"

"Yes," I say, gulping back the wetness in my mouth.

"Eight o'clock?"

"Yes."

"I'll see you then." He leans over and kisses me one last time. Short and soft. "Goodbye..." he says and kisses me again.

"Goodbye..." I'm holding on to the doorframe in a dizzy state.

"Bye then..." His lips are still touching mine.

"Bye..." I breathe on to his lips.

"See you next Saturday..." he breathes back.
"Bye..." I don't mean it. I don't want to say 'bye'. I want him to stay.
"Bye... I've got to go..."
"Go... you should go..." I whisper.
He breaks away and steps back. "Next Saturday..."
"Yes," I reply and nod. "Next Saturday."
He turns and walks a few steps away. "Bye..." he lifts a hand and waves at me before carrying on.
"Bye... and thank you Ryan..."

***

I've been out with Ryan twice now. Last Saturday he had a new phone which I kind of felt a bit guilty about, but we exchanged numbers for the first time, which was really nice. He has sent me at least one text every day, just to ask me how my day has been. He's very sweet.

So, last Saturday we went into town and had a few drinks in a bar and then we went to a nearby Indian restaurant. The same thing happened as the week before (not the toilet/phone thing). We had a bit of a kissing session at the front door as he was leaving, but that was all. He's a real gentleman, which is almost a shame because I seriously want to rip his clothes off and have mad, passionate sex with him all around my flat. Maybe that will come later. I have wondered, when he was kissing me, if sex has been on his mind too. I'm sure it must have been – he's a man after all.

Anyway, it's Saturday again and we're spending a whole day together today. You know, Saturdays seem to take twice as long to come around these days since I've been seeing Ryan. Anyway, we're having a day out at the seaside, as the weather is beautiful at the moment. Ryan has planned the day out with some fun activities like, boating on the lake, crazy golf, a walk along the pier, afternoon tea (afternoon tea – can you believe it?) and a visit to the funfair. Then we will nip back to my flat, get changed and then visit the theatre to see *Buddy – The Buddy Holly Story*, followed by an evening meal of my choice. Wow – what an itinerary. And he won't let me pay for a single thing. He tells me that I've got enough to pay out for, what with owning my own flat (I still haven't got a flatmate yet) and he says TAs don't get paid what they deserve anyway. He is just such a gentleman and I really like him. A lot.

***

What a day. What a night. I have enjoyed every single minute. We have walked along the seafront, hand in hand, had such fun playing crazy golf and screamed our lungs out on the rides at the funfair. It was totally amazing. Then, when we came back here to get changed late this afternoon, we almost didn't make it back out of the front door as things got a little steamy. We had rather a long session of full-on, steamy snogging and literally had to tear ourselves apart. His hands wandered around my torso, my neck, my thighs and my bottom but never actually went anywhere else. Trust me, my other parts were screaming out for him to touch them.

We're back at the flat now, having seen a fantastic show and then stuffed ourselves with Indian food. I'm making coffees while Ryan is flaked out on the sofa.

I did notice earlier that he placed his phone on the coffee table...

Yes, I'm still after getting at that message to delete it (even more so now as I like him a lot and don't want a stupid, drunken message to jeopardise our new relationship) but I haven't dared try a trick like the last time. I don't think I'd get away with it twice. I have found out that he hardly ever uses *facebook* though, so I guess I should be relieved by that, but I still want to get rid of that message, just in case.

I finish making the coffees and carry them through to the living room. I'm quite shocked to see him stretched out on the sofa, asleep, as I place the mugs on the table. I nudge him gently to wake him.

"Wake up – I've made a coffee for you," I whisper.

He opens one eye and smiles at me. "I wasn't asleep – I was resting my eyes."

I laugh, just before he pulls me on top of him and wraps his arms round me. He kisses me passionately. Oh gosh – we've never kissed in this position before. It's always been in a respectable upright position...

Oh dear... it's going to happen. I know it is. I can feel a hardness pressing into me. Oh gosh...

With his mighty strength, he lifts himself up while holding on to me and I instinctively wrap my legs around his waist. He carries me out to the hall, still kissing me madly. "Which way...?" he breathes on to my lips.

I point to the first bedroom. "There... in there..."

***

OK, I know I've said it before but that was the most beautiful thing ever. It really was. Gentle and gorgeously slow. I think I'm in love. He's absolutely awesome.

He's lying next to me, curling a strand of my hair around his fingers and gazing, through the dim light, at my face. I'm looking back at him but we're saying nothing. I'm sure we don't need to. What just happened said enough.

He closes his eyes and stops curling my hair. It really doesn't matter that he's fallen asleep. He can stay the night. I want him to stay. I want to wake up tomorrow and see his handsome face looking at me. He's amazing. *It was amazing.*

I think I've found someone new. Someone to care for. Someone who will care for me. This could be the beginning of a beautiful relationship. A new life. New hope and dare I say it – stability?

A future.

I don't know what to do about the message – he's asleep, and now would be the golden opportunity to get his phone. I can't do it though. It feels so wrong and besides, I want to stay here, next to his warm body and fall asleep too.

***

Clair – it's finally happened. Ryan stayed the night. I feel like a new chapter is just beginning in my life. I look forward to telling you all about it, next time we meet. Love from Susie xxx

PS I miss you xxx

******

Susie Satchel will be back next year...

Thank you for taking the time to read this book
I would be hugely grateful
If you would leave a short review on Amazon
Kindest regards
Tara